The Part of Me That Isn't Broken Inside

Kazufumi Shiraishi

THE PART OF ME THAT ISN'T BROKEN INSIDE

Translated from the Japanese by Raj Mahtani

DALKEY ARCHIVE PRESS

Originally published in Japanese by Kobunsha as *Boku no naka no kowareteinai bubun* in 2002.

Copyright © 2002 by Kazufumi Shiraishi
Translation copyright © 2017 by Raj Mahtani
First Dalkey Archive edition, 2017.

Library of Congress Cataloging-in-Publication Data
Names: Shiraishi, Kazufumi, 1958- author. | Mahtani, Raj, translator.
Title: The part of me that isn't broken inside / by Kazufumi Shiraishi ; translated by Raj Mahtani.
Other titles: Boku no naka no kowareteinai bubun. English
Description: First Dalkey Archive edition, 2017. | Victoria, TX : Dalkey Archive Press, 2017.
Identifiers: LCCN 2017006165 | ISBN 9781943150250 (pbk. : alk. paper)
Subjects: LCSH: Meaning (Philosophy)--Fiction. | LCGFT: Philosophical fiction.
Classification: LCC PL875.5.H57 B6513 2017 | DDC 895.63/6--dc23
LC record available at https://lccn.loc.gov/2017006165

www.dalkeyarchive.com
Victoria, TX / McLean, IL / Dublin

Dalkey Archive Press publications are, in part, made possible through the support of the University of Houston-Victoria and its programs in creative writing, publishing, and translation.

Printed on permanent/durable acid-free paper

1

Friday, November 10th. Eriko and I went to Kyoto.

It had been very cold that day, and by the time we boarded the six p.m. Nozomi, my body was completely numb, exposed to a northerly wind while waiting for Eriko at the Shinkansen platform of Tokyo Station.

It was my twenty-ninth birthday that day.

But the trip wasn't in any way meant to commemorate the beginning of the final year of my twenties. It just turned out that both our holidays as well as my birthday happened to fall on that weekend.

When we arrived at Kyoto Station it was 8:14 p.m.

We traveled by taxi to an old hotel in Kawaramachi, and after checking in there, we had drinks in a restaurant with a panoramic view of the city to celebrate our first trip together.

It was rather disappointing: to Eriko I was already twenty-nine years old; she'd already given me an expensive-looking summer sweater in the summer as a birthday gift, so there was no gift, let alone wishes, from her that day, the day of my actual birthday.

This regrettable outcome was thanks to my tendency to lie a little while shooting the breeze.

Back in the early days when I'd just met Eriko, we began having a conversation about each other's star signs, as couples often do. On a whim, I declared my birthday to be this particular date in the summer because its zodiac sign was in perfect alignment with Eriko's, giving her the impression that we were a match, astrologically speaking. While I'd been thinking about coming

clean in the course of a casual conversation, I hadn't been able
to tell her the truth just yet, believing that it was rather useless
to do so; after all, many people tend to get strangely worked up
and broody once it comes to light that they've been lied to, even
if that lie happens to be a white one.

At any rate, in addition to that little deception, there was an
ulterior motive at play behind this trip; the excursion had, in
fact, been the fruit of a small, spiteful maliciousness on my part.

I'd planned it entirely by myself and I'd also personally taken
care of presenting the tickets to the attendant inside the train
so that Eriko would remain clueless about our final destination
throughout the railway journey. And so, as expected, when she
stepped off the train at Kyoto Station she appeared slightly
baffled—it was a subtle and momentary change in her demeanor,
the kind of change I'd never ordinarily detect, but it didn't escape
my notice because I'd been observing her closely, anticipating.

"What do you want to see tomorrow?" I asked Eriko while
dining at the hotel. "Are you familiar with Kyoto?"

"Not at all," she said, turning her eyes away a little. "You
decide."

"Right. In that case I'll be happy to guide you on a complete,
leisurely tour of Kyoto. The fall foliage is just around the corner.
By the way, I often used to come to Kyoto in my school days for
fun."

"Is that right? I never heard you say that before."

"Yeah, I guess not."

Truth be told, I never actually used to come to Kyoto for
fun. How could I, when all of my school days were spent
moonlighting?

"But I thought you were more familiar with Kyoto than me,"
I said.

"Whatever gave you that idea?"

"I was under the impression that you used to come down
here often for film shoots and such."

"Just occasionally, really, and since it was for work, I'd return on the same day. I hardly even had the chance to take a stroll through the city."

"I see," I said, nodding.

Frankly, until recently, I'd suspected that Eriko had been visiting Kyoto frequently. That's because her lover, with whom she broke up two years ago, lives in the city.

This ex is a popular graphic designer and in these past several years he's been attracting much media attention for his art while lecturing at the Kyoto City University of Arts. Requisitioning an old townhouse somewhere around Fuyamachi and turning it into an atelier, he enjoys an elegant living as an artist. Since he often appears in magazines and TV shows to offer his expert views on life in Kyoto, I can't help but take notice of his physical appearance and the aura he projects; he sports a goatee, even though he's about my age, and he's also slightly plump.

But it's not that I particularly dislike him or anything. After all you can't come to like or dislike someone you've never seen in person.

It's just that in my mind I felt there was something wrong with Eriko, that she was a very strange woman to have had an affair with such a man for nearly three years.

Before we began to sleep together I'd asked her once about the guy. "I said goodbye to that part of my past a year ago," she'd answered before adding, "We went out for nearly three years though."

When I went on to ask about her ex's line of work, she snapped and said, "Don't call him ex!! I hate that word. Besides, I don't want to remember anymore."

Of course I didn't poke my nose any further, and since then I've managed never to ask about her ex-boyfriend again.

However, just because I didn't ask her about the guy, I hadn't lost all my interest in him, her former partner. On the contrary, the very fact that I'd simply withdrawn at the drop of a hat should've been enough for her to suspect that my interest in the affair was genuine, that it remained alive and well with a single-minded focus.

We work in similar business circles, she and I. So I'm sure she must have been fully aware of the fact that I was capable of easily discovering the existence of another man in her life.

And even though I expressly chose Kyoto as the destination of our first trip to make my point, to make insinuations that were for the most part venomous . . . Eriko was just relishing her food, appearing blissfully ignorant.

But I'm perfectly confident that she was fully aware.

I was sure that in her heart of hearts she was breaking out into a cold sweat at that moment, and come tomorrow morning, she'd take pity on me, for the state of mind I was in.

Eriko was tenderhearted like that.

The next day, we didn't embark on a sightseeing tour around Kyoto. Instead, I rented a car from a company near the hotel and we headed for Hikone in Shiga Prefecture.

"Hey, we're not in Kyoto anymore!" Eriko said in a perplexed tone once we reached the Yamashina area after leaving Kyoto city.

"I've changed my mind. Let's forget about Kyoto and see Hikone Castle instead."

"Why?"

"Why? Well, there's a chance you'll get sentimental if we hang around in Kyoto. I really wouldn't know what to do if you got sentimental. That'd be a problem."

I suddenly swerved the car, parked it at the shoulder of the road, and turned to face Eriko in the passenger seat.

"And besides, it'd be awkward if you ran into your old lover, right?"

She fell silent for a while and stared back at my face. "You know, it did occur to me that you were up to something like that," she said, sighing. "Wow! I guess you picked Kyoto on purpose after all. Why would you do such a thing? Why would you come up with a ruse like that? Why would you go to such lengths?"

I slammed on the horn abruptly. Eriko was surprised, to say the least.

"You never talk to me honestly about your ex, so I just thought I'd honestly let you know that I knew, okay?"

"What are you getting so worked up about?" she said, laughing. "I think nothing of that creep anymore and even if I did run into him I couldn't care less really. Come to think of it he was a really dull and absurd man. I realize now how utterly foolish it was to have gone out with him. It was such a waste of my time."

I let go of the steering wheel and edged toward Eriko. She held me in her arms and calmly stroked my hair.

"Don't you think worrying about exes is entirely pointless? I for one am not the least bit interested about the women you dated before me."

I moved back to my original position and took a good look at Eriko again.

"It's not pointless. Not if your interest in a person is genuine, if it's something that wells up from your heart. It's only natural to want to know everything about that person's past. If you're telling me that you have no interest in my past relationships with women, well then, you're practically saying that you're not into me. That's what I think!"

Eriko beckoned, so I leaned my body toward her again. "There, there," she said, laughing again. But then she said, "Let's say I ask about your past. You wouldn't tell me a thing, would you?"

"Of course I wouldn't!"

"So what are you getting mad at me for?"

I straightened myself up again.

"Look, you're free to snoop without my permission."

"Just like you snooped?"

"Precisely."

"What good would that do? Do you want me to investigate and report what I dig up and then cross-examine you, interrogate you? Would that make you happy?"

"Look, it's not about what happens or what doesn't. It's about the act itself; the very act of going to the lengths to investigate and examine. That's what's important."

"But how can I even begin to investigate when you've never even taken me to your room?"

She was sidestepping the issue, but this time it was my turn to sigh.

"You're such a tiresome person," she went on. "But you know something? I'm willing to fully appreciate who you are to me: you're my lover, the person who associates with me, the man who keeps me company. I've made up my mind to believe in my eyes, you see, to believe in what they see," she asserted flatly in her characteristic tone.

We crossed the Lake Biwa Bridge and arrived at Hikone before noon. In stark contrast to the day before, the sunlight was warm and the wind was blowing gently. We left the car in the parking lot of Hikone's city hall and—after passing through the gateway beside the Gokoku Shrine and walking a path that ran alongside an inner moat—we entered the castle. The maple and ginkgo trees in the courtyard had already changed color. I led the way and turned left at the Tamon Tower to head for the site of the Umoreginoya ruins. The place used to be the palace where Naosuke, the fourteenth male heir to the House of Ii, spent his fifteen ill-fated years, from seventeen to thirty-two. It also served as one of the principal settings in Seiichi Funahashi's novel, *A Flamboyant Life*.

Once we passed through the front gate with a large sign above it that read, "The Imperial Family School of Naosuke Ii," we beheld a range of simple and elegant one-story houses. The place was terribly quiet, except for three or four tourists gazing over a bamboo fence into a room whose sliding *fusuma* paper doors and *shoji* screens were left open.

"How marvelous! Only someone as honorable as Naosuke Ii could live in a place like this," Eriko said, impressed.

But I knew better and said, laughing, "By the living standards of those days this amounts to nothing more than the mansion of a middle-class clansman."

There was a life-sized panel replica of Naosuke installed in the living room, and Eriko was enthusiastically reading the explanatory note attached to it. I was watching her from behind, wondering whether she had any real interest in subjects like the Treaty of Amity and Commerce or the Ansei Purge or the Sakuradamon Incident.

"Have you read *A Flamboyant Life*?" Eriko asked suddenly, turning around.

"Yes I have," I answered.

"My, you're really well-read, aren't you?"

"Not really."

"What's the story like?"

"Well, it hasn't left much of an impression in my mind, but the protagonist, rather than being Naosuke, was this person named Suzen Nagano, his aide who was responsible for carrying out the Ansei Purge, the mass executions that took place in the Ansei period. The lives of these two revolve around Taka Murayama, a woman of unsurpassed beauty; in a way I suppose it was a novel about a love triangle."

"How about that!"

I then recalled my most favorite lines from *A Flamboyant Life* and recited them from memory.

There is an old saying, is there not, that says that there is nothing in this world more confusing to the human heart than carnal desire. The hermit of Kume loses his magical powers at the sight of the whiteness of the legs of a washerwoman; in the entwining net of a woman's hair can often be found entangled even the mighty elephant; and by playing the flute made from the clogs worn by a woman, an autumnal deer is said to approach always. Verily, the woman herself is a thing of the evil spirit. The heart can rarely forgive.

Eriko was eyeing me, looking absolutely shocked. "I wonder how your head works, really. I always wonder about that."

"It's a scene where Kazusuke, the owner of an inn in Kyoto speaks his mind to Shuzen Nagano, who's getting carried away by his lust for Taka Murayama. Put simply, he's saying that a woman with the kind of hair you have can even catch a whale with it, and if you hold those shoes you're wearing at this moment and begin to bang them together repeatedly, you'll probably attract panda bears as well."

Since I'd strained to pull this data from the library of my memory, I felt as if the core of my brain was worn out, but having mused on this passage for the first time in a long time, I was struck by the truthfulness of the words, by how remarkably they hit the bull's-eye.

Woman, a diabolical spirit, an enchantress. Nothing seduces man more than the allure of sex . . .

Ichiro, the pro baseball player who got transferred to the Mariners a few years ago, had a falling-out with a mistress he was seeing during his time with the Orix, and when she ended up revealing his affair with her in a tell-all exposé in the magazines, the mistress in question said that Ichiro had aptly uttered something like, "You can't hold down a man with sex alone."

Reading the news story about the affair, I was deeply impressed, convinced that this genius, who had impeccable control over the baseball bat, had no control whatsoever over his own bat; that is, the one hanging down between his legs. But now I'm even more convinced that a beautiful woman can indeed be a thing of terror, just like Eriko must surely have been at that time, standing before me.

That reminds me, I had some drinks this Monday with the managing director of a certain publishing house with whom I co-represent a certain writer, and he'd said, "Every morning I have to masturbate. I can't come to the office if I don't. It's been like that for years now."

"So you watch some porn videos or something while doing it?" I asked him. "Sometimes," he said. "But I do it in bed when I'm about to wake up, losing myself in wild fancies of this and that nature."

This man was a managing director, but he was still thirty-eight. When I thought about ending up like him in another ten years, I felt slightly blue. Haruki Murakami's novel *Norwegian Wood* came up, how the main character in the story also masturbates before going out on dates. It occurred to me that I masturbated on nights I didn't sleep with Eriko, and in addition, on those days when I didn't meet Tomomi or Onishi.

Still, for married men, it must be a major hassle to hide that habit from their wives. I wonder how they manage. As for the wives, if they're in the house all the time they must be taking care of the urge by themselves whenever they like, and in some cases—in a desperate attempt to cope with the dissatisfaction of their faded married lives—become prostitutes or join one of those dating sites trending nowadays.

Why, just last week I came across an elderly man in his fifties who was driving the taxicab I hailed at Urawa Station—where I'd gone to collect a manuscript. He was repeatedly checking text messages on his cell phone. When I asked what he was doing, he said with pride, "Well, two housewives, see. Both of them in their twenties. One's twenty-four, the other's twenty-six. They tell me they're scared of young guys, so they're happy to go out with me."

I said, "Matchmaking site, eh? The success rate must suck though."

"Tell me about it!" he answered, his voice rising a little in excitement. "I only scored these two chicks after hitting on dozens of them."

The central tower of Hikone Castle was truly magnificent. It was about to be abandoned and destroyed, but the famous Shigenobu Okuma, who had visited the site to inspect it just before its demolition, was so moved by its dignified appearance he personally appealed to Emperor Meiji to have the tower spared. But actually the castle tower was just a reconstruction, having been removed from Takatsugu Kyougoku's Otsu Castle, and, come to think of it, the Tenbin turret found here was also formerly the turret that had graced Yukari Hideyoshi's Nagahama Castle.

I was relating this story to Eriko while taking in the view of Lake Biwa that spread northwest, just below our eyes. Once we'd breathlessly climbed steep flights of stairs to reach the top floor of the three-tiered castle tower, Eriko finally said, "So you're saying they used to properly recycle in the old days as well."

"Of course they did," I snapped back. "Castle-building was an enormous undertaking after all, requiring vast expenses. Even though the castles were set on fire every time a battle started, they used to salvage any unburned materials and stone walls and reuse them. If they hadn't it would've been a very costly affair in terms of both time and money."

"Wow! I guess those warring feudal lords knew a thing or two about what made good economic sense."

"Obviously! They led far sounder lives than we do today."

"But they were always at war, weren't they?"

"Which is why they knew death. A person can't hope to lead a decent life without knowing what it really means to die, don't you think?"

"And you know what it means to die?"

"Nope. I'm just someone who lives every day thinking he should never have been born."

"There you go again with your weird nonsense. You're so full of it."

Eriko takes my hand and gazes at the cloudless scenery with me. The lake was serene and devoid of rippling waves. After falling silent for a while she spoke again. "You should never say such a thing. It's bad luck, surely. There are many who can't go on living even when they want to, after all."

Hearing her words I suddenly remembered my mother. I wondered if she too, at this moment, was praying for her life to go on, lying in a hospital bed.

"Just how long is long enough for such people?" I murmured. "How long do they have to live to feel they've had enough of life?"

I wasn't really talking to Eriko, but she nonetheless asked, "What do you mean by 'such people?'"

"You know, people who want to go on living even when they can't."

I grasped Eriko's hand without taking my eyes off the glittering surface of the lake.

"I believe I could happily give away my life," I said, "to anyone who badly wanted to live; that is, as long as they didn't mind having the life of someone like me. But even if I were to somehow find a way to hand over whatever's left of my days to such a desperate someone, it'd only be a matter of, say, a few dozens of years before doomsday starts to feel imminent again, against his or her will, and the protesting would start again, 'I want to live longer no matter what!'"

"But anyone who's about to die is probably hoping for another year at least, don't you think?"

"So you're saying then that it's okay to die a year later, that it'll make a difference?"

"Yeah, emotionally speaking. I mean, by wishing for another year, what they're really asking for is a little more time to get ready to accept their own passing."

"I doubt it . . ."

I ponder a little further. Is it possible to prepare for death? Speaking of preparation, isn't life itself a preparation for death?

"I don't think it'll be like that," I said. "If you could extend your life by an extra year, you're going to desperately try to do just that, certainly, and when the time to die does come, all that's going to happen is that you're going to find yourself more fully reconciled to your fate than you were a year earlier. That's all."

"But that's the point, that's what's most crucial—the reconciliation!" Eriko responded without hesitation.

But I didn't agree. Reconciling—or in other words, giving up—can't be all that important, and honestly, it isn't a big achievement. To give up, after all, is being ready just for an instant. What's more, if giving up is supposed to be so "crucial" then there's nothing wrong with believing that I should never have been born. Why should it be bad luck to say such a thing?

The things Eriko says usually sound plausible if you don't pay too much attention to them, but upon closer examination, you see that they're groundless and inconsistent.

We had a late lunch at the Hikone Prince Hotel and then drove to Azuchi, where we visited the site of Azuchi Castle. In recent years, thanks to dedicated excavations and research, and the use of computer graphics, the complete architectural story of Azuchi Castle has come to light; while the magnificent scale of the castle and the gold-encrusted tower attract much attention to this day, as far as the actual ancient castle site is concerned, only the stone walls remain, appearing distant and abandoned on a slightly elevated hill. Nevertheless, just by following the path through the area of the ruins we were able to arrive at an understanding of the castle's extraordinary scale.

While ascending a flight of stairs that rose endlessly toward the crest of the ruins of the main keep, Eriko grumbled, "Why is each step so wide? It just makes it even more difficult to climb up. They should've put a little more thought into their construction, don't you think?"

"They're probably wide on purpose to let horses climb up too. What's more, if an invading enemy approaches, a soldier with a spear's got to be able to spread out his legs to effectively confront the invader—the stairs have to be wide enough for him to do just that."

"Wow! Really?" As usual Eriko was fascinated.

When we arrived at the site of the castle tower the sun was rapidly setting as a cold wind began to blow. Both of us were sweating profusely, which didn't help because the sweat made the bitter cold even worse. We went down the hill hastily and— upon Eriko's suggestion—hurried back to Kyoto. Although we ended up having a late dinner, I was happy; she'd taken me to a restaurant by the Kamogawa River, where the food was delicious, and she'd also taken care of the bill.

"For your information," she said as we entered, "there's no need to let your paranoid imagination run wild regarding this restaurant."

She was alluding to what was better left unsaid, so I responded, "I feel really bad. I did behave offensively. I'm sorry." When I apologized Eriko bit her lip and looked a little sad.

After finishing our dinner, I in turn took Eriko to a *zashiki* bar in Gion. It was a tatami-floored watering hole where I'd drop in whenever I visited Kansai. The proprietress of the place was the former mistress of the father of a certain young writer I represent, and for some reason she was always friendly. Her physique, which was rotund like a fat cat's, and her skin, which was fair and slick like a brand new bar of white soap, were reminiscent of the writer, so I suspected she was his mother.

That night the proprietress welcomed us both, and when

I introduced Eriko to her she remarked repeatedly, "What a ravishingly beautiful woman! Good for you, Mr. Matsubara, good for you!"

When I began to drink in earnest, the proprietress called Eriko over to the corner of the counter and the two talked in hushed tones for quite some time.

On our way back to yesterday's hotel—inside a taxi—Eriko said, "Mama-san—that proprietress—was telling me that underneath your tough-looking exterior, your difficult-to-please looks, you're actually lonely, that you couldn't go through life alone, and that, surprisingly, someone like that has nowhere to go."

Upon hearing this I remembered that a while back, when I was alone in the bar there and getting helplessly drunk, she let me stay in her room on the second floor. The image of how pathetic I was at the time had probably been seared into her mind. Granted, I may have behaved disgracefully, bursting into tears and letting my face fall on her knees, hollering, "I'm lonely, I'm lonely." But that's the kind of thing one should try out now and then. In fact, I engage in such behavior at most bars at least once, in an experimental spirit. Admittedly, it's a silly habit, just like a dog's habit of pissing on whichever telephone pole it happens to come across.

At any rate, the mama-san was being meddlesome, talking to Eriko about me. What a disappointment she was! Still, Eriko seemed to be in a good mood, so I certainly kept a lid on my feelings.

2

AFTER RETURNING FROM KYOTO I decided it would be better to stop seeing Eriko for a while.

Having had a lot of sex, our chemistry was strangely heightened, and although our trip had only lasted a weekend, our experience of being together from morning to night, without any time apart at all, would undoubtedly have a significant impact on our future relationship. I had probably become a stronger, more solid presence in Eriko's eyes and in turn Eriko's presence had become all the more distinct to me.

To be sure, it wasn't anything unpleasant at all. But as far as I was concerned, at that juncture in my life, I wanted to break off contact with Eriko for the time being. By doing so I wanted to make Eriko incomprehensible again. To maintain human relations, in general, I feel it's vital to try to understand the other person at first, and after that, avoid arriving at a full understanding. Once you finish a book you don't want to read it again, do you? If you do you get tired of it. Relationships with people are like that as well.

A long time ago, when I explained this to the girl I was going out with at the time, she said, "Human beings aren't books, and anyway, there definitely are books that are interesting no matter how many times you read them. Besides, if you're going to use the metaphor of a book to describe a human, then I'd say it's a long, long, never-ending story.

"To begin with," she continued, "no matter how much you try to understand, the printed matter we call 'a human being' is riddled with illegible characters and ciphers, so your reading of a person will always remain incomplete, no matter how many times you try. If you ask me, I think it's more apt to compare a human being to a piece of music, a sort of living repository containing an entangled mess of tens of thousands of different kinds of sounds, varying from person to person. And I'm sure this music is really complex, changing your impression of it every time you give it a listen, you know."

For several days I seriously tried to understand what she'd said.

But it was no use—I ended up concluding that there just wasn't any book so fascinating that you could read it over and over again without ever losing interest, and I also thought that a never-ending book was a fanciful, fairy-tale notion. Worse still, to compare a person to a piece of music was going a bit too far, I felt, even if she were just being whimsical.

And then I had another thought.

If you wanted to read the same book again and again, the only way was to forget the details you'd read, from cover to cover.

I'd come to know Eriko's body by then. I'd also come to know about the man in her past, and about other things as well.

It was time I started forgetting a little.

To that end, from the following day, I began killing my nights with booze.

On the first day I drank the night away with my colleagues in Shinjuku, and just went straight to work from there. But keeping company with a bunch of people you don't particularly like or dislike is boring and a terribly troublesome affair, so from the second night onward I began to drop by several familiar watering holes by myself. Most of the time I'd drink until about 3 a.m. before returning to my apartment.

Meanwhile, my cell phone buzzed with many calls from Eriko, but I never answered.

The fifth morning, a violently painful toothache woke me up.

My lower-right tooth in the back, my wisdom tooth, whose treatment I'd abandoned about half a year ago, must have festered, thanks to my nightly drinking. The pain—a hammering sensation near my temple—was quite intolerable. I rushed into the dental clinic, realizing how ungrateful I'd been for the existence of this place all this time. As expected I was told that the tooth was in a terrible state, and in the end it was extracted.

Nevertheless, I went out drinking that night as well. The hemorrhaging had stopped one hour after the tooth was pulled, and since I'd downed, all in one go, an entire three days' worth of the Voltaren they'd prescribed me, the pain had disappeared in no time. I skipped lunch, but went to Yanagibashi in the evening to eat with a certain essayist I'd asked to join me. I had about three bottles of sake but no particular harm was done; I was doing all right.

The essayist and I parted company at about nine, but an hour later I was opening the door to "New Seoul" near Morishita Station in the vicinity of my apartment.

There were no customers in sight, just Tomomi wiping a glass alone.

It was a small shop, approximately seven stools lined against the counter, a U-shaped brown sofa, and a square table at the back of its narrow interior.

I'd bought a stuffed figure of the children's manga character "Trotting Hamtaro," which was displayed under the eaves of a general store near the exit of the Ryogoku side of the subway station.

Since it had already been a month since my last visit, all Tomomi did when she saw me was give me a deadpan look and mumble, "Oh."

I sat on the chair facing her, placed the stuffed toy on the counter, and asked, "Is Takuya asleep?"

Tomomi fixed me a glass of whiskey and water in silence and didn't open her mouth until she placed the glass on the counter.

"He's a real handful these days, having turned into a night owl!"

She then shouted in the direction of a gloomy, sharply rising staircase found at the right end of the counter, "Takuya, that nice mister's here!"

"Your hair, you've dyed it," I said, noticing for the first time her strangely red and disheveled hair.

"Kind of odd, don't you think?"

"Not really."

I heard footsteps running down the stairs. Tomomi finally looked at me straight in the face and smiled.

Takuya was in his pajamas and when I handed Hamtaro to him he was delighted. He was a frail kid, catching cold all the time, and even though he'd already be five when the next New Year holidays came around, he still ran a fever once a month without fail. His build was also far more fragile than that of most children his age, and he had a pale complexion. His large, bulging eyes, just like his mother's, made him look even sicklier.

A customer entered, and Takuya shot a mean look at him for a second, since his arrival meant the boy had to return to the second floor. But when Tomomi jerked his chin up he embraced the stuffed toy and climbed up the stairs without any further fuss. The visitor was an elderly man in his fifties, wearing a tired-looking brown business suit, his forehead riddled with wrinkles. I'd seen him in this bar from time to time.

While Tomomi picked up this man's bottle, which was on reserve for him, and began preparing a strong glass of whiskey and water, I leaned over the counter and said to her in a low voice, "How about going to Disneyland this Sunday, the day after tomorrow?"

After serving the man, Tomomi refilled my glass, which I'd already emptied.

"I wonder, she said, "who was the one wearing a long face all day long at the Ueno Zoo last time?"

"Hey, it was awfully cold that day! Come on, let's just go. I've got free press passes—we're talking unlimited free rides here, and get this, the passes also come with food tickets! And you know what else? DisneySea's opened next door, and there's Ikspiari too, so we can also have fun shopping!"

I was being insistent with her, as always. "Come to think of it we've never bothered to go there even once. Takuya's a big boy now so he'll be able to ride any kind of ride—it'll be great, so come on! Takuya's going to be super pleased for sure!

"Yeah, I suppose so," Tomomi said, apparently taking my offer into serious consideration.

"I'll come pick you up by car at ten the day after tomorrow."

"Hey, I can't just drop everything and leave on such short notice! I've got plans . . ."

"Sure you do. I'll come pick you up anyway. If you can't make it at that time, no problem. I won't mind."

Then I drank quite a bit. The regular customer left after thirty minutes or so and was soon replaced by five or six other people, each of whom merrily sang two or three karaoke numbers before leaving.

The customer traffic stopped, and a few minutes later it happened again; my toothache. It was intense.

Seeing me in pain, Tomomi apparently thought that I was only joking. But when my groaning began to resound throughout the bar she did finally get seriously worried. When I related, in fits and starts, twisting and writhing in pain, the details of what had transpired that morning, she began to rebuke me, saying that I'd been reckless.

But by that time blood was spilling all over from out of my mouth, forming a few small pools on the black Decola counter. There was so much blood even I was horrified.

Tomomi went around behind me in a hurry, removed my jacket, loosened my tie, and wrapped a large towel around my neck. Then she swiftly went upstairs and came back down with something in her hand. It was a box of Twining teabags. She took out two bags and, after removing their wrappers, tied them into a bundle with the attached strings and thrust them under my nose, telling me to bite into them.

"Tea contains an ingredient that can stanch bleeding. Be sure to sink your teeth in, even if it hurts."

As I reluctantly pressed the edge of the towel to my lips, she moistened the teabags a little with water, and then forcibly shoved them into my mouth.

However, after desperately applying the teabags over the gap previously occupied by my wisdom tooth and clenching my teeth, the pain, which made me feel as if the flesh of my cheek was about to tear apart, only sharpened. I became confused, clinging to the counter, and my eyes blurred with tears.

The teabags had become blood-soaked, oozing out a rotten-smelling juice that spread throughout my mouth, making me nauseous.

I couldn't go on breathing, the alcohol was taking effect all at once, and although I was burning up inside, feeling the heat surging toward the surface of my skin, it was as if each and every pore in my body was blocked, making it impossible to vent the heat. My vision turned slightly hazy and everything before me began to lose clarity.

Tomomi went upstairs again and I began hearing the sound of heavy footsteps right above my head, going thump, thump, thump! After returning approximately five minutes later, she started to close up shop early. The abrasive, screeching noise of the seven stools being dragged across the concrete floor seemed to rub my throbbing nerves the wrong way, irritating the hell out of me.

She ended up taking me to her room on the second floor and laid me down on the futon, which was already made-up there.

While going up the stairs, borrowing her shoulder for support, and after hunkering down on the futon, I kept complaining, "The tea's made it worse! The tea's made it worse!"

"Cotton, cotton," she said in a panic before fetching from a dressing table a box of cotton strips she used for her makeup. Handing me several layers of them at a time, the box was empty in the blink of an eye, the cotton strips stained red, one after another, before ending up scattered all over the tatami mat.

"That's it! No more cotton," Tomomi declared, and when she held out some tissue paper as a substitute, I just couldn't tolerate her bungling ways anymore.

"Why don't you have a steady supply in your house," I complained, "of something so necessary as cotton? What are you going to do if Takuya gets injured? Look, it's all right. Just forget about it and leave me alone."

Tomomi placed the tissue box beside me and left without a word.

A little later she returned with a tub of ice and a cold wet towel. When she gently pressed the cool towel to my cheek I felt the pain dissipating somewhat. At the same time, at twice the speed, I felt the drunkenness inside me fade away as I fell into a wonderfully peaceful state of mind, just like when you're about to doze off.

After she'd changed towels several times, the pain had subsided for the most part and I was humming, as I usually did out of habit. Even though I was still hemorrhaging, I thought to myself, "Man, the world's opening up its doors to me again."

And then I felt foolish for having such a hackneyed line flit through my mind. I realized I was thinking clearly again.

When I considered falling deeper into my drowsiness—my body all curled up and cozy—I suddenly realized that Tomomi, who should've been at my side, was nowhere in sight. I raised my head in a panic, looking around.

She was sitting in a corner of the eight-mat room, looking

down apologetically. For a moment I thought she was crying, but then I noticed that both her hands were moving earnestly over her lap for some reason.

I slipped into a reverie, musing that her red hair didn't look good on her at all, that it seemed frivolous even, and when she was looking down, I saw that the shadow of her face mercilessly revealed the fact that she was a woman in her thirties, her wrinkles beginning to stand out at the edge of her makeup.

Tomomi was five years older than me. The thin nape of her neck was pale, reminding me of Takuya, whose breathing I heard as he lay sleeping in the next room.

After a while I couldn't stop wondering what on earth she was up to, so I rose from the futon, the towel still pressed against my cheek, and approached her, crawling on my knees.

There was a small box placed on her black skirt. It was a box of sanitary napkins and in her hand was a small, slender white thing. Tomomi was working hard to untie this hard lump of cotton with her manicured red fingernails.

Noticing my line of sight, she slowly lifted her face.

"Just hang in there for a bit longer, okay?" she said with earnest eyes. "I'll have some decent substitutes for cotton ready. I just need to do a little more disentangling."

3

THE NEXT MORNING I got up early and went to the dentist.

Although the pain was completely gone, I was anxious about the fact that the next day was a Sunday. Besides, I dreaded the possibility of finding myself in a similar predicament again that night; I'd have been devastated and mired in deep despair. So it was absolutely necessary to secure a large quantity of painkillers.

I didn't want to wake up Tomomi, who was asleep on the futon next to mine, so I quietly sneaked out of bed, put on my pants, and, on the back of a furniture store's leaflet I found on a low table, began to scribble with a ballpoint pen some words of regret for staining her pillow case with blood, along with some words of gratitude for nursing me last night, when suddenly Tomomi woke up and called out to me from behind, giving me a jolt of surprise.

Tomomi's face, which was resting on her pillow, no longer showed any traces of makeup. I wondered when she'd wiped it off last night.

Her large, languid eyes were lit by the pale light streaming through the curtain, dimly betraying the fatigue that had settled in them. But she was looking rather attractive nonetheless. In fact, her face, devoid of any seductive allure, had a strong, down-to-earth charm, with its small wrinkles, and a texture you could see in fine detail. Her sharp eyebrows, her long nose and her thick lips, which always made those other features, in contrast, look a little sloppy, matched her tired expression well. I recalled the faces of Eriko and Teruko Onishi and realized that

Tomomi was quite different from them. She was endowed with a particular beauty of her own.

When our eyes met, she said, "Thanks for the doll."

"I'll come pick you up tomorrow at ten," I replied.

To which she said, "Uh-huh," nodding like a little girl.

I pulled my wallet from the inside pocket of my coat in hand, took out three ten-thousand-yen bills, stacked them up on the leaflet, placed the ballpoint pen lengthwise, splitting into two halves the face of Yukichi Fukuzawa, the man on the bill, and faintly waved goodbye to Tomomi before softly tiptoeing down the stairs.

The apartment I rent is about fifteen minutes walking distance from Morishita Station in the direction of Monzennakacho. It's a temple town close to the Kiyosumi Garden, crowded with small buildings and stores, taking a while to reach even after crossing the lofty bridge straddling the Onagi River, which merges into the Sumida River. New Seoul is in the direction of Ryogoku, which is in the opposite direction from Morishita Station, and if you were to go there on foot it'd take you nearly thirty minutes. I usually take a cab, but that morning, since my dentist was located near the bridge, I reluctantly decided to walk over there.

I had a checkup, got my medicine, and returned to my apartment, once again on foot.

It's an old, three-story concrete apartment called "Corporate House Nagisa." Nagisa means beach, so it seems like an odd name to give an apartment by the river, but apparently there's no deep meaning behind the name; it's just the name of the landlord's granddaughter. At any rate, the place is just a shabby accommodation made up of three floors, each with the same 2DK layout.

I went up the perpetually dark stairs and turned the doorknob to my room, located at the end of an open corridor.

As I opened the unlocked door it occurred to me that it had been a while since Raita and Honoka had dropped in.

I took off my shoes and entered the room. After walking into the kitchen and placing on the table an envelope bulging with five days' worth of painkillers and anti-inflammatory drugs, I put the kettle on to make some coffee and then opened the refrigerator door—there was no food in there, only beer. I went on to slide open the door to a six-mat Japanese-style room connected to the kitchen.

Looking inside the dimly lit room with the curtains closed, it didn't seem like anything had changed since around ten days ago, when I'd stepped into the room to ventilate the place after Honoka had stayed and gone home. Just to be sure, I opened the closet and checked the position of the futon mattress, but because Honoka was always scrupulous when it came to folding the mattress, I couldn't tell whether it had been used since then. Still, chances were that it hadn't been taken out and put back in there that many times, since the sheets and pillow covers weren't all that wrinkled, so I supposed she hadn't come in here, after all, for ten days.

As for Raita, I knew for certain that he hadn't turned up recently because we made it a point to sleep together in the eight-mat Western-style room across the corridor, removed from the kitchen.

At any rate, I was a little worried about Honoka, wondering what she was up to.

It was nearly six months since I'd begun allowing her to visit my apartment freely, and she used to stay at least once or twice a week without fail—until now, that is. This was the first time she'd been absent for so long. I feared she may have found a more convenient place to crash somewhere else, but then again, I never considered her savvy enough to pull off something like that.

The kettle rang out noisily behind my back so I banished Honoka from my mind and returned to the kitchen.

It was no use getting worried; it wasn't as if I could contact her or anything. Besides, I wasn't close to Honoka, or even Raita for that matter; my ties to them weren't deep.

I poured myself a weak cup of coffee, sat down at a table for two, and absentmindedly gazed out the window until my cell phone began to ring inside the pocket of my suit jacket.

I pulled it out and looked at the screen. It showed Eriko's name and her cell number. Although I hesitated for a moment, I pressed the Start button and brought the phone to my ear. Eriko's voice buzzed as I peered at my watch—the hands pointed to about nine twenty.

She was asking what I'd been doing all week, pretending not to be worried. Her tone suggested she really couldn't care less, but there was an underlying anger seething in there, betraying how upset she was over my failure to answer, no matter how many times she'd tried calling. But I couldn't help thinking tenderly of her, hearing her voice after a long absence. I told her that I'd been bingeing on alcohol all week, that I'd had one wisdom tooth pulled out, and that until just a little while ago I was in a dental clinic, reclining in a chair.

"It was no big deal," I said.

"Are you eating well?"

"Yes, I am."

"So it doesn't hurt anymore?"

"No, not anymore. Besides, they gave me lots of drugs."

"Oh . . ."

"But hey, anything the matter? Anything urgent?"

"Why?"

"Well, apparently you've been calling my cell phone a lot lately."

At this point, for a fleeting second, I sensed Eriko holding her breath.

"Then why the hell didn't you answer or return my calls?" she said.

"I'm sorry. I just didn't feel like talking over the phone. Besides, I was probably drunk whenever you called, since I've started drinking early in the evenings."

The cell phone was all I had, having never gotten around to installing a landline in my apartment.

"So what if it was an emergency? What were you going to do then?"

"Was it an emergency?"

Eriko didn't answer.

"At times like that," I went on, "you should just call my office. Even if I'm out, you can leave a message with the operator."

I heard Eriko letting out a small sigh at the other end.

"Oh for God's sake! The least you could do is set up a PC in your office. You know it's out of the question for me to call your company."

Ever since I got transferred last April to the publishing division from the editorial department of the monthly magazine where I'd worked for two years, I hadn't used a PC at all. In the magazine's editorial department, where I had to proofread on a monthly basis and where manuscript submissions piled up at deadlines, email was indispensable for carrying out all the back-and-forths regarding manuscripts. But for the present job, which only requires me to proofread at most around ten books a year, there was no need to use email at all.

"I distinctly remember telling you quite some time ago that I detest email," I said.

"Yes, you did," she chimed in before going on to say, "but if you'd answered the first call, I wouldn't have bothered calling you that many times, so it would've been a good thing for you too, don't you think?"

"In theory, sure. But look, after returning from the trip, I just wanted to put some distance between us," I said candidly, at which she scoffed straightaway and said, "What the hell are you saying? There you go again with your weird nonsense."

"You think?"

"Oh yes, for sure! Look, have you become fed up with me?"

"It's not like that."

"Then why do you say such a thing?"

"I only thought that we needed to keep our relationship fresh, that's all."

Eriko laughed again.

"What's funny?" I tried asking assertively.

"You're kidding, right? You can't seriously believe that meeting once or twice, now and then, is going to keep a relationship alive, do you? That's absurd."

"You think?"

"Absolutely! Liking someone and being able to feel like the relationship is always fresh means that you and your partner are able to understand each other pretty well and discover new sides to each other. Genuine freshness in a relationship is something that naturally emerges in the course of keeping company. It's really not the same thing as enjoying your favorite game or book, you know. When two people are together, the relationship's constantly evolving, and that's what keeps the love alive, what keeps it fresh. So if you stay away from your lover—if you keep a distance—the romance would just fade away, wouldn't it?

"Hmm."

I was impressed by what Eriko had said, but I didn't necessarily agree.

"What's the matter? You're not disagreeing. That's unusual." Eriko seemed amused.

"I just thought it was quite clever of you."

"In that case will you please properly answer my calls from now on?"

"Yeah okay, I'll be sure to do that."

"Fine."

I listened for a while to Eriko's account of her week.

Eriko was in charge of planning magazine campaigns at a mid-sized PR firm rather well known in the fashion business. She'd started working as a stylist in her college days attending the Tokyo National University of Fine Arts and Music, then joined a magazine publisher owned by a major apparel maker, working first as a fashion-magazine stylist and editor. But she said when the parent company of the magazine fell into financial trouble two years ago and was acquired by a French publishing conglomerate, she transferred to her present company. Even so, she only entered into an annual contract with this company and apparently managed other work at the same time, as a freelance stylist. According to colleagues of mine working in the editorial department of a women's magazine, Eriko is a charismatic presence in the fashion world, but I'm clueless about that trade, so I've never really been able to form any kind of opinion about her in that regard.

Eriko was talking about various things, like how she'd traveled all the way to the Inubozaki Lighthouse in the Choshi Peninsula to attend a shooting session on location there, only to see it ruined by sudden rainfall, or how a certain female celebrity, whom Eriko turned to for advice, became desperate thanks to some trouble with her new boyfriend—apparently this celebrity came uninvited to her apartment late at night, dead drunk, and Eriko had ended up letting her stay overnight to lend a sympathetic ear.

It was about twenty minutes before she finally came to a pause, at which point I seized the opportunity to interrupt her.

"Listen, do you remember my face?"

"What do you mean?" she said, sounding perplexed.

"It's just that, since we haven't met for a week already, I thought you surely must have forgotten what I look like by now, ha, ha."

After a slightly long pause she answered, "I see."

"What do you mean 'I see'?"

"Well, I understand now what you meant when you said you'd like our relationship to stay fresh."

She wasn't making much sense to me.

"So what did you understand?"

"It's like if we're able to forget each other's face, we can meet again as if we were meeting for the first time, right?"

"What I was saying isn't that simple really."

Having said so, however, I also felt that's what it really boiled down to in the end.

"So, how'd it go for you?" Eriko said. "Were you able to forget my face entirely?"

"Regrettably, I remembered just a short while ago. Bummer."

"You're such a fool, aren't you?!" Eriko said, laughing.

"You think?"

"You bet. One week's absence can't be long enough to make you forget, mister."

"But until yesterday I'd forgotten completely, you know. I was sloshed all the time, after all." I spoke jokingly, but Eriko suddenly fell silent.

"What's the matter?"

Her voice eventually returned, but only after she sighed heavily.

"I always remember you," she said. "Even when I'm having lunch I wonder if you're also eating at that time, and at night, when I'm in a meeting at work, I think you must also be in a meeting, talking with a writer or a college professor. And get this, sometimes I even break out laughing when I'm alone, imagining how you must be putting on a fake smile for people you bad-mouth all the time—those folks you call dimwits and ignoramuses. Oh, and did you know that whenever you laugh with your mouth closed you look nasty? It's so obvious that I'm sure people notice. Anyway, my point is that's how much I think of you, how well I remember you."

"Is that right?"

"Uh huh. So I call you sometimes when I want to listen to your voice. But you never answer. All I want is to be able to hear your voice, just like I'm doing right now, and that's why I don't need any reason to call. What matters isn't what we talk about, but the fact that we do."

It occurred to me then that if there really were no value in what was being said—that is, in the content of a conversation—then there mustn't be any value in talking itself, and anyway, I also didn't know what was so important about "the fact" of talking to each other.

"You know, if that's the case, you really should've called the office. You'd have been able to at least just talk then, I think."

"What? And have an involved conversation like this one? Over your office phone? Impossible."

"But the details don't matter, right? At least we'd be able to make small talk."

"Jumping to sarcasm again, are we? It just goes to show that you lack conscience." For some reason Eriko said this in an awfully steely tone.

I decided to change the subject. "Are you on a break today?"

"I've got a photo shoot now, and I won't be done until evening. What about you?"

"I'm on holiday."

"Shall we meet somewhere?"

"Not tonight. I'd like to take it easy, you know, because of the tooth."

"I'm on leave tomorrow—want to catch a movie?"

"Sorry, I've got something planned for tomorrow."

"Work?"

"No, not work."

"Going somewhere?"

"Uh huh."

"Where?"

"Don't know yet."

"Traveling alone?"

"Yeah."

"Is that fun?"

"Not in the least."

"So why go?"

"Hell, I don't know! No reason, really. Travel doesn't have to be about having fun all the time, does it? What about you? What's your plan?"

"Hmm, let's see. I suppose I'll go see a movie after all."

"Now that's what I call not having fun, seeing a movie alone."

"Not necessarily. In fact, you can enjoy movies and plays more freely when you're alone—you don't have to have any scruples or anything."

If that were the case, I wondered why she'd wanted me to accompany her a while back.

"Why don't you ask someone else to come with?"

"You want me to?"

"Not really, but I thought it'd be nice if you went out with a friend or two, you know."

"Well, why don't you go out with your friends too then?"

"I don't have any."

"You know that's not true."

"It's true. I've never had a single friend. You, on the other hand, probably have plenty."

"Why do you say that?"

"Say what?"

"Why does it seem to you like I have a lot of friends?"

"Well, don't you?"

"That's not the point. I just want to know the reason why you think that."

"No particular reason. It just seems that way."

"You're lying!"

"About what?"

"About the fact that you don't have any reason. I bet you

don't actually believe in friends, do you? I bet you think anyone convinced that he or she has a lot of friends is just a mindless fool."

"That's not true. You know there's a saying that goes 'The bells that bless romantic love are the death knell of friendship.' I just thought it'd be better if you went out with your friends sometimes because you start losing them by getting too absorbed in romance."

"Here we go again with the mumbo jumbo."

"It's not mumbo jumbo! Even Francis Bacon said, 'It is a mere and miserable solitude to want true friends (that is, to lack true friends); without which the world is but a wilderness.' There's also a quote that says something along the lines that love and friendship repel each other."

"Francis Bacon, my ass," Eriko said, finally laughing.

I laughed as well and added, "But most importantly Aristotle put it like this: 'A friend to all is a friend to none.'"

"You see what I mean? You're making fun of me after all."

"All right, I'll take back the word 'plenty.'"

"So what does that make someone like you, someone without a single friend?"

"That makes me, as Confucius said, 'A clear stream that's avoided by fish.'"

"Huh?"

"It means common people avoid clearheaded, wise men like yours truly, which is why I'm friendless."

"You're such a twit."

"I suppose so."

At this point I suddenly felt something like a fragment of a genuine feeling welling up inside me. It was a conviction that this presence called Eriko, who didn't mind all the random back-and-forths we were having then, was a very important friend. But I held back from saying so, since it felt as though she'd, on the contrary, take offense if I did.

"Well, talk to you again next week. This time I'll call you for sure. Let's meet somewhere."

Eriko muttered in a tiresome manner, "I don't know, maybe I'll take the day off today. I don't feel like going to work right now."

"I'm sure," I chimed in.

"Why?" Eriko said suddenly in a brittle voice again.

"Why what?"

"How could you say 'I'm sure' so offhandedly?"

"Because work isn't fun. I for one think about ditching the office every day, and I mean every day!"

"That's not what I'm talking about."

"Guess you're upset again."

"Thanks to you."

"If so, I apologize. I meant no offense. It's just a matter of semantics, really—just a misunderstanding. Please don't get so excited. Here's another saying: 'Without any intention to forgive each other's faults, friendship can never be realized.'"

I was fed up with the conversation by then and was half-laughing, hoping to calm her down. But this breezy manner of mine only backfired and she ended up getting even more excited.

"What are you saying? I'm not your friend?" Her voice kept getting sharper and sharper.

"But Chekhov says, 'A woman can become a man's friend only in the following stages—first an acquaintance, next a mistress, and only then a friend.'"

"Oh my God! What's wrong with you? Do you really think I want to listen to all that laughable smart talk of yours, so full of jumbled up knowledge? Why can't you give me straight answers—you know, the serious kind, *in a sincere way?*"

At this juncture I just wanted to hang up the phone. Partly for this reason, I decided to mount a somewhat decisive counterattack. I was also sure the reason why Eriko had suddenly flown into such a rage was because her sixth sense had detected—like sonar picking up a faint vibration—the genuine feeling of friendship I'd experienced only a few minutes ago.

"Eriko, I've been giving you serious answers. But remember what you said about talking? That what's important isn't the content of a conversation? In the end all language ever really amounts to is a medley of jumbled up knowledge and information. And it's not just me. That's the way it is for absolutely everybody. You yourself said that what counts is the act of talking—the fact that we engage in the act, that we experience it, right? So why get upset? By your own account, there's no need at all to get mad over anything I say, and basically, there's no way you and I can ever, as you put it, understand each other through the medium of language alone, right? But all you keep doing is asking, why, why, why, and, frankly, it's starting to get on my nerves a bit. In the first place, you never even tried to understand why I stopped contacting you for a while. All you did was treat me with contempt. If as you say the actual experience of talking is important while what's actually being talked about is immaterial, why'd you phone me to talk like this in the first place? You know, if you really want to talk you should just come see me in person. Getting together anytime this week wouldn't have been a problem. All you had to do was come visit me in my office. It's not as if I'm trying to run away or hide from you after all. You know why we end up having this kind of idiotic quarrel? It's because when you want to talk to me, you simply place a thoughtless phone call. Let me ask you this. When you talk about the importance of the act of talking to each other, you mean the importance of the act of talking itself, right? So if that's so important, we should be talking to each other face-to-face, right? As long as we're talking over the phone like this, we can't check each other out, monitor changes in our facial expressions and body language, the look in each other's eyes even, nor can we detect each other's breathing or the way we smell—over the phone, it's mostly just meaningless words going back and forth; words for mindlessly swapping pieces of random information and half-baked feelings from the gut. But while you say the content of what you talk about isn't important on the one hand, on the other hand, you find fault in a single phrase and begin to criticize me and talk to me as if I hated you. So what the hell do you mean when you say, 'give me straight answers?' I mean, what's up with that? You're the one who's being insincere, who's not playing it straight. Besides, I've apologized properly and if you still need to lash out so much, you should've never called me like this to begin with. And what's up with the 'I'm not your friend' line? Just what is it that you're saying I am to you then? If what you want to say is that I'm your lover, why don't you first of all clearly define in your head what the difference between a friend and a lover is before you say such such a thing? For your information, I consider you a true friend of mine, and to put it simply, in true Chekhovian fashion, you're my best friend, and, right now, I even think of you as my lover. Of course, that's not all there is to what I think about you."

Eriko was silent at the other end of the line. But it didn't feel as though she sympathized with my views. She was most likely confused, terribly weary of being argued down by my rather unusual logic.

"My tooth's starting to ache," I said, "so I'm hanging up. Hey, look, I was wrong. I'll make amends. I'll be sure to call you next week."

I pushed the End Call button and turned the cell phone off, just in case.

Moments later I poured myself more coffee, which had completely cooled down, and had a few sips while gazing at the view outside for a while.

By the way, regarding the proverb I quoted by the German Nobel Prize-wining author Paul Heyse? The one that went 'The bells that bless romantic love are the death knell of friendship'? Well, I have to confess that it wasn't altogether accurate. The correct quote is 'The bells that bless marriage are the death knell of friendship,' but for the life of me, I couldn't utter the word "marriage" to Eriko, so I just replaced that bit with the phrase "romantic love" before delivering it.

But in the end I realized, looking out at the view beyond the veranda, that such a concern was unnecessary and not worth giving a damn about.

4

THE FOLLOWING WEDNESDAY I was in my office until late, reading a manuscript before setting out for home on the last train. As I walked down Kiyosumi Street from Morishita Station toward my apartment, I was thinking about this manuscript. The author was a female nonfiction writer who, when she was thirty-nine years old, saw her mother suffer a cerebral hemorrhage that robbed her of the ability to move and speak. The manuscript painstakingly relates the author's thirteen-year battle to look after her mother, waged together with her aged father, before her mother passed away half a year ago—the work was, in part, as powerful and moving as a fictional first-person narrative—an "I" novel.

The final chapter vividly describes the author's experience of attending to her mother until her final moments.

Late at night, in a dim-lit room, I was alone with my mother, seated by her bedside, rubbing her hands. Her chest was making a heavy sound like the one a pair of bellows makes. She seemed to be in constant pain. Although nobody said so, I was aware that Mother was approaching death. She no longer responded to anything I said, and her facial expression didn't change anymore. Her bulging eyes were staring vacantly into thin air. Mother seemed like she wanted to take a rest now. I imagined she wanted to fall into a peaceful sleep. But it was as though her body didn't allow her, as though it was forcibly detaining her, saying not yet, not yet.

But Mother seemed to be suffering now. She even seemed to be saying, 'Enough already.' I breathed in sync with Mother's heavy breathing but couldn't share the pain with her. Mother was fighting all by herself. From start to finish, it was a lonely battle.

I could no longer tell her to hold on. If it were up to me, I'd have removed the breathing tube reaching into her windpipe, cut off her oxygen supply, and ended it all for her right there and then. Mother was just running alone toward a goal she could never turn back from. As I continued to watch her suffer in such a hopeless state, the concept of time collapsed in my mind and I lost all track of it.

It was around half past seven in the morning when the doctor called. After I reported that there was no change in her condition, that she constantly seemed to be having difficulty breathing, he told me he'd dispatch a nurse first thing in the morning.

It happened soon after that. Mother's breathing became heavier, more intense. She was gasping for breath, sounding like a locomotive train desperately climbing a steep slope, sputtering, her entire body rising as her chest heaved. I was overwhelmed by the intensity and before I knew it I threw myself at my recumbent mother and embraced her, desperately calling out to her. In my arms Mother breathed deeply, her chest creaking. And then, suddenly—like a locomotive suddenly coming to a halt—she ceased to breathe. For an instant, the room became enveloped in silence, and then the tube slipped from her lips.

"Papa, Mother's stopped breathing."

Father was standing there, stunned.

"Is that so?" he finally said.

How hard it is to grow old, to die—how heavily it weighs on us. Whether your family is by your side, or for that matter whether anyone is by your side, in the end it's a lonely battle, one that each and every one of us must ride out on our own.

And that's why, on that day, Mother had taught me, and only me, what dying is all about, telling me, in her own way, "This is what it is to die, my dear."

Don't worry, mom. I can, surely. Just like you, I can too, in the same way, I can.

I read this prose again and again in the office, breathlessly. The author says that death in the end is a solitary battle that everyone must ride out on their own, adding her declaration that she too could brave her own death. But then it occurred to me: if death were a battle, then exactly what purpose did it serve and for whom? Furthermore, what did it really mean to ride out death on your own?

I wondered whether Momma would be able to ride out on her own—like this author's mother, or even the author herself—this very difficult thing called death.

Pondering this as I walked along, I felt my chest tighten. Death must actually be a phenomenon of no great significance in the scheme of things—nothing really worth bothering about; the suffering expressed during death is stage-managed so that what's essentially just a turning point ends up becoming a heroic tale of a bitter and hard struggle, and all those accumulated memories of the past end up luring the dying into a deep swamp of regret and lingering affection, dragging along those standing near them.

But that's just a peripheral effect, as it were, of the phenomenon called death; it's not the thing itself at all.

Death's true substance is found in its inevitability: the fact that it happens, without fail, to everyone. In other words, it's something tantamount to birth: an absolutely singular phenomenon. Beyond that, nobody really knows anything. If I were asked to give an accurate description of death, I'd have to say that it's nothing more than an insignificant, common, and ordinary event after all.

But I could never leave it just at that. I believe that we all must make strenuous efforts to consider what lies beyond, even if it's impossible to do so. If death were something to "ride out" or survive—as this author suggests—we must grasp by any means possible the identity or true nature of the thing to be found at the end of the ride.

I became lost in thought, just thinking how absolutely impossible such a thing is for Momma to achieve, that she isn't capable of "riding out" death safely.

When I arrived in front of my apartment building, there was light spilling out from the window of my room on the third floor. I assumed Raita or Honoka had dropped in for the first time in ages.

But when I pulled the doorknob, I found that the door was locked.

I never locked my room. I didn't even lock it from the inside when I was alone in there. I never felt the need to; I'd never lived in a residence where I was likely to be inconvenienced by a break-in. When I was a child though, when I lived together with my mother and younger sister in an apartment in Kita Kyushu, I admit I used to be in the habit of locking up on account of the fact that the apartment was a predominantly female-run household. But ever since I graduated high school and came to Tokyo I've never used this thing called a key. Back in my college days when I went about my days frantically trying to scrape together money to cover my school fees and living expenses, I'd never keep any valuables in my room—those personal effects that'd get me into trouble if they ever got stolen. And even after I found a job and began to lead the workaday life of a wage earner, the key still proved unnecessary because I'd stash valuables like my bankbook and signature seal inside my locker at the office.

However, in the case of Honoka, I'd strictly told her to keep the door locked and the chain set in place whenever she was alone in my apartment. It was only natural that I should.

After sounding the chime, the door opened a few moments later.

"Welcome home, sensei." It was Honoka, whom I hadn't seen in about two weeks.

"Yeah, thanks," I said as she released the door chain. "It's been a while! Have you been well?"

Honoka mustered a vague smile, her long hair wet, suggesting she'd just had a shower. I entered the apartment and went straight into the eight-mat Western-style room instead of following her into the kitchen.

I got out of my suit and headed for the bathroom to take a shower. After washing my hair and body I changed into my loungewear and then opened the door to the kitchen.

Honoka was writing something at the table, several books spread out before her. When I tried to take some beer from the refrigerator she spoke from behind me.

"There's some salad and stew in there. You can have them, if you like."

"Yeah," I answered, grabbing a can of beer and two small plastic-wrapped bowls before putting them on the table and sitting down on a chair opposite her. Honoka didn't even lift her face, her pen racing across the writing pad.

I gazed on this present situation while sipping beer and pecking from the two bowls. The salad was a potato salad made with onions and carrots, and the stew contained shiitake mushrooms, lotus roots, chestnuts, and fried bean curd simmered in a sweet broth. Since I made do with a light meal of delivery soba for my dinner that day, my chopsticks got busy picking through her offerings.

Honoka is a strict vegetarian, but she's quite the expert at seasoning side dishes like these, which she'd prepare from time to time for me; they were all quite tasty for sure.

"I became disgusted with eating animal meat," she's told me since I've gotten to know her. "I don't care what it is—beef, pork, chicken, fish or whatever! I've just become sick of the idea of killing animals for food."

Perhaps influenced by Honoka, even Raita—someone who never ate fish anyway—seems to have considerably cut down, too, on his intake of meat—like beef, chicken, pork—these days.

Back when I used to tutor Honoka, there was a time she looked dreadfully hurt when I killed a mosquito that had strayed into her room.

A few minutes later, Honoka, the junior high student that she was then, said with a self-conscious laugh, "I'm incapable of even killing an insect, you know." But then she surprisingly added, her face turning stony, "A person like that can't live for long, I suppose."

Her attitude regarding living things isn't a bad one, I think. But I also feel she's right in her belief that people with such an attitude end up having short lives. It's just not instinctive, and the whole idea of not killing living things goes against the preordained condition of human existence.

"There's really no need," I recall saying at the time, "to lead a long life if it means you have to put up with things you don't want to."

I used to moonlight as a tutor for a while even after I joined my company. My early years in the firm had proved costly in many ways: there was the obligation to send money to my mother and younger sister, which I'd been doing since my school days, and my younger sister, who is four years younger than me, made her way into a local junior college. Even though the take-home pay from a publishing company is considered high, the entry-level wage I received was hardly enough to manage the hefty entrance fee and school expenses for my sister, along with the living expenses she sustained leading a single life.

I was first assigned a post in the accounting department. The others who'd entered the company with me all hoped to get into the editorial department, but not me; just because I chose to work at a publishing house, that didn't at all mean that I was bent on becoming an editor. I'd taken the entrance exam for my present company simply because the salary was attractive. And, after getting admitted, when I expressed my interest in the operations division, they assigned me to accounting, just as I wished. Thanks to that, I wasn't burdened with any overtime other than twice a year when I had to prepare financial reports, so I was basically free to spend my evenings moonlighting, just like in my school days.

Honoka was in the ninth grade when I tutored her. It lasted for a year, from the end of my second through my third year at the company.

It was rather grueling, giving her lessons—for three hours, from seven to ten in the evening—on how to pass the entrance examination. But it was worth it, since she passed with flying colors and was admitted into the Keio high school for girls. Today, she's a junior at Keio University, majoring in literature and psychology.

As for me, after working in the accounting department for two years, I was transferred to the editorial department of a weekly magazine without my say-so, and since then working part-time really has become impossible. Still, there was no need to moonlight anymore because I began to earn loads of overtime pay during my years at the weekly, and by the third year in the company, my salary was well above the amount for even a manager of a blue-chip corporation, so financially speaking I was pretty sound, until three years ago when my mother fell ill and her medical bills began to pile up.

It was exactly half a year ago, some time during the valley of the Golden Week period—the holiday-studded week in May—when Honoka suddenly called my office out of the blue. I hadn't heard from her at all since the day we met to celebrate her success with her high school exam.

I met Honoka again for the first time in five years.

Back in her junior high days she used to be an unstable girl, mentally and physically, repeatedly suffering from alternating bouts of anorexia and bulimic bingeing, but even after becoming a college student it didn't appear as though she was quite relieved of her plight. We met in a restaurant in Ginza. As ever, she only ate vegetables, but even then, only a small amount, taking one or two dainty bites after prodding the food with her chopsticks, gulping down beer most of the time. She'd grown remarkably, to a height of nearly 170 centimeters. Upon inquiring she told me that she weighed approximately forty kilos.

The fact that her disorder was rooted in her household environment had been clear to me since I began to visit her at home. Her father worked for the National Aerospace Laboratory and was renowned as the leading authority on rocket development in Japan, but he spent most of his time away from his family, living in the United States or Tanegashima, neglecting them for the most part. The mother was a musician, and she too was absent from the home for a third of the year, performing at recitals or presenting lectures at local music colleges. Despite her absence, this mother was a tyrant to Honoka and a brother three years younger than her, putting the siblings through a regimen of hyper-education.

Even while we ate, Honoka remained silent about why she'd called me up suddenly. As long as she didn't say anything, I was unable to broach the subject myself, but judging from the fact that she hadn't changed—she'd gotten completely drunk in a matter of two hours—I simply couldn't let her return home, so I brought her back to my apartment.

On our way back, in the taxi, Honoka was breathing painfully in her inebriated state and said, "Even today, at the station, on the platform, I saw a young mother scolding her small child like a crazy person. The kid was crying her eyes out but the mother didn't give a damn, shouting at her as if she'd really gone insane. If she was going to be so cruel to her own child, she should've never brought her into the world. It was terrible! The world is a miserable place," she said to no one in particular, sighing.

"Such a mother should die early for the good of the child," I said, and she fell silent for a while. Then she muttered, "Still, to that child, she's the only mother she's ever going to have."

I spread out a futon in the six-tatami mat room, laid her down on it, and slowly and carefully wiped her face and the back of her neck with a cold wet towel to sober her up.

"I'm sorry, sensei, for being such a nuisance," Honoka said, closing her eyes as she let out a heavy sigh.

"Hey," I said after a while, "do you want to die?"

"I don't know," she answered.

"If you do, you should die in this room. No one's going to stop you. If you're feeling lonely dying alone, let me know. I just might be able to help."

Without saying a word, she winced, tears from her closed eyelids spilled down the cheeks of her gaunt face.

"Nobody was there. I thought about calling someone, but there wasn't anyone I could call."

I gripped her hand. It was a bony and cold hand.

Honoka cried quietly.

She continued to cry for a very long time until, suddenly, while wiping her tears away with the towel, she asked in response, "Do you want to die too, sensei?"

When I said, "I don't know," she said, "Obviously."

Finally wearing a faint smile, she just fell asleep as though she'd dropped dead. While gazing at her skinny, sleeping face, I felt that she probably thought about dying often. To many of us living in this day and age who are still considered young, especially like her, and rather less like me, it's probably just an ordinary fact of life. It's certainly true that this world is terribly unappealing to live in, but that's been the case throughout the ages. I distinctly felt, however, that I wasn't as inclined to die as Honoka was. I don't think there's much overlap between feeling like you should've never been born and hoping for death.

THE PART OF ME THAT ISN'T BROKEN INSIDE   49

It's just that, since way back when, whenever I'd confess to someone something like "I wish I'd never been born," or "I never asked anyone to give birth to me," or "I'd be more comfortable dead!", in the few experiences I've had, the kinder this someone the more predictably he or she would respond by saying something like, **"So why don't you go ahead and die already!"**

If you think about this a little, such a response is a prime example of the power of reverse psychology: basically, the person saying such a thing, after saying such a thing, would go on to listen to my story with deep appreciation, and then reveal all kinds of stories related to his or her own experiences, earnestly and warmly and wisely comforting and encouraging me in the process.

But I was always disappointed by those very words they uttered. In fact, I used to be so thoroughly disappointed that I hardly heard anything they'd tell me afterward.

First of all, there's no reason to tell me to die just because I said that I wish I'd never been born. But let's just say that I went even further and had actually declared that I wanted to die. Still, who the hell has the right to then bluntly advise me to die?

If you're going to sing such a brutal tune, you should at least add, "In that case I'll die together with you."

It's often said that there's no way to stop a person who insists on dying, that there's no hope to save a person attracted to death. But that's false. A suicide can be prevented if a person continues to be kept on watch twenty-four hours a day, even if you have to divide the work with others. I've always thought it's possible to sharply reduce the suicide rate. The failure to do so has mainly been due to the strange hesitation exhibited by the people around those who commit suicide, and I'm convinced that what lies at the root of this hesitation is the evil trend spreading today: the worship of Western individualism.

As I heard Honoka breathing in her sleep, I wondered which question was more important to ask: "Do I really want to die?" or "Do I really want not to die?" To us mortals—for whom death is inevitable—I felt the latter was the far more important question.

I wonder what people would generally say if they were asked, "Do you really don't want to die? If so, what's the reason?" If you ask me, no matter how much I think about it, in however many ways, I feel that I won't be able to work out any reason per se that'll prove convincing enough to me, or to other people for that matter. However, people who have someone they love, or people with a family near and dear to them, most likely will answer that they wouldn't want to die for the sake of such people, vaguely leaving it at that, not giving the matter any further thought.

Among them, some will also probably say it's because they want to enjoy themselves, become happier, confusing our human destiny with death, evading the question altogether. Such a person is averting his eyes from the fact that he's going to die, but I'm sure when his moment arrives, he'll pay the price for sidestepping the issue and, consequently, will suffer all the more.

According to the writings of a certain physician, the number of suicides has increased since 1998 over a period of three consecutive years to over 30,000, indicating the third wave of sudden spikes in suicide rates recorded since World War II. The physician wrote:

The first wave, which peaked in 1958, transpired at a turbulent time when the revision of the US-Japan Security Treaty was imminent, with young people below the age of thirty accounting for over half of the overall suicides. The second wave occurred just before the nation rushed headlong into the period of the bubble economy that lasted from 1983 through 1986. The sudden increase back then was attributable to the same age-group. In the case of the third wave, which began in 1998, however, although an increase was registered in all age-groups, records show that the total increase was mainly accounted for by the Baby Boom generation whose members were in their early fifties.

So, apparently, this essay infers that at least ten thousand people below the age of thirty, like myself, in the first half of the third decade of the Showa era (1955—1965), committed suicide every year. I was surprised to read this statistic, thinking the figure was exaggerated. If it was accurate, it would mean that twenty-seven people were dying every day, which in turn meant that one young man or woman had committed suicide somewhere in Japan every thirty minutes without fail.

The physician also wrote:

However, the trend of seeing youth below the age of thirty accounting for half of all suicides has diminished since then. As of today, they only account for a little over ten percent. Young people have stopped committing suicide.

After reading the above, I wondered why it was that young people had stopped committing suicide, but I couldn't find any good reason.

However, on the other hand, I was also utterly struck by the following thought at the time:

Why is it that I don't commit suicide?

I couldn't readily find an answer to that question.

Seated in front of Honoka, I drank beer for half an hour. She didn't lift her face even once, her attention fixed on the writing pad. When I glanced at the wall clock, the hands were pointing to eleven. Although I didn't know what she was writing, it was probably a report she had to finish for one of her classes. I was fed up pursuing any text outside of work, so I rarely read a book these days. If I did read anything it was at most the work of an author I was in charge of, or reference material that was required reading for work. So I didn't feel any interest in whatever prose Honoka was composing before my eyes, though it's still interesting to observe somebody at close range pouring their heart into their writing. The reason I liked tutoring wasn't because I got to teach, but because I got to see how earnestly students like Honoka poured themselves into their studies.

A pleasant and hazy buzz spread throughout my body, making me feel drowsy. I quietly got up, washed the two small bowls at the sink, carefully crushed the beer cans and threw them into the disposal bag reserved for them. Before Honoka started frequenting the apartment, the great many cans of beer and bottles of wine and whiskey that Raita and I used to consume and throw away were left mixed up inside a massive trash bag which took up considerable space in the kitchen, but with the appearance of Miss Methodical here, before we knew it we were obediently following her rules, separating the trash and taking them out for disposal.

About to retire to my room after placing the tableware in a basket and washing my hands, I heard her voice saying, "Shall I make some tea?" I turned around and saw Honoka looking at me, her face relaxed. The writing pad was already put away, the books closed and stacked up at the edge of the table.

"All right," I said. "I'll boil some water then." I poured mineral water into the kettle and put it on the stove; Honoka stayed away from tap water.

She came to my side and took out two glasses from the closet above the sink. Next, she fished from a small drawer attached to the sink a silver bag stashed with tea.

"What's up with those?" I asked, eyeing the glasses.

"After I found the tea the last time I stayed, I told myself I'd get proper glasses. I just bought them today in fact; three of them, including one for Raita."

They were clear, wide glasses.

"Sure look pricey!" I said.

Honoka laughed. "Not really. They're recycled—just 300 yen a pop."

"Is that so?"

"You know, I've noticed something about you, sensei; as a consumer, you're as bad as it gets."

I left the sink first and returned to the table.

"This tea is far more top-notch," Honoka said, cutting open with a pair of scissors the seal of the vacuum-packed tea bag. "Who bought it?"

"My girlfriend. That reminds me, even she had nice things to say about the tea."

"I know, right? It's sold by this Chinese teashop that's all the rage in Aoyama right now. I think a hundred grams of this will probably set you back around five thousand yen."

Honoka dropped some leaves into the glass with a spoon and slowly poured boiling water until the glass was about half full. "Ah, smells good."

She held the rim of the glass and placed it before me, and then seated herself in a chair opposite mine after bringing her own glass.

I positioned my face close to the steam and detected a subtle honey-like aroma tickling my nostrils. It smelled nice indeed. The fine tealeaves, covered in something like downy hair, opened up slightly in the boiling water, their hue changing into a bright yellow and green in the transparent glass. One sip revealed a thick, sweet flavor.

"Hmm, this is good," I said.

Honoka also seemed to be enjoying her sips.

"It's called Luxueyinzhen," she said, glancing at the label on the tea bag.

"What's that?"

"The characters stand for green, snow, silver, and needle—together they spell the name, Luxueyinzhen. I guess you're not good at Chinese, are you sensei?"

"Guilty as charged. I'm absolutely clueless."

"Actually you're quite clueless about a lot of things, aren't

you! Such a shame. You seemed to know about everything back
when you tutored me," she said, sounding oddly impressed.

"Obviously!"

"But Kanji's great, don't you think? There's a certain panache
to it. In English, you'd just call this Luxueyinzhen tea green
tea, and as for the names of black teas and coffees, well, they're
mostly just derived from place names—you simply don't
come across such a wonderful name like Luxueyinzhen now,
do you!?"

"You think?"

"Oh yes, most certainly! And that's why I don't like English.
Why, just today in class we were asked to translate from Japanese
into English, and the word *robai* came up. What do you think
the correct English translation for this word is?"

"Well, the word *robai* translates to something like 'confusion'
or 'the state of being upset,' doesn't it?"

"It translates to 'don't know what to do.'"

"Right, okay."

"But that completely fails to capture the finer nuance of
robai, don't you think?"

"The finer nuance?"

"Well, the kanji characters for *robai* contain the radical for
'beast' and the characters for 'ryo' and 'kai,' right? So both
characters in *robai*, that is both *ro* and *bai*, are a reference to
wolf: *ro* is a wolf with long front legs and short hind legs, while
bai refers to a wolf with short front legs and long hind legs.
These two usually move around in pairs, but once they get
separated, they both falter and start panicking. And that's why
robai means confusion. Didn't you know?"

"Nope."

"Really? It's common knowledge."

"Sorry about that."

"There's no need to apologize. I mean it's not as if I'm
blaming you or anything."

When I saw her earlier at the door she looked her usual sullen self, but apparently she was in a good mood tonight. She was even enjoying her hot tea with great relish, blowing on it to cool it down. She picked up the tea bag and examined it again.

"I'll buy you a *chakoro* next time. I know it's belated, but it'll be my gift to you, okay? If I remember correctly, sensei, your birthday is on the tenth?"

"What's a *chakoro*?"

"My dear teacher, perhaps you're under the impression that tea is just for drinking?"

When I refrained from answering, the look on her face turned all the more amused.

"The *chakoro* is a tea incense burner; you place some tea leaves on a plate inside it and warm the leaves from underneath with a candle." She pointed to the tea we were drinking. "These tea leaves should give off a pleasant aroma. It'll be so soothing for the soul."

"Soothing for the soul, eh? Hmmm."

"Oh stop with that condescending look of yours. You're always quick to give me that look."

She appeared genuinely amused.

"I'm not making fun of you, but all that talk doesn't really interest me—that talk about what's soothing for the soul. It's all just wispy mumbo jumbo to my ears, and hearing it from your mouth makes it sound all the more incredible."

"Why, how rude of you, sir! I hope you can see that I'm not always depressed, you know, and that's because I have latitude in my life, you see, and latitude is the most important thing you can have from day to day. Tea can give you that latitude, so can a fragrance, so can kanji."

I then remembered. Eriko had similar things to say when she'd given me the tea.

This tea's really tasty. You can prepare it just by putting it in a cup and adding hot water, so why don't you try some when, for instance, you've had too much to drink. It'll be a great way to take a break. I've always felt you lacked a certain peace of mind that would allow you just to relax and genuinely take pleasure in what's pleasurable.

"Latitude, huh?"

"Yes, latitude."

Honoka's smile—as I always felt—was somehow tinged with mystery.

5

THE NEW YEAR BEGAN all too soon, while I was swamped with work.

Publishing gets busiest during the year-end. In the case of a magazine's editorial department, we have to finish the New Year's special issue and the Early Spring issue (the February issue) in less than a month, from the end of November through the middle of December, and on top of that, it's also necessary to prepare half of the table of contents for the March issue (released in February). Even books, pressured by the situation at the printing press, the deadlines for finishing the proofs of titles, planned for publication in January and February, follow a tight schedule. Furthermore, with the year-end settlement of accounts approaching in March, the top brass mandate company-wide increases in sales, so the number of releases we're expected to make at the very beginning of the new year is usually considerable, and what's more, in a major publishing house like the one I work for, we have to come up with at least several eye-catching products worthy of the honor of being the first releases for the year, and therefore worthy of gracing the newspaper ads running on New Year's Day. The year-end season is a showdown, so to speak—the moment of truth when each and every editor finally sends out into the world the fruits of their year-long labor, including full-length novels by bestselling authors, over-sized books, and the first releases in a series of collected works or of theme-based compilations.

Even in my case, I had to compile more than thirty studies done on educational issues by experts of various fields—studies

I'd invested about half a year in collecting—and I also had to finish at a stretch the memoirs of the former Prime Minister whom I used to be on familiar terms with during my days working at the monthly magazine. For this reason, I ended up staying overnight through two-thirds of December, in the basement of the office, which was, for all intents and purposes, the napping room.

On Christmas Eve I enjoyed French cuisine with Eriko at a hotel in Toranomon. We'd dined there the previous year as well and Eriko was feeling slightly sentimental about the fact that she was spending Christmas Eve with the same person for the second year in a row.

"It's been a year already since that rainy day, hasn't it?" she said wistfully. When I pointed out that it was *only* a year, she appeared happy nonetheless. The food wasn't good at all; it was merely expensive, just as it was last year.

On Christmas Day we held a party at New Seoul in the evening. When I arrived around seven with some cake, champagne, and gifts for the mother and child, Tomomi was in the middle of roasting a chicken in a microwave oven placed on the counter—she'd taken it down from the top of the shop's refrigerator, where it was usually kept.

After draping a white tablecloth over the table, the three of us sat down on a U-shaped sofa, popped open a champagne bottle, and set off crackers. While tearing out a piece of chicken, Tomomi remarked that it was the third time she'd eaten chicken like this with me. Since it was the most fragrant chicken I'd ever tasted, its skin roasted to a crisp, I praised her a number of times.

She told me that Ilgon Park had brought presents on Christmas Eve. Takuya began to spin the many Beyblade tops he'd gotten from his father on the small floor of the shop, and I joined him, getting absorbed in the game too.

On December 29th, Eriko returned to her childhood home in the town of Suwa. I saw her off at Shinjuku Station.

Tomomi also left with Takuya for her parental home in Sendai on the thirtieth. I saw them off at Tokyo Station in the daytime.

Raita was to visit on New Year's Eve in the evening. I awoke around noon and drove to the liquor store in Monzennakacho to purchase some alcohol. Although I consider myself a heavy drinker, Raita gets quite hilarious and thrilling when he drinks; I doubt I'll ever meet a heavier drinker than him. After purchasing a large quantity of all sorts of liquor and grabbing a bite to eat at a revolving sushi bar, I returned to the apartment and spent my entire afternoon reading a book. It had been a while since I read for pleasure, but when it occurred to me that neither Eriko nor Tomomi was in Tokyo, my mind quieted down and I was able to lose myself in the book.

Raita arrived a little past nine. He'd brought a large platter heaped with food, and after he placed it in the center of the dining table, we began drinking at once. He told me how he'd spent the entire day preparing the food from leftover ingredients he'd gotten from the restaurant where he worked, which had closed for the year the previous night. Raita had prepared food for last New Year's Eve as well—his cooking tasted great, being quite the chef himself. This year he'd prepared so much more than last year that we couldn't finish eating everything in a single night.

When I remarked how gorgeous the food looked, he appeared bitter and said, "The customer traffic's been bad; the amount of meat and vegetables left over was double last year's."

He then went on to say, "I'm fed up with all those structural reforms that bully the people—I say protect employment, protect the small and medium-sized companies from the politics that prioritize large corporations over the weak."

He pauses to laugh. "Seriously though, your proletarians about town are in deep trouble, you know. Even my boss is getting really worried, with the traffic of regular customers steadily fading and all."

Raita dropped out of high school after his sophomore year and became a live-in attendant at a yakitori shop in Nakano called Torimasa. He just turned twenty this year. His father had been a long-time board member of the Communist Party of the Tama area and was now serving as a city council member of Inagi City. Raita and his father apparently got along well and on his days off Raita would help out the political party with their activities.

I'd become acquainted with Raita after a TV producer called Terauchi, an acquaintance of mine, tried and failed to recruit Raita while he was handing out flyers for the Japanese Communist Party in the streets of Shinjuku two years ago, in the spring.

Terauchi was plainly turned down, but he didn't give up and managed to get Raita to disclose where he worked. Since then, Terauchi kept visiting Raita at Torimasa every single day to persuade him, but in the end it was to no avail. It was on such an occasion when I was invited by Terauchi to visit the yakitori shop with him. I'd accompanied him just for fun when I met Raita there for the first time. It happened two years ago in the month of June.

Raita claimed, with a swagger in his voice, that his hobby was class warfare and that his favorite book was *The Communist Manifesto*. Terauchi was mystified, but of course, Raita was no Marxist at all. Even though his father had apparently urged him to join his political party, I'm certain the chances of Raita complying were zero.

Apart from Raita's questionable nature, though, there was nothing unreasonable about why Terauchi was so driven to offer Raita a role in a drama he was producing; Raita was a beautiful young man; so much so that the word "breathtaking" applied literally in his case. Even I was captivated when I beheld him for the first time, despite being told what to expect from Terauchi.

When I went to the shop alone the next time, I was able to have a decent conversation with him and I found out that apparently proposals from talent scouts like Terauchi had been incessant since the time he was in high school.

"With those looks of yours, life's probably not that easy, huh?" I said, and Raita nodded and laughed, saying, "Yeah, I guess . . . Well, once I get old and get used to living a life of poverty, this face of mine, the looks I have now in my youth, is just going to tumble downhill, right? It's just going to look drab and lackluster, you know. Until then, I just have to be patient I suppose."

"Yeah, I guess so," I chimed in. "I think there's something slightly wrong with people who become singers or actors on account of their good looks—they get carried away. But then again, those guys who go to The University of Tokyo and become bureaucrats or scholars just because they've got good heads are even worse; they really have a problem."

"Yeah, sure seems that way . . ." Raita appeared to agree with my words, slightly raising the flesh of his cheeks while carefully grilling skewers of meat over the charcoal fire. It was a fearless expression bordering on a sneer, marked with an unquestionable trace of violence, inspiring dread and trepidation in anyone who beheld it.

Later on, after the shop closed and the two of us went barhopping, Raita spoke his mind, asserting, "Naoto-san, you said something's wrong with scholars and government officials, but I think it's the entertainers and politicians who're the real scumbags, the lowest of the low. No one knows scholars and bureaucrats—they're lost in obscurity. But entertainers and politicians? Now these guys are engaged in the petty business of selling their faces for a price, right? That's like such an uncool thing to do, yet they think of themselves as being cool or great, and that upsets me sometimes—I mean I get this feeling that they're unforgivable, see. I'm like, what the hell do they think they're doing, you know, like how can they get it all so wrong? There's nobody more unruly, I believe, than someone who's convinced he can see everything about himself all by himself. Don't you agree, Naoto-san?"

"What do you mean by 'see everything about himself all by himself?'" I asked in return, my interest slightly sparked by that line.

"Well," he said, "the thing about the business of selling your face is that the initial sales strategy concerns whether the person selling himself can successfully control the person he's actually selling, right? It's all about how much you can sell this product called yourself for. So you can say it's a business transaction, an act that allows you to profit, right? But if you ask me, what it all boils down to is the fact that anyone who commercializes the self just ends up with this make-believe self who's supposed to manage the commercial product—the commercial self—and in so doing, such a person ends up completely removing all the imperfections, vagueness, and all the fuzzy relativity inside him and gives himself permission to subject his entire existence to the dogged pursuit and acquisition of wealth and power. But you've got to be out of your mind to do something like that, right? After all, no matter how hard you try, there's no way you could ever truly know yourself, right? But these people carry on wheeling and dealing anyway, peeling off the surface appearances of the selves they're completely clueless about—at the end of the day they're nothing more than shameless strippers of the human psyche. That's all you can say about those bozos, really."

While mulling over Raita's half-baked words for a while, I remembered the following passage in a book by Erich Fromm that I'd read.

How are we to come to terms with the fact that subjectively speaking our actions are motivated by self-interest while, objectively speaking, we serve purposes other than those for ourselves? How are we to reconcile the spirit of Protestantism with the spirit of modern individualism?

It seems to me that Fromm has concluded that individualism isn't self-love, but simply another form of greed.

So I said to Raita, "I don't think it's really necessary to argue in your roundabout way to point out that entertainers and politicians are uncool. At the end of the day we're all just sellers, all of us human beings. Just as you're doing business by selling yakitori, the grocery store sells vegetables; the fishmonger sells fish; the butcher shop sells meat; those guys at the GS gas station sell gasoline; the car dealer sells cars; the electronics store sells electrical appliances; the bank sells money; scholars, artists, and various other artisans sell whatever know-how they've mastered; entertainers sell acts; politicians sell policies, and that's all there is to it. Everyone's just the same in that respect. To eat, everyone's just stripping off various resources from this planet. Sure, when you talk about someone selling his face, you could certainly call it the commercialization of the self, but simply put, what you really mean to say is that—as a seller—an entertainer or politician lies more than a grocer or fishmonger, right? When the product you're selling is fish and vegetables there's not much scope for lying, and you don't see that much deception either in the skills and techniques of artisans. However, with entertainers and politicians it's a different story: the products they sell are often vague and don't assume any kind of shape that easily, so these guys attempt to boost their commercial value through ostentatious displays, see. Now what you're saying is that this obvious avarice and deception, to us buyers, look awfully shameful, right? After all, there's a saying that goes 'Show me a liar, and I'll show you a thief.' So in brief, those people who upset you are simply good-for-nothing liars—that's what you basically want to say, right?"

"Well, yeah, I suppose so. But hey, doesn't it really piss you off hearing those phonies call each other 'artist' or 'sensei'? It's a sign this world's going to the dogs, that it just keeps getting more and more rotten to the core."

"But it's not just the world today that's rotten to the core, is it now? I mean the world's been rotten throughout the ages—through all time—so saying that it's getting rotten is a bit naive in my opinion, pal."

A month after we met, Raita began staying at my apartment occasionally, and we've continued our friendship for more than two years.

We watched the *Kohaku Uta Gassen,* the Red and White Song Battle, on TV and had loads to eat and drink. When it was past twelve Raita tidied up the glasses and tableware and went home after saying, "Well then, Naoto-san, I think it's time for me to call it a day."

For the next three days after New Year's Day, in order to prepare an annual New Year's guest list of the politically powerful, the cameraman from my company's photography department and I were in a rental car, circling around the homes of politicians—the Premier's official residence, Ozawa's house in Fukazawa, and Hatoyama's original house in Gokokuji—to monitor the traffic of luxury automobiles with black-tinted windows entering and exiting through grand, imposing gates. For several years getting this job done was apparently a major struggle for the company, since nobody readily volunteered to take it on. But this problem was solved once I joined the company.

During those three days I used the car phone four times, placing three calls to my younger sister in Kitakyushu, and one call—my first one—to Mrs. Onishi. When I called her at six in the morning on New Year's Day, the missus said in a still half-asleep, groggy voice, "Happy New Year!"

I promised to meet her on the evening of the fourth at the usual hotel and hung up.

Every afternoon, inside the car, when the traffic of political guests would come to an end and the cameraman would begin to put away his film, I'd open the book I'd started reading on New Year's Eve and lose myself in its world. The book was a collection of essays written by a certain wealthy female Buddhist scholar in her later years, recounting the teachings of Buddha in such a lucid and eloquent fashion that it was worthy of multiple readings. Her prose was that marvelous. For example, in the passage titled "What It is To Live," after introducing the famous Buddhist story titled "Sights From the Four Gates During A Stroll"—the Shimon Yukan—she writes as follows.

In the days of my youth, the legend seemed like a cold and distant fabrication when I heard it. At times, I even felt repelled, questioning whether it was appropriate to depict the sacred Lord Buddha as someone so sickly and ignorant of the world. However, having lived for nearly seventy years now, and having indeed reached old age, which inevitably brings illness and the clarity of my own demise that lies beyond the affliction, I find myself utterly admiring the truth of each and every word expressed in the legend—yes, yes, absolutely, I keep telling myself, this is what it means to live: if you thoroughly scrape out from human existence, using a bamboo whisk perhaps, all things that pass and fade away, including youth, beauty, love, emotions, material wealth, social status, and worldly abilities, the skeletal frame that remains in the end will be merely made—for everyone alike— of old age, illness, and death. Everyone, including myself, realizes this for the first time only after facing old age, after facing illness, after facing death. But perhaps, we die without ever becoming aware.

Buddha, however, was still in the flower of his youth when he'd understood—one beautiful day when his hair was still jet-black in hue—the absolute skeletal frame of life itself to be the 'suffering' caused by old age, illness, and death. What's more, he understood this suffering to be common to all living things and renounced the world to pursue the spiritual path to transcend this suffering. What cosmic sensitivity, what cosmic kindness! What delights me even more is the fact that the youthful Buddha has articulated exactly what lies behind our aversion to old age, illness, and death, which are inescapable truths for all of us. He said,

When young, one is subject to aging
when healthy, subject to illness
when alive, subject to death.

In other words, he'd realized that behind our denial lies our subconscious belief in our own superiority—our arrogance. Ahh, who else on earth could ever speak into my ear these words that tear open my chest and expose so plainly, so logically, how rotten my heart has become in the course of living and harboring it for seventy years.

In the latter part of the book, she writes about her current state of mind as follows.

If 'life' were clothing you put on a skeleton that bears old age, illness, and death, then I'd like, if possible, for this clothing, worn only for a while, to be beautiful and graceful. If one thinks of the way one lives in life as the way one dies in life, one is fortunate. If you understand that living with exuberance is to go on to die with exuberance, you'll have peace of mind.

I was inside a taxi on the night of January 3rd, returning to my apartment, when I suddenly had chest pains. My breathing got rough, my heart began to pound, and every time I breathed my throat made a whistling sound before my entire body began to shiver. It felt as though several of the tubes of my lungs were clogged, preventing oxygen from properly reaching into the depths of my chest. Eventually I became incapable of exhaling properly, of blowing out puffs of breath, as it were. My entire body felt like a deflating lifebuoy, its air being forcibly released through a pinhole.

I had to loosen my tie, unbutton three buttons of my shirt, remove my belt, take off my shoes, and lie face down on the mouton-matted rear seat of the car. Amid such a pressing situation, the driver called out to me many times, but I explained that I was just a little tired, having eaten hardly anything the past three days.

After getting off I went up the stairs of my apartment but had to stop and crouch down three times to take deep breaths.

Several years of hard work were taking a considerable toll on my heart. Every time I pushed myself a little these days, I started suffering symptoms of angina. My family doctor—a graduate of a women's medical college—said it was cardiac neurosis, judging from the symptoms I was experiencing of cardiac arrhythmia and chest congestion. She occasionally prescribed for me a mild vasodilator and children's aspirin. At any rate, the pain was rarely this excruciating.

The room was chilly but I didn't feel like turning on the heater; my chest was yearning for fresh air. So, without turning the light on, I opened the window first.

I looked up into the dark, starless sky of New Year's Day. The breath I let out flickered white in the dark. I stretched myself out by the window, my jacket still on, and probably breathed over a hundred times a minute for nearly an hour until I felt heavy with sleep. I then closed the window and lay down on the bed, but my chest pain remained.

Feeling as though I'd swallowed a clock gone haywire, I simply remained still, not moving a muscle.

In the pitch-black room I embraced my own cold body with all my heart, feeling terribly sad. It had been quite a while since I'd felt this way, I thought.

The next morning I called the family doctor and asked her to give me a checkup right away. As usual, she took an electrocardiogram and X-rays of my chest.

There was nothing terribly abnormal about my heart, the middle-aged, bespectacled doctor told me. But an examination of the X-rays indicated that there was some accumulation of fat around the heart. She gave me seven days' worth of drugs and tranquilizers.

On my way to the office from the clinic I kept imagining the yellowish fatty substance stuck around my heart. I wondered if that fat was also an integral part of me.

When I arrived, the several hundred pictures taken three days ago of men and women in full formal attire were ready: old men sitting up straight with a cane in hand behind smoked-glass car windows; ladies in heavy makeup and fur, greeting guests with dramatic flourishes at the front gardens of the Hatoyama and Ozawa residences. I began writing down their names and titles with a soft-leaded blue pencil on the flipside of the copy paper of each photograph. I wrote down the names of cabinet ministers, ordinary members of the Diet, high-level bureaucrats, the brasses of local support groups, and the executives of large corporations. I was able to confirm half of the guests, but that still left two or three hundred of them nameless in the end.

The task took me a full six hours to finish, and when I noticed the time it was one hour past my appointment with Mrs. Onishi. When I called the hotel the lady was in the usual room. I apologized for the long wait and told her that I wasn't feeling too healthy, and that I wanted to call off the rendezvous tonight. Her voice sank with disappointment as she asked for the details of my condition, so I answered, "It could be that I'm just playing sick."

"In that case, come!"

The missus was waiting for me, as usual, with the "Pink-Rotar"—a love egg vibrator—inside her vagina. There'd been a gap of more than a month since our last tryst, so she was horny as hell, the sight of her downright disgraceful.

"You told me to stick it inside the moment I got up this morning," she said, clinging on to me as soon as I entered the room. "So it's been in there for twelve hours already, you know."

I'd completely forgotten, but come to think of it, I may have commanded her to do such a thing on New Year's Day, in the morning, over the phone.

Detecting a faint vibration in the abdominal region, which she began rubbing against me, I listened closely and heard, indeed, the hum of the quivering love egg.

"You've been a good girl, haven't you?"

Due to my state of health I refrained from being a tease as usual and immediately got down to the nitty-gritty. Completely turned on already, the missus didn't particularly seem to mind either.

At first I made her crawl naked, and after fishing another, fat vibrator from her Louis Vuitton bag and throwing it in a random direction, I made her retrieve it with her mouth, like a dog, from the carpeted floor. We tirelessly played this game of fetch for about thirty minutes, but I intended to clear out early that night, so whenever she came back with the thing in her mouth properly, I had her face her butt toward me to reward her with a good jiggle of the love egg peeking through her vagina. With the fat vibrator crammed in her mouth, the missus let out a queer-sounding muffled cry and continued to come multiple times without getting tired.

Next, I tied her arms tightly together behind her, using a rope she'd also brought along, and then went on to gag her, slip a mask over her eyes, throw her down on the bed, and smear jelly lotion all over her body while pulling out the love egg and shoving the vibrator instead, deep into the base of her vagina, turning the dial to maximum intensity before thrusting it in and out. The missus was drooling, and, by turns, sobbing and screaming; in that way, even though she took intermittent breaks to wipe her vagina with a hot, wet towel, she continued to come incessantly for more than two hours. Casting a sidelong glance away from the missus, who was lying now on her back with her mouth open like a slob, drifting off to sleep, I looked at my watch and noticed that it was nearly eleven. Both my arms were starting to get numb by then, and even though I was now down to just my undies, I was sweating bullets all over my body, partly because the room's heating was set too high. I sensed then, in the area of my chest, a faint warning of an impending seizure, so I decided to wrap it up for the night with some foreplay the missus had recently taken a particular liking to.

After untying the rope at her back, I made her legs split wide open and fastened her ankles to her wrists with two short ropes, tying each into multiple knots. The missus resisted, but only outwardly; that's how she reacts every time, and the moment I yell, "Don't move!" she immediately becomes tame.

Reinserting the lotion-soaked love egg into her vagina for the time being, I left the bed, removed a nail clipper from my briefcase, and carefully clipped the fingernails of both my hands, one nail after another, clipping the forefinger and middle finger of my right hand particularly short.

Taka Kato, the porn actor, in a popular series titled "The Squirting Club," had emphasized that the secret to making your partner achieve a successful squirting orgasm was to properly cut your nails in such a way. A close-up of his right hand clearly showed that his fingernails had been cut short; I remember being impressed by this testament to his dedication, to the thoroughness of his professionalism.

When I returned to the bed and pulled out the love egg, an unbelievable amount of liquid spilled out from the missus' vagina.

Lodging, at once, the forefinger and middle finger of my right hand in there, I fixed the balls of my fingers to the upper part of the vaginal wall, where the wrinkles were the most prominent, and began to apply strong pressure, rubbing from the bottom up. At the same time, with my left hand, I stimulated the clitoris, turning it like a small screw after, once again shamelessly and without any hesitation, peeling back its hood.

As I made the lower half of her body convulse intermittently while gently calming her as she tried to instinctively release her hips from my grip, I fingered, with a single-minded focus, a single point on her vaginal wall for nearly fifteen minutes, when her abdomen surged suddenly and she began to writhe with waves of ecstasy rippling through her, letting out a sad scream, sounding like a child crying—aaaahnnn. At that moment, a torrent of liquid gushed out from between her legs, soaking my right arm.

Once women get started like that they lose all control and turn incontinent. In the end, the missus thrashed about so much that the sound of the bed creaking resounded throughout the room as she repeatedly spouted out more urine from between her legs, as if to empty her stomach, while her wrists and ankles turned crimson red with bruises, and the gag I'd made her bite chafed both ends of her lips. She finally passed out, looking horrible, the veins of her forehead bulging.

Taka Kato, in one of his video appearances, while watching actresses he'd just met for the first time on set falling prey to his technique with great ease, losing control of their urinary tract and fainting, said, "Wow! I really envy women. How is it possible that they can feel so good, experience so much pleasure? I'm so jealous!" He casually dropped this line over and over, but you could tell that he was being candid, judging from his half-amazed expression and manner of speaking. It's often said that the more you master sex the more it approaches sport. I couldn't agree more.

I didn't hate Akiko Onishi, nor did Akiko me, I think. But we were never in love. The affair was nothing more than the result of some goodwill toward each other. But if such a faint link is all it takes to propel a man and a woman toward engaging in acts of shameless debauchery, just what on earth is the point of a sexual relationship anyway?

That night, on my taxi ride home, I remembered Raita saying, "Sex is just like eating and sleeping: it's a momentary, flash-in-the pan performance. And, like, the only reason you could keep doing it over and over again is exactly because it's so fleeting and forgettable! You know what I mean? Like if you think about it, how else could we all just go on eating, sleeping, and fucking throughout our lives without ever getting bored, right? In that sense I don't think it's even a game, this male-female relationship thing. You don't hear anyone saying eating or sleeping's like a game, do you?"

I also remembered Honoka saying, "I think liking a person and having sex with that person are, in reality, two unrelated things. But still, men and women get so caught up with the idea of how deeply these two must be connected and eventually get old without ever arriving at a decent understanding of what it really means to like a person, or for that matter, of what sex actually is, don't you think?"

6

ON THE NIGHT OF January 6th, after I did some light shopping at the convenience store nearby and went up the stairs of my apartment, at the end of the dim open corridor of the third floor, just in front of my room, there was someone standing. It did occur to me that it could just be Honoka or Raita, but they'd have entered the room at once. Suspicious, I approached slowly and carefully without making a sound, when the other person detected my presence and turned around to face me.

To my slight surprise, it was Eriko. There were two large paper shopping bags lined up in front of the door and a black travel bag placed at her feet.

Why was she here at such a time? I'd never brought her to the apartment, so how'd she come to know about the place? In the heat of the moment I couldn't find any answers.

Before I knew it I'd trotted over to her and said, raising my voice, "What's wrong? Something happen?"

Still, seeing that face of hers after a long absence, my heart filled with nostalgic yearning.

Although I was feeling physically well again, the exchange I'd had with Mrs. Onishi the day before yesterday put me into a melancholic mood, and I just couldn't snap out of it. The deed I did with her—which was as exhaustive as constantly turning the switch of a blender on and off—had left me considerably spent.

"I left Suwa on the limited express in the evening and transferred to a subway line at Shinjuku to come visit you here directly, but this apartment's really hard to find from Morishita

73

Station, isn't it? On top of that, all that was written in my new
address book was your mobile phone number, so I got really
lost before finally arriving here; the only thing I could count on
was my vague recollection of the address I used when I wrote
you a letter once. So you can imagine I'm really pooped right
now." Eriko spoke calmly, as if she'd just made good on some
promise.

"I've brought you some New Year's treats in lacquered boxes.
You're not eating properly anyway, right? Okay then, come on,
let's get inside quickly. It's cold out here."

Now that I thought about it, I did recall receiving a letter
from Eriko once, and hearing her tell me afterward that she'd
gotten my address from a colleague.

"How long have you been waiting?" I asked, and she took
a peek at her watch and said, "I arrived just before nine, so
around an hour." I looked at my watch too. It was ten.

"You should've called."

"But I decided to just come on a whim."

Sidestepped by her nonchalant air, I lost all will to berate her
for this sudden visit that felt like a surprise attack. More than
that, I felt sorry for her, having had to stand there in the cold
and the dark for an hour.

"It's a royal mess inside though," I said, turning the knob
and opening the door.

"What about the key?" Eriko said without hesitation, leading
me to believe that she'd possibly already pulled the knob once
and noticed that the door was unlocked.

"I rarely lock up."

"Why? That's not safe, it's careless." She gave me a dubious
look.

"There's nothing valuable in there."

"But . . ."

"Come on inside, please. But it's rather cramped, I have to
say."

I went ahead and took off my shoes. Eriko appeared cautious at first, apparently wondering if anyone else was already inside, but after I locked the door from the inside and she entered the room along with me, she seemed to have banished such a doubt. We sat at the kitchen table, facing each other. I boiled water and served a glass of hot Chinese tea, placing it before her.

"Guess you've been enjoying it, huh?"

"Yeah, quite often. Hey, I lead a leisurely lifestyle after all—even when it doesn't really suit me."

"Oh come on, of course it does. Look, if you liked it then I'll buy some more."

The two of us opened the nest of lacquered boxes Eriko had brought and ate sumptuous New Year's dishes. The food seemed like something catered from a restaurant, but she told me that everything was in fact her mother's homemade cooking. In particular the caramelized carp, a Suwa specialty, seemed to melt in the mouth; the fish, for the most part, was devoid of the small bones for which carp are known.

"This carp's incredibly easy to eat!" I remarked.

"You cut them into round slices, you see—" she said and stopped, resting her chopsticks on her plate before fixing her eyes on the fish and drawing her face nearer to it with a jerk. "And then you pull out," she continued, "the small bones one by one, using tweezers, together with your mother, very delicately so as not to disfigure the body."

She then lifted her face and said, smiling, "From morning to night, you spend an entire day doing just that, ending up with a stiff neck and numb hands; I get sick of it every time."

I'd heard that Eriko's folks run a precision machinery company in Suwa. So I imagine Eriko and her mother have been preparing such luxurious food for the New Year holidays year after year, very likely in the spacious kitchen of a large residence.

"You're lucky. I envy you," I said.

"Why?" she asked in return.

"Just that New Year's must be properly celebrated at your home."

"How's that? How does one celebrate New Year's properly?" Eriko was laughing lightly, looking curious.

"So, like, on the morning of New Year's Day, for example, you arrange New Year's dishes like these, drink the spiced *toso* sake together with your entire family, eat *zoni* soup, make a New Year's visit to the shrine, welcome relatives and guests— you know, like in those New Year's holiday moments you often see in television dramas. It just occurred to me that you guys back in Suwa must have actually been doing stuff like that."

"And your home wasn't like that?"

It puzzled me how she could be so thoughtless.

"If my home were like that," I snapped, "I wouldn't have said that I envy you." I immediately regretted the outburst. I wonder why on earth I got upset over such a trivial matter. I think it must have been because I was so tired from the past several days.

The two of us fell silent for a while, until I said, "I'm feeling rather restless, how about you?"

Frankly, I'd been extremely uneasy since the moment I invited her into the apartment. Eriko didn't respond.

"Shall we go out?" I continued. "There are places open until late in this neighborhood, or if you like, we can use the car."

"But it's very cold outside."

Eriko appeared amused, her confident look making me depressed all the more.

"Let's go outside, all the same. Besides, someone might be dropping in soon."

"Someone?" she asked instantly.

"I have these two acquaintances who come over sometimes to stay overnight—that is, just once or twice a week."

Eriko became prickly, the question of the key still lingering in her mind, naturally.

"Are these two your friends?"

I politely explained about Raita and Honoka. I didn't want Eriko to get the wrong idea about them, let alone about Tomomi. Besides, by clarifying matters I felt my mood lifting a little.

Eriko was listening with a serious look when it occurred to me, as I watched her, that she was always way too serious like that.

"So that's why you don't lock up, huh?" she interrupted.

"No," I answered, "that's just a habit of mine from way back when; it's got nothing to do with those two."

After listening to my talk, Eriko seemed to understand to some extent. There was no indication that she doubted my relationship with Honoka. But then she said, "If that's the case, this room might be too small, I guess. You should think about moving to a larger place, you know." Her input was a bit too much for me.

"Why should I go to such lengths just for them?"

"Why not?"

"Look, it's not as if I'm letting them freely come and go to help them out with their lives or offer support or anything like that."

"Then why do you do it?"

"No reason."

"That can't be."

"Well, you probably wouldn't understand. When you don't have a place to go to, even if it's just for a temporary stay, it can really devastate you. I believe a person exists only when a place exists for them."

"A person exists only when a place exists for them?"

"Right. It's the most vital ordering principle of the world."

"There's nothing sadder," I continued, "than never having a

place to go to. I've always felt so since I was a child. I never had a proper, respectable home to return to, nor did I have proper parents, you see. And that's why I kind of relate to those two, Honoka and Raita."

"What was your home like, your family?"

"It was terrible. Among other things my home was poor, the kind of place you couldn't possibly imagine, I'm sure. You know, this is why I get restless whenever I let someone like you into my apartment. I've actually never lived in a house where I've felt comfortable enough to invite friends."

Eriko was nodding but I needed to clarify.

"Now don't get all philosophical and start saying something like 'If you stop to think about it there's really no place anyone can really go to,' all right? What I'm talking about is a far more practical and unsentimental matter."

"You know something? You've never spoken so much about yourself."

"Yeah, I guess not. Your visit's also probably making me panic or something. I never thought I had any explaining to do to you about my past. All I've got are miserable and shameful memories."

Eriko mumbled slightly, but swallowed whatever words she'd started to say. Then, wearing a gentle smile, she spoke in her usual point-blank manner.

"I don't think you have anything to be ashamed of in your past."

I gazed intently into Eriko's face; at that moment she brought back memories of a person I knew a long time ago—someone who once admonished me the way Eriko did just then.

After we finished eating, Eriko gathered the leftovers on one plate, took both boxes, which had been emptied, into the kitchen and washed them with a practiced hand. While listening to the sound of running water it occurred to me that she was intending to stay overnight. I wondered if that was a good idea.

So far I'd never let anyone I was seeing stay in my apartment. Tonight was the first time we'd even had dinner together here.

When Eriko finished washing she removed a small, white towel from her bag and wiped off the wet boxes before stacking them up, together with the box containing leftovers, and putting them away in the kitchen's hanging closet. She then neatly folded the towel and hung it over the rim of the sink. Vacantly watching her move about in her element like that, I lined up in my mind words like "procedure," "habit," "regulation," "order," and "control."

With just that single piece of small, white, wet towel hanging in the kitchen, my apartment didn't feel the same anymore. There was a certain quality, a certain ambiance that was fundamentally different from the one that had been there while Honoka was still washing.

I felt strangely suffocated then, as if something were clogging my lungs.

Eriko, who had returned to my side, hastily switched off the heater she'd turned on a while ago and took out pajamas from her bag before saying, "Right, let's go to sleep." I stood up and obediently led her to the eight-mat room where the bed was.

Without saying much we changed our clothes, took turns going into the bathroom to brush our teeth, made sure of when each of us planned to wake up tomorrow, and turned off the lights before getting into bed. A few minutes later, with my back turned, Eriko snuggled up her body against mine, her lukewarm, gummy femininity clinging onto my ass, feet, and back. At that moment I thought what a bother all this was.

A line from "What It is To Live" I'd read three days ago came back to life in my mind. If "life were clothing you put on a skeleton bearing old age, illness, and death," then what point was there for Eriko and I to take the time and trouble to enter into a relationship? Life, after all, was just a flimsy piece of clothing, according to the book.

I really couldn't find any reason.

Remaining silent, I suddenly turned my body to face Eriko and leaned on her, as if to pin her down. With both hands I seized her slender arms and crossed them above her head, binding them together with the cord of a bedside desk lamp I'd been using for ten years. Eriko resisted, but not for long. After peeling off her underwear, nearly tearing them, I folded her pajama shirt up to her shoulders and completely covered her face with it.

After that, until the sky began to turn bright with the light of dawn, just like Lady Onishi, Eriko continued to raise her voice nonstop. When I finally untied the cord, she fell asleep, resting on my arm, blacked out from exhaustion.

After that, for around thirty minutes, I stared at a stain on the ceiling while chewing the ball of the forefinger of my right hand. The more I stared, the more it appeared like a really small square.

The blurry light of the morning glow slowly colored this square faintly purple.

Why did this person take the trouble to enter such a small, stuffy room? What on earth would motivate her to do something like that? I was beginning to think clearly again, feeling like I'd finally regained myself.

She must be lonely, I thought, just like me.

But you didn't need to follow the teachings of Buddha to see that we're all lonely and that it's no one's fault, just an inevitability we were all born to bear. So if that's the case, no matter whose help you seek, you can never cure your loneliness.

Doesn't this person understand even that? Moving my eyes from the ceiling, I gazed at Eriko's face as she continued to sleep on my arm: appearing dead, it looked truly sad, filled with a deep resignation in its calm and peaceful stillness.

7

THE SEASON OF CHERRY blossoms arrived again.

During the winter I shared four holidays with Tomomi and her son. The three of us went to the Museum of Maritime Science, the aquarium in Kasai, and a movie theater in Kiba. When March began we went for a drive to Kamakura.

Eriko had started, after her first visit, to come to my apartment once a week. She even came to know Raita and Honoka by sight, and while I was away once, she talked them into agreeing to keep the apartment door locked. Consequently, I was made to hand over duplicate keys to the three of them.

For some reason, Raita and Honoka had completely opened up to Eriko, so instead of visiting less frequently out of respect for her privacy, they ended up coming and going more frequently than ever before.

In brief, Eriko had brought some sanity into our lives.

Because Raita and Honoka grew up without normal families, I can safely say that they got their arms twisted easily by Eriko, being the sort of person she is. Having lost his mother immediately after he was born, Raita has been living all the while with just his father. Honoka also was never blessed with the love of two parents. You could say even my situation was somewhat similar.

Although Raita is miserable for having no memory of his mother, I know for a fact that children with mothers in their lives can end up even more miserable, if, at the end of the day, they were never loved.

Honoka calmly spoke about her mother once. "That woman

left me with a nursery school soon after I was born, when I was only one and a half months old. It's not illegal or anything; society approves of such behavior, and plenty of other mothers do it. But, frankly, I don't know what to make of mothers like that; mothers who entrust others with the care of their own children who are so young they're barely able to cry properly. Of course, under special circumstances, I believe it would be unavoidable. But in the case of most mothers, the situation isn't bad like that at all, right? I mean most of them don't particularly need to work to bring up their baby. My mother was typical in that sense. But if you stop and think about it, I think it's a real shame. Any baby, if he or she could speak, would get upset and say, 'you must be joking!'"

"I have no intention at all," she also asserted, "of accepting that person as my mother! Sure, she's remarkable, I believe, as an individual human being, as a lover of independence and freedom above all else, as 'a friend to no one but herself.' According to her, the most important thing in life for a human being is 'to live all by yourself.' But in reality no one is capable of such a thing. Even when, from the outside, it may seem as if you're totally self-reliant, in reality, somewhere unseen, there's always somebody paying a large price, someone being sacrificed, for such arrogance. I think that someone is always a child.

"After leaving me with a nursery when I was just a newborn baby, and after having strangers nurture me en masse with the children of other strangers most of the time, day after day, it's really annoying to see her wear the face of a parent now. The sight of a baby in the streets or inside a train gets me all worked up, you know. I keep being reminded of what she did to me when I was a baby; I keep thinking, 'It's incredible how that person could've done such a horrible thing.' I don't think I could ever do the same—it would be impossible for me. When she made the choice to give birth, it was only for herself. She wanted to become a mother without ever having thought about how the child might turn out—her decision to give birth was just a whim."

As I listened to Honoka it occurred to me that it wasn't necessarily the case that her mother was being completely thoughtless; it was probably, more than anything else, a failure of imagination. This world's ultimate ruin will no doubt be triggered by the decline in serious, deliberative thinking, but in the course of reaching this decline what will emerge first is a shortage of ordinary imagination, as seen with Honoka's mother. When Honoka's mother became an actual mother, she must have been horrified. Just as Honoka finds it unbearable to sacrifice herself for her mother, it must have been unbearable for the mother to sacrifice herself for her child.

I'm sure it was the same with my mother too.

However, while Honoka's mother and my mother were given a choice, we—as their children—were not. The fact that they made the wrong choice stems from nothing more than the lack of genuine, childlike imagination, but that's all the more reason why the consequence was monumentally grave—the consequence of having been brought to life.

Well, all I can do is resign myself to the fact that it was bad luck to have been born to such a mother.

My favorite writer, Komao Furuyama, has reached the ripe old age of eighty, and based on his experience of being dragged around Asian countries as a lowly soldier in the Imperial Japanese Army, before barely escaping alive and returning home, he recently wrote the following account.

I've given up on luck. I do not entertain such fanciful notions like the idea that luck is talent, or that luck is something you can carve out by yourself. Luck isn't something a person can bring about on his own. We have no choice but to live at its mercy, letting it make fools of us.

Although we humans may talk big, and are even creatures markedly different from other animals, when it comes to luck, we're powerless. One should, while being aware of the very fleeting nature of existence, go on living as long as one is kept alive, and then simply proceed to die. People urge you, among other things, to be optimistic and forward-looking, encouraging you to live life energetically even in old age. But while I won't hold anything against you should you think like that for yourself, don't go compelling others to think the same. There's no need for every one of us to be positive, to be full of life and energy; it's okay to be gloomy and blue, it's okay to dream your life away. A person has the right to think the way he likes, to live the way he likes. Life has a way of failing to turn out as planned at times. When your wishes don't come true, there's nothing else to do but give up.

Ultimately, no matter who you are, in the end, surely all you can do is give up. But in the case of a parent and her child, the choice is the parent's to make, so the parent should be the one, in the first place, to give up; I suppose this is the point Honoka was trying to make in particular.

Among my acquaintances is a man named Minegishi. He's an official at the Ministry of Finance, now on loan to the Cabinet Office. But until a few years ago, he was serving as a paymaster in the Ministry of Finance, put in charge of the budgetary affairs of the Ministry of Health and Welfare. Although he's far older than me, ever since interviewing him when I was in the editorial department at the monthly I've been enjoying drinks with him a few times a year. This Mr. Minegishi once told me an interesting story from his years as a paymaster.

"You know about my place, right? It's a double-income household with two children. In those days, we'd just had our second son, and my wife was employed at a government office, so you can imagine how hectic it was for the old lady and me; we were living in an official residence at Takanawa, but public childcare centers were all booked up so we were left with no option but to hire a babysitter for our baby boy. As for ferrying our eldest son to his nursery school and back, whoever happened to have the time that day would do so. But come budget preparation time, something like that was out of the question for me. As for my wife, since she was the head of the division in the Department of Labor promoting gender equality, there was no way she was going to be accommodating. I was exhausted, I tell you. Then I found out that my colleague in the Ministry of Health and Welfare was in the same boat. He says to me, 'Mr. Minegishi, this is a major problem! Unless we find a way to increase the number of public childcare centers, this nation's productivity is going to hell in a handbasket.' I too at that time sincerely believed so. That's why the two of us ended up persuading each other's government offices, to allocate for the expansion of childcare facilities, a budget the size of which would make your eyeballs pop out—an amount so exorbitant it's too much even for this age of zero-ceiling.

"The day the original bill passed and the budget document was approved in a Cabinet meeting, the two of us went to Akasaka to celebrate, applauding and cheering, we did it, we did it! But unbeknownst to us at the time, we had, in actual fact, committed a terrible mistake. I became aware of this only recently. Last time I had a drink with that colleague of mine he muttered suddenly, out of the blue, 'Mr. Minegishi, for some reason, we seem to have committed a fundamental error. At that time I certainly believed that we should make the budget pass no matter what, for the welfare of working parents, but in reality we appear to have misidentifed our most important clients.' Having seen how my sons have turned out over the years, I was keenly aware of what he said, so I asked him, 'Are your kids weird too?' He nodded dramatically and said, 'Oh yeah! When I look at my kids all I see are automatons; it's as if they're emotionally bankrupt.' He said that he felt, compared to our generation, they were decidedly inconsiderate, and were far more introverted and fearful of laying bare their true colors in any strong, impassioned way. And that's so true, don't you think,

Matsubara? Essentially, we'd gotten our clients wrong. Sure, parents like my wife and I were initially grateful that the budget helped boost the number of childcare facilities, you know. But don't you think that public funds reserved for education should be primarily spent for the benefit of children? The clients, after all, aren't supposed to be the parents; they're supposed to be the children themselves, you see.

"But what did we do? Did we take into consideration the welfare of such children? Not at all! Instead, we went full steam ahead with a budget allocation that just prioritized the parents' convenience. In effect, without ever listening to the voice of our true clients—the children—we ended up providing a service that was utterly useless for them. If you stop to think about it, there's no way we could ever help society as a whole benefit by building a system that makes it possible for parents to part with a forty-three-day-old newborn baby and leave him or her with a stranger. In the event you actually build such a system for society, you shouldn't complain if your kids turn out strange; it's not surprising to see that there'd be something wacky and helter-skelter about them. Still, we failed to realize this essentially simple truth, so I can't help thinking how truly screwed up we were back then, that there was something terribly wrong with us, you know."

I related Mr. Minegishi's story to Honoka after she talked to me about her mother.

Honoka then told me with an ironic smile, "I guess when something goes irreversibly wrong, it's not just partially wrong, it's totally wrong."

Every time Eriko visited she brought along small things: a folding table; tableware; a mirror; a pillbox; an electric pot; her clothes; and clothes hangers. At first, various objects innocuously occupied a corner of my room, but before long they ended up laying down the law.

Finally, on the morning of the first Sunday in April, a massive three-door refrigerator arrived. I was fast asleep when the doorbell rang an umpteen number of times, rousing me from bed. When I opened the door, I saw before me a brand-new refrigerator wrapped in white vinyl, its receipt stuck onto the door of the vegetable compartment with adhesive tape. In no time at all, two delivery guys conveyed it into the kitchen by hand and left with the small refrigerator that I'd been using until then. Momentarily, the interior of the new refrigerator filled up with a plethora of things: cans of beer, bottles of white wine, yogurt and cheeses, tomatoes and apples, eggs and balls of udon noodles. Eriko, Honoka, and Raita—they'd all gotten busy filling up the fridge.

On the Saturday of the week the refrigerator arrived, we had Raita and Honoka over so that the four of us could make some sukiyaki and enjoy it together—Eriko had taken the trouble to return to her apartment to bring back, for cooking sukiyaki, an iron pan I'd bought for her as a souvenir from Morioka, where I'd gone on a business trip.

At the table, Eriko enjoyed very pleasant exchanges with Raita and Honoka, but what I found surprising was that Honoka, the vegetarian, had joined the rest of us around the sukiyaki frying pan without any trepidation. When Eriko told me, rather belatedly on the day of the occasion, "I've invited those two as well," I said, "Honoka won't eat sukiyaki dishes."

"So what?" she responded quite apathetically. "We shouldn't be indulging her, right? If she won't eat meat, she can just have vegetables."

Honoka didn't show any signs of being dismayed. Instead, she earnestly began to serve into her small bowl and eat with great relish all the vegetables Eriko had tactfully set aside for her: dried bean curds, shredded kuzu cakes, tofu, mushrooms, and plenty of garden greens.

I went on meeting Mrs. Onishi once a month at the usual

hotel. And every time I did, I had to ask her for some money. My mother's condition had worsened and my younger sister, in her desperation, was trying out various folk remedies, leaving me with more medical bills than I could handle.

In the beginning of April, when Tokyo's cherry blossoms were in full bloom, and when prime-time news programs began reporting on their sites in various areas up north, I made an appearance at New Seoul for the first time in two weeks. When Tomomi saw me she said, laughing, "I had a feeling you'd show up sometime today." She then remarked that I'd gained some weight, that my face had become rounder.

After telling her that I'd slim down and restore my former physique soon enough, I asked, changing the subject, "How about Shinjuku Gyoen this year?"

Last year we took a trip all the way down to the large botanical garden in Musashino, but the park was right in the middle of carrying out maintenance work, so cherry-blossom viewing was out of the question.

Prohibited from even approaching the trees lined up right before us, where the petals were falling wonderfully, both Tomomi and I were very disappointed. The grounds were being irrigated with massive supplies of water and a power shovel was digging up the soil with a deafening roar, so the entire park felt damp and miserable, prompting the three of us to retreat immediately after opening the lunch boxes, which Tomomi had woken up early to prepare.

"My, my, my!" she said. "Year after year! You never get tired of cherry viewing, do you? Isn't there anyone else you could invite?"

Tomomi had said some such thing last year as well. I answered that I didn't get tired of it necessarily, that I didn't want to go cherry-blossom viewing with anybody else.

When I visited her bar for the first time around four years

ago, it was just around this time of the year. I was still working as a reporter for a weekly magazine back then and was brought to the place by a freelance writer who was working with me in the same editorial division.

In those days, I used to live in an apartment in Higashiojima, and New Seoul, which is in Morishita, was on my way home. At any rate, ever since that first visit, I began frequenting the bar almost every night, emptying the most expensive bottles available there at a rate of one every couple days. In the first two months I'd racked up a bar tab of around five hundred thousand yen, but, as I recall, I settled the bill in full with the bonus I got in June.

What got me interested in Tomomi at first was her awfully high-pitched laugh, which she'd put to good use in the company of her customers. The laughter had a hollow ring to it, as if small pebbles were rolling inside a flimsy and transparent barrel. I thought I'd heard such a sound a long time ago, and when I pondered over it, I vaguely recalled that my mother used to laugh in such a way when she was still young.

The second reason behind my interest in her was the fact that I was terribly surprised to hear from the freelance writer that she was actually a mother. Severely inebriated, the writer pointed up at the ceiling of the watering hole in an exaggerated gesture and said in a somewhat angry-sounding tone, "At this very moment, right above our wasted brains, sweet little Tomomi's baby lies fast asleep, breathing peacefully. You can hear him if you listen carefully." At that time Tomomi looked very young—she was far from looking like someone who was shouldering the burdens of motherhood. In my eyes her face looked so dignified, and I couldn't possibly imagine that a baby's large head, along with its body, had been wrenched out from between her legs. That night I just couldn't keep my eyes off her belly.

On the fifth day after first visiting the bar, I'd bought my first present for Takuya before dropping in. Since I knew neither the name nor the gender of the child, I had the attendant at the department store choose some bright yellow children's attire for me.

Suddenly presented with such a thing by a customer who had been gulping down whiskey night after night without saying a word, Tomomi seemed a little bewildered. I'd finally found an opportunity to start a genuine conversation, but it occurred to me that I didn't particularly want to know anything about Tomomi, so I couldn't find anything concrete to talk about in the end.

But apparently I'd gotten drunk soon enough and had posed as a palm reader, inspecting her lines and telling her, "Mama-san, you should devote as much of yourself as possible to someone born in the Year of the Monkey, and have someone born in the Year of the Rat reward you for that devotion." I had no recollection of this whatsoever, but the next day when I visited again, Tomomi began to tell me that I'd said so. The year of the Monkey, which I'd blurted out at random, in fact turned out to be the year Ilgon Park was born, and of course, the Year of the Rat was the year I was born.

She then went on to talk about her relationship with Park in some detail, but I wasn't that concerned, so I was hardly listening, and I've never since then asked about the man.

I think it was probably ten days after I started visiting her bar, since it was around the end of the cherry-blossom season, just prior to the garden party that year, on a Sunday, when I invited Tomomi to a cherry-blossom viewing.

Together with Takuya, the three of us went to the Shinjuku Imperial Garden. With Takuya strapped to her chest in a baby sling, her long hair gathered into a knot at the back, a large bag slung from her shoulder, Tomomi came to Shinjuku-Sanchome Station, our rendezvous spot. When we arrived at the Imperial Garden in the early afternoon, I draped Takuya in the jacket I was wearing and seated him by my side before lying down next to Tomomi on the lawn of the Imperial Garden, gazing up for a long time at the clouds drifting to the north across a beautifully clear, springtime sky.

At the Imperial Garden's restaurant I ate curry and rice and Tomomi had a thin, hardened offal steak, but it didn't seem tasty. I'd borrowed from a colleague of mine a single-lens reflex camera, so I used up three rolls of thirty-six-exposure film to take continuous mother-and-child snapshots—at the train station platform, inside the train, amid the crush in Shinjuku, by the park's pond, atop a big sky-blue bench blanketed with cherry blossom petals, and at the base of a cherry blossom tree. Whenever I pointed the lens at her, Tomomi would smile, and with Takuya in her embrace, she'd change the boy's position every which way before striking a pose with him. Takuya slept comfortably, his hair teased by the spring breeze.

We ate Chinese food in Shinjuku and on the train ride home I carried Takuya, strapping the baby sling to my chest. Tomomi laughed dramatically, amused by this sight.

It was five days later that I had one of the many finished photographs enlarged and made into a canvas print before taking it to Tomomi's bar, along with the nearly one hundred remaining standard-size photos.

Tomomi was behind the counter, tirelessly looking over the photographs in which she appeared with Takuya. She'd repeatedly put them away in a drawer only to goggle at them again whenever business slowed down, her back turned to the few remaining customers.

Since that day, I've brought in various other things as well, and after a while, after she closed shop, we began to drink beer together, just the two of us, helping ourselves to sushi that I'd buy.

It was in the autumn of that year when my relationship with Tomomi turned sexual. One night I was talking a lot about

silent films, which I'd acquired a passion for in those days: Mary
Pickford, Janet Gaynor, and Lilian Gish in *A Romance of Happy
Valley*, a story about John and Jenny, two people leading quiet
lives in a peaceful valley in Kentucky until John foolishly sets
out for New York, swept away by the tides of ambition.

At first, Tomomi was silently listening to my commentary,
but before long, she began to comment on the actresses in detail
herself.

"Although Gish was famous for her role in Griffith's
masterpiece, she was really more impressive on stage in her later
years. Gaynor in *A Star is Born* is surely peerless; no one can act
better than that. I like Pola Negri more than Pickford—*the* Pola
Negri, who became involved with Rudolf Valentino!"

I was astounded by how well informed she was. And then
I remembered her telling me around the time we first met
that she'd been an actress in a small theatrical company once,
performing in plays. Anyway, even after closing shop, we kept
guzzling down gin and sounding off until dawn about silent-
film actresses.

Eventually both of us became completely drunk, and before
I knew it, we had climbed up to the second floor. At that time,
in Tomomi's room, there used to be an old sofa for two, and
when I laid back on this sofa and relaxed with my suit still on,
Tomomi, who was laying out a futon with shaky, staggering
steps, suddenly said loudly, "I'm going to take a bath!" and
became stark naked in front of me. Then, when she crouched
down at my feet, as if sapped of all her strength, she began to
take my clothes off, muttering "Hey, let's take a bath" without
looking at my face. Gazing down into the deep gulf between
her largish breasts, and taking in the sight of her kneeling down
like a slave girl, I became very aroused.

After we finished, Tomomi murmured out of the blue in
a sober voice, lying face down, taking sips from a cold can of
Coke, "Yup! Still a woman, just like any other."

As for me, I was finding it a major hassle to get up and get dressed again to return to my apartment, so I pretended to be asleep. But Tomomi didn't ask me to leave. We just fell asleep together, embracing in the nude.

8

AFTER I MADE TOMOMI promise to go out cherry-blossom viewing next Sunday, I brought up the topic of the television drama in which Ilgon Park was appearing.

NHK's Hisashi Nozawa had written the show for the Saturday evening serial-drama time slot, and nearly ten episodes of it had already been aired to high acclaim.

Park in particular had attracted a great deal of attention for playing one of the three protagonists in the drama, in what was his first television appearance. Having been a stage actor specializing in art-house theater until then, he was apparently regarded highly in the world of stage dramas, but otherwise, as far as the general public was concerned, he was practically a nobody. But after being cast for the television role suddenly, at a time in his life when he was past thirty, he began to try to sell himself as a major character actor. Of course, he was known under a Japanese pseudonym, and the fact that he'd had a wife once, and that he was a father to a boy who was about to turn five, all remained under wraps. Whenever I mentioned Park's current circumstances, which I'd gleaned from magazine articles, Tomomi simply responded with a nonchalant, "Oh well."

It was past twelve when I left New Seoul, but on the way back to my apartment I was overcome by fatigue. It was so sudden and intense I couldn't walk any further; I had to crouch down by the side of the road and throw up twice, after which I felt considerably better, but then my foot went numb. I somehow managed to crawl into a small alley, where a row of tenements stood, and sat down on the ground, hugging my knees.

I felt myself plunged into a quiet world just then, a world without wind, heat, or light.

While rubbing my sleeping foot, I muttered how tired I was, reflecting on how weary I felt about the manic life I'd come to lead these past several years: about all the different things I did with Eriko; about seeing Mrs. Onishi regularly; about bringing gifts to Takuya; about going somewhere with Tomomi and the boy, acting like they were my real family.

In the end I wasn't really accomplishing anything, I thought.

I kept still for probably ten minutes. I tried to stand up but still couldn't get my foot to move, so I dropped to the ground again and wondered how to go about killing some time until my foot recovered. To fend off boredom, I tried to contemplate my future with Eriko, but that train of thought failed to advance even an inch, barricaded at the entrance gate, as it were.

So I said to myself aloud, "Sure wish something nice would happen to me." But my voice sounded like someone else's. I thought about what I was supposed to do tomorrow, but there wasn't anything in particular. I'd just handle all the small tasks written into the column for tomorrow's date in my day planner, and at night, end up drinking in Shinjuku or Morishita. That was all.

Without anything else to do, I decided to remember the time when Eriko and I had first met. I was feeling guilty for not being able to think about my future with her, so I wanted to at least prevent my mind drifting away from the thought of her. That's what I did whenever I felt down—ruminated over somebody I'd come across in my life. To me, it was one way of finding solace. Perhaps this was the only reason I'd kept company with Eriko, Mrs. Onishi, Tomomi, and various other individuals in my past. If you sometimes wallow in your misery—your rock-bottom feelings of despair—and endure them, then everyone in your past becomes illuminated in the buoyant radiance of nostalgia.

Eriko used to turn up in my office sometimes because of her work, mainly associating with the people in the women's magazine section. But she was nonetheless popular and much discussed in the office.

She was an exceptionally beautiful woman, after all.

She used to frequently drop by the women's magazine editorial desk, which was partitioned off from my editorial division by a single glass screen. She needed to carry out photo shoots for photogravures in the basement studio, so she'd bring along dozens of fashion models, one after another, but not one of them, except perhaps in terms of height, could hold a candle to Eriko. She was that beautiful.

The moment she stepped into the editorial office, all eyes, with the rhythmic regularity of waves, would fall upon her. Meanwhile, it seemed business as usual for Eriko as she went about her affairs in her inimitably practiced, artless way.

Although her voice sounded slightly childish, I was occasionally impressed by how terse and pithy she was, listening to her nearby. She clearly had a certain steadiness about her, the kind of presence of mind possessed by only those seasoned in the art of attracting attention.

Eriko began paying frequent visits to my office at a time when it was decided that the editorial desk of the women's magazine would put out a special edition. It was she who made the first move then, the one to break the ice. I was compiling for an essay some shorthand notes from a certain interview, using the wide writing desk usually reserved for senior staff writers. The substance of the interview was about a well-known French scholar of comparative literature analyzing Yukio Mishima's philosophy of self-determination from the perspective of the classical Japanese view on life and death derived from a Buddhist text, *Ojoyoshu*, or *The Essentials of Rebirth in the Pure Land*. To turn this university professor's boring talk into prose, I'd loaded onto the desk several books by Mishima and a copy of his father's memoirs, riffling through relevant parts while putting pen to paper. It was quite late at night by then.

I sensed a presence before the desk, and when I looked up I saw Eriko standing there, picking up one of the books, holding it with both hands, and looking at it. It was a hardcover copy of Mishima's *Runaway Horses*, a first edition released more than thirty years ago, which I'd found in a secondhand bookstore in Hongo.

When Eriko became aware that my eyes were trained on her, she looked my way to say, Mishima, right? I put my pen down, leaned back in my chair, and after briefly explaining what I was doing, I asked whether she liked Mishima. Eriko just smiled without answering. So I asked her whether she knew what Mishima had said to his mother the night before he died. As expected, Eriko didn't say anything; she just faintly shook her head.

"You know, he'd said, 'So far, I haven't been able achieve a single thing I've set out to do.' Funny, isn't it? In the summer when he died he'd written in an essay, 'When I think about the twenty-five years inside me, I'm surprised by how empty they are, so much so that I can hardly say that I've lived. I just passed through those years, pinching my nose.' He adds, 'I'm fully vulgar, and even endowed with the gambling spirit to an excessive degree, yet I can't put myself into a state of mind that would help me engage in what is commonly known as play. I wonder why? It puzzles me so much I've come to doubt myself, my heart. For the most part I don't love life.'

"Among Mishima's writings, I like this one best of all. What about you?"

Eriko finally opened her mouth to say she was interested in knowing what the French scholar's interpretation of Mishima's death was.

"Out of all the dull things he said in the interview, only two things stood out for me."

I slowly leafed through the thick stack of shorthand notes to the beginning and started to explain. One was the fact that, although Mishima appeared to take no notice back then of the intellectuals who used to mock him as a right-wing buffoon, in reality he was stewing inside, finding them intolerable. And that by actually dying, he'd compellingly asked, "With my corpse before you, do you still intend to say that I'm just acting in a play?"

The other thing was a typically French observation, suggesting that since Mishima was homosexual, his suicide by disembowelment—his seppuku—was in the end an act meant to establish his own sexual identity. As evidence of this, the scholar highlights the fact that when Mishima made his speech from the balcony of the headquarters of the Japan Self-Defense Force in Ichigaya, he made frequent use of the line, "Can you still call yourself a man?!", arguing that we should consider this line as a question being posed to himself, rather than to the soldiers. For this reason, he asserts that Mishima was, in effect, asking himself, "Am I man? Am I man?"

As I babbled on leisurely, it struck me as terribly funny that a gorgeous woman was quietly devouring me with her eyes, with a copy of Mishima's *Runaway Horses* in hand, eagerly listening to what was essentially tripe.

I asked her once again if she liked *Runaway Horses*. Eriko tilted her head slightly and began to leaf through the book. Her eyes seemed to be meaningfully scanning the text, but at the same time, she also seemed to be feigning interest, so I was getting pretty irritated. I suddenly stood up then, taking the book away from her and telling her I only liked one part of it, before turning to the page where that part appeared and handing it back to her.

It was the part where Shigekuni Honda encounters Isao Iinuma, and comes to believe that Isao is the reincarnation of Kiyoaki Matsugae.

I often remember even to this day the episode written in there about the "four successive existences." One of them is the existence between death and the next birth, when the spirit, assuming the form of a child, has a glimpse of a man and woman copulating. Fascinated by the body of the shameless woman who would become his mother, while harboring resentment toward the man who would become his father, as soon as the father ejaculates his impurity into the mother's womb, the child sees his opportunity to get reincarnated. This story strikes something of a chord in me. It's probably the only part of the book that smacks of realism.

When Eriko heard me say this she laughed, so I added that I didn't believe there was another writer who was as dedicated as Mishima was to the quest for the truth about this world, even though it was in vain.

In a slightly discontented tone, Eriko said she wanted to know why I thought so.

Noticing how confident she looked, as if to test me, I got suddenly annoyed, thinking to myself—she's been standing there, not saying much herself, yet she's got this suggestive manner about her. What the hell's going on?

So I told her that there was no particular reason; I'd said so because I simply thought so, but it came out, even to myself, sounding terribly blunt and cold. I looked away from Eriko and returned my gaze to the manuscript paper. I then sensed her quietly placing the book on the desk before leaving for her assigned place.

Thereafter, our eyes would meet now and then. That is, Eriko would be constantly looking in my direction, and, sensing her eyes were on me, I'd look up sometimes. Whenever our eyes met like that, Eriko would give a small smile; her timing was off, though. After a few more such awkward moments I began to slightly wave my hand in return, but such gestures never got us talking to each other again.

9

It happened two years ago, on an October day, as I was walking around the city of Tokyo on business, utterly exhausted. I hadn't slept a wink the previous night, troubled by the symptoms of gastrospasm, a chronic, neurological disease involving stomach cramps. In the morning I was in the National Diet Library looking for source materials on the Russian government's economic policy for a paper a certain university professor was attempting to write. In the afternoon, I paid a visit to the Textbook Administration Division of the Ministry of Education to report on some issues for a paper being prepared by a different professor, concerning high-school textbooks on Japanese history. After that, I met up with a farmer from Akita, with whom I had a passing acquaintance, at a hotel in Yaesu where we exchanged opinions on the post-liberalization challenges faced by rice farmers before I left to visit a newspaper firm in Otemachi, where I interviewed, for approximately an hour, a certain figure who was said at the time to be the prime minister's brain.

Although I'd left this newspaper about five in the evening, I was so tired my gait was unsteady. Still, I had to go to the office of a design firm to receive a photogravure whose layout I'd asked them to handle, so I hastily made a connection to a subway line from Otemachi and went to the station near the design office.

And then, by pure chance, I ran into Eriko.

The station was a hub for many metro lines, and since the line I'd used was a new one, the platform was located at the station's deepest underground level. Access to the ground was possible only via one of four adjacent escalators, alternately moving up or down.

I stepped onto the ascending escalator with downcast eyes, my head drooping, the tie I loosened feeling too heavy around my neck. When I casually looked up the well-lit stairs above my head, after surrendering myself to the sedate motion of the escalator, I noticed just then a couple stepping onto the descending escalator to my right. One of them was Eriko, dressed in bright red clothes, and standing next to her was a fortyish mustachioed man, wearing a gray suit that clearly advertised, at a glance, his involvement in the fashion business. There was a distance of around thirty meters between us, but nobody stood in between to obscure the view, so Eriko also noticed me instantly as she gradually approached, her eyes motionless and fixed on me in the usual way. It was the first time that I'd seen Eriko's figure from such an angle, but the view of her, her jawline, was like beholding before your very eyes the perfect curve found in a Lautrec painting in all its exquisite beauty—a detail that had been lost on me whenever she came to my office, wearing incredibly thick layers of makeup that made her look artificial.

I was shaken up a little, running into her so unexpectedly; it also didn't help that I was dead tired. So the moment I thought I saw my reflection in Eriko's eyes—the reflection of a young office worker in a tired-looking suit with a sweaty face turned up vacantly, burdened with a big bag hanging down from his shoulder, which clumsily bulged with the things he'd shoved inside—thick wads of photocopying paper, a tape recorder, an automatic camera, and several notebooks of varying kinds—I averted my eyes and looked down. But at the same time I began to feel something like a resentment brewing inside me toward Eriko's beauty—a beauty that made someone like me—someone who had nothing to do with her—feel small. It was audacious of her, after all, to remain nonchalant while casting a piercing glance on another person's face. I lifted my eyes.

Something white jumped into view.

It was Eriko's right palm, resting on the black rubber of the escalator's handrail, the nails of her shapely, slender fingers manicured with a thin enamel, shining. I consciously and slowly traced my eyes from her hand to her shoulder, to her throat, and then to her face before finally looking into her eyes, deadpan, fully returning her stare. The ten or so seconds that followed, while we were approaching each other, seemed to last an eternity. The moment we were in alignment, when my hand was thirty centimeters apart from hers, I reached out toward her palm resting on the handrail sliding in the opposite direction. Eriko attempted to swing it away at once, but I seized it before she could; her palm was surprisingly soft.

After I let go and the two of them had passed me by, I heard the man next to Eriko say in a wildly impulsive, high-pitched voice, "What the hell just happened?"

I met Eriko at the office after that, but we didn't talk.

It was only a month and a half after the chance encounter that we had an opportunity for the first time to have a lengthy, prolonged exchange.

A year-end party was held annually in honor of a certain female author, and it was held that year, as usual, in Tokyo on an evening in the beginning of December. The writer had specially traveled from the countryside to attend the event. The draw was a restaurant in the outskirts of Roppongi, which had been entirely reserved to make it a closed-door affair.

Praised to high heaven by industry insiders about her serial novel in progress or her other works adapted for film, the kimono-clad author, on cloud nine by then, would get drunk, watching the party guests belt out a tune, one after another. That's what the usual proceedings were like.

For the occasion, every publisher, scrambling for the rights to her manuscript, attempted to send in as many of its own people as possible. Naturally, since the target of their attention—the author—was a single, middle-aged woman, they'd bring out the youngest male employees they could. Consequently, I was nominated to attend last year.

I was near the entrance, seated at a corner table, on a round red chair that resembled a stool for a dressing table, taking sips from a glass of whiskey and water, when Eriko entered the restaurant, accompanied by a young man who seemed my age.

No sooner had the singing begun than every VIP of every company had finished taking turns grabbing the microphone to offer their greetings. There were perhaps fifty people gathered there. A band had been specially arranged, providing accompaniment upon request.

When Eriko and her date arrived, the publishing director of Kobunsha was just in the middle of singing a Frank Nagai tune. Urged by her companion, Eriko sat by the writer, exchanging some pleasantries with her for a while, as if the two were old acquaintances.

Even in the dimly lit restaurant, Eriko's beauty stood out and, as usual, I could see many eyes drifting in her direction.

After gazing at her for about five minutes, I gave myself up to alcohol. At times like this I made it a point to get drunk early and keep my eyes and ears closed.

Around an hour later the party had reached the stage where all the veteran editors were done singing, and the young ones began to be called out to appear on stage, against their will. They called out my name once too, but I was seated far away and declined with a shake of my head. Fortunately, that was the end of that, since a guy from some other company cut in and started to sing of his own accord.

That's when Eriko, having apparently noticed for the first time that I was there—when my name had come up— approached me. But I'd completely forgotten about her, having had plenty to drink by then.

Standing before an empty seat, she asked if she could sit next to me. I ignored her for a while, after lying that the seat was taken by a girl who had gone to the restroom. But she didn't look like she was going to leave me alone, so I reluctantly raised my head and suggested moving over together to a vacant counter nearby if she liked. In one long pull I drained the rest of my glass of double whisky and water, which the bartender had made for me just a moment earlier, and stood up, feeling somewhat unusually wobbly.

We sat down on the stools at the counter, side by side, our backs turned to the stage, and began to talk.

The first thing Eriko said was a question: she wanted to know why I hadn't sung a while ago when I'd been named. Even I rolled my eyes at this question, and even though I was feeling unwell, partly thanks to my plastered state of mind, I nonetheless said, "I don't think it's any of your business, but if you must know, it's because I'm exceptionally tone-deaf."

By then I was getting so liquored up that my entire life was starting to drag me down, so I just began to speak about how music had never been one of my fortes, raising a few examples in the process. In grade school, the teachers used to always make us take these song tests at the end of the term, so I had to sing in front of everyone. For each such test, I'd practice desperately the night before, but just when I'd reach about the fifth measure, the teacher would invariably stop me to remark, "Rearranging the song without permission, are we, Matsubara?" Laughed at by the entire class, I'd feel ashamed and want to cry.

"And it wasn't just the singing! I also sucked at playing the harmonica, the flute, the organ; everything was way out of tune. At the school arts festival when I was in the fifth grade, my entire class performed Friedrich Silcher's *Die Lorelei* together, purely by whistling, but I sucked at that as well, incapable of whistling satisfactorily. Here, look at my front teeth; there's a huge gap between them even when my jaws are closed, right? The sound just escapes, turning my whistling into a travesty. Come practice time I'd always fake-whistle and fool everybody. I thought I'd get found out one day, though, feeling uneasy for nearly a month. In fact, I got so paranoid I thought I was going to die. Really. And because I got so worried, in the end, my stomach started aching in the morning, and I was unable to go to school for some time. But on the day of the arts festival, my teacher took the trouble to come pick me up, insisting that all the effort I'd put in would be wasted if I didn't show up—so I ended up delivering a performance after all, whistling—no, actually hissing—through my breezy dental arrangement. Totally pathetic, right?"

Incidentally, I also informed her that I've always been timid since I was a child, and that my friends used to tease me and make me cry all the time. To illustrate, I made up a few examples again. Eriko laughed at each one of them before remarking, "Where does a spineless person like you get the nerve to touch me the other day at the subway station?"

She was being so predictable I found it funny. I told her that her palm was very soft and pleasant to the touch, as if the bones were as pliable as a straw. Eriko then told me that after the incident she was badly razzed by the designer acquaintance standing next to her. I nodded, sure that that must have been the case, before going on to explain that there was no particular motive behind my gesture so she shouldn't be concerned, and begged her pardon if it had upset her.

"You're different," Eriko suddenly said, adding that the moment she saw me for the first time at my company she felt there was something slightly off about me, that I was the only odd man out in there. I responded by telling her that it was just her imagination, that it only seemed that way because she found it monotonous and boring to be in that office every day, so even a subtle change in mood would prompt her to see me in such a light, and that was all. I then told her, based on my observations of her, that her present job didn't seem to suit her at all, that I had been of this opinion for a long time.

Puzzled, Eriko wanted to know why, saying that it was the

first time anyone had said such a thing. I said I just thought so, and added that only she knew best what the reason was. Then I asked her to refrain from using the word "why" in front of me because I found that word to be rather lacking in decorum.

"Regardless of who you're talking to," I explained, "if someone doubts you, you should first of all carefully contemplate the reason for that doubt inside your own head, and only when you can't come up with a decent answer yourself should you approach your doubter to ask 'why.' But, honestly, before you do, you should first take a day to come up with an explanation of your own to throw at the guy, to see how he'll react. But you know something? If you really take the trouble to work out the reason yourself you'll find that, in most cases, it'll be unnecessary and meaningless to ask. Listen, you're a grown woman, and you can't expect this world to go on being a school forever—and no one's obligated to be your teacher or anything like that either, you know."

Eriko was listening silently, but after I finished she asked if I wanted to drink some more, so I answered that I did. She left the counter and returned with a glass of whiskey for me and one for herself.

At that moment a certain editor in chief at my company's magazine bellowed out my name from the stage. This man was sort of emceeing the occasion and he was the kind of character you often spotted in my line of work: an asinine fan of Ango Sakaguchi—the kind of manic and strung-out individual who was convinced that showing off one's flaw, say an uptight, nervous disposition, was a defense mechanism. Apparently this editor was practicing the principles set out in Ango's book, *Playing Hysterically*, but he simply struck me as an idiot and a royal pain in the ass.

He shouted in a raucous, tipsy voice, with the microphone turned on, "You're one heck of a funny guy, aren't you? Think you can come here just to hook up with some gorgeous dame on the sly? Without even singing a single ditty? In the old days, all the young greenhorns, chosen or not, would gladly belt out two, three songs without complaining. So get your ass up on the stage right this minute, rookie, and start entertaining. That's an order!" Alcohol always brought out the worst in him.

I turned my stool to face the man and told him loudly that it was against my policy to sing at a place like this because I was a terrible singer, and that enforcing this policy was the only way to guarantee that the evening wouldn't get spoiled for everyone. Momentarily, the place exploded with laughter, but his royal highness wasn't too pleased.

"Quit stalling," he shouted again, "and hurry the fuck up!" He must have mistakenly believed that I'd mocked him. The party dried up all at once. Eriko was facing the counter, looking awfully embarrassed. I whispered in her ear, "This is all your fault" and got down from the stool to walk over to the stage.

I was handed the microphone but placed it back on its stand and, instead, borrowed a classical guitar from one of the band members and began to slowly sing the full chorus to "April Come She Will." Eriko watched me, amazed.

Following a huge round of applause, the boorish editor in chief, with a cigarette pressed between his lips, gestured for me to sing another tune, but I returned the guitar and went back to my seat next to Eriko's. After emptying in a single gulp her glass of whiskey and water, in which the ice had already melted, Eriko rested her chin on her hand and fixed her gaze on me.

"You're a big fat liar," she said. "You can actually sing well, and you're probably, like, really versatile, so what's with that long face of yours? Why do you always look so jaded? It's so yesterday, you know, that dark and broody air of yours."

I glared at Eriko and thought about getting teary-eyed, but that was too much trouble, so I decided on a slightly different tack.

"Momma has terminal cancer," I said. "She was admitted last summer and had an operation once, but it didn't go well. It's going to become critical soon and the doctor said she might not be around to enjoy the next New Year's holidays. I grew up in a fatherless family, so it was always just her and me. I can't help feeling weighed down."

Eriko's face turned grave. "I'm so sorry. How horrible of me."

"That's okay."

"I feel so bad. But thank you for telling me. If you hadn't, I . . ."

Seeing her get so timid, I burst out laughing.

"Like I said, you're convinced too easily. My god, you're so gullible! One moment you're calling me a liar, the next you're getting duped again."

For a moment Eriko looked confused, trying to make sense of my facial expression, and finally went on to say in a serious and strained manner that such a lie was unduly vicious. I dismissed her comment and excused myself, telling her that I needed to get outside for some fresh air soon because I was seriously drunk now. Eriko said she'd leave with me, so I got annoyed, but when I asked where she lived she said Ningyocho, which was in the same direction as Morishita, my place of residence.

"Hey, we're neighbors, huh?" Eriko said rather happily, getting down from the stool first.

When I stepped out and felt the cold wind blowing, I sensed my body straightening up, and then said, "I know just the place for someone like you. Want to go?" Eriko nodded so we walked for approximately ten minutes until we reached Azabu.

The place I brought her to was "Mister Donut." When I told her that a glassed-in, well-lit shop like this one—which was brighter than daytime inside—perfectly suited someone who resembled a mannequin like her, Eriko looked terribly uncomfortable. Seeing her like that, I laughed, saying, "You're such a hothead!" and then sank my teeth into a sticky doughnut that was nothing but sweet. I suddenly felt nauseous, however, and rushed into the toilet to vomit.

Around ten minutes after I'd crouched down in the restroom, undergoing so much pain and discomfort that I'd completely forgotten about my date, there was a knock at the door. "It's unlocked," I said.

Eriko entered and was about to rub my back but I brushed away her hand, stood up immediately, and went outside the shop.

We then took a taxi to a bar in Nihonbashi where I was a regular, and drank until early morning.

At that shop I began to talk, slightly at length, about Yukio Mishima, the topic that had begun our acquaintance. Eriko seemed to have read Mishima's novels in her own unsystematic, hopscotch fashion, but was unfamiliar with his superior essays. In a rather unintentionally condescending manner, I explained the evolutionary journey his ideas had gone through, beginning with his call to action and ending in his ritual suicide by disembowelment, his *harakiri*.

I told her that this is what Mishima wrote.

Life works in such a way that unless it becomes comfortable with the risk of death, its true power can never be evidenced, along with one's inherent, human tenacity. Just as you can't prove a diamond is a diamond unless you test its firmness by rubbing a hard, composite ruby or sapphire against it, to test the firmness of life, or to show proof of existence, life perhaps needs to collide with the definitive concreteness of death. Consequently, any life that gets hurt and broken the moment it comes into contact with death perhaps amounts to nothing more than brittle glass.

However, where life is concerned, we live in an ambiguous age. Except for perishing in car accidents, we rarely die these days, completely sustaining ourselves with medicine while managing to entirely elude the threat of tuberculosis, which used to threaten sickly men and women, and the threat of military service, which used to threaten healthy young men. And in a realm devoid of the danger of death, the impulse to affirm your life, to prove your existence, inevitably gets sublimated into the mad exploration of sex on the one hand, and into political action for the sake of violence, on the other. And then, amid such a situation, there is born a frustration so restless that even art ceases to have any meaning. This is because art is meant to be enjoyed by the fireside.

Watching me recite Mishima's prose from memory, Eriko flashed an envious look. I had to explain to her then that, just like her good looks, her envy was of no consequence in the grand scheme of things. "So perhaps," I then said, "Mishima, having made his own life collide against his own death with all his might, had, in the end, been instantly shattered like glass. But even if that were the case, I believe he lived a life imbued with more integrity and honesty than any writer of this nation, dead or alive."

10

AFTER THAT DAY, WE met three times in two weeks. But our dates never lasted longer than two hours; we used to part ways as soon as we finished dinner. Although Eriko would return straight home, I'd hurry back to my office to manage my ever-increasing workload; it was the year-end, which was a busy time for me.

Our fourth date took place on December 14, which fell on a Friday I believe. Eriko arrived a little late at the restaurant where we agreed to meet, and as soon as she sat down across from me, she conveyed the news—which she herself had learned only yesterday—that the two of us had become the talk of her office. Apparently, an acquaintance of hers had spotted us eating at an incredibly expensive restaurant in Nogizaka on a previous date.

I told her that it was no big deal, that everyone at my office already knew about us anyway.

Looking surprised, she said she'd been to my office the day before yesterday, but no one there was talking about us.

"Of course not," I said. "No one's so tactless as to bring up the subject in front of you to see if the rumor's true. But, I can tell you for certain that, in my office, we're a hot topic, you and I. It's a bit of an incident, after all."

"How'd they come to know so easily?"

I found it funny how suspicious Eriko was all the time.

"The answer's elementary. I let everyone know about us."

I went on to explain that my stock had risen just because I was going out with her, and then laughed, saying that it went to show, I suppose, how much she'd been feared all this time. Eriko slowly raised the coffee cup, which had just been brought over to her, and after taking a sip, she fell silent for a while. I told her that if she was uncomfortable, we didn't have to see each other anymore, but I also added that we weren't doing anything wrong.

"How could we?" she asked.

"How indeed," I answered.

After leaving the coffee shop, we took a cab to Asakusabashi and ate sushi at a shop where I was a regular. While drinking sake, I reminded her repeatedly about the sequence of events, that at first she'd been interested in me, constantly looking my way, and that only then did I start to gradually take interest in her before we ended up meeting together like we were then.

"It was you who began speaking like we were old acquaintances when we first met," Eriko argued at first.

But she got drunk soon, and by the time we left the shop she didn't give a damn anymore about the matter, admitting, "Yeah, it's more or less as you say."

After that I was led to a bar in Harumi, which was apparently a hangout for Eriko and her friends. There, I sat down on one of the uncomfortable, long-legged chairs lined up in front of a glass counter, downing many glasses of bourbon and soda while silently listening to Eriko talk about various things. Every now and then, she'd glance at my sloshed, vacant face to say, "Hey, are you listening?" Each time I'd reply, "And then what?" to urge her to go on, but truth be told, for the most part I was just calmly taking in the view of the busily changing expressions on Eriko's face, not listening to anything she was saying.

Since we both drank a lot, we ended up laughing very loudly, and Eriko would, over and over again—every couple of minutes, in fact, while pushing back her hair from her forehead with both hands—open her mouth widely and burst out laughing. This gesture was, in a word, stagy. While drawing a picture of a rabbit with drops of booze spilled on the counter, only to erase it and draw it all over again, I wondered why nothing ever penetrated deep inside me; everything just got repelled, like all this water on the surface of the glass counter.

Having become awfully tired, when I boarded the taxi to get home, I rested my head against the window and fell asleep at once. I awoke with Eriko shaking my body. The car had stopped in front of a building I'd never seen before.

When I asked, "Where is this?" Eriko said, "My apartment."

"I'm sorry for the hassle," I said, "I think I've gotten completely drunk."

The taxi door opened and Eriko attempted to pay the driver. For an instant, I thought about restraining myself, but out of my mouth, in a very sleepy tone, came words that were totally opposite to such an intention.

"Could you let me," I said rubbing my eyes, "have a cup of coffee in your room, if that's okay?" Eriko nodded, so both of us got out of the car.

After passing through the entrance to a large, newish apartment, we got into the elevator, where I gazed on Eriko's profile illuminated by the bluish light of a fluorescent lamp. I wondered whether I was going to make love to her tonight in the tired condition I was in, both in terms of mind and body. There wasn't an iota of excitement left in me, but the moment the offer of soft flesh is made, the due formalities for the male-female transaction are semi-automatically set in motion.

I recalled a passage in a novel I'd read.

Desire, you know, always comes from the outside. It's not the case that people choose to entrust themselves to their own desires. Desires choose the people they want, and then people just get on board. Fear, humiliation, desire—they're all just roller-coaster rides that come to a screeching halt before you. These guys are our bosses, see, and we're not even their drivers. They're, see, always taking us for a ride, is all.

Although Mishima wrote that launching a mad exploration into sex is how people can affirm their lives—or prove that they exist—in this day and age when death is far removed from everyday reality, I for one can't possibly imagine sex to be so noble a thing as to warrant some label like "exploration." Sex is just like alcohol or narcotics; for both men and women, it's like being dosed with an injection and becoming mindless.

Eriko's apartment consisted of a living room and a dining room the size of around twenty tatami mats and a bedroom of around ten tatami mats with a huge walk-in closet. After making a general survey of the place and receiving a cup of espresso from Eriko, I sat down on a leather sofa in a corner of the living room. The bitterness of the coffee coated my mouth, relieving the drowsiness I was feeling until a moment before. I looked at a large photographic portrait hung on the wall. It had caught my eye as soon as I entered the room; in fact, I was so astounded by it I wondered what she was thinking by having that stuff up there. Eriko sat next to me with a large mug in hand. I stood up and approached the wall. After scrutinizing the portrait I looked back and asked, "What the hell is this nonsense?"

Putting her unfinished cup on a small table before the sofa, Eriko wore a slightly embarrassed face, and then mentioned the name of a certain well-known photographer, adding that after she stood in front of his camera for a test shot during a studio shooting, he'd taken the trouble to enlarge the positive of that shot to its present a gargantuan size and gave it to her as a gift.

Unsatisfied with her account, I walked around the wide living room while sipping my coffee. Upon careful examination, I realized the place was filled with snapshots of Eriko, taken on a trip to some foreign country, framed and displayed on the dining table, shelves, and even on top of the television set.

"Looks like you're a frequent flyer," I said after returning to the sofa.

I simply couldn't understand how she could go on living so unfazed, gazing at her huge self-portrait every day, and I also couldn't appreciate the fact that she'd travel overseas often just for the sake of bringing back picture-perfect memories, which she could then carefully frame and preserve.

"What do you do there, in all those foreign places? What do you see?"

"Don't you like to travel?" Eriko responded, genuinely amazed by my question.

"Not sure. I haven't traveled that far, other than for work. Besides, I've never felt there's really anything worthwhile to see out there that would make me want to spend a bucket load of money, or go out of my way to make the time I really can't, you know. It's not worth the trouble. The thing about people is that while they're yearning for faraway places and things, they tend to fail to really see anything all that well, when in reality, they need to be paying attention to what's near them. What I'm saying is that there's really nothing important a lavish use of money can ever help us achieve—nothing that really matters, that is."

"Besides," I added, "I'm tired enough here, so I can't even begin to think about going anywhere else."

Eriko picked up the mug again, and, wrapping both her hands around it, thought for a while. And then she stood up from the sofa to sit up straight on the deep-pile carpet below, with her legs folded underneath, before looking me straight in the eye and saying, "Even so, I'm never satisfied with anything until I see it with my own eyes. When I travel I always gain something, and even though I have no idea how it'll benefit me, I get all kinds of impressions on the spot, and I think about those impressions later, in retrospect, see, which is why I try to travel alone as much as possible, whenever I travel far."

"You gain something, huh?" I said. "Just what kind of gain do you attain by seeing things with your own eyes?"

Eriko broke her posture, stretched her legs, muttered "Yeah," and began talking, but not before shyly prefacing with the words, "it's not really anything serious.

"For example, when I went to a rural town in Thailand, I saw that all the dogs there were afflicted with skin diseases. Their hair had fallen off from various parts of their bodies, and they were all skin and bones. They all had adorable faces though, with such lovely eyes you've never seen in your life, always teary. You just want to, like, get close to them and lift them up and hold them in your arms. But when you see their bodies, all swollen red and scab-ridden, you just can't get yourself to touch them. You just can't get up the nerve to, you know, because you feel like you'll catch whatever they have if you touch them, even though all the Thai kids don't mind pulling their cheeks and slipping them into their inside pockets, you know. Since public health over there isn't properly run like it is in Japan, you find a lot of these stray dogs wandering all over town. But I can't help thinking that, with our achievement in sanitation, we ended up losing something precious in the process."

I got down from the sofa as well with my cup in hand, and sat down on the floor to face Eriko across the table, deciding to listen to her story with an erect posture.

"When you travel in Europe, even trains have international routes, right?" she went on. "It's all a single continent, and the nations are actually accessible from one country to the next. When I was standing in the train station in Paris, I could see multitudes of different skin colors, eye colors, and hair colors, surging into the platform, each of them carrying just one small piece of luggage.

"But you know what? The only thing truly different about them was their language. Anybody and everybody was laughing in the same way, embracing the people they were expecting to see in the same way, all the while speaking in entirely different languages. Even though the scene—once you get used to it—ceases to appear strange, the voices you hear never do, the babel of tongues clashing against each other, never becoming one. Do you know what you end up actually hearing when a lot of languages get jumbled up? A sharp, piercing cry, as sharp as a splinter of glass, the kind of noise that makes you want to cover your ears; it's all so unbearably hideous to me.

"I've always believed that the problem doesn't lie in skin color, but in this weird cacophony of languages that sounds like the buzzing of bees. Even though Europe has turned into the EU, unless the language becomes one, the invisible boundary of words can never be removed, I think."

When Eriko finished talking and gave a small sigh, I closed my eyes and was able to let her sigh sink into a deep place inside me, a deep place inside my heart. I reflected on the person I'd been to her until this moment, the guy who had been going out with her, halfheartedly, just for laughs, treating the whole relationship like a joke. Although my memories of my moments with Eriko were still few, I ruminated over them, and vividly confirmed in the depths of my consciousness that the woman called Eriko had a beautiful heart, and that she was an honest soul.

However, after a while, even that vividness like the glint of a sunken pebble scooped out of water.

My cup was empty already, and all I should've done after that was to bend my left elbow and take a look at my watch, but instead I said, "Listening to your story's kind of making me tired."

Eriko gave me a strange look, so I moved the table with the two cups in front of me to the side, crawled over to her, across the carpet, and said in a firm, unwavering voice, "I guess the time for lecturing is over," while raising my hips to bring my face close to hers and stare intensely into her eyes.

Without averting my gaze, I draped my body over hers, but Eriko seemed to have been waiting for me to do just that from the beginning. The scent of her perfume, infused with alcohol, turned me on. After thinking in the corner of my mind that this scent was all there was in the end, I laid my lips against hers.

We fell down on top of each other on the carpet, kissing intensely, over and over.

But that was all.

I arose before long, and took a look at my watch.

For nearly ten days after that, we didn't have any kind of contact whatsoever. I sometimes thought about calling her, but when I began to think about what I should say, it became troublesome so I gave up on the idea. In the first place, I didn't know Eriko's cell number, nor did I know her apartment number. Eriko didn't know my cell number either. We'd agreed just to call each other's offices if we needed to communicate, having already decided on a time and place for our next appointment when we parted company. We were both punctual people, and mutually understood that the both of us were looking forward to our next rendezvous, that we considered it a top priority. Still, it was slightly surprising to realize that we were both unaware of each other's cell numbers, so I was thinking about keeping it in mind to make sure that we asked each other about the numbers when, on December 22, the ninth day since we'd last met, a letter from Eriko arrived in my apartment's mailbox.

It was a square envelope, formed by folding a sheet of letter paper four-fold; its front was white but its back bore a pattern of pink stripes and the seal was decorated with golden letters that formed the words, MAY YOU HAVE SWEET DREAMS TONIGHT. It was a somewhat long telegraph, explaining in concise terms that she'd been waiting for me to get in touch with her, that she wanted me to contact her soon—if I still liked her— and that she wanted to see me again. It really read like a template for polite prose.

I was quite surprised that a woman in this day and age would even send a letter. What's more, the style was so clear and direct— completely free of flowery expressions—that it even felt clunky. I imagined when she might have written this, and wondered about the look on her face at that time, and found it all very amusing.

On the evening of that day, I called her office at once. Without touching on the letter, I just suggested dinner at a hotel the day after tomorrow, on Christmas Eve. Speaking in a businesslike tone, she told me she was already booked for Christmas Eve, so I suggested she simply come up with some excuse and cancel whatever it was, but she replied that it was impossible.

I abruptly began to talk about the weather.

There was a cold wind blowing that day, but otherwise the weather was clear, and it appeared likely that it would be the same tomorrow and the day after, but I asked her to have dinner with me if it rained. Eriko finally softened her tone and said, "Reminds me of that story about Kanichi and Omiya," adding, while laughing, that she found it hard to believe it would rain when the fair weather was lasting as long as it was. I told her that in this world there's rarely an engagement you couldn't break off and conveyed the name of the restaurant of the hotel and the time I'd be there if it rained. After replacing the receiver in its cradle, I came under the impression that if it didn't rain, I'd probably never get to meet her alone again.

And then, two days later, Tokyo was hit, from early in the morning, by a sudden downpour.

When we finished dinner and went into the room I'd reserved, I trotted over to the bed, which was neatly made up with a dark brown bed cover and two layers of blankets. Folding these blankets over fully to both sides, the dark room, lit only by a pale light filtering through the lace curtains, suddenly seemed to brighten a little because of the exposed bedsheets.

Eriko was standing at the entrance, watching me in action.

I removed my jacket and tie and sat on the bed before beckoning her over. Eriko placed her bag on a small chair in a corner of the room and came very close. Lightly tapping the edge of the bed twice, I motioned to her to sit next to me. Eriko straightened her long skirt and politely complied.

In the dim hotel room, where only the faint noise of the ventilation could be heard, we kissed. Her tongue fluttered in my mouth like a slowly flickering flame, and I sucked in the saliva by moving my lips round and round in circles before slowly tracing her gums with the tip of my tongue. In the gap between her lower lip and the base of her teeth, there was a lot of sweet-tasting drool, so I carefully sipped it.

Taking as much time as possible, I undressed Eriko, one piece of clothing at a time, and Eriko undid the buttons of my shirt, one by one.

Turning on the bed lamp and marshaling the full attention of each and every one of my five senses, I carefully and thoroughly reaffirmed Eriko's limbs, which were like works of art. Without showing many signs of shame, she just quietly surrendered, with her eyes closed, to my modus operandi and, in time, began to respond with satisfaction.

After we finished I was smoking a cigarette when Eriko, lying on her stomach next to me, peeked at the nightstand's digital watch and said, "It's eleven already." Two hours had already passed since we'd entered the room.

"I'm totally spent," I said, letting out a smoky sigh. "A while ago, just as we were finishing, the roots of my teeth tightened all at once; they were throbbing and it hurt like hell. I never experienced anything like that."

"You must have been trying so hard." Eriko was chuckling, her bare breasts on my back, her fingers slowly stroking my forehead and hair.

We took out a can of beer from the refrigerator and enjoyed it together, passing the liquid from mouth to mouth.

"The beer that goes into your mouth comes out much colder," she said happily, as if she'd just stumbled upon a life-changing discovery.

A little after dimming the lights Eriko confided, out of the blue, as if remembering her distant past, "I wonder why I've come to like you." When I remained silent, she grumbled, "You're probably going to tell me there's no reason anyway, right?"

I said, drawing her shoulder close, "If you came to like me, it's probably because I didn't think anything of you—a person like you can't stand that."

"You always say the oddest things, in that perfectly composed voice of yours, with that wise-ass look on your face."

"But I guess that's the part of you I like, Eriko—"

"But you've got to become a little more agreeable from now on, like this person here."

Eriko rubbed against my dick, which had become erect again, with the inside of her soft thigh before falling on me and pressing her lips for a kiss.

It seemed to be raining outside again, as I heard some light pitter-pattering against the window.

"But . . ." Eriko said, releasing her lips and pushing back her long hair, ". . . to think that it really rained."

At that moment, I flinched somewhat, finding in her eyes infinite points of light, glimmering like distant stars. I thought I was going to lose myself in their brilliance, and before I knew it, with my eyes closed, I was winding my arm around her neck and aggressively drawing her slender body closer.

11

ON THE MORNING OF the Sunday we promised to go out cherry-blossom viewing, the incessant ringing of the telephone awoke me. Climbing out of bed, I picked up my cell phone from the charger on the bookshelf and pressed it to my ear.

"I'm sorry. I just can't make it today."

It was Tomomi, speaking in a frail voice.

"Oh . . ." I said, half-asleep, unaware at first that I was even standing.

"I'm sorry," Tomomi said again.

With the grogginess weighing down on me, I wanted to hang up quickly, but that impulse, if surrendered to, seemed to betray the truth that I really didn't give a damn about cherry-blossom viewing from the very beginning, so I immediately changed my mind and pressed myself to properly play the part of the disappointed friend.

"What? You can't make it?" I began, sounding discouraged before reading the hands on the alarm clock beside the charger. It was still seven.

"Why? Anything urgent come up?" My mind finally began to clear.

"It looks like I'm about to find the right nursery at last," Tomomi said.

Lately, she was frantically trying to find a nursery school for Takuya. The boy had been unable to get adjusted to the nursery he'd begun attending in April last year, and since the new year began, he'd been absent for days. Even though Takuya liked this particular nursery's policy of permitting the kids to remain barefooted all year round and play to their hearts' content with just one shirt on, even in winter, it still didn't suit him in the end, apparently. So Tomomi had to look for a new nursery, but there were only a few in the neighborhood, which all happened to be full. She ended up welcoming the new year without any closure on the matter.

But then, she told me, late last night she received a call from an acquaintance who had been helping out with the search, and she was going to go together with this person this morning to the office of a certain member of the ward assembly to ask him to negotiate her boy's entry into a particular nursery on her behalf.

"Actually, we were already rejected once by this place, but my friend told me, with the help of this ward member, we stood a chance, even though it's still all up in the air."

When I told her, in that case I could just go see the cherry blossoms with Takuya alone, she responded very coldly, "I'm supposed to take Takuya along too."

"Well, I guess it can't be helped then. The cherry blossoms are going to be mostly gone by next week, so I guess there'll be no flower-viewing this year."

Having said that, I was still pleased about the prospect that Takuya might get into a new nursery, so I added, "Hope it works out well," and hung up.

I canceled the alarm setting and slipped into bed. While privately thinking what a lucky break it was—since I'd been extremely tied up with work this week and had gotten exhausted more and more—I fell asleep again.

When I woke up, it was one in the afternoon.

I got out of bed, went to the kitchen, pulled out a can of beer from the refrigerator and sat on the table and drank. No sooner was I halfway through the beer than I turned my face away from the budding brightness pouring through the veranda, toward the empty, six-tatami mat space, where the partitioning was open. I suddenly felt down, taking in the dismal darkness I saw in there.

I wondered why the beer tasted terrible. I thought I should've gone out to see cherry blossoms today, no matter what.

I felt that if it was going to turn out like this, I should've invited Raita or Honoka to come along.

Eriko was in Los Angeles on a ten-day trip since the previous week. Apparently, she was put in charge of handling the styling of a certain singer's promotional video, and was excited about it when she left. She'd terminated her contract with her company at the end of last year and gone completely freelance from this April. She was very pleased to have landed a major project right away.

Honoka and Raita rarely visited these days. Honoka seemed to be quite exhausted from all the job-hunting she'd begun since the latter half of last year. Apparently, she'd been turning to Eriko for advice about one thing or another, even staying at her place sometimes.

"But she's finally thinking about her own future, so I feel she's become very emotionally strong." Eriko was being optimistic, as always.

Raita, on the other hand, had no choice but to live precariously from day to day, with Torimasa having gone bankrupt. While the recession was partly to blame, the primary reason for the shutdown was because his boss suffered a stroke as soon as the New Year holidays began, and even though his condition had improved, the left half of his body remained paralyzed, making him unable to attend to the demands of running his store in the way he used to. Consequently, the boss, along with his wife, was preparing to retire to Kagoshima, his birthplace, sometime next month after selling off the store and the land. Raita had to search for an apartment immediately, as well as worry about finding a new job, and since he had to scrape up the money to take care of the moving expenses, he seemed to be working part-time jobs all day long, every day.

I had some drinks with him last week in Nakano—the first time in a month—but he didn't seem all that well; his cheeks had become hollow and he had a constant hacking cough. As usual, we both guzzled down the drinks, and I was drunk halfway through, but Raita was heatedly cursing the producer, Terauchi.

"That old fart, he goes—'Good riddance! That damn shop going bankrupt is the best thing that could've happened to you. It'd be a shame to see a man like you waste away in obscurity, hidden in that damn shop. You agree, don't you? Deep down inside, you see what I mean, don't you?'—I tell you there's something wrong with that dude, never opening his piehole without saying, that damn shop, that damn shop."

Having finished, Raita turned toward me and said, "Naoto-san, could you believe that guy? The nerve! Here's what else he said"—Raita put his arm all the way around my shoulder and spoke into my ear in a weird voice, mimicking Terauchi. "'Hey there, Kimura, you know you can become a way bigger star than that Kubozuka guy in no time at all, so why don't you just take my word for it and jump into the world of television, huh? Come on now, why don't you?'"

Laughing, I wriggled out of his grasp and teased, "Hey, you never know! Surprisingly, you just might have the talent to become an actor."

Raita became straight-faced and spat out, "Stop it! You're making me sick!!"

Knowing how tenacious Terauchi could be, I'm sure he took the opportunity to try to persuade Raita again when he heard he was out of a job. It wasn't surprising, really, seeing how driven Terauchi was to win over Raita, but it still was a tough break for the guy, considering that it was Raita whom he was trying to persuade—the young man was one heck of a hardheaded dude. Perhaps it was just as well, though. For someone like Terauchi—someone who unwaveringly believed that everyone in the world wanted to get on television and become famous—

being rejected by Raita may have been just the lesson he needed all along.

I got to know Terauchi at a seminar on politics and the economy, which was sponsored by a certain media insider. I thought it was rather unusual for someone in the drama field to come to such a seminar, but according to him, "The people working in drama today are such shameless ignoramuses. Without knowing the difference between the House of Representatives and the House of Councilors, they blissfully have actors refer to Councilors as Representatives."

We became friends only around the end of the year, after we both attended the year-end party held by the organizer of the seminar. Although the first party ended without incident in an Akasaka restaurant, when we stepped into a room of a gorgeous mansion in Motoazabu specially arranged for the second party, there were five topless porn actresses, dressed only in loincloths, waiting for us to take the party in a completely vulgar direction. Still, up to the point when the girls put on a clumsy travesty of a striptease, things stayed charming. But shortly thereafter, after the alcohol started to take effect, when the tensions of about fifteen partygoers began to ease, the entire scene began to show signs of a wild orgy. Even the men began to strip down to their waists, one after another, and take turns putting the girls on their laps; among them, there were those who untied the loincloths of the girls against their will—it took three to do that—and there were even those who began an impromptu photo session with a small instant camera provided by the organizer.

I was exercising tact in my exchanges with the girls and waiting for the right time to leave, when Terauchi, who was seated next to me, put on a sour expression and said, "Mr. Matsubara, let's flee this hell hole, double quick."

The two of us slipped away from the room and drank the rest of the night away in Roppongi, having become kindred spirits. It was that night when I came to know, plainly from his mouth in the form of a confession, that he was gay, and that he'd never laid a finger on a woman in his life.

"Although that's not the reason why I entered the world of show business, I must say that for gays like myself, showbiz is someplace like heaven . . ."

I came to like him at once, finding his strangely warm manner of speaking novel and fresh.

"Well, he's not such a bad guy at heart, you know."

When I thoughtlessly defended Terauchi in that way, Raita got worked up, which was unusual for him.

"But who the hell does he think he is, telling me he was happy to see 'that damn shop' go bankrupt, that it was good riddance? The boss and his wife have always gone out of their way to protect that shop, you know. Maybe I've already talked to you about this, Naoto-san, but eighteen years ago, the boss lost his only son, who was four years old, to cancer, and ever since then he's been taking care of his wife, who's been constantly on the verge of a breakdown, while breaking his own back to keep the shop going. As for me, he said he loved me like his son, believing me to be his stand-in, and began to train me from scratch at a time when I was going astray. Then here comes this insensitive faggot with his rude remarks, hardly aware of the circumstances. At any rate, the bottom line is that folks like Terauchi, and even you, Naoto-san, are elites, right? You fellas graduated from first-rate universities and entered first-rate companies and earn top-notch salaries, right? People like that can never understand the hardships of folks who survive by skewering several hundred pieces of meat every single day, charging just a hundred yen per stick."

When I heard Raita say these words, I remembered my mother saying something along those lines in the old days. When I passed my entrance exams and was about to leave for Tokyo, she handed over a meager amount of money and said, "Now, you'll never, ever understand me."

"I feel like something's snapped," Raita muttered when I fell silent.

"Snapped?" I said automatically.

"Yes, that's right. When the boss and his wife suddenly decided to close shop and return to Kagoshima, in the beginning, I was, like, resigned to that and simply thought to myself, like, oh, so that's how it's going to be. But lately, I've been getting this sense that it's not something so simple, that this thing like a cord that's been barely keeping me tied to this rotten world until now has finally snapped. My life until now, let's face it, has just been about living in my bro Kohei's shoes, right? Although he was my cousin, he was like an older brother to me. Now that two years have gone by since his death, I've been thinking what a disgraceful life I've been living. As I've been saying for some time, there's nothing I really want to do in this world, right? The boss asked me to inherit the shop, but I've never thought about running my own business; I was just working my ass off there because he and the missus had let me stay with them. Like you said some time ago, Naoto-san—this world's a genuine hell? Well, I really think so too, because no matter where you go, I don't think you could possibly find any other world that's made to be so stifling as this one, that before you're finished you're made to suffer and suffer, only to be made to suffer again; there's no end, you're never excused. When we let Kohei die I became convinced, like you, Naoto-san, that this here is where hell is."

By that time I was sloshed, and half of Raita's story had slipped out of the other ear. Raita didn't seem to mind, though, going on and on as he pleased.

"You know what'd be great?" he went on. "To die by doing something really rad and flashy; go out with a bang, you know!"

Raita seemed dead set about that, so I decided to give him a piece of my mind.

"Don't place conditions on dying," I said. "Only idiots say I want to die in this or that way."

"You think? I mean, if you're going to die anyway, wouldn't it be okay to go out in a really messed up way? Honoka and I talk about stuff like that a lot."

Raita looked embarrassed now.

"Honoka's been saying such things too?"

"Yes, she has."

"Fools, the both of you." I decided that's what they surely were and laughed loudly.

After spending about thirty minutes at the kitchen table, staring into empty space, I changed clothes and went out.

With lunch on my mind, I was walking down toward Morishita when I saw Tomomi and Takuya near an intersection; they were approaching down the sidewalk on the other side. It was surprising, considering that it was already past two. Perhaps they were returning from the ward official's place, but what I found puzzling was that Tomomi was holding a large bouquet. What's more, the two were walking side by side toward Morishita Station, which was in the opposite direction from New Seoul. When I hid under the eaves of a watch store and saw them disappear into the subway entrance, I hurried down there myself, having made up my mind to follow them.

At the platform, I spotted the two standing at the Shinjuku-bound side. Keeping a safe distance, I observed them from behind a column. Takuya's legs, exposed by his shorts, were so thin they seemed like they'd break any minute. Tomomi was holding the bouquet in her right hand while holding her son's hand. Her hair was rough as usual.

I wondered where she was going with such a large bouquet? At the very least, it didn't seem like the ward official's place. A train bound for Hashimoto pulled into the platform, and when I made sure that the two of them boarded this train, I jumped onto an adjacent car.

The two got off at Meidaimae and transferred to the Ino-kashira Line from there. Of course, they remained clueless to the fact that I was shadowing them.

They ultimately got off at Shimokitazawa Station.

I finally had an idea about where they were going, and the bouquet, fluttering in and out of sight amid the bustling crowd in the lively street just outside the station, seemed unusually vivid now.

As expected, they disappeared into a small playhouse located approximately ten minutes away on foot from Shimokitazawa Station.

The place had only a few seats, but it was a historic theater, equipped with the very latest stage sets. There were several garlands lined up at the entrance, and young couples were streaming through there. Apparently, on that day, the playhouse was featuring the opening performance of a small theatrical company, which had only recently shot to prominence. A flashy billboard, using only primary colors, was on display, pasted with a particularly large photograph of the leading actor. Naturally, the face in the photograph was that of Ilgon Park.

After Tomomi and her son were out of my sight, I smoked a cigarette in front of the playhouse and went back the way I came. There was a Hiroshima-style *okonomiyaki* restaurant in front of Shimokitazawa Station I used to go to sometimes back in my college days, so I had one helping of a large *okonomiyaki* pancake called *oban*, and had two glasses of oolong tea highball before returning to my apartment.

Three days later, at night, I arrived at the door to New Seoul, bringing along three special admission tickets to Korakuen Stadium's Children's Day shows, which I'd purchased from a ticket agency in Ikebukuro in the afternoon. But, for some reason, I was unable to pull the door open. In the end, I decided to just let go of the handle and walk back home.

On the way back I pulled out the tickets, which I'd stashed

inside my wallet, and tore them to pieces before throwing them into the trash bin of a convenience store found along the way.

I decided to end my association with Tomomi and Takuya.

Until then, I'd always thought that I'd lose touch with Eriko first, so it occurred to me, as I walked along, that the order was reversed.

That night, I had a hard time falling asleep.

For some reason Takuya's face kept drifting through my mind, unsettling me terribly. For some reason it was heart-wrenching to imagine what Takuya would think if I stopped turning up suddenly. By getting to know Takuya, I learned that children lived in a completely different world from the world of us adults. However, this small world of theirs was always being crushed to smithereens for our self-seeking convenience.

Lying there in bed, I was remembering the time when just Takuya and I went up to Okutama last summer for a swim in the river there. It was a hot day, and Takuya was down to his underpants, wearing a small straw hat and crouched down in a babbling brook, playing in the water, never getting tired. Sitting on the riverbank, which was scorched by sunlight, I was, despite feeling dozy, keeping a cautious eye on his really small back.

Meanwhile, around thirty minutes later, a middle-aged man appeared and began fishing right next to Takuya. Takuya was drawing water into a beach bucket he'd brought from his home, dumping sand into it and emptying the bucket into the river whenever it got heavy; it was a game he was repeating over and over. Every time he did so, he generated a small splashing sound on the shore.

A little while after the man had lowered his fishing line, a sharp voice reached my ears, which were still fuzzy with sleep. Snapping out of my reverie at once, I took a clearer look at Takuya in a hurry, afraid for a brief moment that Takuya might have become stuck in the river. But that wasn't the case. Instead, the fisherman was gesturing to Takuya while shouting, "Move over more, boy!"

Surprised, Takuya looked up at the man and ran back toward me, on the verge of tears. I don't think I've ever felt more rage than I did just then. In fact, I thought I clearly felt the blood in my head boiling.

Approaching the man, I raised my voice and shouted, "Move the hell out yourself, asshole!" and grabbed a big stone on the riverbed and hurled it at his fishing line with all the strength I could muster. The man gave me an indignant look in return, so I seized his lapels suddenly and pushed him away with brute force. He fell back into the rapids, and when I took a further step forward I kicked his jaw with my right foot without much hesitation. Blood gushed out of his nose as he began to pack up his gear and hightail it out of there, looking disoriented and helpless. But my anger didn't subside. I grabbed yet another sizable stone, and began to run after the guy, just when his back was receding far into the distance. Flinging away his rod and cooler on the way, while yelling out expletives and looking behind over and over again, he managed to escape. Only after I'd mercilessly chased him in this way—and after breaking in two the fishing rod he'd thrown away, knocking the cooler into pieces with the stone, and making sure that he was nowhere in sight—was I finally able to regain control of myself.

When I returned to the part of the riverbank where I'd been originally, I found Takuya still frightened, so I encouraged him to resume his playing in the water. This time I joined him and the two of us together caught small fish and built a sandcastle as well. Takuya was delighted and, squatting down, played on and on by the riverside. When he'd occasionally turn his face toward me, laugh innocently, and wave, he'd look relieved and return to playing by himself.

And then, for some reason, watching the way Takuya was at that moment, I felt, for the first time in decades, that old misty-eyed sentiment of feeling wanted.

I was just beginning to doze off when my cell rang.

Since Eriko was supposed to be coming home that night, I answered the phone, thinking it was certainly her, but it was Tomomi instead.

"I'm sorry to call so late," she said in a sad voice. Apparently, Takuya had been in bed since three days ago, running a fever. Although she closed the shop today to nurse him, his temperature was fluctuating wildly and he was weakening considerably. Since she got worried about how strange his condition was, she'd ended up calling me, apparently.

It then occurred to me for the first time that New Seoul's sign wasn't lit up tonight. If I'd pulled that door handle even just a little, I'd have realized for sure that the shop was closed.

This disturbed me quite a bit. I'd carelessly overlooked something I usually wouldn't have. I've always loathed such negligence.

"I'm on my way."

After hanging up the phone and going out to the street, I climbed into the car parked in the lot behind the apartment. While driving, I thought about the steps to take if Takuya's condition was serious. I remembered the whereabouts of a general hospital in the vicinity and concluded that calling an ambulance would be more reliable than driving Takuya over to the hospital.

Then, suddenly, I had another thought.

If I hadn't overlooked that sign, I wouldn't be hurrying over to Tomomi's place in such a state of panic. I also thought that perhaps I'd bought those three tickets with the intention of tearing them up from the beginning—but I couldn't give a damn about such things anymore.

The room smelled of illness. Takuya was lying on a child's futon with a wet towel placed over his forehead, but was coughing intensely in intermittent bursts. He was half-asleep, and his forehead was terribly hot when I removed the towel and placed my palm over it. Yet he looked pale, his breathing was fast, and the wings of his nose quivered with each breath he took. A part of the sheet was stained, and when I asked Tomomi about it, she answered, "He vomited as soon as I called you. But it must have been only water, since he hasn't eaten since the day before yesterday."

Tomomi squeezed the towel over a washbowl and placed it over Takuya's head, covering his eyes. Apparently, he'd started running a fever Sunday night, which was three days ago, and since his temperature rose considerably the day before yesterday, she'd taken him to see a doctor and was told that it was a cold. After administering the medicine she received, the fever finally went down yesterday, during the day, so she was feeling relieved, when it rose again. It's been repeatedly going up and down, all day long, ever since. When it was evening, the strange, wet cough started, and he seemed to be suffocating. Even though he tended to catch cold, she'd never seen him like this, so she'd become unbearably worried at once.

Takuya's state was clearly odd. It appeared that he was semi-conscious, rather than asleep. I put my arm under the futon and, tucking up the hem of his pajama top, placed my hand on his skinny belly. Even though he'd been avoiding food, his abdomen was noticeably swollen.

"It's probably pneumonia. A little severe even." The moment I said so, Tomomi crumpled up her face and seemed to be on the verge of bursting into tears.

"He must have caught a nasty virus," I went on, "that day at the ward official's office. The human traffic at places like that is intense."

At a loss, Tomomi covered her mouth and looked into Takuya's face by the pillow, and began to call out his name again and again.

I got up, went into Tomomi's adjacent room, and called for an ambulance.

After being wheeled into a hospital in Sumiyoshi on a gurney, Takuya was immediately put into an oxygen tent, where they began to administer an IV treatment after piercing his thin arm with a long needle. Overwhelmed by the gravity of the situation, Tomomi lost it and began biting into her handkerchief while sobbing impatiently.

"It hasn't led to pleurisy, so there's nothing much to worry about," said the doctor on night duty in his office while examining X-rays of Takuya's chest, displayed on the viewing screen. Nonetheless, Tomomi said vehemently, "Doctor, please save Takuya!" Naturally, the doctor seemed a bit troubled.

I learned his name from the nametag on his chest and called my office from the lounge of the emergency room. A junior reporter I'd worked with in the past was still there; the weekly magazine's final proofs were due that day. I had him look up the doctor's history in the directory of physicians found in the reference library on the fifth floor. When I learned that the doctor was formerly on duty for a lengthy period of time at the medical office of a well-known university, I conveyed the information to Tomomi to comfort her, to allay her fears.

Takuya was moved to the children's ward on the third floor, and Tomomi and I spent the night there, seated on steel chairs that we arranged by the tented bed where Takuya slept. An hour after he was administered a transfusion, I could see, even through the tent, that the look on Takuya's face was mellowing. Hearing his breathing become more regular, Tomomi finally looked a little relieved.

"If anything were to happen to this child, I wouldn't be able to go on living," Tomomi murmured, so I said reprovingly, "Saying such a thing could make it come true, you know." And then added, "He'll probably be hospitalized for two, three days, but everything's going to be all right. I'll pay a visit tomorrow with a big bouquet in hand."

Tomomi reacted to my words by casting a dubious look, and seemed to be on the verge of saying something, but kept quiet.

When I told her, after a while, that it would be appropriate to tell Park about this matter, Tomomi told me that she could manage on her own from this point on and that she wanted me to go home and get to bed, ahead of her.

"That won't be necessary," I responded, without taking my eyes off Takuya's sleeping face.

12

Two days later, I visited Takuya's hospital room and found Park there.

Takuya was already quite well, sitting cross-legged on the bed, eagerly playing with a toy car that Park had apparently bought for him. On top of a small closet used for storing small personal effects was the large bouquet I'd brought yesterday, arranged in a blue vase.

After introducing myself to Park I said, "Where is Tomomi, if I may ask?"

He answered that she'd returned in the evening to Morishita to open up shop, and that he intended to stay here tonight. When I asked Takuya, "Isn't it great that your father has come?" he nodded very happily.

"Would you like to have a smoke in the lobby downstairs?" Park offered, polite in speech, gentle in bearing, tall in stature. His face, with thin eyebrows and strangely large eyes, was angular. The bridge of his nose was smooth like a beveled surface, and his reddish hair, kept long, was parted in the middle of his forehead and left hanging down all the way to his ears. He had a voice that was thick and penetrating, and he had a figure that was so impressive it could leave a lasting impression even from a distance. Seeing Park up close for the first time, I realized that Takuya in fact took after this man, and not Tomomi.

We descended the stairs together. It was already late, and there didn't seem to be any other visitors around. The dry sounds of our slippers flip-flopping resounded throughout the stairway. The lights in the outpatient lobby were already turned off, and, with the green light of the emergency sign and the light from the medical office in the back providing the only illumination, the place was dim and silent. There was a large houseplant in a pot placed by a massive television set, and a surprisingly large, black wall clock hung on the wall, displaying in golden letters the name of a drug company and the word "Donation" on the glass door encasing a swinging pendulum. Next to it was a replica of Hanjiro Sakamoto's "Three Horses in a Pasture," fit in a frame whose gold leaf gilding was starting to fade away here and there.

We went over to the corner designated by a sign that said "smoking corner," and sat down next to each other on one of the green-vinyl-covered settees there.

He removed from the breast pocket of his heavy-looking, multi-pocketed shirt a packet of cigarettes and pulled one out for himself. To offer me one as well, he shook the box and let the tip of one more poke out. I pulled it out as he held out his lighter, but I declined with a wave of my hand and lighted up with my own cigarette lighter.

For his first puff, Park inhaled sharply and exhaled slowly, as if he were taking a deep breath of fresh air. "I've heard a lot about you from Tomomi. She tells me that you've been helping her out in many ways, and I'm grateful for that."

I told him that I found his formal tone somewhat surprising, and that I didn't really do all that much, and that I didn't think I was in any position to receive any gratitude from him.

"But," he said, "even this time, had you not been around, Tomomi would've been at a loss."

"No, it's all merely having neighborly relations with her, and nothing more."

Park looked my way and gave me a strange smile that bordered on a frown.

The two of us smoked in silence for a while, but since I had nothing particular to say to the guy, I just waited for him to speak, believing that he wouldn't have invited me down here unless he had something on his mind. Park methodically extinguished his cigarette, stubbing it out on the rim of a one-legged ashtray before lighting up his second one.

"Takuya is a frail child, you see," Park began. "When he was born, I was traveling around Shikoku on a promotional tour of the provinces, and I only got to see him for the first time a month later. Apparently, the jaundice he had at the time of delivery was severe; it spoiled his complexion."

Listening to his low, sonorous voice, I thought, possibly because of his profession, there was something theatrical about the way he talked.

"Perhaps you may have already heard," he went on, "but Tomomi was my senior in the acting troupe, and age-wise, she's also a year older. Although I know I've always been a heavy burden to her, I still had the nerve to make her abandon the theater so that she could deliver Takuya.

"Back in those days, I was a zero. A zero human being, no matter what he does, stays a zero in people's eyes, so I thought I could get away with whatever the hell I wanted. So when a child was born to me—a zero human being—it felt incredible, frankly."

I couldn't quite understand what Park was trying to tell me, but every word, which he seemed to articulate with the intention of engraving it in my mind, was driving me up the wall, so I told him that it wasn't as if he was the one who gave birth to Takuya. Park laughed out loud before resuming his talk.

"The only time Tomomi said anything selfish in her life was when she insisted on giving birth to Takuya. Even her parents in Sendai were dead set against that at the time, and I was at a loss. There's also the issue of my nationality, and I hadn't had my name entered in the family register to begin with. Tomomi was quite frantic by then. It was terrible. At a time when the pregnancy wasn't that conspicuous yet, she named the baby

Takuya, a boy's name, and loudly declared that she and Takuya, just the two of them, would live together alone. She appeared like a beast in my eyes, behaving in such a way. Nonetheless, at the end of the day, she's actually very ordinary. And it seems to me that you don't understand this part of her very well. What's more, with the age gap between you and her even wider than in my case, you probably see her as more of an adult than I do."

I was starting to get fed up with him, having suddenly realized that he was in the middle of saying "something profoundly important." In effect, he wanted to meddle, fancying himself a nice guy. But I couldn't stand the jerk. Sure, he might have taken a benign interest in me, but I'm simply repelled by anyone who tries to so simplistically, so shamelessly, spew out dime-store tales of what they've seen or experienced in their lives, even if those stories aren't that pushy or in-your-face.

"I'm sure such things happen often," I said. "Just because someone's ordinary doesn't mean that person's weak, and there are tons of women out there who carry themselves perfectly well even after being dumped by a man."

"But when Takuya falls sick in this way . . ."

"He may be ill, but he's not seriously ill, right? Contrary to what you might think, a father is a good-for-nothing, and if he's not around from the beginning, kids aren't going to have a problem with that: they're just going to go on living, indifferent to his absence, never thinking there's anything unnatural about not having a father around, and women can lead surprisingly fulfilling lives with just one child in their lives. At the least, children serve as a sufficient excuse, after all, for living. That's the impression I get even when I see Tomomi-san. If you're worried sick about the two of them, well, I feel you're just wasting your time."

Park was listening to me with a blank look on his face, but he suddenly said, "My God, you're interesting!" He then said that Tomomi was right when she remarked that I was terribly awkward at keeping an appropriate social distance between people. "Apparently, you don't understand human relations. I suppose it's because you haven't come across that many hardships," Park said, conclusively.

I was about to burst into spontaneous laughter at how old-fashioned he just sounded.

"You're the type that wants to get along with anyone and everyone, aren't you?" I said to Park.

"Yeah, whatever," he said, pausing for a moment. "At any rate, what I wanted to talk to you about isn't me, but you. I just wished to know your feelings for Tomomi. She's concerned about you. The last time we met she said she was unsure about the way you thought of her, but she felt certain that you love Takuya. She seemed amazed, though, by how you could be that way."

I didn't quite understand what Park meant to say.

"Why are you interested in all this stuff?" I said. "To this day, I've never wondered whether I'm in love with somebody, you know, not even once. You can't figure out something like that, no matter how much you mull it over—it's just something that gets validated by your actions, more or less."

Park laughed again. "Look, if you aren't comfortable saying, 'I love you,' that's okay. There's nothing wrong with that. What I'm really trying to ask now has nothing to do with what you think; I just want to know whether you've imagined Tomomi's feelings for you."

"Why, it would be rude of me if I did. Her feelings are her feelings," I answered.

Park nodded with perfect understanding, as if I'd just confirmed his suspicions about me. He said emphatically, "Now, that's what's generally seen as a sign of not being in love. Frankly, I think the concept of acceptance is alien to you. All you do is think about yourself, but you still poke your nose into Tomomi and Takuya's affairs. In the end, all you do is enjoy the kinds of exchanges with them that can never hurt you, or put you in a vulnerable position."

Although I was more or less unfazed, I detected a touch of rage in his words, which felt like a ball of shit brushing past the outer layer of my heart. The one who couldn't think about anybody but himself wasn't me, but Park. In my dealings with people, I've always been wary of pushing any uncertain or shallow emotions, while also being cautious about never accepting any impositions of such emotions from anyone— emotions that invited delusional and careless thinking. But what I've been upholding above all, to maintain this principled attitude, at whatever times, in whatever situations, are the inviolable rules of never prioritizing my interest, and of never bargaining.

When I said, "I think you can never genuinely love anyone, as long as you keep hoping, self-indulgently, for your own feelings to be understood," Park said, glaring into my eyes, "So then why would you have sex with someone you just got to know by chance? Why would you occasionally give money to her? Why would you take care of her in so many ways? Don't you think that by acting like that you're only playing with her feelings?"

"Of course not! Even if I did something for Tomomi-san, it shouldn't matter at all. In the first place, there's no such thing as a coincidence in this world, and no one can really play with another person's feelings."

"Don't you know that Tomomi occupies a weak position in society, that she's actually starved for kindness? Don't you think you're taking advantage of this weakness of hers?"

It was starting to get unbearable, listening to the discordant, off-key remarks of this guy who wasn't much older than me.

"Look, talking like that amounts to insulting Tomomi-san, all right? I'm sure she'd lose her temper if she heard you."

Park sighed pretentiously and stood up, and after clenching

the cigarette that had burned down to the filter between his forefinger and middle finger, he went over to the vending machine by the dispensary and pulled out two cans of coffee and returned, the cans suspended in his left hand.

Park turned gentle, smiling with friendly eyes. Deep down, I found the sunny actor's mask unforgivable. As he stood there, he pulled the tab off of one coffee can, and then the next, and then held out one can before sitting next to me again.

"At any rate"—it was the second time he'd said that—"I heard from Tomomi today that you found out that she'd gone to see my performance after standing you up. Apparently, she's very uneasy about it. Look, Tomomi likes you, but she's got a child, and she's older than you, so I believe she's completely at sea about her future, you know: she just doesn't know what to do."

Gazing at his impressive profile, I was thinking that the only way this character could ever think about anything was to mix things up in his head. His extraordinariness, in short, was only skin-deep. He was simply incapable of distinguishing between himself and Tomomi, or even between himself and me. It was clear to me that Park, in the end, was nothing more than a misguided, muddled Joe Blow you found loitering around here and there everyday, supremely self-confident in his self-knowledge, when, in fact, his self-knowledge didn't amount to knowing anything about even a single strand of hair on his head.

"For sure," I said, pausing as he did earlier, and then began breaking down my rationale, mainly for myself.

"For sure, when I came to know that Tomomi had deceived me to go see your play, I did think about saying goodbye. But it wasn't because I hated her for betraying me. It was just that I'd decided on my own to end it, just like that. You can keep looking for a reason to explain such a decision, but you won't find it anywhere. I've always tried to suppress any anger in me, no matter how I'm offended, trying not to take things too seriously. This is because I believe others, just like myself, can't clearly account for their own actions. A person's emotions are like the fleeting glimmerings of a fireworks display, and each and every action arising from those emotions hasn't a shred of consistency in it to begin with. So if that's the case, who could blame anyone for their deeds, and for what reasons? If I'm in any way different from others, it's only because I don't get upset over the results of my decisions. Unlike you, I don't get all bothered and behave miserably. I never engage in such stupidity. You're the type of guy who's always repenting or reflecting; in a restaurant, the moment your dish arrives at the table, you start regretting, falling into a panic-stricken state, thinking to yourself I should've never ordered this crap. To me, the decision to end my relationship with Tomomi and the decision to eat curry and rice in my company's cafeteria at lunchtime are the same things. They're simply decisions for which I'm entirely responsible. The only problem here is you can't understand that. Even though in the end I didn't break off my relationship with Tomomi and Takuya, it's not in any way because I forgave her; rather, it's merely the result of the fact that there were no grounds, in the first place, for my decision to part from them. You see, people tend to do such things over and over again."

Park had been listening to my long-winded talk in silence, but he didn't really seem to have understood anything.

"Listen, dude, it's all fine and dandy for you to get so fancy-pants and la-di-da about the relationship, but Tomomi can't afford to be like that. In fact, that lady isn't like you at all. What you're doing is involving an innocent woman and her child in the drama of your big fat worthless ego. Your babbling is irritating, by the way, and there seems to be a serious hole in your heart, and I don't want you to do anything silly like have Tomomi around just to fill that hole."

He looked down, and began to speak in a slightly quivering voice. "We broke up five years ago, but she never visited me, not even once, of her own accord. Only I'd visit her with many toys, like some kind of Santa Claus, after finding some kind of a pretext like an anniversary or a memorial day. She used to often tell me that, come summertime or Christmas, Takuya would always remember me.

"Then, out of the blue, that Sunday, for the first time really, she came to visit me, of her own accord, holding a big bouquet. After the show ended, I took the both of them out to dinner. She let me know of the tough time she was having in finding a nursery school for Takuya. Apparently, the social worker at the child welfare office kept making snide remarks, finding fault with Takuya's nationality, his fatherless household, and with Tomomi's bar business. Apparently, in the end, the meeting just blew up into a big fight, with Tomomi kicking her seat. And because of that, she had no choice but to make a round of visits to the bigwigs of the ward assembly to seek their help.

"I personally haven't given Takuya's nationality any thought, but she said that she was now unbearably sad for him, imagining such harassment could happen again many times in the future as well.

"Do you know why she came to see me that day? She came to ask me to give up being a father, which was when she suddenly confided in me about the presence of another man in her life, about you. It's rather negligent of me, I know, but these last five years, I had no idea at all that there was another man in her life.

"At any rate, you must have already figured out by now what's going on in her head, right? You can't go on pretending like you don't anymore."

"As I've been trying to say for some time now," I said, "such talk is meaningless. Granted, she might have become a bit fainthearted, and so is likely thinking about getting married to me, but it's a passing phase."

In reaction to these words of mine, Park crushed the can he was holding and immediately spoke in a despairing voice, brimming with melodramatic tones, hammy enough for the stage. "What the hell are you saying!?" he boomed. "Something's seriously wrong with you. Such talk isn't meaningless! Such talk is rife with meaning! It's terribly significant! Look, just answer this question—can you categorically say that you're going to marry Tomomi and become Takuya's new father? Can you swear you will? Can you tell me if you're absolutely ready for something like that? Well, can you?"

I took my first sip of the sweet coffee, and said, "Ready? I don't know about that, but I don't have a problem with becoming Takuya's father."

"But I don't think she's seriously wishing for such an outcome," I continued.

Then, with some emphasis for the first time, I added, "I believe you're a conscientious person, but isn't there a part of you that's underestimating women and children? Anyway, I couldn't care less."

After parting from Park, I paid a visit to New Seoul. The store was crowded and Tomomi was moving about busily behind the counter. I told her that I'd talked with Park in the hospital, and that although I knew she'd gone to see Park that day, I really didn't mind at all.

"On the evening before the visit," Tomomi said, "I was reading the paper, and as soon as I spotted a small article introducing Park's performance, somehow I got this urge to show Takuya what his real father's like when he's at work, you see. It came to me suddenly, this urge."

And then Tomomi said, under her breath, "I'm sorry."

I told her that such an urge was common and could arise in anyone, and then I left the shop after saying, "Once Takuya is discharged, let's celebrate somewhere nearby. I'll make reservations."

After stepping outside, I realized I didn't even take a single sip of the whiskey and water she'd served me. It occurred to me that it was the first time that I hadn't drank in that bar. I went on to kill about two hours in a pachinko parlor near the station, and after roaming about the shopping area in Takabashi, I returned to Tomomi's place. She was just in the middle of closing up shop.

While helping her clear up, I said, "You said 'real father' a while ago, didn't you? Well, how do you feel about a fake one?"

I didn't quite understand why I asked such a question, but Tomomi didn't answer anyway. Instead, she turned toward me and wore a smirk on her face and said, "Hey, how about going to a hotel from now on?"

We took a cab ride to Kinshicho, drank a lot of sake at a yakitori joint, and then entered into a hotel district, arms around each other's shoulders. It had been a while since I last slept with Tomomi in a place other than the second floor of New Seoul.

Standing in the reception, in front of a panel displaying available rooms, the two of us chose the most expensive room listed there; it was called Paradise, and it certainly lived up to its name.

We bathed in a glass bathtub, washing each other's bodies, and messed around on a round bed that revolved while moving up and down. Our figures were reflected in the mirror on the ceiling.

I straddled Tomomi's face and swatted her cheeks with my hardened thing—which went splish-splash. And while looking down at her creased, pained expression and listening to her gasp and moan, I became terribly excited, somehow, strongly desiring to finish inside her for the first time since I'd begun sleeping with her.

When I asked, while thrusting my hips, "Can I come?" Tomomi screamed, "Yes, yes, faster, faster." When I said, "You'll get pregnant," she said, "Yes, yes, let me get pregnant, let me get pregnant, please let me get pregnant," and ad infinitum.

When I pulled out my dick in a wild frenzy, I discharged an unusually large volume onto Tomomi's stomach.

After we finished, Tomomi's face was radiant. She even looked two or three years younger. I then felt, while comparing the sight of my semen scattered across her lower abdomen with the sight of that glowing, rejuvenated face of hers, a chill coursing through the depths of my heart.

13

WHILE HAVING BREAKFAST IN the coffee shop of our usual hotel, I talked to Teruko Onishi about the commotion over Takuya's hospitalization.

"Oh my! Tomomi-san must have been very worried then," the missus said, frowning with a really pitiful look.

Any story concerning Tomomi always drew her attention. Though her circumstances had nothing in common with Tomomi's, the missus appeared to feel particularly sorry for her. While I'm not really sure why, I'd once taken her to New Seoul to introduce her to Tomomi. Perhaps that one-time encounter had left a strong impression on her. Of course, she seemed to figure out that night, at a single glance, that my relationship with Tomomi was physical, and to the missus, this fact had apparently served as a springboard for diving headlong into the kind of X-rated relationship we began to have.

Bedeviled by sexual dissatisfaction, Teruko was hungry for some no-strings-attached sex; she had to have it, by hook or crook. In that sense Tomomi's presence was the best insurance against the collapse of her marriage.

It was on a summer evening, about half a year before I got to know Eriko, when I first asked Teruko Onishi out on a date.

I told her to come out to Nihonbashi from Takanawa, where she lived, so that I could take her to a small *izakaya* pub. I used to work part-time during my college days, for around two years, at a large wholesaler specializing in medical supplies in Takaramachi, and the *izakaya* was where one of my senior colleagues used to take me. The proprietor used to be a professional cyclist, and, perhaps because he tired of making money, he used to let penniless customers like us enjoy delicious liquor and fresh fish at amazingly low prices.

The missus, who wasn't much of a drinker, got drunk soon. Her face all red, she seemed to be in pain, so we left the place early and took a very long stroll. Exiting out of Kayabacho, we passed through the shopping district of Monzen-Nakacho and walked further toward Kiba.

As we walked, Mrs. Onishi began to sober up from the fresh air, and she became amused by the lively early-evening ambiance of the downtown area on a balmy summer's day. Turning left at the intersection in front of Kiba Station, I led the missus by the hand into Kiba Park. The sun had gone down, and a cool wind was blowing from the sea. A large bridge resting in the center was lit up, appearing serene in the evening's twilight.

"Oh dear! I never knew there was such a vast park here," the missus said, impressed.

"That's the Museum of Contemporary Art," I said, pointing to a gorgeous building on the left, presently crouching under a deep black, overhanging gloom.

"Is that right?" The missus nodded, pushing back, with both her hands, her long hair streaming in the wind.

Crossing the large bridge, we headed for the park's plaza. When we reached the area with a grove of trees, there was no other soul in sight; with even the streetlights sparse, a thick darkness was enveloping the periphery. We sat down together on a bench beside some trees and bushes.

Perhaps someone was blowing on a trumpet in the grove, rather incompetently, as we occasionally heard the grating, high-pitched sound of a brass instrument.

I proceeded at once to put my hand into the missus's skirt, having become hopelessly filled with desire, as soon as I felt the soft flesh of her upper arm when we were seated in the bar at the small counter. As I kissed her while rubbing my fingers against her panties, moving them up and down, right and left, her wetness reached the pad of my middle finger in no time, filling my heart with gratitude.

When I pulled out my hand I stood up hastily—afraid she might dry up soon—and then, as I assumed a crouching posture, I took her hands and, in the spirit of pulling open a drawer, drew her into the bushes nearby. The missus got on top of me, and I felt the cold summer grass, along with the night dew, on my back, penetrating through my shirt. There was a large stone at my back, around the area of my belt, bugging me, so, with the missus still over my chest, I shifted my left arm to my back, grabbed the stone, flicked it to the side, and immediately repositioned my body.

But the moment I slid my hand under her blouse to play with her breasts, the missus began to resist suddenly. Even when I pressed my lips to hers, she kept her teeth clenched, and when I tried to pry them open with my sharply stiffened tongue, it was no use.

In the end we just got up and returned to the bench.

I talked for a while—"Hey, did you know that the novelist, Mr. Yoshimura, lives with his wife in an apartment that's just a stone's throw away from this park? He likes sushi, and oh yes, his favorite sushi bar's also nearby. The food there's delicious. You like sushi? If you're up to it, we can drop by. What do you say?"—I was talking a lot but the missus, appearing tired and sluggish, was taking no heed. So I reluctantly ended up inviting her to Tomomi's store.

"Can't hear the trumpet anymore," the missus muttered, standing up.

On the way to Morishita, inside the taxi, I briefly explained about Tomomi and Takuya, and at the shop each of us drank two, three glasses of whiskey and water. Tomomi and the missus also exchanged a few words, all harmless pleasantries.

While walking up to the crossing after stepping out from the bar, the missus was completely drunk and kept saying over and over again, "That mama-san's so like me!" Each time she said so, I shouted into her ear, "Not at all!"

The next day, when I showed my face at New Seoul, Tomomi said she found the missus to be "a beautiful person," so I talked to her about the lady—"There's a small concert hall in Takaido, and just the other day, a well-known concertmaster of a large orchestra held a private recital there. He has a women's-only fan club, made up mainly of his students, and most of these members are wives of the owners of blue-chip companies or the wives of doctors and lawyers or their daughters. I was there at the event with a photographer to cover it for my magazine, and that was when I came to have a nodding acquaintance with the woman from last night. She's the daughter of a director of a certain maker of musical instruments, and is apparently married to an international trader twenty years older than her. The husband's always off in Europe for half a year, so she spends all that time alone with just her maid in a huge mansion in Takanawa. I know it sounds like the setting to some cheap melodrama, but such ladies of leisure actually exist. Last night, completely by accident, I ran into her alone at this bar in Ginza, and, while drinking, she made me listen to her life story. I ended up bringing her here just for fun. I hope you didn't mind, Tomomi."

Mrs. Onishi devoured her breakfast, finishing everything on her plate, which was unusual for her. But what's more, she went on to order papaya for dessert. I ordered the same and continued to talk about Takuya.

The boy had left the hospital five days ago on a Thursday, which was a week after he'd been hospitalized. That evening, I took the mother and child to a large Korean restaurant in Tsukishima, treating them to some Korean barbecue in a private room. Takuya was very well, eating a lot of meat, to Tomomi's delight.

We left the restaurant around nine, and after placing Takuya on the saddle of the bicycle Tomomi had walked over with, I straddled the rear deck and pedaled with my outstretched legs. Grasping the handles and stiffening up, Takuya was in high spirits as we fooled around, accelerating to overtake his walking mother, only to cross her path.

When I pumped the pedals with all my strength to race the cars flowing through Kiyosumi Avenue, Takuya hollered with such gusto that it seemed as if his sharp cry, so peculiar to children, echoed across the clear, star-sprinkled night sky. After nearly fifteen minutes of goofing around, we finally began to walk alongside Tomomi. I got down on the sidewalk and walked while pushing the bicycle with Takuya still riding on it. Turning left at Tsukuda, we entered River City, which was lined with high-rise condominiums. Takuya was gaping up at the blocks of apartments shining like huge Christmas trees with the lights lit up in each of their rooms. The night breeze, streaming through the valleys of buildings from Tokyo Bay, pushed against our backs. The flowers of every cherry tree, planted on the shoulders of the road, had fallen, but thick growths of bright green foliage were rustling in the wind.

Although April was already over, the night air of this neighborhood still retained a chill. Concerned about Takuya, who was just starting to recover from his illness, I turned the bike around and we all returned to the main street.

We stopped in the middle of Aioi Bridge, which straddled the Harumi Canal, and looked up at the sky together.

There, in the center of a cloudless sky, was floating a big round moon in all its splendid glory, its patterns clearly visible.

When Tomomi pointed and said, "See that, Takuya? It's the great big moon," Takuya said with admiration, "Wow, you're right! It's the moon!" Even when we began to move again, he just sat there quietly on his saddle, staring at the moon all the time, eyes squinted, as if rays of moonlight were dazzling him.

"Isn't it beautiful, Takuya?" I asked, and he murmured in a small, enchanted voice, his face still turned to the sky, "I want to go to the moon on this bicycle."

Tomomi turned to me and smiled. I lowered my eyes calmly. The moment stood still just then, and it was captured with precision, somewhere far away in the evening sky, like a photograph, I thought.

I had a rare glimpse that night, I said to Mrs. Onishi, into a child's mind. It felt as surprising as encountering a ghost in the city, but I was convinced, for the first time, that it was the one true thing you could ever find in this world. The missus was listening while laughing, and then said, "Remember E.T.? What you said reminds me of a scene in that movie, and I tell you I just cried uncontrollably." I complained, "Don't lump my story together with that fairy tale! What I said just now isn't some kind of a figure of speech or a product of my imagination, or some kind of a parable to teach moral lessons."

"Whenever you speak about Tomomi-san, you wear this cold look, as if you didn't give a damn about her, but when it comes to little Takuya you always look earnest," she said, adding, "You told Tomomi-san and her former husband that you only love Takuya-chan, right? Well, I think that's right on the mark."

"Takuya's a child, and there's no way I could ever compare him with Tomomi, an adult," I argued, but the missus showed her usual pale and nasty smile and said, "Such a manner of thinking speaks volumes for the deep affection you have for Takuya-chan, you know. But if you can get all teary-eyed about a child who's not even your own, you really should consider giving more thought to your mother in the hospital."

Here we go again, I thought, inwardly tut-tutting her triumphant air. While the missus also liked to hear stories about my mother, lately she'd been all too eager to lecture me.

"My mother's an entirely different matter."

"Is that so? She's someone who gave birth to you, isn't she? No other son would feel fine not paying a visit to his ailing mother in the hospital for over two years now. Why, poor thing, her health must have considerably declined. Listen, if you don't return to see her soon, it might be too late, and you'll be scarred for the rest of your life."

"There's no need for that. Why can't you understand that, Teruko-san?"

"Let me ask you this then, what do you intend to do about Tomomi-san and Takuya-chan? You'll probably end up getting together with Tomomi-san and becoming a father to Takuya-chan. Even though it doesn't sound like the sort of thing you'd do, I still feel that's what's going to happen in the end."

I fell silent. The missus scooped up several spoonfuls of papaya, and after conveying them to her mouth, she suddenly lifted her face and leaned forward and whispered, "If you want a child I can give birth to one for you, you know."

"Stop joking!" I demanded. But for some reason the missus wouldn't stop. "Oh, so you prefer another person's child, do you? You don't want your own, do you?"

Her harassment was exceptionally shocking. After all, she was the type of person who usually said things like,

"I'm someone who totally lacks concentration and conviction. Whatever I do, I've never been able to keep it up for long, and whatever I think about, I've never been able to get it organized in my head. I get tired just like that, you see. Even hating people, or, for that matter, loving people, there are times when you have to try so hard, you know? Make an all-out effort. It would be wonderful if there were a step-by-step program you could follow from beginning to end, like piano lessons, but the reality is that, when it comes to matters concerning you personally, there's a one-off finality to them, right—like you only get one shot at them, without any chance of a redo, and you need to make up your mind about them, once and for all, right? I lack the concentration to do something like that. Seriously! And that's why I think I got married to my husband, even though I didn't particularly like him."

"Of course not!" I responded. "Having my own child is absolutely out of the question, no matter what happens!"

The missus raised her voice, and said, in a single breath, as if she'd been waiting a long time to say it, "Even if I bear your child, you have my word that I'll never trouble you. I could make the little one my husband's child, or if you want I could even get a divorce and raise the child on my own. I mean it!"

"There's something wrong with you today, Teruko-san," I said, feeling an eerie, oppressive sensation around my chest at the sight of her eagerness.

The missus then cooled down and sighed, and in an offhand tone explained, as if to vindicate herself, that her husband has a new mistress, but that this time she might really separate. And then, after falling impressively silent, she began speaking again heatedly.

"Yesterday, before I came here, I met an old friend from my college days for the first time in a long while. She had her first baby this year in January, you see, but the delivery was a difficult one. Apparently, there's a postpartum complication that could develop, and, as odd as it sounds, to this day if she suddenly runs she leaks pee. It seems she's stuck with this condition for life. I was really surprised, you know, because the person I knew back in the old days would have hung herself over something like that, but she was calm, saying all was fine and dandy because the baby was all right, and that it can't be helped if her condition was the price she had to pay.

"As for me, I don't feel like bearing my husband's child anymore. But I'm thirty-two this year, right? So I feel like, if only for the baby's sake, I should give birth now."

"You're talking like there's a baby inside your stomach already."

"I'm not as maternal as that friend of mine, but even with a woman like me, there comes a time when you naturally feel that way. Funny, isn't it? But yesterday, I seriously realized that."

"In a novel I read some time ago," I began, "there was this scene where a woman, after being reproached by her husband for having an affair, assumed a defiant attitude and said, 'No matter how many men I sleep with, the only child I'll ever give birth to will be yours. That's a firm decision I've made. For a woman, staying true to such a thing is of the utmost importance.' I was pretty impressed, but in the end I realized it was just another lie."

Even though I'd managed to change the topic, the oppressive sensation around my chest remained.

"Yeah, I suppose you're right," Teruko Onishi said plainly.

When I received money from the missus, I was asked about my mother's condition as usual, so I answered, "She's using many alkyl-based anticancer drugs, but she's terribly depressed because of their side effects—her skin's festering in many places. My younger sister phoned to tell me so."

The missus urged me again to go see my mother soon.

"She's certainly in the terminal stage," I said, "and I wouldn't be surprised if something happened to her any time now."

"I'm amazed you can stay so calm," she said. "You're odd."

"I send enough money every month. Half of it is your money, though, Teruko-san."

Shrugging her shoulders, the missus said that, unlike her, I might be overthinking things a little, that I might be making them more complicated in my head than was necessary.

While looking at her face, I thought what she said sounded like what Eriko would say. In fact, she'd said something similar last week, when I'd met her for the first time in a long time.

If I remember correctly, after emphasizing that women tend to try harder than men to arrive at a deeper understanding of their partner, she solemnly said, "For instance, I've been observing you all this time, and there's something I've been meaning to tell you. It's something I've written about in my diary a little bit, after traveling to Kyoto with you. Anyway, then, as usual, you didn't seem to be having fun, right?

"See, the thing about you," Eriko continued, "is that you're always trying to find radically unique answers regarding various things about this world—answers that are all your own. You hesitate to engage in everyman's joy, in everyman's contentment, or even in everyman's sorrow. Instead you're always complaining that there should be a brand new kind of happiness out there waiting just for you, or a sorrow that only you can suffer. For example, after we make love like we did a while ago, there's this mild inertia we experience like we're experiencing now, right? Well, I had an urge to snap out of this inertia, and so I thought about falling asleep by your side tonight, holding you tight in my arms. But when I look at you, all I sense is that you've been driven to despair by this inertia, this listlessness. I like you, you know. In the beginning, I think I was simply mad about you, and that was that. But now, it's a little different. I think I'm gradually turning into a coward, just doing everything I can not to dislike you.

"I realize there are things we'll never see eye to eye about. But to me, there's comfort and solace in the willingness to gloss over that fact, to forget about those things we can't understand in each other. In fact, that's the way I feel right now too. Don't you think that the inertia can, with a little thoughtfulness, give us peace of mind and room to grow? But what do you do? Just like a child who doesn't know the rules, just like a first boyfriend, you keep crazily attempting to comprehend, to make sense of things—until you lose interest. I'm not saying your thirst for knowledge is wrong. In fact, that's what's great about you. But I sometimes get worried that you'll never gain those insights you crave if you keep using that simple method of yours."

14

After parting from the missus, walking down the hill toward Akasaka, I remembered her shameful conduct the previous night.

With her hands and legs tightly tied up as usual, she was down on her hands and knees on the bed with a big vibrator shoved into her vagina, allowing her large ass to be mercilessly violated by me. Her anus, holding fast my condom-covered penis, exhibited a powerful outside-in suction every time I thrust it in and out. When I pulled out my dick, a cavity opened up, and the flesh in its periphery underwent massive spasms while shrinking. When I thrust into her again just after this cavity closed, the folds of her intestinal wall climbed all over my penis to put it through its paces. Overcome with a pleasant sensation—like an electric current shooting up to the crown of my head—I thrust my pelvis tirelessly.

The missus implored, screamed, foamed at the mouth, thrashed about her restrained hands and feet, pressed her blindfolded and gagged face against the bed—as if to crush her nose—and wailed. In the end my condom split apart, and the massive volume of semen released poured straight into her anus.

After pulling out my soiled dick, I carefully washed it in the bathroom before returning to the bedside. But the missus, whom I'd just left lying there, was letting the white liquid drip down from her pushed-out buttocks, while continuing to come, the vibrator still entrenched in her vagina, endlessly stimulating her.

I mounted the bed, wedged the drooping vibrator into her butt crack, and, using the base of the vibrator as a fulcrum, lifted her ass. The semen inside was already sticky, but thanks to this swift motion, a residual quantity spilled out of her anus to the bed sheet, creating a puddle.

Mindful of this puddle, I scooped up her legs with my left arm, and, holding her by the waist, flipped her over and made her face me.

"Ahhhn," the missus moaned. Grasping her long hair tied into a knot at the back with a rubber band—supporting her small head in the process—I stretched out my right hand and firmly inserted the protruding vibrator into her vagina again. I then removed her blindfold and gag, and lifted her chin. With her makeup ruined by sweat, tears, and saliva, she looked back at me with vacant eyes. I half rose and held my freshly washed dick over her half opened lips. Reflexively springing at it, she began to let out a moan again.

"Taste good?" I asked.

She nodded her head subtly.

"Answer me properly!"

"It tastes good, sir," she said in a muffled voice.

After making her suck for nearly five minutes, I pulled out my dick and used it to smear the bubbly saliva around her mouth all over her face.

"Well then, let's have you lick something more delicious now."

Seizing her hair, I pushed her head down and drew it close to the carefully preserved puddle of semen near my knees.

"Go ahead, lick it, and don't you dare leave a single drop, you got that?"

The missus was just gazing for a while at what was there before her eyes, but when I pressed her for an answer, she said, "Thank you, sir" and stretched out her tongue and began to lap up the fluid.

"Is it yummy?"

"It's delicious, sir."

"Wrong answer!"

"It's delicious. Thank you, sir."

I untied the missus while she kept her face pressed to the bedsheet, and after moving behind her and making her assume a proper crawling stance, I slowly worked the vibrator in and out of her vagina. The missus, while awkwardly licking up the semen, writhed violently, and continued to come, over and over again.

While making use of the vibrator in such an interminable fashion, I was, as usual, thinking about something else entirely.

Of course, I don't recall everything, but I believe I'd remembered a certain assistant professor from my college days, who used to be fond of me for some reason.

Although I was a law student, he was teaching German when I was taking general education courses, and we became close after I submitted a dissertation in German. We began to meet outside the campus to have drinks together, talking about novels often, since he was an aspiring novelist. I wonder how much whiskey he treated me to back in the day, when I was spending all my hours moonlighting to come up with the money for covering my school and living expenses. He was really talkative, shooting the breeze about various dull things, which I hardly remember anymore. But while playing with that vibrator yesterday, I suddenly remembered something he used to often say.

"A woman's body is a treasure. Everything else about a woman is unpleasant. So going out with a woman is all about how much you can tolerate those unpleasant things, for the sake of the treasure. With sex, the more you see your partner as an object, the more you'll get better at it, and the more she'll cling to you."

One day, just prior to graduation, he invited me to an old-fashioned bar in Kanda, where he repeatedly said, "You think you're smarter than me, don't you? Well, perhaps you're right."

But then he added with conviction, "You'll likely self-destruct, though, if you're actually much smarter than me. I've known two guys like that before now. You're the third."

If I recall correctly, I think he went on to say that one of them had committed suicide or something, but I'm not sure. That year, he'd at long last won a certain well-known literary prize.

I headed toward my office, walking down a lonely back street devoid of traffic even though it was nearly lunchtime.

The reason why my mind drifted to the past last night wasn't because I was seized by some silly nostalgia for my college days. Not to put a damper on Teruko Onishi's enthusiasm for having a child, but it was because I couldn't help thinking that childbirth, in the end, results from the sort of contemptible acts she and I had engaged in.

At the risk of sounding like Honoka, I feel that, where sexual intercourse is concerned, men and women are driven merely by their libido, which is fundamentally different from love. Nonetheless, both men and women avert their eyes from this basic physiological mechanism, forcing themselves into a romantic union, rationalizing their denial.

But here's what I think. You can never get at the truth unless you look like crazy, unless you look hard, unless you fix your gaze on the naked truth. Eriko said that she was someone who had to make sure of things with her own eyes, that she had to see things for herself, or else she was never satisfied. But when it comes to her relationship with me, she says she finds comfort and solace in turning her eyes away. Now, have you ever heard anything more selfish and contradictory than such an attitude?

When I told her—some time ago—that everyone reluctantly goes on living, she rejected this notion at once. When I asked her to elaborate, she said something silly like, "There may be people who live reluctantly, but there certainly are others who live vibrantly." Even then, my heart—fluttering in my chest—burned with a small rage. When I say that everyone goes on living reluctantly, I naturally and absolutely mean that there exists not a single person in this world who does not live reluctantly. I didn't articulate those words so casually that Eriko could negate and dismiss them in a few words. I pride myself on always being accountable for the words I speak. But in the case of Eriko's words, I found this all-important sense of responsibility—this gravitas—utterly lacking. Which is why she's always quick to laugh and make light of a situation, making groundless arguments with a smug look on her face. Frankly, I can't stand this attitude of hers.

Eriko says she gets listless after having long, drawn out sex, that she feels inertia. It's the same with me. Which gets me wondering about exactly what lies beyond this shameless act, in which a person isn't treated like a person. I can't help wondering about what the hell it is. But then Eriko says I shouldn't look at this listlessness, this inertia, in a negative light, and that if one gets obsessed over it, harboring dark and backward doubts about it, one will lose the will to live. I certainly agree with her. But another question immediately occurs to me: so what if you lose your will to live? What's the big deal? What's going to happen as a result?

What I want to know has nothing to do with sensory constructs like volition, or freedom of action, or peace of mind. Whenever I meet Eriko, whenever I sleep with her, I'm always asking her questions, deep inside my heart: what will become of me, always being together with you? By staying together, how close will you and I ever get to the ultimate meaning of life itself, transcending concerns like the will to live, freedom of action, peace of mind and comfort? To what extent can you reassure me?

Where on earth will we be heading, having a family and living together all the time? Can you even vaguely see the destination? If you can, please tell me, please stop hesitating and just tell me! Honestly, I can't see the destination very well at all. So I'm uneasy, terribly uneasy. This boat we climbed aboard is really small, floating in the middle of the great big ocean. Sure, just as you say, there's a warm wind blowing, and if we look up, we can see that we're enveloped in the azure light of the sky. Still, I'm unable to shake from my mind how tiny the boat is, and how ominous is the sea, where anything can happen. What's more, I'm unable to banish the thought that one day one of us will abandon ship, ahead of the other. This isn't an issue of making choices, as you suggest. It's a more important, more fundamental matter—one that precedes the choosing. It's a terribly dispassionate and heartless matter that transcends time, and there's no room in it for human emotions like love and compassion and sympathy.

Still, there's not a scrap of an answer to be found in Eriko's loquacious talk. She doesn't offer answers. She doesn't even share her views about what I'm saying. And yet she concludes that what I'm seeking can't be found with the kind of simple method I apply. Does she then have knowledge of some complex method that can help me in my quest?

But I understand.

Put simply, she doesn't want to know anything; she just wants to feel, just like Tomomi, just like that Park, just like Mrs. Onishi—just like everyone.

15

HONOKA, WHOM I HADN'T seen in a while, was hardly recognizable.

Her body, which used to be skinny, had become remarkably more fleshy around her shoulders and chest, while her legs, clad in jeans, retained their slender charm as before, making her physique appear all the more feminine. Even her looks, which used to be memorable for the prominence of her large eyes on an angular, lackluster face, had become really lovely, her now plump cheeks and lips hiding the former sharpness of her features. Even if Eriko were to stand next to her, you'd be hard-pressed to notice any striking differences between the two, as there had been before. Even her tone of voice, eye color, and facial expressions exuded a cheerfulness that made it hard to believe she was the same Honoka I used to know. Although I'd heard rumors, seeing her in person like this only filled me with admiration for Eriko's astuteness.

Raita also, compared to the time I drank with him in Nakano, was looking fine. Working part-time to pay off his debts while simultaneously managing a change of residence, he couldn't hide his fatigue, but he still seemed ready and eager to face the day when he'd finally leave Torimasa to embrace his new future.

These past several days, it seems Honoka had worked hard, having undertaken full responsibility for packing his luggage and handling particular arrangements at the new address.

According to Eriko, the relationship between Raita and Honoka had rapidly progressed since the year began.

"So you think they've bedded each other already?" I asked every time the two came up in our conversations. Eriko would always laugh and say, "That's all you think about, isn't it? Apparently they're putting off things like that until later."

She also emphasized that it was Raita, and not Honoka herself, who deserved the credit for her dramatic change.

"A woman changes, after all, when she applies herself to her main profession," Eriko said with feeling once, so I asked her, "What do you mean by main profession?"

"You fool," she yelled. "I mean men, of course."

The apartment Raita rented was in a place that was about fifteen minutes away by foot from Seibu Shinjuku Line's Numabukuro Station, in the direction of Ekoda. From Torimasa it would take less than twenty minutes to reach, moving directly north along the Loop Seven Kanana road. Raita's baggage wasn't that considerable, and so it was decided that the four of us would help him move on May 3, when my holiday coincided with Eriko's.

We promised to assemble at Torimasa at nine. Although I drove away from my apartment before eight and picked up Eriko at Ningyocho before heading for Nakano, the roads in Tokyo were almost completely empty that day—since it was the middle of the holiday-studded week—so we ended up arriving in less than forty minutes. I went around to the back of the shuttered shop, pulled open the old, unlocked wooden door there, and climbed up a steep and narrow staircase, ahead of Eriko. It was silent inside the house. I'd heard that the boss and his wife had already retreated to Kagoshima before the consecutive holidays began. At the top of the stairs, to the right, was a space for drying clothes, and there was a refreshing breeze blowing through an opened window. On the left-hand side of this space was the couple's suite, apparently, and with its sliding *fusuma* doors already removed, a vacant two-room interior was visible. Raita's room was on the right. When I knocked on its *fusuma* door I heard Honoka's voice calling out, "Coming," so I slid the door open and saw the two of them peacefully eating their lunches in a room littered with huge piles of cardboard boxes. Lined up on the tatami mat were two cans of oolong tea, and when I inquired, it seemed that Honoka had prepared the box lunches, waking up early in the morning.

Eriko and I also sat down on the tatami mat and waited for them to finish eating.

Honoka was attending to Raita in various ways. Whenever his paper tray was empty, she'd serve a side dish from a large lunch box and swiftly hold out an *onigiri* when he was done with one. At times, appearing cheerful and happy, she'd also stop to gaze at Raita's neat face. To be sure, Raita's good looks—now accentuated by his sunken cheeks—had acquired such a formidable, bad-boy charm that you couldn't help but admire them, even if you weren't his girlfriend.

A little after half past nine, Raita pulled up a pickup truck in front of Torimasa, which he'd borrowed the day before from the boss of a wrecking yard, who had been a regular at Torimasa. It had been decided that Raita would start working, for the time being, at this wrecking yard after the consecutive holidays. It was this boss who had found the next apartment for him, on account of the fact that his company was located in Ekoda. On the door of the pickup was, indeed, the name of the company: Nakagaki Industries.

After loading all the baggage in about an hour, Raita and Honoka set out in the pickup ahead of us. We were to stay behind and finish up cleaning before following them in our car.

But we didn't need to be all that meticulous, since the building was slated to be demolished as soon as it was handed over. The window frames were sash, but the rest of the place was made of wooden mortar from around thirty years ago, and parts of the tatami mats, where Raita's bed and bookshelves used to stand, were discolored by sunlight. We vacuumed the place briefly, wiped the floor and windows, removed the nails and hooks stuck in walls and decorative *nageshi* beams, and then called it a day.

Sitting down on the vacant space of the six tatami mats, I smoked a cigarette, using an empty can of oolong tea as an ashtray. From a window flung open, two light gauge steel apartment buildings—also old-fashioned—were visible across a parking lot, a clear blue sky spreading out above their rooftops.

Extinguishing the cigarette, I lay down on the tatami mat. Eriko, who had been standing by the window and also taking in the view from there, came back and sat next to me. Without saying a word, I moved my hips, placed my head on her lap, closed my eyes and distinctly felt the sunlight pouring in on my face and palms.

"When I'm in this kind of a room, I feel at peace."

"Is that so?" Eriko said with a hint of wonder in her voice, smoothing back my hair.

"Until high school, I lived in such a room with my mother and younger sister, just the three of us."

"Is that so?" she said, this time in a tone that was gently stimulating.

"I suppose the name Tobata doesn't ring a bell for you. It's a town in Kitakyushu City—next to Yawata—where you find steel foundries. In this town there's a small bay called Doukai Wan with a large bridge there, and nearby there are a lot of these small factory towns subcontracting work from Nippon Steel, and the apartment I was living in was in a corner of a district with clusters of these factories. It was the size of six tatami mats with one restroom for all, and no bath. I was raised there until I graduated junior high. Mother would hardly come back home, on account of work or men, leaving me to take care of my younger sister from grade school onward.

"But what was really sad was that I couldn't serve her a proper dinner. Although I've forgotten the details, the memory of that sadness I felt in my juvenile mind, that indescribable vexation and hurt, remains unforgettable to this day. My mother was one miserly woman; she'd give plenty of money to her boyfriends, but when it came to me and my little sister, her own children, she was such an awful penny-pincher: she'd never let us have any money. I bet you haven't eaten canned food all that much. You usually have food like that when you're climbing mountains or camping. But my sister and me, we were different. I'd buy canned foods from the supermarket with whatever pittance Mother handed over, and eat them with my sister as side dishes. Day after day, it was just canned food and white rice, so you can imagine how fed up we were, right? But our mother, whenever she could be bothered to return to the apartment, would pick up an empty can of boiled mackerel from a pile of other cans in the kitchen, and say something like, 'You know what, kids? All canned foods are delicious because they're made seasonally, when the ingredients are harvested in large quantities.' Only at the time of a school field trip did our mother allow us to buy pork. We'd be overjoyed then, getting up early in the morning, roasting the pork—which we'd leave pickled overnight in plenty of ginger soy sauce—and then putting it on top of the rice in our lunch boxes before heading out for the excursion. This was, to us, the best treat we could ever have. Nonetheless, even back in those days, I thought that it was rare to see anyone leading such a pathetic life, a life of such poverty . . ."

I wondered why I was talking about all these things. Perhaps because the sight of this cheap apartment awakened a nostalgia in me, or perhaps I was moved by the light and wind and all too crystal-clear sky of the day. But then I had a thought. It occurred to me that I was confiding all these stories to Eriko— stories I'd never confided to a soul since coming to Tokyo— because I was happy, probably, and that feeling of happiness I was experiencing was probably quite substantial. What exactly was I so happy about? I knew immediately. I was terribly glad to see Honoka, whom I hadn't seen in a long while, looking happy for the first time. And I was also feeling deeply grateful to Eriko for helping Honoka become that way.

"Must have been tough," Eriko said in a particularly relaxed tone.

"Yeah, it sure was. Even though I was born to a parent like that, I was honest and serious. During junior high, there was a time I badly wanted to become a juvenile delinquent, but my younger sister was there, and I never had fun strolling about town with the gang. I also did well in my studies, so in the end, I was lectured by my buddies not to follow in their footsteps because I was different from them. I felt very lonely."

"What swell friends you had!"

"Not really," I said, taking a deep breath and stretching, my head still on her lap. "They were friends just for that time; I don't have anything in common with them anymore."

I then looked up at Eriko's beautiful face, only to see another face superimposed. It was the face of a certain person, who was totally different from Eriko in every possible way, including looks, age, and demeanor. Yet, there she was, perfectly superimposed over Eriko.

"But," Eriko murmured, wearing a thin veil of a smile, "I'm kind of ashamed."

"About what?"

"Well, while you were going through hard times, I was leading an ordinary life, day to day, unable to do anything for you."

"How could you? It's not as if we could've met way back then."

I was laughing, but on the other hand, I felt she was right. Eriko was three years younger than me, and she'll be twenty-seven this year. Just when she was leading a happy and blessed girlhood, I was accumulating formative years that I don't care to remember anymore.

"Ordinary, huh?" I said. "Ordinary family, ordinary life, ordinary youth—I envy all those things about you. Still, it frightens me, such ordinary happiness."

"Frightens you?" she said, suspicion appearing in her eyes.

Closing my eyes again, I breathed in the air of the quiet room through my nose. It smelled like dry grass.

"Yeah, I don't think there's anything more frightening than the ordinary, because the ordinary sticks to you and never leaves, and the more ordinary you are the more difficult it gets for you to abandon yourself."

I then spoke for quite some time, keeping my eyes closed.

"A great unhappiness makes it easy for you to renounce your despairing self, and a large happiness is always accompanied by an impulse to reject the much-too-happy person you find yourself to be. Frankly, in my childhood, I badly wanted to be reborn into a different family. I wished so many times to start over again. I wanted to become another person, and I had no regrets about my present self vanishing. I think it's the same for other people who are also truly unhappy in their heart of hearts. When humans become filled with happiness, for some reason they want to freely give it away to others. But an ordinary, mediocre happiness isn't like that. An ordinary happiness clings to you forever. Eventually, it begins to rot and make you sick. As long as you continue to indulge in ordinary happiness, you'll never be able to change this thing called the self until the day you die; nor will you be able to abandon yourself. And when you're like that, despite being able to have sympathy for another person's misfortune, you can never have empathy. That's because empathizing requires you to abandon yourself. Understanding another person isn't about loving one another, sympathizing one-sidedly, or even being happy together. It's about leaving yourself behind to become another self. Mediocrity makes that impossible, surely. You keep telling me that you want for us to understand each other, and that a relationship is meant to draw people closer to each other. But I don't think people could ever understand each other by just getting close. If you really want to understand someone, you must completely abandon yourself and become that person. You must take in everything with that person's eyes, ears, nose, mouth, and skin, breathing with that person's lungs, thinking with that person's head, and feeling with that person's heart. Only then can you for the first time draw another person's happiness toward you and make it your own. But no one's really capable of such a thing, let alone someone so steeped in ordinary happiness."

Eriko was listening to my talk in silence.

"After my junior high school days ended, perhaps because my mother had, as might have been expected, begun to feel a little guilty, we moved to a municipal house in Kokura. But neither my sister nor I could open up to our mother. It must have been the same for Honoka as well; the bottom line was that it was too late."

I stood up and glanced at my watch; nearly an hour had passed already.

"We better get going soon or else Raita and Honoka are going to get tired of waiting."

Standing up at the same time as me, Eriko grasped the palm of my hand, looked into my eyes, and said, "Let's do the best we can, you and me together, yeah?"

"Yeah, let's," I said nodding, grasping her soft palm in return.

The flames of the bonfire were beyond expectation, flaring up so wildly that all of us simultaneously edged back nearly a meter to escape the gusting hot winds.

Raita's old wooden desk and chair, bookshelf, manga books and magazines were all burning away in a magnificent blaze.

The four of us just stood there in silence for a while around the open-air fire, breathlessly transfixed, in the light of the afternoon, by the raging, semitransparent flames—which contained luminous, bright red inner cones—and by the emanating shimmering heat haze.

Raita's apartment was in the neighborhood of a large metropolitan housing complex, standing in a cluttered area where stores, residences and plots of tillable land coexisted with each other. When we arrived there, most of the luggage had already been carried inside, and the only task remaining was to clear up some oversized refuse. Raita said he was planning on rearranging the apartment later at a leisurely pace with Honoka, so we all got in the pickup together and drove over to the scrapyard. Apparently, Nakagaki Industries was renting the land lot here, and situated on a fringe of its considerably spacious premises was a solitary shack, and in an adjacent parking lot, which was the only place where the land was leveled, there were parked a medium-sized excavator, a bulldozer, and three dump trucks. The rest of the place was dotted with piles of household scraps, large bundles of copper wire, old tires and rusted household electrical appliances, among other junk.

Raita unloaded some luggage from the pickup, picked out some combustible materials, and busily carried them over to a slightly sunken area in the middle of the lot. He then proceeded to unlock the door to the shack and bring out a polyethylene tank from inside it. Stuffing those materials—manga books and magazines—into any gaps found around his desk and chair, he sprinkled the contents of the tank over them. And that's when I finally realized that he was going to burn them. When he threw a lit match, a towering flame shot up in no time, prompting Eriko and Honoka, who were on the pickup's rear deck talking, to cheer and rush close to the bonfire.

"Hurry, Hono-chan!" Raita, who was standing to my left, called out suddenly to Honoka, who was standing next to Eriko, diagonally opposite us. Honoka nodded and put her hand into a large paper bag placed by her feet and pulled out several notebooks. Raita went behind me and approached Honoka.

Together with her, he took out more of these notebooks from the bag.

"What the hell are those?" Eriko asked Honoka.

"They're diaries," Raita answered on Honoka's behalf. "They're Hono-chan's diaries."

Eriko was curious, looking at the notebooks and peering into the bag.

"That's a whole lot of diaries."

"I know, right?" Raita spoke again. "She's been keeping them since she was in the fourth grade, and there are twenty-four of them in all."

"So like, you're going to burn them all?"

"You bet."

"Why?" Eriko said, surprised.

"Because, she's written nothing but crap. It's just full of whiny complaints. When she made me read everything once, I got super nauseated."

Honoka, standing next to Raita, was staring in silence at the cover of one of her diaries.

"I told Hono-chan that it's no use cherishing something like that. Since this seemed like a good opportunity, we both decided to burn them today."

"Are you sure you're okay with that, Honoka-chan?"

Honoka turned to Eriko and said, "Yes, I'm okay. I was thinking about doing it anyway."

"All right then, let's get this show on the road." Raita removed the remaining notebooks from the bag and handed over a few to Eriko before returning next to me. "I'd like you to help out too, Naoto-san," he said, holding out five or six notebooks. I accepted them and looked at the cover of the diary on top of the stack. It was neatly inscribed "Honoka Suzuki" in a handwritten script I suddenly thought I'd seen somewhere before, but I couldn't remember.

Raita went ahead and casually tossed his share of the

notebooks into the flames. The diaries began to blaze up at once, and their pages, licked open by the flames, blackened while curling up. Following his lead, I threw in my share. Then Honoka, and finally Eriko. No one turned to any page before throwing the diaries.

"Sometimes, when I was little," Eriko said out of the blue, "I used to wonder how I'd feel if my house burned down in a fire."

"I've also wondered about that myself," Raita said. "But I've always lived in an apartment, so I couldn't picture it all that well."

"But there really exist people whose homes have been reduced to ashes, right? I wonder how they feel."

"They probably feel refreshed, you know," Raita said without averting his gaze from the heap of diaries being reduced to ashes.

"Yeah, I suppose you're right," Eriko said pensively. "At first, they're probably terribly shocked, though."

"I think so too," Honoka spoke. "You know what? I'm kind of feeling refreshed right now."

"I know, right?" Raita said, turning to Honoka.

When the desk and chair were carbonized, the fire subsided and its flames finally began to settle into an elegant dance. Raita returned from the shack, holding four cans of beer. We were all sipping our beverages while talking around the fire, when around thirty minutes later, a car entered the site. It was a cream-colored Toyota Estima and it approached slowly, coming to a stop right near us.

A door—its window smoked glass—opened, and a woman around thirty and a small girl stepped out. From the driver's seat a stern-looking middle-aged man also emerged.

Raita placed his emptied can of beer by his feet and took a deep bow toward the man. The man flashed a smile on his suntanned, wrinkly face and raised his hand to say hi.

"Looks like you're nearly finished," he said in a gentle voice that didn't match his face. Although he was dressed in a pair of khaki cargo pants and a loud orange trainer, his close-cropped hair at the back gave him a formidable, masculine aura. He seemed to be in his mid-forties.

"Anything the matter, sir?" Raita asked in a relaxed tone.

"No, it's nothing. You were talking about lighting a fire so I thought I'd just drop by to have a look."

The woman and the girl, who had gotten out first, were already by the bonfire and had begun talking with Eriko and Honoka.

"Naoto-san, this is President Nakagaki. The two over there are his wife Yoriko-san and his daughter Moe-chan."

My attention was caught by the wife and child, so the president ended up bowing ahead of me. Embarrassed, I returned a bow in a hurry and offered my greetings.

"I'm Naoto Matsubara. I hear that you've kindly taken Raita under your wing. For that, I'm truly grateful. That's my friend over there, Eriko Fukasawa, and the other one is Honoka Suzuki."

The president nodded with appreciation and said, "I'm the one who's grateful. It's sad to see Torimasa gone now, but with the present times being the way they are, there was nothing that could be done to save it. Raita was really doing a fantastic job there, though. I have no idea how much help I can be to him, but I'd like him to give it his best shot at my company." He was speaking in a truly polite manner.

"With this dismal economic climate," I said, "business must be rather challenging for you too, sir."

"Yes indeed. We can't survive on demolition alone. The business of reconstruction has gone down the drain, so right now we're somehow eking by since expanding into repairs last year. But you can imagine how meager our margins are, since we're basically sub-sub-contractors."

Eriko and the others approached us. All four of them had reddened cheeks from exposure to the bonfire.

The president's wife, Yoriko-san, was beautiful. Moe-chan looked as though she might be around Takuya's age. She was endowed with pretty features herself, taking after her mother. With Eriko up close, President Nakagaki became wide-eyed for a moment, but immediately returned his gaze toward his daughter and wife.

Moe-chan was clinging to Honoka and giggling.

"That Kitty-chan hair clip is really cute! Who bought it for you?" Honoka said to Moe-chan, touching her fancy hair clip.

"Mommy bought it for me."

Honoka then said with an exaggerated gesture, "That's so nice, I want one too."

Moe-chan showed an elated smile before throwing her arms around Yoriko-san's knees. While patting her daughter's head, Yoriko-san said to President Nakagaki, who was in the middle of a conversation with me, "What about those things, Daddy?"

"Oh, yes, yes." The president headed toward the car and came back with a large *furoshiki*-wrapped parcel.

"I don't know if you'll enjoy them, but my wife prepared some bento lunches. You all must be exhausted from the move, so please feel free to dig in. She'll be delighted."

Raita, Honoka, Eriko, and even I let out shouts of joy, all at once.

"Sir, I'm grateful to you, as always," Raita said. "With your permission, we shall indeed dig in."

As if embarrassed by Raita's moving tone of voice, President Nakagaki turned to look at the bonfire, which had become small, and said, "Well, it's about time we take care of that and pull out of here, don't you think?"

16

As soon as the holidays ended, I got bogged down by trouble.

A brand new full-length novel by a certain mystery writer, which was to be published in September to commemorate the company's seventieth anniversary, was suddenly snatched away by another company. My superior and I had secured the promise of this very writer two years ago, and had been steadily preparing for the novel's publication since then, investing abundantly for its publicity. If published, this work of his was expected to sell 300,000 copies, at a minimum, so we found the suddenness of his broken promise all the more jarring.

Along with the director of the literary division, we visited the author's office on a daily basis and urged him on many occasions to reconsider his decision, but he wouldn't budge. What bothered us the most, though, was his refusal to clarify the reason for his change of heart. In the end I was on my knees, together with my boss, pleading for an answer, but he nonetheless kept his mouth shut. Judging from my personal association with the writer, I could tell that it wasn't for any ordinary reason like dissatisfaction with the slated number of first-edition copies or the advertising plans to be executed after publication. While he was no different from other bestselling authors in being selfish or moody, I knew for a fact that he wasn't the kind of person who'd break a promise that easily once he made it—he was a man of his word.

Of course, we sounded the new publisher out about the matter, but they appeared rather bewildered themselves, since the author had apparently approached them out of the blue.

We were at our wits' end.

In the office, various rumors spread about me and my boss—"One of them must have been careless in his dealings with the author and upset him," it was rumored, or "The project was being steamrolled ahead when nothing had been decided in the first place." The project was supposed to be a flagship for the first half of the year, so the mystery of the defection bred ever more suspicion, driving us into an untenable situation.

When we came to know the truth, the month of May was already drawing to a close.

A call suddenly came in to my cell from the author, after which my boss and I went to his place that evening. For the previous two weeks, in order to make up for the loss of the full-length novel, we'd been scrambling about trying to engage other authors whose prospects for generating sales seemed favorable, so we weren't all that thrilled to be summoned so late in the game, but the author—opening the door to his office—had apparently heard about our predicament at our company, and so after he led us into his room with an openly apologetic demeanor, he dropped his head in a deep bow.

And then, he said, "When the dust settles, I promise to give my next work to you, but for now, I beg you, please take the blame for my desertion. Now, there's something I must confess. But what I'm about to divulge, I do so in the strictest confidence. I want absolute assurance of your silence!" He made us promise again and again, as he conveyed a summary of the events that led up to his betrayal.

After hearing the story, we just sat there, stunned.

It was nothing more than a love affair.

He'd never worked with the new publisher until then, but a new, twenty-three-year-old female agent had paid a visit to say hello sometime in the month, after which a small association had begun. However, this association with the young agent had unexpectedly—according to the author—developed into a physical relationship.

When he first mentioned her name, I couldn't recall anyone by that name among my contacts, but in a few minutes I remembered vaguely a freckle-faced, awfully quiet girl.

"Apparently she's been a fan of mine since high school," the author said, "and has read everything I've written, and well, at any rate, she came to see me with a lot of enthusiasm."

And then he got her pregnant.

He was told of her pregnancy during the holidays, apparently while taking a stroll with her somewhere in Tohoku. The rest is just absurd, but after much wrangling over whether to give birth or not, she threatened the author, who was notorious for being a henpecked husband, that she'd disclose their affair to his wife.

Hence the change in publisher.

"But that's still no reason," I began, "to hand over your manuscript to her, is it? It's patently ridiculous! First of all, such a response can only be a temporary fix, and it's only going to embolden her. Even the matter of having an abortion or not is all up to her, isn't it? I mean it really depends on how she personally feels about that. It's unlikely that a twenty-three-year-old woman would willingly give birth to a child fathered by someone she's not married to. Bottom line, she just used her body to reel in your manuscript, don't you think? If you continue to deal with her so timidly, you're bound to be preyed upon from now on." I realized that my company had covered the costs for his research trip to Tohoku with the preposterous woman.

"I understand," the author said. "You don't need to tell me that, but things like this never tend to follow reason, do they?"

The author appeared downhearted and exhausted, but I felt that he was faking it, that he actually didn't regret his decision at all.

"Sir," my boss began, "you're naturally planning to break up with her, aren't you? If you go on like this, you're bound to get caught by your wife sooner or later. And when you do get caught, the problem's just going to get worse, because this tart appears to have no scruples; no decent woman would kick up a fuss about becoming pregnant soon after you start dating her." My boss was certainly insinuating that he had doubts about the agent's claim of pregnancy.

"Of course, with this incident having caused an awful amount of trouble for you both, I intend to set her straight soon."

An author, in many cases, is an individual who puts himself in a warped, closed environment, never sufficiently exposing himself to the winds of society. Thus, more often than not, lacking in the department of love, he makes passes at an insignificant, yet accessible, member of the opposite sex, and at the depressing end of the affair, falls into a severe psychological crisis.

Believing that he wouldn't break off ties with her that easily, and not counting on his promise regarding his next work, we refrained from grilling him any further and left his office.

We then went to Ginza and drank.

"Even though he wants us to keep our mouths shut," my boss began, "we've got to let the brass know up to a point."

"Naturally," I answered. Even though it was an outrage that he was duped by the agent of another company—a twenty-three-year-old minx, no less—when I thought of how a small life, whose light was now lit in the mother's womb, was going to get snuffed out in exchange for a single full-length novel by that miserable wretch of a writer, I felt nothing but utter contempt and disgust. There's no limit to human vulgarity.

"I'm amazed," my boss then said, "at how he can keep writing novels with so many murders in them, when no one in his life has been murdered, not to mention the fact that he himself hasn't murdered anyone. What's more, he hasn't even seen a corpse, nor has he had a long talk directly with a murderer, you know. Frankly, whenever I meet mystery writers, I can't help thinking there's something's wrong with them. They have zero sense of reality, in reality. I haven't met a murderer myself, but if a murderer actually read any of the stuff mystery writers put out, he'd find their works totally phony, don't you think? But then again, murderers don't read books."

He then went on to curse recent novels and novelists incessantly. I was overcome by about half a month's worth of fatigue, bearing down on me all at once, and so couldn't keep up with all his yammering.

In the restroom of a small bar we went to next, I threw up for a long time.

Even after I returned to the counter, just looking at the sweaty glass of whiskey and water made me feel sick again. Such a thing rarely happened with me.

For the most part, I've never considered alcohol to be all that tasty while drinking it, but on this particular day, I was simply shocked that I'd been pouring the foul liquid into my gut for all this time. Just what was it about booze that made you dent your wallet anyway? All it offered in the end was misery. I tried searching for the reason while holding back the mounting urge to vomit again. It felt as if there was some profound meaning to be found, so I couldn't help pondering. But there's no answer to be found to such a question.

I rose from my seat, told my boss that I was ill, left the shop, and flagged down a taxi. Inside the moving vehicle, the prospect of going home to that bleak apartment became unbearably tiresome, so I changed my destination to Ningyocho. I'd stayed overnight just three days ago, but since I'd never visited without a warning, Eriko might get a little surprised, I thought.

I felt sick again, leaning against the wall in the elevator of Eriko's apartment building, mumbling her full name over and over again. For some reason, in the short time it took for the elevator to ascend to the ninth floor, I came to believe that of all the people I knew, she'd surely be the one to relieve me of this suffering. When I stood in front of Eriko's apartment door and sounded the chime, it was already past twelve.

Eriko opened the door and stepped out, and I snuggled up to her without saying a word. I think I was testing my limits, and as I convinced myself that I wasn't actually so sick that I'd collapse to the floor, I pressed my cheeks against the smooth nape of her neck. But it turned out that I was just kidding myself. The moment I leaned against Eriko's body, my knees collapsed, my body began to shake, and I became paralyzed. I was panicking inside as I tried to stand up again, but she held my body as firmly as she could, and when I realized that she was making an all-out effort to convey me to the bed while stroking my back, despite the unnatural posture I was in, I felt at ease and fulfilled, so I let go and entrusted my entire being to her.

She laid me to rest on the bed ever so gently, and I became enveloped in the sensation of being submerged in a lukewarm pool. Close to my ear, I faintly heard the sounds of music streaming through a satellite radio channel, but it stopped soon. A magazine-like object near my head was carried away by a slender arm crossing over the tip of my nose.

Eriko's palm covered my forehead; it felt cool and nice. I saw her face as she untied my necktie. Apparently, I just fell asleep then.

I woke up suddenly. It seemed like a long time had passed, but it might have been only a short while. The room was bright, but the fluorescent light on the ceiling, in fact, was switched off, and the only light in there was spilling out from the kitchen. Still, the snow-white ceiling, the creamy walls, and the sheets, whose whiteness pressed against my peripheral vision, seemed to glitter brilliantly, washed in the spilling streaks of light. I felt as if I'd been thoroughly disinfected and dried. I was comfortable.

Eriko was watching. Seated by the bed, she had her face turned toward me.

I tried to speak but my throat was stinging, so all I could do was let a hoarse lump of sound roll over my tongue. Trying to smile, I grimaced.

Eriko brought her face closer, looking ponderous, as if she'd failed to catch something I said.

"Feeling a little comfortable now?" she said, the palm of her hand before my eyes. I finally realized then that a cold towel had been placed over my forehead. Next thing I knew, the slight weight got lifted from there and I heard, from somewhere unseen, the sounds of ice clinking in a washbasin and a towel being squeezed, fizzing with foam. Then, once again, the cold weight returned to my forehead.

"Somewhat." I coughed, my voice having gotten extremely hoarse. "I feel like I'm in a hospital."

I thought about what I just said and added, "It's as if you're nursing me as I lay here dying."

Eriko laughed.

"You're so kind," I said, thinking how true that was—from the depths of my heart.

Eriko drew her mouth close to my ear and whispered, "This is the first time you've praised me for something other than my looks."

Listening to her humbly tell me so, I wanted to cry for some reason. And when tears began to well in my eyes I became genuinely surprised.

"I'll be looking after you, so why don't you get some more sleep?" Eriko said before pulling the thin blanket up to my neck and covering my shoulders.

I closed my eyes, and in that moment, sensed a few teardrops brimming from my eyelids and dampening my eyelashes. I wondered if Eriko saw, but my hold on consciousness thinned again.

Next morning, we sat facing each other across the dining table. Eriko, sinking her teeth into a slice of toast, looked into my face and said, "You seem worried."

I wasn't worried about anything, so I shook my head.

I finished eating and stood up to reach for my coat and necktie hanging on the wall, but Eriko prevented me, saying "Just a minute," and crossed over to the closet and returned with a brand-new shirt and a beige and purple pin dot tie. Thanking her and receiving the two items, I placed them on the sofa and took off my shirt illustrated with baby birds. Meanwhile, Eriko picked up the new shirt, broke open the seal of its packaging, spread out the shirt, and unbuttoned it before handing it over to me as I stood there. I thanked her again and wore the brand-new shirt. Grabbing the new necktie, I put up my collar and wound the tie around my neck, but then I stooped down, picked up the tip of the necktie and thrust it out to her. She happily went on to tie it with a deft hand and said, "It suits you well." I suddenly kissed Eriko on the lips and doggedly sucked her tongue, but she removed her lips, as if to escape, and said, laughing, "You still smell of booze."

While she changed, I read the morning edition, standing up. There was a long article in there by a correspondent in Jerusalem reporting on the signs of a power shift happening in the corridors of power in Israel, so I read it carefully, ruminating on the subject.

The two of us left the apartment a little past ten. As Eriko was locking the door, the door to the neighboring apartment opened and a jeans-clad woman in her early thirties stepped out. She was carrying a large sketchbook under her arm. Eriko said "Good morning" and she too said "Good morning" in return. She glanced my way and then walked past the both of us.

"She's a storyboard writer for TV commercials," Eriko said, depositing her keys into a pocket inside her bag.

"She drops by my place to drink beer sometimes. Until around five years ago, she was a magazine model, you know. I haven't worked with her though. Now she's into riding her 750cc motorcycle; the big one that's always parked in front of this apartment."

Eriko continued to talk about the woman during the elevator ride, and while we were walking as well. For the most part I just listened in silence.

Since the two of us didn't have anything planned that morning, we entered a Starbucks near an intersection in Ningyocho and I ordered an Americano while Eriko ordered an iced latte.

We settled into a sofa on the basement floor. Eriko had a sip of her latte and began to discuss my holidays in July. Having worked nonstop without a break since the beginning of the year, I thought about settling the matter of the blunder regarding that author within the next month, and then taking a paid week or more off as soon as July began. I'd already spoken to Eriko about that.

Eriko said that if I were to take a vacation in the second week of July, she'd be able to take four days off in a row from the eleventh. She paused and then invited me to visit her parents' home in Suwa for three days, from Friday the twelfth, if I didn't mind.

I was bewildered by her sudden suggestion.

I immediately asked where I'd stay.

"It's an old house," Eriko replied, "but it's got plenty of rooms. There's no need to worry." She then added that her parents wanted to see me.

You must be joking, I thought. But considering how intimate we'd been for the past couple months, I believed it would be prudent not to reject her invitation outright, or even give the impression of doing so.

But then she said, "I suppose it's somewhat sudden, so if you're not up for it, I wouldn't particularly mind." If that were the case, she went on to say, we could go somewhere else together.

"I'd hate to disappoint you again, as I did during that last trip to Kyoto," I said.

"Oh, that was fun in its own way," Eriko said, laughing a little.

"So, hey, what do you want to do?" she asked again. I fell silent and tried to search for a suitable answer, but I began to feel ridiculous. I took a deep breath, cleared my mind, and said to Eriko, locking my eyes on hers, "I don't understand. Why do I have to meet your parents?" I wasn't able to prevent my voice from quavering with emotion. "I hardly think our relationship has reached such a stage. But don't get me wrong: I'm not saying that I don't want to meet your parents. I only feel I'm probably incapable of meeting your expectations and your parents' regarding polite formalities—I suck at things like that. What's more, I'm associating with you, not your parents, and I have no intention of associating with them in the future. I think I told you before, but I don't believe in families at all."

Halfway through my diatribe, Eriko's expression changed suddenly. When I finished, she was looking down and seemed like she wanted to run away, rendered speechless, her slender shoulders shaking slightly.

But rather than feeling sorry for her, the sight of her like that was getting on my nerves. It was as though she was inflicting a subtle form of violence on me.

"I don't think it's a matter of whether I'm up for it or not. If I may say so, with regard to our relationship, I feel you're more irresponsible than I am." I felt my anger rising steadily. "On the day of Raita's moving, remember what you said? You said let's do the best we can together, didn't you? What the hell did you mean by that? Were you in fact saying that we should do our best together in order to meet your parents? If so, I believe there's been a terrible misunderstanding."

Eriko, still looking down, let out a small sigh. Taking the bag she'd kept on the chair next to her and slinging it over her shoulder, she stood up with the unfinished cup in her hand without saying anything. And then she looked down at me with serene eyes. Looking back at her, I let out an obnoxious sigh and leaned back into the sofa.

I could tell that my actions had made her hold back the words she was about to say.

"I'll take off, then," she finally said, wearing a crooked smile as she slowly turned her back and walked toward the dim-lit stairs of the shop. Holding my breath, I endured waves of anxiety and regret surging through my heart, while cursing at the figure of her receding back: "Get the hell out of here."

17

THE FUNERAL HALL WAS a small ceremonial hall at the edge of Urawa.

I rode the Keihin-Tohoku Line from Tokyo Station to Minami-Urawa, transferred to the Musashino Line from there, and got off at Higashi-Urawa Station. The spacious station plaza was—possibly because it was a little too early to be crowded with office workers going home—completely deserted, hit by the rain that had been falling nonstop all day long. On the other side of the street, except for a McDonald's and a pachinko parlor, there were no conspicuous structures in sight. Underneath the dark clouds of the rainy sky, the entire town seemed submerged, smelling of despair.

The rain wasn't letting up at all.

I pulled out from my bag the fax Eriko had sent to my office and stood by the ticket counters to check the whereabouts of the funeral hall. Apparently, I needed to turn left from where I was and keep walking straight for less than ten minutes.

Opening my large umbrella, I began to walk down a paved road where the pedestrian traffic was sparse. I kept looking back and forth to see if there were others who appeared to be making a condolence call like I was, but no dice. The intense rain immediately made my shoes and the hem of my black pants soaking wet.

Although I'd met the deceased only once, when it occurred to me that I'd be offering my condolences in such a bleak place—a place that was so remote from my everyday life—it made me sad. According to Eriko, only the older brother of the deceased was living in Urawa. The wake and funeral service naturally ought to be held, therefore, in the vicinity of Ekoda, where the deceased's company was located, or in Hitachiota, where the deceased was born, but apparently circumstances conspired against that.

The sign, "Ceremony Mall Higashi-Urawa," appeared. There was a parking lot just before an antiquated, box-shaped building, but the only vehicles parked there were a car and a station wagon, and there was no reception tent in sight.

The eaved entrance was slightly spacious, and the front door was on the right-hand side; it was a set of double automatic doors, but they were made of frosted glass so you couldn't see through them.

Even in this area, though, there wasn't a single reception desk to be found—just a large, rectangular panel hung on the wall, which had these words written in deft calligraphic strokes:

Memorial Services for Susumu Nakagaki

Right under this panel was fixed a metal plate that read "National Funeral Hall."

For a while, as I stood under the eaves and wiped away the raindrops from my black mourning attire with a handkerchief, I waited for someone to come out from the other side of the automatic doors. But no one appeared.

I glanced at my watch. It was already past six. On the panel it clearly indicated that the wake was to be held on June 17th from 6:00 p.m., and the funeral service on the 18th from 11:00 a.m. However, there were no comings and goings around the entrance area, nor was there anyone else arriving.

I reluctantly passed through the automatic doors and entered.

The place was the size of about ten tatami mats with two tall screens partitioning off the left side, and when I peered through the opening between the screens, I saw a marvelous altar. The portrait of the deceased and a coffin, laid in state, were decorated with many chrysanthemums. The smell of incense filled the air as quiet music flowed from the ceiling. The seats for the bereaved were found to the right and left of the altar, and behind these seats were steel chairs for about thirty people, but only a smattering of figures—around five or six—outfitted in mourning dresses were seated there.

In the front was a glass-tiled wall, and the reception desk was right before it.

Raita and Honoka were sitting up straight, looking somber.

I removed from my pocket an envelope containing my condolence gift of money and stood before the two. Raita's face was pale, looking back at me with vacant eyes.

"It's the wake and these are the only people who showed up?" I said, signing my name in a guest book that was mostly blank.

"It appears they haven't told anyone, except family members and employees," Honoka answered in a low voice.

"But this is so sad—so very lonesome."

"Yes, that's true . . ." Honoka said, eyeing Raita, but he was looking down.

"Has Eriko arrived?"

"Yes, she came some time ago. I believe she's sitting over there now."

A line had formed behind me, so I said, "See you both later," and left the place. Raita, in the end, hadn't spoken a single word.

I hadn't noticed earlier, but when I faced the altar now I spotted Eriko seated in the right-hand corner of the row furthest to the back; the refined posture of her back was a dead giveaway. I approached her with muted steps and sat on the seat to her left.

Until the phone call this morning, we hadn't contacted each other since parting ways in Ningyocho that day.

I spoke first, saying, "I'm worried about Raita."

"He's taking it very hard, apparently. Honoka says that until a little while ago he was in a state of confusion."

"But . . ."

The first phone call from Eriko in half a month had rung at six in the morning.

According to Eriko at that time, it was Honoka who had broken the news to her, and she'd called from the hospital that President Nakagaki had been brought into. She said that Raita had gone mad and was out of control, so Eriko had also rushed over to the place. When she gave me the call she was already at the hospital herself.

It was Raita who had found President Nakagaki dead in his car.

Raita and the wife, Yoriko-san, had been desperately searching for him after he'd gone missing the day before yesterday, a Saturday morning. Finally, on the night of the following day, Raita discovered the president inside his car, parked in the Tetsugakudo Park. He was dead from carbon monoxide poisoning, having inhaled the fumes of the exhaust gas.

It had been raining heavily since midnight the previous day. When Eriko called I was just getting out of bed, roused from sleep by the sound of the rain striking violently against the windowpane. I could imagine, as I listened to Eriko over the phone, the impact the sight of the president's horrible figure, appearing in the light of Raita's flashlight, must have had on Raita, after he'd run all over the pitch-black park, soaked to the skin in the driving rain.

". . . you must be exhausted too," I said.

She must have gone straight to work from the hospital before coming here. No wonder she looked so worn out. Without saying anything, Eriko kept staring at the portrait on the altar.

"He seemed so kind," she murmured.

I saw Yoriko-san seated in the section for the bereaved, her shoulders drooped, and her face, swollen from weeping, had turned pale, making her look like another person entirely. Seated quietly next to her was Moe-chan, dressed in a black dress.

Two priests entered and the sutra-chanting began at once. Many seats remained vacant; counting Eriko and me, there were only a total of eight people present.

While waiting for my turn to light an incense stick, three more people arrived, but even then, not five minutes passed before the line leading to the square incense burner broke off. Eriko went to fetch Honoka and Raita at the reception desk, and they were the last to make an incense offering.

As soon as Raita stood facing the coffin, a strange thing occurred.

The flames of the two candlesticks set in front of a low table, where some servings of rice and dumplings were also found, went out one after the other, beginning with the right one; there was no wind blowing.

I saw Raita's back shrink. The incident caused a faint stir among the bereaved kin, as they also seemed to take notice. Raita put his hands together in prayer and after he calmly pulled a lighter from his pocket, he approached the altar and lit the candle over the right railing before slowly walking over to the railing on the left, stretching his arm, and lighting the remaining one.

When he returned to the portrait at the front, he closed his eyes, joined his hands in prayer, and stood there, motionless, for nearly five minutes.

I was watching everything unfold with a heavy heart. As for Eriko seated next to me, I could tell that she'd stiffened and was trying to catch her breath.

"Machiko-san." I called out this name in my heart.

"The spirit of Mr. Susumu Nakagaki is here with us now. Please guide his soul so that he may be able to leave his worldly misfortunes, miseries, and regrets behind and depart peacefully for the place he must return to."

I prayed in earnest.

In a room on the second floor prepared for serving ritual meals, I talked a little with Yoriko-san and other family members.

"Raita had been such a great help . . ." she said, choking up.

Last spring, the president had started a new line of business, offering renovation services. He was basically subcontracting work from the renovations division of a major housing construction company, and what had driven him into a tight corner was the sudden bankruptcy at the end of last month of an engineering firm, which was the primary subcontractor. The charges he'd accumulated this past half-year for construction work, which he'd undertaken on credit, remained unpaid, and Nakagaki Industries apparently became short of funds in no time at all. Needless to say, he had a tough time repaying the business capital for which he'd overreached and borrowed, let alone pay the wages of the craftsmen he'd employed, so when June came he made an all-out effort to raise money. But with the bank also being merciless in its demands, it was all over for the company. On Friday, his request for a loan that would've served as a stopgap fund was declined by a credit union he'd associated with since he'd established his business. It was his last resort, so that night, the president came home dead drunk, apparently.

He went missing the next morning, and by the time his family had woken up he was nowhere to be found.

Yoriko-san immediately called Raita, who lived in the vicinity, and the two of them searched for him everywhere they could, but in the end they couldn't account for his whereabouts over that day and a half.

"It's just like him," the older brother spoke haltingly as he wiped away his overflowing tears with the palm of his hand. "He sealed up the windows of the car with packing tape so thoroughly it was incredible, and he'd properly written three suicide notes; an extra long letter each for Yoriko and Moe, and one for clarifying how he wanted his company to be disposed of. I suppose his mind was made up a long time ago. Ever since he launched his company fifteen years ago, he has said, 'Bro, if something happens I'm going to see to it that things get cleared up with a life insurance policy. I don't want to cause any trouble for anyone.'"

Eriko too was sobbing incessantly, next to Yoriko-san.

It seems that the president had tied a vinyl pipe to the exhaust vent of the Toyota Estima he was driving when he'd brought lunch for us that time, letting the exhaust leak into the interior of the car.

Honoka was going in and out of the room while looking after Moe-chan. Raita was looking quite calm now and was drinking together with the condolence callers, of whom there were many more starting to show up. I was watching him from a distance, impressed by how freely he was interacting with people again; it just went to show how seasoned he was in entertaining customers. After he'd lit up those two candlesticks again, he'd become so sunny and energetic that you could easily mistake him for another person.

But I was nonetheless feeling slightly anxious about this transformation of his.

At a little past eleven, Eriko and I rose from our seats. As we were leaving, I finally got to exchange a few words with Raita, who had come to the entrance, along with Honoka, to see us off.

"Naoto-san, Eriko-san," Raita said, bowing deeply, "thank you for coming today."

Eriko said, "You've got to find a job again, don't you? If you like, I can help, so feel free to let me know, okay?"

"Thank you. Hono-chan is there for me, so I'm good."

"Take it easy, you hear? I'll drop by tomorrow as well," I said.

"Yes, sir."

"I'm certain the president's at peace now," I said. "He's free at last from this trouble-ridden world, after all."

Just then, Raita's face warped, making me think he was on the verge of tears, but I was wrong, because his odd expression momentarily morphed into a smile.

"Yes, I feel the same way," Raita said. "He must have been fed up with living in a world where hard work never pays off—hard work carried out by people like the president and my old boss."

After Eriko and I said our goodbyes and stepped out of the entrance hall, the never-ending rain had finally let up, and the night sky was studded with stars.

"Won't you look at that?" I said. "You stray from Tokyo a little and this is what you get: such crystal-clear skies."

Eriko quietly took my arm and we walked down the road to the station.

"Thanks for contacting me today. I feel bad about the terrible things I said last time," I said, expressing both my gratitude and regret in one breath.

"I'm sorry for having called you so early in the morning."

And then, after hesitating for a while, she added, "I feel bad myself you know, for asking for such a selfish thing that time. I'm sorry," Eriko apologized again.

In this small exchange, I felt as if I'd gained a glimpse of the essence of my relationship with her: at the end of the day, I was the self-centered one in the relationship, I thought, behaving selfishly and being a constant pain in the neck.

"When was it that you were planning to travel to Suwa? Was it the twelfth of next month?" I said before adding, "I'm looking forward to joining you."

"Really? Are you sure you're okay with going there?" Eriko said, peering into my face.

"Uh-huh," I said, nodding. "But I'd like you to let me stay at your apartment tonight, because I want to sleep with you."

After we sat side by side in the train whisking us home, Eriko asked me to tell her about Kohei, for whose death Raita blames himself, so I explained what Raita had once told me in brief. Eriko seemed to have heard only bits of the story from Honoka, since the first thing she asked me was "What kind of accident was it?"

"Apparently it happened more than a decade ago. Raita was still in the fifth grade or so, and Kohei, his cousin, was a high school student, it seems. One day Kohei and his parents, and Kohei's younger sister, and Raita himself—the five of them—set out for the shores of Minami-Boso for some beach fishing, and that's where the accident happened.

"Fishing was a family pastime in Kohei's household, and they often used to head to the beach during fishing season. Raita had joined them for the first time that day. With the ocean calm, the day was absolutely ideal for fishing. At the beach, there were other anglers scattered across a rocky stretch with their rods cast. Raita partnered up with Kohei and the two of them took up positions at a certain place in the stretch, while Kohei's parents and his younger sister cast their lines from another location.

"It was some time after their lunch break when the waves began to rise. While Raita and Kohei were having a hard time scoring any catches, the other team led by Raita's uncle, at a slight distance from the two, had already caught a number of huge sea chubs.

"It was Raita who had urged Kohei to come along with him to the edge of the rocky stretch. The man who had been fishing there had left, making the position available. Having seen that this man's fish basket was full, Raita got excited and restless. But apparently Kohei was hesitant, since, just then, the waves had become rougher. But Raita persisted, leading him forcibly by the hand to the edge.

"Before they could even fix their chairs, a high wave attacked the two. The one who got swept away was the light-weighted Raita.

"Kohei jumped in and grabbed hold of Raita, just when

he was about to drown at the trough of a wave. Kohei then desperately tried to cling to a rocky surface, but the riptide was vicious and the waves were higher than he'd expected. The two of them were flung against the reef many times and were pulled underwater by returning waves, over and over again. The trace of a deep laceration remains on Raita's right arm to this day—it's a wound he suffered being hurled against a sharp rock at that time.

"The fact that the two had fallen was immediately noticed by the other three. Raita was pushed up by Kohei, and somehow the uncle managed to pull him out by the hand. But Kohei, after making sure that Raita was safe, was swallowed up by a wave, perhaps because he'd exhausted all his strength.

"The uncle jumped in, and several other anglers, who had rushed over, also plunged into the sea without delay.

"But Kohei was beyond saving by then.

"His corpse was found the next morning, washed up on a neighboring shore beyond a promontory."

"And that's why Raita never eats fish."

I smiled wryly at Eriko's off-kilter remark and said, "Maybe that's why he and Honoka get along."

"Yeah, you might be right about that. Both of them are deeply wounded individuals."

"Raita in particular."

"Yeah, I feel that way too."

I was remembering the word Raita had repeatedly muttered when I had drinks with him in Nakano in April; he kept saying "snapped."

". . . this thing like a cord that's been barely keeping me tied to this rotten world until now has finally snapped . . ."

That's what Raita said at the time, and so I feared, if he was like that back then, what his mental state must be like now. What kind of psychological impact was President Nakagaki's suicide having on him now?

I saw, through the train's window, the darkness of a pitch-black night open out.

"Everyone dies in the end," Eriko said, sighing.

"Yeah, everyone does. I'll die eventually, and someday, you will too, and so will Raita and Honoka, and even the currently grieving Yoriko-san. And let's not forget little Moe-chan; she too will certainly die."

"So it's really pointless to take your own life then, isn't it?"

"You're wrong," I said to the reflection of Eriko in the window on the opposite side.

"Nakagaki-san didn't take his own life. All he did was kill himself, the way one murders another."

Eriko's reflection appeared baffled.

"He was the victim of his own murder. Just as murder is wrong, I believe it's a sin to kill yourself. That is to say, to kill yourself is the same thing as killing someone else. If you approve the act of killing yourself, you also approve the act of killing another. War is the basis of that idea."

"But isn't war carried out for the purpose of killing people?"

"No, it isn't. As I believe I told you when we went to Hikone, war is homicide premised on your own death: if you decide to put your own life at risk—that is, if you decide that you don't mind getting killed at any time—the guilt you feel for killing someone else disappears without a trace."

I closed my eyes and waited for the question to arise in my head, the question I continue to think about every day.

Why is it that I don't commit suicide?

I believe it's simply because, just as I have no right to take away another person's life, I have no right to take away my own. People often fall under the illusion that they're living by themselves, relying solely on their own willpower, their own strength. But this is preposterous; humans don't possess such a capability. Birth itself is unrelated to self-will or any individual gumption; while you may feel supremely confident about your own willpower during the height of your life, it becomes utterly powerless at death's door, just as it was when you were born. So essentially, human beings, from beginning to end, are incapable of determining anything for themselves. For this reason, they really don't have the right to end their own lives arbitrarily, nor do they have the right to take the lives of others. People don't live; they're merely being allowed to live.

All this reasoning leads to the birth of yet another question.

Why do human beings seek to bring about a new life?

If there is one place we humans can act of our own volition— that is, demonstrate our own will—it's in the realm of creating another person's life, I think.

But I can't quite understand why we end up doing such a thing. Why should we, when bringing about the life of another person is tantamount to bringing about the death of this person? Giving birth to a person is also to murder him or her.

This isn't a feeling; it's the truth.

A human being who fails to grasp the profound meaning of the fact that he will die one day will, without fail, end up having to choose between either killing himself or killing another. The alarming cruelty of this world lies entirely in the fact that we're compelled to face such a dilemma.

A good example of this is women.

Just like my mother; just like Honoka's mother; just like Teruko Onishi, who began to talk about wanting to have a child on a whim; just like Tomomi, who goes out with me while still having half-hearted feelings for Park after bearing Takuya against everyone's advice; and just like Eriko who wishes to take me to Suwa to see her parents and eventually marry me; and just like all those mothers who entrust the care of their forty-three-day-old newborns to total strangers, women are so obsessed with their own desires they simply can't forsake their egos. They're neglectful of their own deaths and continue instead to readily bring about the deaths of others.

It never occurs to them that having a child is, in the end, an act that results in the death of the child. And it's likely that they never realize, not even for a fleeting moment, that they themselves, in this sense, are the true murderers.

I was bothered by such benightedness in women.

The world is filled with people who lead reluctant lives because they never had to be born; nobody possibly can—while he or she is on the way to fulfilling a fate of certain death—find any contrary evidence in him or her that could disprove this truth.

Just as that lady Buddhist wrote, ". . . if you thoroughly scrape out from human existence, using a bamboo whisk perhaps, all things that pass and fade away, including youth, beauty, love, emotion, material wealth, social status, and worldly abilities, the skeletal frame that remains in the end will be merely made of—for everyone alike—old age, illness, and death." This is absolutely true.

Even my mother, even Honoka's mother, even Teruko Onishi and even Tomomi and even Eriko all avert their eyes from this telltale and unavoidable skeletal frame of life common to us all; instead, they succumb to the allure of their unconscious sense of superiority, their arrogant thoughts as they thirst for short-term happiness, driving those whom they should be loving and cherishing the most to the brink of their cruel deaths.

The Lord Buddha accepted all this as suffering, and preached deliverance from this suffering. And Machiko-san, on that day, a long time ago in my distant past, said to me, "You don't have to be ashamed of yourself at all, Naoto-kun, as long as you witness yourself feeling ashamed. Eventually, there will come a time when Naoto-kun will part from Naoto-kun to merge with a whole lot of other people who have passed away, and then, Naoto-kun, you'll become a gust of wind somewhere. So that's why I want you to, while you're alive, forget about yourself as much as possible and become the kind of human being who thinks for other people. You see, the Lord Buddha teaches us that everything in this world is all one and the same. Humans, animals, even stones, flowers, and the air—they're all like one big connected dream. I believe everything—before birth, while alive, even after death—must be all one and the same. I'm sure you are me, and I'm you, and anyone about to be born is me, and I was once someone else who died a long, long time ago. Perhaps you're still too young to understand, Naoto-kun, but there's no difference between you and a stone, a blade of grass, an insect and an animal; they're all, in the same way, just you, so in reality, there really isn't anything to worry about. If you think you're suffering, then you're suffering; if you think you're having fun, you're having fun. That's all you can say about this world. And so, even though someday you and I will die, Naoto-kun, there's nothing sad about that at all. You really don't have to be sad about that—you don't have to grieve. If I die, you'll go on living, and if you die, there will be others who will go on living, right? If you think like that, you'll see that there's nothing to be afraid of. And that's why I want to abandon myself and be considerate to others, to take care of them, to cherish them, no matter who they are. Just to be clear, it has nothing to do with whether I like you or not, Naoto-kun. I'm only being nice to you because of my belief. There's no need for you to thank me at all. I'm merely doing it for myself, and believing that, in doing so, it would eventually be good for you too."

Ever since that summer night, I've been ruminating over Machiko-san's words, thinking about them again and again. And the more I pondered them, the more I felt they were loaded with meaning.

I also firmly believe that Raita will soon come face to face with the significance of those profound words left behind by Machiko-san. At that time, I wonder what kind of answers he'll find. This thought was troubling me. There was so much sadness in his life right now; it was overflowing with misfortunes that could easily lead him to false answers. For one, there was his relationship with Honoka, a girl who was deeply wounded because of her parents; then there was the sadness of watching his former boss fall ill and ultimately retreat to his hometown with his wife, laying to waste all they'd built up over the years, even while suffering the pain of losing their child; and then there was the death of President Nakagaki this time. However, what was even more troubling was the fact that Raita was convinced he'd killed someone.

All I could see was the figure of Raita driven into a corner, teetering on the brink of self-destruction.

Eriko suddenly tapped me on the shoulder and I lifted my face.

The train had apparently arrived at Tokyo Station while I'd been lost deep in thought. The scenery through the window—completely changed from before—was filled with the brightly lit view of the comings and goings of a throng of people moving across the station platform.

"I hope the weather clears up tomorrow," Eriko said in a lifeless voice, rising from her seat ahead of me.

18

ON JULY SEVENTH, IN the middle of the night, my sister informed me over the phone that my mother's condition had taken a sudden turn.

Although I'd heard that she'd been suffering from complications of a cold and hadn't been able to eat anything, I didn't expect to hear that she was in a critical condition. Fortunately, I was slated to take a one-week vacation beginning the following day, which fell on the eighth, on a Monday, so I packed my bags and boarded the first flight next morning to Kokura, Kitakyushu, my hometown.

From Fukuoka Airport I rode a taxi straight to the general hospital where my mother was hospitalized and found her moved into a single room, receiving no treatment save for an oxygen mask placed over her mouth.

My younger sister was seated beside the bed, her face haggard. She told me that Mother had suffered throughout the night, but she was now sleeping with the aid of painkillers and sleeping pills; according to the chief physician, since her heart had completely weakened due to pneumonia, it was only a matter of time now. Her consciousness was already drifting from confusion toward a comatose state.

My mother, whom I hadn't seen in two years, had lost a lot of weight. The folds of her dark blue *yukata* gown with floral patterns were slightly parted, exposing her chest, and there was a light cotton blanket covering her up to her waist, but the thin bulging outline of her legs, from the waist down to the tips of her feet, now appeared as thin as withered branches, laying bare for all to see the tragic state of a body whose life was for the most part worn away.

Her face, chest, hands and feet, which literally looked skeletal, were ridden with innumerable pockmark-like blisters—the adverse side effects of drugs—appearing all dried up and scabbed now.

The next day, Mother regained her consciousness once before dying; though it might have just been that her eyes had opened reflexively for a moment.

I looked into my mother's tanned, wrinkled face, stared into her eyes, from which all the light had gone out, and gripped her hand. Just then, I thought I saw the subtly quivering needle of her consciousness, but I couldn't tell for sure. I said "Mummy" and kept on crying out to her dozens of times until I'd become mindful of my surroundings, my voice gradually dwindling. I then said, having become tired, "You can relax now, okay? You tried your best, didn't you?" In the end, without showing any response, Mother closed her eyes again, and by the time my younger sister brought the doctor over, she seemed to have breathed her last.

The doctor had no sooner laid his eyes on his watch than my younger sister burst into tears, as if a dam had broken inside her. I too was tempted to cry just then, believing it was all right under these circumstances to get swept away by emotion, and so I imagined that my eyes were actually on the verge of welling up, but the tears didn't come at all.

I tried to think about something related to my mother's death, but before I did, my mind began to buzz with the things I'd been considering throughout the day—the arrangements I needed to make for planning and carrying out the funeral. These thoughts had simply popped into my mind, as if on cue, and so I ended up deciding it would be all right to leave all the grieving to my younger sister for the time being, while I went about handling the requisite tasks.

Not that it really mattered now, but my mother's life had been chaotic and miserable.

I was in a small assembly space of a municipal dwelling house when this thought occurred to me; I was bowing my head, along with my sister, to each and every visitor from the neighborhood offering his or her condolences, wondering all the while what I should say in honor of her memory at the service.

My mother was still shy of twenty when she got married for the first time, and her partner was a student from Kyushu University who used to frequent the bar where she was working. A year later I was born, and apparently this student dropped out of college to work full-time. But just when I was about to turn two, he abandoned my mother and me and fled back to his hometown in Oita. Thereafter, I've not met him, and have pretty much remained clueless about what kind of life he has been leading, or even whether he's still alive. One time, it seems a man who claimed to be his older brother dropped in and left a decent amount of money, and at that time, according to this man, his younger brother had acquired the qualifications to become a lawyer and was doing well. By then, my mother had remarried and my younger sister had been born, so she was able to settle any disputes without much friction.

It was only after the failure of my mother's second marriage that her life began to go downhill.

Her bar, which she'd started in Tobata with a loan, went bankrupt, and after my mother's promiscuity drove my younger sister's father to leave, she repeatedly got into so much trouble with money and men that even she herself was shocked. Although she kept blaming her parents for her inability to keep an honest job, saying that they never gave her a satisfactory education, as far as my sister and I were concerned, it was just her slovenly nature that kept her from leading a sound and steady life.

When Mother was working as a bar hostess in Kokura, we

were living at the back of a factory zone in Tobata, in a filthy apartment the size of six tatami mats, but it wasn't a place you could relax in the daytime, with all the cacophony. Fed up with the apartment, Mother used to repeatedly stay out, so whenever my sister and I returned from school, we always ate tofu, instead of a proper snack, and killed time outside at the grassy field beside the factory.

I'd fallen in love with a guitar my neighbor, a young bartender, had given to me when he moved out, and it was on that very field that I came to pluck the strings of that guitar for hours on end, every day. If I remember correctly, I was in the third grade at the time. The gentle melody would get muffled and drowned out in the din of the factory, but not before reaching my ears. The experience taught me that, no matter where I was, at whatever time, it was easy to create a small, silent stillness in me, just for myself.

Once in a while my mother would return to the house, and whenever she did she'd prepare a scanty supper in a hurry, and instead of joining us kids at the dining table, she'd get dressed in a flashy outfit and rush back to a bar or to a man again.

By the time I entered high school, she rarely came back home, having settled into a footloose and fancy-free life as the mistress to a president of a real estate company who was many years older than her. Perhaps she finally regretted how bad she looked in the public eye, having her children raised in a shabby dwelling, so—thanks to the connections of the real estate tycoon, her new patron—she got approved for a municipal apartment in Kokura and made us kids move out abruptly, not giving a damn whether our studies were affected in the process.

Although she parted company from this patron after two years or so, she continued, as ever, to get entangled in complicated relations with men, even after I'd moved to Tokyo.

Her wild adventures with men did finally come to an end three years ago though, but it was because she was diagnosed with uterine cancer. Mother was grief-stricken by this sudden illness, but, frankly, neither my younger sister nor I were able to feel sorry for her.

When the disease was discovered the doctor repeatedly insisted on performing a complete hysterectomy. But I suggested radiation therapy and anticancer drugs. I'd decided this was the best option after I turned to a few doctors, whom I personally knew, for their opinions, showing my mother's test results to them. But she wasn't persuaded and went ahead with the operation, putting her faith in the doctor. The operation backfired though, bringing about unfortunate results; her recovery was unexpectedly poor, and with her entire immune system crippled by the invasive surgery, the cancer cells, which were lodged in her abdomen, ended up metastasizing to the liver in less than half-a-year's time.

When it became clear that she'd suffered a relapse, I seriously thought about quitting my job and returning to Kitakyushu to find some other work there so that I could devote myself to nursing my mother, but it wasn't economically feasible, and when I thought about it carefully, I saw that such an urge was, for the most part, meaningless. There was actually no link between me and my mother's death, and I concluded that, in effect, all she could really do was to pass the one or two remaining years of her life alone, in her own way.

I left the nursing to my younger sister and returned to Tokyo, never to return to Kokura again, except the one time when the doctor performed an embolization of the hepatic artery. Mother was discharged three times in the meantime, but only for a short period each time.

As for my not returning to see her, I had no particular reason. I was busy and tired all the time, and just didn't want to return. That was all.

And so, in the end, for these past twenty-nine years, the total number of times my mother and I'd come into direct contact

with each other—not counting my early childhood years—
was terribly negligible. To this day I remain mostly in the dark
about the fifty years of my mother's life, and to a similar extent,
so did my mother about me.

On the day of the funeral, several classmates from my high
school days showed up to offer their condolences. I asked them
to help out with miscellaneous tasks and they saved me a whole
lot of trouble, going to great lengths to complete the tasks. But I
parted from them without having a decent conversation. Many
of them looked into my eyes and nodded slightly, but I found
this gesture, performed in lockstep by pretty much all of them,
quite laughable. After we nailed the coffin shut, we moved in
sync to the melody of the funeral march, loaded the corpse into
the hearse, and left for the crematory.

The crematory was in a valley about forty minutes away
from Kokura, but the rain had graciously let up on the day of
the funeral, July the tenth, letting the cloudless blue sky stretch
out for the first time in a long while. But while everyone was
invariably happy about the fine weather for the sake of the
departed, I didn't feel a thing.

As my mother burned, I sat down on a wide and luxurious
sofa, the kind you might find in a hotel lobby, and let my entire
body bask in the sunlight pouring through a bay window. I got
lost in thought, musing that the rays were declaring an end to
the rainy season, and then dozed off, partly because I'd been
sleep-deprived for the past three days or so.

It then occurred to me that even when Machiko-san died,
the world was awash in a bright light like this, even though
it was the middle of winter then. At that time I was moved
by how the light was truly in character with who she was—
remembering this, I thought Mother, setting out on her journey
to the other world, would surely, just like Machiko-san, become
beautiful and peaceful before returning to heaven.

In the immediate vicinity of the municipal apartment in Kokura, there was a huge temple called Koboji. I'd always pass by this temple on my way to school; beyond its magnificent main gate stood a splendid, old-fashioned *hondo*, the main hall, and on the left-hand side of the spacious temple enclosure there was a cemetery where you could see row after row of gravestones ranging all the way back, and on the right-hand side, there was a tenement house—also antique-looking—which was where the abbot of the Buddhist temple lived.

On my way back home from school, I often used to walk into the precincts of the temple, sit down under a huge camphor tree, and read a paperback book. Koboji's main hall was open to the public, so I occasionally read in there as well. In this hall, where the Sakyamuni Buddha—the principal object of worship—was enshrined in the center, the lights were always bright and it was usually silent and deserted too, so whenever I was in there my mind would magically quiet down. The hall was connected to the tenement house via a covered passageway, and in a Japanese-style room—the size of around fifteen tatami mats—found at its entrance, there was a bookshelf, filled with many books, taking up an entire wall. Not only was it lined with works on Buddhism, but also an entire series of world and Japanese literature titled "Masterpieces of the World" and "Masterpieces of Japan," and the complete works of Soseki, Ougai, Takeo Arishima, Saneatsu Mushanokoji, Soho Tokutomi, the Luha brothers, Yukio Mishima, Takehiko Fukunaga, and Masao Yamakawa.

Having had no choice in those days but to borrow books from my school library or the city library, or buy a paperback sometimes from a secondhand bookstore for a hundred yen a copy, I simply couldn't contain myself when I stood in front of this bookshelf for the first time.

Before I knew it, I'd stepped into the room, found a copy of Baien Miura's *Gengo*, which I'd always yearned to read, and held it in my hands. As I frantically flipped through its pages, I heard a voice behind me and looked back in surprise.

Standing there by the doorway was a petite, middle-aged woman wearing a smile.

And that was Machiko-san.

"You like books?"

I was trying to put the book back on the shelf in a hurry, and I nodded shyly.

"You're the student always reading under that tree over there, aren't you? It's a rare sight nowadays to see someone doing that," she said rather condescendingly. "Please forgive me," I said, returning the book and passing by her side to exit the room when she powerfully caught hold of my arm. I got annoyed and was compelled to confront her round, freckled face. However, looking into her big, dark eyes up close, I quickly realized that she wasn't accusing me at all, or getting angry with me in any way.

"Where are you going in such a hurry?" Machiko-san said, laughing with her mouth wide open.

My association with Machiko-san began that day; it was about one month after I'd moved in, when I was in the tenth grade, in the month of May.

I came to frequent Koboji to pore through the books on that bookshelf, and before long, I was also bringing along my younger sister and doing my homework or watching TV in one of the many rooms of the tenement house, which was surrounded by a large garden; sometimes the two of us would even join Machiko-san to enjoy the dinner she'd prepare.

Machiko-san was the eldest daughter of the temple's abbot, and although she'd been married and had left the temple, she was diagnosed with a debilitating disease and ended up parting from her husband and returning to Koboji, her childhood home. She was forty-five but appeared very youthful, looking about the same age as my mother. Her affliction was Parkinson's disease, and at the time several years had already passed since she'd contracted it, with the light shaking of hands and palsy starting to set in.

Machiko-san, without a doubt, taught me a lot of things. She'd looked after my sister and me for less than three years, in the last years of her life, when her condition was inevitably taking a turn for the worse. So it should've been a harsh time for her, when an onslaught of severe symptoms would surface, robbing her of her physical freedom. But looking back on those years now, I have absolutely no recollection of her suffering in any way. Machiko-san was always lively and gentle. The only recollection I have of her that's in any way related to her disease is the memory of her eating salted loquat seeds often, while reading books. And if I, or my younger sister, wasn't feeling all that well, she'd shake out, with great care, these seeds from a bottle she used to carry, one black seed at a time, and feed them to us.

"Doctors can't cure my disease, you see. But the loquat takes good care of me."

Machiko-san went on to explain how good the loquat was for the body. She told us that she never went through a day without undergoing thermotherapy—a treatment made possible by loquat leaves; she'd make compresses out of the leaves and apply them to her hands and feet, which tended to stiffen. She even showed us, more than once, these loquat leaves fixed on her waist and shoulders. They were literally just leaves stuck onto her affected parts with adhesive tape, so I wondered if they really worked at all. The only other thing that reminded me of her illness was the fact that the rice she used to serve was always unpolished rice, cooked with a mixture of black soybeans, adzuki beans, and *hato mugi*.

The reason why my younger sister had gotten all worked up over treating Mother with alternative medicine was because she'd seen Machiko-san championing it. So, naturally, my younger sister eagerly went about administering a regimen that made use of loquat leaves. But apparently it didn't work.

"Whatever I do, deep down inside, Mom doesn't believe," she told me once, regretting how different Mother and Machiko-san were.

It was Machiko-san who first taught me that humans are born without a purpose.

Being ill herself, Machiko-san was an ardent admirer of Ichiro Tsuneoka, a man who had narrowly escaped from a death due to tuberculosis before devoting himself to relief work for war orphans in Fukuoka.

Oftentimes, she'd talk about him, referring to him as Tsuneoka sensei, and sometimes she'd even hand over a copy of his writings for me to read.

I've forgotten most of it, but there's one part that remains etched in my memory to this day. It's a Q&A titled "Why Are People Born?", which went as follows.

Why Are People Born?

Q: Next spring, I'll graduate from college. I'll be entering society. I'll be entering the world of adults. However, having seen the world made by adults so far, I can't say that I have respect for it. Whenever I see or hear about it through newspapers, radio programs, and magazines, the world seems to be filled with too many sad things and too much nonsense. Dishonest and sly people make their way in the world, and people of high social status throw their weight around, practicing corruption and skillfully getting away with it. It's totally disgusting. Why should people have to go on living in this world, when it's so unfair and underhanded? It absolutely baffles me. What I'd like to ask you is, "Why are human beings born?"

A: Such a question really bothers me. I can't give you an answer.

Q: Why not?

A: Because it's something I don't understand myself. I have no idea why we're born.

Q: What? Even someone like you doesn't know the purpose of being born? Someone who goes about working every day with such zest, such energy?

A: That's right. I don't. I was born without a purpose after all. I came into this world devoid of thought, devoid of power; I didn't wish for a thing, and I didn't seek anything either. I'm sure I was born without intention and without a plan. Therefore, instead of saying that "I was born" I should be saying that "I was made to be born" by some other will than my own. And so you see, I'm not qualified to provide an answer to your question, what my birth was for.

Q: Indeed, I see. I suppose you could then say that I'm also someone who was made to be born. So just to be clear, you're telling me that humans aren't born of their own accord, but are compelled to be born?

A: Yes, that's right. The young philosopher, Misao Fujimura, said, "Life is incomprehensible," before jumping into Kegon Falls and ending his life. He'd gone around asking the question, what's a person's birth for. He'd read books. But he never arrived at any kind of understanding, and so he died, you see. So perhaps you should stop asking me why a person is born, and instead ask me, "Why is a person made to be born, what do I think about that?" If you do I'll be able to offer an answer.

Q: Fine. So why is a person made to be born?

A: So that he or she can grow, probably.

Q: Wait, what? Grow? What makes you say such a thing?

A: It's plain to see that people keep growing. Their minds and bodies, year after year, experience growth. Anything that doesn't grow will fall into ruin and die. Anything that doesn't die will go on to grow. And that's why I primarily believe that a person is made to be born in order to grow. Now, one must consider how one achieves this growth. The answer lies in achieving harmony by synthesizing dual contradictions. After you breathe in, you always breathe out. You ceaselessly continue to do so, even late at night, without ever feeling reluctant about it. You always harmonize these two conflicting actions of inhalation and exhalation. After you eat, you get hungry. After you get hungry, you eat. You wake up, and then you sleep. You sleep, and then you wake up. You repeat these processes energetically, cheerfully, punctually, and, consequently, harmonize. Isn't this how we achieve growth every day? To understand how our human world has grown until now you must see the cycle of birth and death, of death and birth; you must see that life and death are two faces of the same coin. It's taught that the world has been reborn many times prior to arriving at the state it's in today. If you realize this, can you not also then see that there's a road to growth made possible by being made to be born in a place where all dualities collapse? Where a thesis and an antithesis can collide to achieve a wonderful synthesis? The face of a human being always faces outward, toward a distance, does it not? There's no one who has his or her face turned toward himself, you see. When two people talk to each other, the reason why they can reach an agreement is because they're, in effect, two individuals with outwardly looking faces, facing each other. However great or smart a person may be, no one can see his own face all by himself. It's only when he looks into the mirror that he can for the first time gain knowledge of his own face through the reflection that appears there. So without the mirror, even though the face of others will always be visible to him, he'll die without ever having seen his own face. Now, just as you need a reflection to know your own face, you also need a reflection to know your inner self. And the mirror that will give you this reflection of your inner self is religion, I believe. Let me clarify this point with a simple analogy. For instance, let me talk about the daikon, the Japanese radish. If I ask, Oh Daikon, why have you been born, the daikon will answer, "I was born for no reason. I was brought into this world without any purpose, without any intention of my own. My birth was brought about by divine providence. And I was cultivated by humans with the utmost care." That's what the daikon would say. Now, if I were to ask, why do you think you were brought into this world and cultivated, the daikon would likely say, "I was probably brought into this world to be eaten by humans, and the humans seem to have cultivated me for that very purpose. But you may wonder how I can say such a thing? Well, I can because my ancestors, the Clan of Daikons, from generation to generation, have been eaten by humans. Therefore, I believe that I too will most likely be eaten by humans eventually, just as all my descendants will. Yes, I believe that I must have been created and cultivated to be eaten by humans." That is how the daikon would answer. Now, let us assume that the daikon looks into himself and thinks of only his own interests. "My ancestors," he will think, "were also eaten by humans. I too will be eaten before long. My offspring will be eaten too. So come to think of it, my life is wretched and lamentable. The relationship between human and daikon is that of archenemies: we can't co-exist. It would be fair if we'd been eating them too; the score would be even then, but our relationship is one in which only we daikons are consumed. It's absolutely shameful. I must avenge this ancestral injustice and deliver my progeny from this evil; I must take revenge. And so I'll become a terribly bitter daikon. If I become so bitter that the person who eats me will learn a lesson, I'll surely be taking revenge then. However, humans will consequently decide to never again produce a daikon as bitter as me, condemning my offspring to a fate of extinction. And so I think that any point of view that arises from taking only my personal feelings into account can only lead me down the road to ruin. In contrast, what would happen if I took the interests of the other party into account? What if I entertain the idea of letting them live? Without the effort and care expended by humans, after all, we daikons would fail to grow. I believe we'll be eaten and killed off by insects while we're still sprouting. The reason why we fortunately mature into ripe daikons is all due to the fact that we're the fruit of human endeavor. So how can I express my gratitude toward humans? How can I make them happy? Well, to this end, I can become extremely delicious. What's more, I can become a daikon that can become the pride of a family. My seeds will then be sent to an aunt in Oita Prefecture, and even to a cousin in Saitama Prefecture. In fact, my seeds will be sent everywhere. Without wishing, without demanding, I'll have set out on the road to my progeny's prosperity. To live and to die, to inhale and to exhale. To sleep and to awaken. To eat and to become hungry. Myself and others. To let live and to be allowed to live. Everything comes in twos, don't they? And so, I'll let people thrive. I'll let my partner thrive. I'll make them all happy. Make them grow. I'll protect them."

Such thoughts and deeds, I believe, form the core of the ascetic training you need to dedicate yourself to, body and soul, every single day.

In this training, I believe I've found a road where I'm condemned and saved at the same time.

Has what I've been saying served as an answer to the question, "Why have humans been made to be born?" In the end, to devote your entire being to emptying yourself, day after day, so that you may give yourself to others, so that you may forgive them, so that you may help them grow, is the road to achieving your own growth. This is what I believe.

After the bones were picked and put into an urn, the funeral service was over. It was the second time for me to experience *kotsuage*, this ritual using large chopsticks to pick bones out of the ashes. Machiko-san's bones were white as snow and beautiful, but in the case of my mother, her pelvis and ribs were terribly discolored. My younger sister, while picking the darkish bones, was sobbing.

"Poor Momma," she was saying, "your bones are so spoiled by the disease."

But I on the other hand, staring at those same bones, felt that the essence of Mother's life had finally been released from "the skeletal frame that had been holding old age, illness, and death," and had flown away to a world without suffering. After returning to the assembly hall and enshrining the urn on the altar, the *Shonanuka*—the Buddhist memorial service held on the seventh day after a person's death—was performed. Afterward, I went up to the second floor and had some food from a catering service with the relatives and neighbors while exchanging cups of sake with them. The gathering adjourned at seven, and I returned to my childhood home for the first time in a long while. As expected, fatigue weighed heavily on my entire body, so when I arranged my futon alongside my sister's and stretched out on it in the six-mat room that served as a living room, I was immediately overcome by an intense drowsiness. Placing the palm of my hand on my mother's urn by the pillow and rubbing its smooth porcelain surface, I slid, before I knew it, into a deep pool of sleep.

The next morning I awoke at six and stepped outside, but only after getting out of my futon carefully so as not to awaken my sister, who was breathing peacefully beside my futon. As expected, with only a spotty number of commuters outside, the morning was quiet, and just like the day before, the sky was clear with a cool breeze blowing through the area. I headed for the Koboji temple. The gates were already open and the deserted precincts were thoroughly swept. Two years after Machiko-san died, her father, the abbot of the temple, had also passed away, and now the eldest son was serving as his successor.

The giant camphor tree was now dense with dark green leaves, creating a deep, airy shade around its base under the powerful light of the early summer sun.

Inside the main hall, a profound stillness reigned supreme.

I sat on the floor, with my back straight, in front of the statue of Lord Buddha, the Sakyamuni-butsu, whom I hadn't seen in three years, and reported my mother's death, joining my hands in prayer while closing my eyes. I also conveyed the same to Machiko-san.

There was now a charnel house built beside the cemetery, and I intended to deposit my mother's bones there. That way, come summertime, during the Bon Festival, Mother will be able to return to me and my younger sister as a gust of wind, and then blow back there again.

As I recall, there was an incident that occurred on August fifteenth of the year Machiko-san died; it was the last day of the Bon Festival. Although the daily routines of my summer vacation usually involved studying in one of the rooms in the tenement house I'd borrow, the spring exams were near at hand, so I used to head for Koboji early in the morning every day, and study there for the exams, nonstop, until late in the evening. Since Mother couldn't afford to let me take summer courses at a prep school, and since I was among the minority who aimed to get into a national university in Tokyo, in a high school where most chose to attend Kyushu University, I didn't belong to any collaborative study group of friends. Even though my younger sister often used to study together with me, at that time, since we were having the Bon holidays, she was staying over at her relative's house in Kumamoto, so I used to go to Koboji alone. In the daytime though, since the traffic of *danka*—the temple parishioners—who came in to pray was ceaseless, there was no way I could stay in the tenement house, so I resolved to visit the temple late at night and study there until early in the morning.

On the evening of the fifteenth, around ten, when I passed through the main gates and went up to the main hall as usual, I found Machiko-san vacuuming the place alone, with all the doors and windows thrown open. Since the Bon Festival saw people coming and going from early in the morning, it was customary to clean up the main hall at night for several days. When I stepped inside, Machiko-san switched off the vacuum cleaner and beckoned me over. She was standing just around the center of the spacious hall. As I approached her, she took my arm and drew me even closer.

The moment the sound of the vacuum cleaner stopped, a profound stillness ruled the main hall.

"What's the matter?" I asked, but she shushed me, placing her forefinger over my lips and breaking into a smile.

"Naoto-kun, do you feel that?" she whispered.

Standing next to her, I followed her cue and listened carefully while surveying the interior of the main hall with wide-eyed wonder. At first, all I could sense was the jet-black darkness that lay beyond the windows, and the pristine, pin-drop silence of the hall. But after a while, I felt a gentle breeze brush past my entire body, streaming through from the opened door and windows, following a direct trajectory to the two of us standing in the center of the main hall. And this strange wind seemed like it was made up of many thin strands, which kept blowing, one after another, into the hall from the open air outside. Once I started to feel these streams, they even began to whistle in my ears.

"Aren't they marvelous? These winds?" Machiko-san said. "When I clean up every year on the night of the fifteenth, I get so many breezes blowing into the hall like this. But whenever I clean up during the beginning of the month, in the mornings, the winds blow toward the outdoors from inside this hall, you know. The spirits of the people enshrined in this temple, whenever Obon approaches, turn into these soft gentle breezes and return to their hometowns or villages, and when Obon's over, they properly come back here like this. I so wanted you to feel these winds for yourself, Naoto-kun. Frankly, I was waiting all day long for you to come here."

I was listening to Machiko-san's words as if they were coming from somewhere distant. They were accompanied, as in a song, by a magical rhythm. I think we probably stood there for nearly an hour, transfixed in a dream-like state, our entire bodies exposed to the soft breezes that kept blowing in, one after another, entangling us in their wispy, whirling embraces before whooshing past us toward the principal deity at the back.

It was around December of that year when Machiko-san died.

One morning, after she didn't show up for some time, the abbot went to her bedroom and found her lying dead, apparently as if she'd just fallen asleep. According to the physician who had rushed over and examined her, it seemed to be a cerebral hemorrhage, but some suspicion still lingered. Nonetheless, since Machiko-san was the daughter of a historic temple, and since she was also a long-time sufferer of a chronic disease, the police didn't demand an autopsy, so Machiko-san's cause of death was never clearly determined.

My younger sister and I stayed with her constantly, attending her wake and funeral. Her face was peaceful, never losing its smooth radiance for the entire three days prior to the cremation.

"It might be a sin to say that my body's such a bother to me now, but I no longer feel like I really need it all that much." For several months before passing away, Machiko-san often used to talk like that. She also used to say something like, "Lately,

I think I've finally realized what it is to die. You see, to die is to pass through. If you're passing through a small tunnel that's all bumpy and rough going, it's going to be quite painful and uncomfortable, but if the tunnel were all smooth and glossy like porcelain, then it wouldn't be tough at all, right? My body may be in ruin now, but as if to make up for that, I feel like all the bumpy things in the tunnel I have to pass through have disappeared, that the tunnel is surely all smooth by now. And then one day, suddenly, I feel I'll be able to quietly pass through this tunnel and leave for another world."

And just like that, just like those words of hers, she slipped away smoothly from this world, leaving me behind.

After we finished seeing Machiko-san off to the distant yonder, we went back home. My younger sister went to school in the afternoon, but I was on a break, so I spent that day alone. The weather during the three days after she died was so warm and bright that you couldn't believe it was winter. For a while, with my legs under the leg-warming *kotatsu* table, I was vacantly basking in the soft light of the Indian summer shining through the window. And then, when I entered my private room, I closed the curtains and sat down on the bed and—for the only time in all my life—wept so bitterly that I completely fell apart, heart and soul.

Sitting down in the main hall, gazing at the figure of Sakyamuni—its black surface gleaming in the morning light, which was getting brighter by the moment—I thought about what Machiko-san had once said; about how humans and animals, and even stones and flowers, and even the air itself are all like a dream, connected as one, and that the people living today, and the people who have died, and even the people who are about to be born, are all merely manifestations of just one single person called you. I also thought about Ichiro Tsuneoka, who preached the daily asceticism of devoting your heart and soul to letting people thrive, letting your partner thrive, making them all happy, making them grow, and giving them protection; and that to do your best to become empty, day after day, so that you may give yourself to others, so that you may forgive them, and help them grow, is to find yourself on the road to your own happiness. I also thought about the lady Buddhist who wrote that you'll be grateful for everything, if you see that the way you live will be the way you die; that you'll have peace of mind if you see that living with passion is to one day die with passion.

They're all trying to say the same thing, ultimately. However, at the time, even though I appreciated their words, I felt as if I was crouched down with my arms around my knees in a place that was far removed from their state of mind.

In the afternoon that day, I returned to Tokyo. From Haneda I called Mrs. Onishi and informed her of my mother's demise.

At the other end of the line, the missus said, "I feel so sorry, sir. You must be exhausted."

Suspecting that her husband was beside her, I briefly thanked her for her constant support and promptly hung up.

19

THE WEATHER IN TOKYO was fine too. The sea off the coast of
Haneda, visible through the window of the monorail train, was
dazzling, as if sprinkled with powdered glass, but the scenery
on the whole looked rather artificial and cheap. I transferred
to the Yamonote Line in Hamamatsucho, got off at Akihabara,
and then walked up to Iwamotocho Station, a stop on the Toei
Shinjuku Line. The city of Tokyo I saw then, for the first time
in four days, was a maelstrom of crowds; whether inside a train,
or on a station platform, or in the electric district of Akihabara,
which I spotted from the corner of my eye when I was in traveling in the train, it was utter chaos, swarming with people, even
though it was a weekday afternoon. An office worker, a college
student, a high school student in uniform, a foreigner, a mother
holding her small child's hand, a young woman with her hair
dyed a brilliant red, a blond-haired boy holding a musical instrument, a rosy-cheeked, middle-aged man with a tumbler of
cheap sake in one hand, a young man continuously muttering to
himself, a woman in a mourning dress, a police officer, a driver
for a courier service, and all kinds of blue-collar workers—in
effect, people of every stripe imaginable, totally unrelated to
each other—were jostling one another in a disorderly fashion,
filling up empty spaces in countless places.

The sight of this urban tableau, nihilistic and mostly lifeless,
instantly awakened in me a sense of futility, suffocation, and
contempt beyond description. It seemed like you could find
everything here, when in reality there was nothing. Even
if everything was one—as Machiko-san had said—even if

each and every individual in the crowd I saw before me was a manifestation of myself, this oneness was only, in the end, emblematic of a cold alienation.

I reached my apartment around five, filled the bathtub with hot water, and took a bath straightaway. As I soaked in the warm tub, heaving sighs of pleasure over and over again, I could feel several days worth of fatigue melting away in the hot water clouded with bath powder.

From the opened bathroom window, the only thing visible was the rough, gray wall of the rice store next door, but the sunlight, which was still quite luminous, was shining in, freely passing through the tiny gap between two buildings. It then suddenly occurred to me that, via this small window, the trajectory of light was seamlessly connecting me to the celestial heights of the boundless blue sky. With this epiphany, I underwent a radical transformation, and gained a far more intuitive understanding of what Machiko-san was saying, at least to a certain extent.

Machiko-san often used to say, "If you run after only those things you can see, you'll end up falling into despair, no matter what it is that you're going after."

It may indeed be the case that we can't see that the truth of everything you find in the here-and-now lays hidden.

After getting out of the bathtub and getting dressed, my cell phone rang. The call was from Eriko. "Where have you been all this time?"

Come to think of it, we hadn't been in touch at all since Tanabata, the Star Festival. Although my cell phone showed some records of incoming calls from her, I simply wasn't in the mood to answer the phone at the time.

Hearing Eriko's voice, I remembered the promise I made to accompany her to Suwa on Friday the twelfth, which was the next day.

"I'm sorry," I said. "I went back to Kitakyushu, after a

long time, since I was on my long-awaited holiday, you know. Besides, you'd said that you were going to be busy with work this week. I just returned a short while ago."

Since she asked about my whereabouts, I suspected that she must have stopped by my apartment, so I answered her truthfully, believing that it would be useless to lie. Still, I really wasn't up to traveling to Suwa tomorrow; it felt downright tedious.

"How unusual," she said, "you, going back to your home-town."

"I hadn't returned in more than two years, after all. By the way, you called me a few times, right?"

"You had me worried, what with the trip tomorrow and my father and mother looking forward to meeting you."

"I got careless and forgot to take the cell phone along. Sorry about that."

"I started to think that you might have just skipped town to avoid going to Suwa altogether, that you couldn't stand the idea of going there." Although she spoke jokingly, her words had a subtle sting to them.

"Not true," I said. "I wasn't thinking like that at all. I mean, I'm back here now, aren't I?"

"But honestly, you don't have to force yourself, you know. You weren't up to it in the beginning anyway."

I was amazed that she could say such a thing after accusing me of chickening out and telling me that her parents were looking forward to seeing me. But on the other hand, I realized how momentous this trip to Suwa was to her. I didn't have the heart to break a promise, and it also felt like a drag to spend the weekend in the apartment, so despite whatever high hopes she had, whatever she was scheming to carry out, I reconsidered and saw that our relationship wouldn't turn into anything decisive just because of one visit to her parents' home.

In fact, now that I thought about it, traveling with Eriko,

which was something I hadn't done in ages, might be just what I needed at the moment; it would be a perfect diversion.

"Where should we meet tomorrow, and at what time?" I asked.

"I've bought tickets for the Azusa departing from Shinjuku at ten. But if you're tired, we could leave on a slightly later train."

"Right. So we'll rendezvous at Shinjuku then?"

"Yeah, let's."

The prospect of getting up alone tomorrow and then going to Shinjuku didn't thrill me. I was awfully tired for sure. I wanted to sleep together with Eriko, at least for the night.

"Well, in that case," I said, "how about staying the night over at my place tonight?"

"Shall I?" Eriko said, sounding delighted suddenly. I felt somewhat relieved.

"I'll come pick you up in my car. First we can shop for gifts for your folks and then have dinner."

"Got it. I'll see you at the usual place in Aoyama at seven."

"Roger that."

I hung up and glanced at my watch. It was already past six. I changed into my street clothes in a hurry and left the apartment.

When I came back with Eriko after shopping and having dinner, it was past ten. As expected, my body felt heavy and I was also feeling this stinging, mental fatigue, so the two of us slipped into bed at once. Eriko was down to her underwear and I was reading a book while caressing her derrière, when a worry suddenly popped into my head, making me close the book and ask her, "Do you think it'd be all right if we slept together like this when we're over there?"

Eriko closed the magazine she was reading, turned to face me, and said, giggling, "Oh yeah, about that. My bedroom is on the second floor, and my father and mother's is downstairs, you see. After consulting with my mother, I've decided to have you sleep in the guest room on the second floor." Eriko then went on to eagerly explain the many different layouts of her house, tracing the bed pad with her finger and mentioning a series of names of the tourist attractions she planned to take me to, saying that we'd be at one place tomorrow and another on Saturday, all the while driving home the point that the plan was, strictly speaking, "just a plan" before adding that her parents weren't going to accompany us on the Suwa tour, but the four of us would, instead, dine on Saturday at her father's favorite restaurant by the Suwa Grand Shrine.

I was silently listening to the detailed plan she'd arrived at in consultation with her mother, but then I blurted out, "So we're going to be sleeping separately, after all."

"No worries. I'm not going to lock my door," Eriko said, looking into my eyes and laughing mischievously.

"Sounds like I'll be sneaking into your bedroom under cover of night," I said, joining her in laughter, and then asking whether her room had a bed. Eriko nodded.

"Well in that case," I said, "we better make damn sure it doesn't creak too much, or else your father's going to come running up the stairs with a golf club in his hands."

Making Eriko lie on her back, I pressed my body over her and rubbed my slightly hardened thing against the area where the round bone of her abdomen was jutting out. I then said, "See, like this," as I jolted my waist up and down.

"Ew! Stop imagining strange things," Eriko said, as she giggled and wound her arms around my neck and drew her lips closer.

When I pulled my body away from her after she came, she wrapped her hands around my still-erect cock with her eyes closed, as usual, and began to stroke it. I caught her wrist, pulled her hand away, and said, that's not necessary. While I had no particular reason to decline, there was something annoying about the warm, raw texture of Eriko's palms.

Eriko had opened her eyes and was looking into my eyes for

a while, when she suddenly got up and tucked up the blanket that was covering the lower half of my body. She then sat squatting like a frog on the bed, before positioning her large butt toward my head and, after inserting my thing into her mouth, tonguing me with heart and soul. Since she still had a lot to learn, her teeth, as usual, were scraping against the shaft at times, so it wasn't all that great, but since I didn't have much of a choice, I bent forward and rammed the tip of my nose right onto the goosefleshed skin in the crack of her ass and sniffed the sweet and sour scent of a woman, while placing my hands around her slender waist and squeezing it tight. Before long I began to ejaculate into her mouth.

While the tip of my penis touched the inner wall of her mouth and her tongue, a whopping four days' worth just kept rushing out, on and on, like water spraying out from an out-of-control, gyrating hose. This was the first time I came directly in her mouth since we began seeing each other.

Eriko closed her mouth, and with her cheeks puffed up in the way they did whenever she took powdered medicine, she looked my way and smiled before yanking out two tissues and spitting out the contents of her mouth. But as I observed her doing so, she put on a show for me by stirring what was still left with her tongue and swallowing it.

As I gazed at this performance, I wondered why she'd even bother. Even though I'd probably get used to it eventually, I was burdened with the kind of guilt you feel when you happen to see a hobo in the street; and, to my disgust, it was just like being with Teruko Onishi.

Eriko snuggled against my chest and curled up, so I hugged her with all my heart, but deep inside, I was wondering whether she was overdoing it a little, whether she'd lost sight of herself.

20

WHEN WE BOARDED THE Matsumoto-bound limited express train departing at ten in the morning, Eriko recounted many stories about when she was little, growing up in the town of Suwa. She also spoke of her junior high and high school days, including her first crush. She was in the eighth grade and the object of her infatuation was her classmate called Kushida-kun. For their first date, they went to see a movie, a remake of *Jesus Christ Superstar*. Eriko said that she still remembered very well how Kushida-kun, on their way back home, had enthusiastically talked about Aleksandr Solzhenitsyn's work, *Cancer Ward*.

"Whatever happened to Kushida-kun, I wonder," Eriko murmured.

"I'm sure, just like you right now, he must be remembering you, and talking about the same thing to somebody."

"He was a bit like you. I've always had a thing, I guess, for odd people."

Eriko then went on to say that she wanted to hear stories about my childhood days, that she'd never heard me speak that much about them.

"As I told you last time"—I went on to say—"I don't have any proper stories to tell; all I have are memories I don't care to recall. We were terribly poor, and until junior high, I used to dream about one day living in a large house. I used to believe that I could make that happen. That's about it.

"I was bright, though. In fact, so bright that the people around me used to be amazed. When I was around three, I was the kind of cheeky kid who memorized Sir Arthur Conan Doyle's *The Lost World* in its entirety."

And then I recited an opening passage of the book, which I still remember today.

"My heart was pounding, as I approached Professor Challenger's living room. If he found out that I was a journalist from the *Daily Gazette* . . . Well, plenty of reporters have already suffered serious injuries, having been punched or pushed from staircases by the professor. When I knocked on the door, an ox-like voice answered back from inside."

I stopped reciting there, and said to Eriko, "By the way, your father's voice doesn't sound like an ox's, does it?"

"Relax," Eriko said, laughing. "My father is a mild-tempered man, and, besides, his room is on the first floor.

"But it's just so incredible!" she went on. "How on earth could you hold all that inside your head for nearly thirty years? I mean, just how does your head work anyway? I've always wondered about that, you know. I've always found it miraculous."

"As I've been saying for some time now," I replied, shrugging, "there's nothing to it—I'm not super-talented, nor do I have some sort of superpower, and it's not as if I tried to memorize all that, you know."

"So it comes to you naturally, doesn't it, this ability to commit to memory? To most people, that's incredible, and enviable."

"No, it doesn't really come to me all that naturally. It's more like an obsession I've had since I was a child; a compulsion, if you will, to memorize anything, and I haven't been able shake it off to this day. What I think is happening is that whenever I memorize, just like any other person, my brain cells are working extra hard, and end up even getting fried. But in my case, I've probably become desensitized."

"Obsession?" Eriko said dubiously.

"It's not as serious as it sounds."

Noticing Eriko's searching eyes, I immediately regretted the trifling remark I'd just blurted out. Until then, I hadn't breathed a word about that to a soul, and it was the first time I'd ever even hinted at it so plainly.

When I stayed silent and averted my gaze to the view outside the window, Eriko suspended her line of questioning and turned her eyes, too, toward the view of the sprawling, lush green rice fields outside.

While staring at her graceful profile, I felt, for some reason, strange and wonderful, as if my heart, deep down inside, was bubbling with joy. I was reminded once again of the gap I'd felt between her and me when the two of us were returning from President Nakagaki's wake. It then occurred to me that I had to get closer to her—and no one else—in my own fashion, at my own pace, however insufficient or flawed the attempt may turn out to be in the end.

The look of happiness, of blissed-out fulfillment clearly shining out of her face at that moment was further amplifying those thoughts reeling in my mind. I felt a certain kind of responsibility, a kind that was unprecedented in my life. It wasn't unlike the feeling that made me want to burst into tears when I was playing with Takuya by the river—the feeling of being wanted.

"When I was little, there was one time when Momma had left me behind," I caught myself saying, unawares. For the first time in my life I was attempting to confide to a soul a part of my past that I hadn't even disclosed to my sister, or even to Machiko-san.

Eriko slowly turned her face toward me, and watched me in silence.

"My mother abandoned me once."

Now that I was recounting, I decided my words should have a more precise impact, so I repeated the same thing. Nevertheless, I wasn't satisfied; I felt I hadn't said enough, so I fine-tuned further.

"That woman dumped me."

I was then inwardly surprised that these words—the very same words that used to freeze my heart and turn my world into a bleak, black-and-white nightmare the moment I uttered them to myself—failed to have much of an impact when I said them in front of another person for the first time.

I realized, unexpectedly, that I was calm. Perhaps it was Momma's death that was bringing about such composure in me.

"I was still two. Momma had just been abandoned by my father, and probably had no idea what to do; she was just a little over twenty then, and was very child-like herself, after all. I think it was just around this time of the year. Momma and I boarded the train together and headed for the town of Hakata, where we were going to have fun at the zoo there; that huge one called Minami Doubutsuen. In those days I used to like animals, and when Momma told me that she'd take me along to a place where I could find plenty of real-life elephants, zebras, giraffes, tigers, and lions, I got so excited the night before that I couldn't sleep. Once there, I was ecstatic, watching all those real animals at the zoo; so much so that at first I didn't even realize that I'd actually been left behind. I remember it well. There was this monkey pavilion, and I was tirelessly watching the monkeys, leaning against a low fence. Momma then said, 'Nao-chan, Mommy's going to buy some ice cream, so you stay put here, all right?' I hardly gave her an answer, I think, since I was mesmerized by the sight of the monkeys.

"After I realized Momma wasn't returning, for six whole days after that realization, I can't tell you how much I regretted not having said, 'I'll go with you too.' I kept telling myself that Momma had gotten separated from me because I was an idiot, because I was careless, and because I was a bad boy. To a child, it's inconceivable that a parent would abandon him, you know. An employee of the zoo came, took me to his office, asked my name, and kindly made an announcement over the PA system, over and over again. You know, the kind that goes, 'We have a lost boy who is looking for his mom. He's two years old and he's wearing a blue shirt. You can find him at our office. Thank you.' Listening to this announcement, I frantically asked the employee to also mention my name over the PA system, telling him that my name was Naoto. You know why, right? Momma might not realize it's me, I thought at the time, if the only description she hears is a boy of around two wearing a blue shirt. And if she ended up taking home by mistake a different boy of around two years old wearing a blue shirt, why, I'd never be able to get back home, right?

"Evening came, the police arrived, and the atmosphere grew stranger and stranger when I was escorted into a police car and driven out of the zoo. Watching from the rear, I saw the front gates of the zoo receding into the distance. I sobbed and began to whine. Because, once I was away from the zoo, Momma would never be able to find me ever again. Still, the police car continued to travel down a pitch-black road unknown to me, and nothing was making any sense to me anymore. Mother used to scold me, after all, that if I left her side without permission, I'd get kidnapped. So I thought that I had, at last, been kidnapped, that because I'd been a bad boy, that day of reckoning had finally come. In retrospect, though, I believe I was taken to the lodging facilities of a children's welfare center. A kind-looking, middle-aged woman was waiting for me there, where I was served a meal; she even let me have some juice and cake. I was then taken into a tatami room, where I was persistently asked about my name and where I lived. But I was just two, so I couldn't remember my surname. The lady nevertheless kept asking me eagerly, 'Naoto-kun, what is your last name?' I'm sure she was thinking that, once she knew my full name, she could look me up in the public records of residential addresses or the family register. But I didn't have any idea what a surname was. In the end, for six whole days, I couldn't recall my last name, Matsubara.

"How did you get here? Did you take the train? Ride the bus? From which station? How long did it take? What kind of house do you live in? Who'd you come with? What's your mother's name? Your father's? I couldn't answer a single question the first day. On the second day, though, I began to calm down a little. As the lady drove me to various stations, I was able to tell her the color of the train I'd taken, and even that the name of the station I'd gotten off at was Hakata Station. But even in my child's mind, I understood that such recollections were worthless as clues. The next day, in addition to the lady, a young man came, and he drove us around Hakata's downtown area. When I burst into tears, the two would say things like, 'Naoto-kun, you don't have to worry. Your mother's going to come get you for sure. There are other kids like you who get lost sometimes, you know. But all their mothers come pick them up in a day or two.' But on the fourth day, both of them stopped saying things like that, and even I understood that my mother wasn't going to come pick me up, that this wasn't my mother's problem, but my own. By that time, even the lady and the young man seemed to have mostly given up. All they wanted me to do now was to tell them whatever I could remember about my home, my parents, my neighborhood, my friends. When night came, I went into the same room of the same building and slept with the lady, but she went to sleep before I did. So, paying close attention to her breathing, I quietly slipped out of the futon to search my memory, in the pitch-black room, for any flimsy threads of recollections. I was so desperate to remember that I thought my head might catch fire. I tried to remember the name that came after my first name; the name of the town I lived in; the name of the station where I got on the train; the name of the bus stop where I got on the bus to go to this station. By the morning of the fifth day, I'd remembered some of these things. While my surname remained a blank, I remembered that the station was Tabata, that the train was Kumamoto-bound, that the bus was a Nishitetsu bus, and that the bus stop was Asao or Asau, or some such thing. But it still wasn't enough, I thought; I had to remember the name of some key place, I thought.

"Around noon on the fifth day, I borrowed paper and pencil from the lady because I wanted to remember the name of the small park Momma used to take me to every day—of course, I didn't remember the name, but I had a faint recollection of the nameplate at the entrance to the park, and, more importantly, of the kanji characters inscribed in this nameplate. The one place I used to visit every single day was this park, after all, where I'd catch sight of the nameplate throughout the year.

"Although I made mistakes over and over again, I wrote the character I saw in my mind's eye. Imagine that! A kid who's just two, writing a kanji character! It was the first character I ever wrote in my life. Incredible, don't you think? Bottom line, I learned that a human being could always do something for himself to get out of a scrape, no matter what kind of a situation he found himself in. The character was *hikari,* the kanji character for light. When I finished writing it I was sure I was right. The place where I always used to play was a park named Hikari Park. Of course, I had no idea at the time about how to read the character of Hikari at all."

When I finished talking, I was unconsciously looking down. For a while I relished the time that gently flowed by, as if time was something chewable. I'd just spoken something I swore I'd never whisper to a soul as long as I lived. I wasn't sure anymore, though, about how accurate it was. Up to what point was the memory fact? From which point in the story did my reconstruction of the events—pieced together after growing up—possibly begin? Nonetheless, I was confident that my memory was probably intact, that it was probably, in fact, all factually correct. This was because, after the incident, I'd accumulated memories of everything that followed it, without losing much detail. That one night in July, when I'd concentrated so intensely that I thought my head would catch fire, something had definitely transformed inside me, and evolved. Since then, unless sleep deprivation or heavy drinking inhibited me, I became incapable of forgetting moments and events, no matter how negligible they were. I came to believe that I must never, ever forget about anything; it wasn't a matter of honing my intellectual capabilities or becoming more perceptive to enhance the quality of my life or some such thing. My survival depended on it. To me, the act of forgetting was potentially critical and life-threatening, and it was out of the question for me to remain passive and entrust my life to the whims and caprices of surrounding circumstances. After all, if there was anything I learned from that little episode of abandonment, it was that if I did forget, I'd immediately suffer a merciless betrayal and lose everything.

I lifted my face and looked at Eriko. Her face appeared hardened, as if she'd lost all emotion.

"And so that's why *The Lost World* is etched in my mind in its entirety. Come to think of it, the book's title, and even the name of the park, Hikari Park, is quite ironic, isn't it? Speaking of Hikari Park, as expected, there was only one to be found in Tobata. So on the sixth day, early in the morning, I was taken to this Hikari Park, where my temporary guardians questioned the mothers who were there with their children and found out where I lived.

"When Momma opened the door to the filthy, one-room apartment, she saw me standing there, accompanied by the staff members of the welfare center, and glared, her sleepiness blown away. As for what happened next, I really don't care to talk about it."

Like most decent people listening to such a story, Eriko had her eyes fixed on me, the teller, but she didn't seem uncomfortable, trying to find the right words to say. Instead, she was reacting to my words calmly, in silence.

"After this incident," I went on, "I became firmly convinced at first that there was nobody who could ever protect me but myself, that to survive in such a terrible world as this, self-protection was essential, not just for me, but for everybody, just like Honoka's mother used to say to Honoka. But eventually, I came to believe that such a thing was a downright lie. Because I never again could consider myself so important as to merit any protection in particular. Don't you agree? I'm a human being who was readily abandoned by his own mother, the very person who gave birth to him, you know. How can there be any significant value attached to such a human being? And when I was finally old enough to understand things, I began to wonder why it is that I was unable to forget about that incident. If I could completely forget about it, I could become much happier, I thought. But then again, I thought, there must be something wrong with my personality, something so rotten to the core about it that it made me doggedly hold on to that memory and suffer such an intense grudge that I could never open up my heart to Momma. But a little while later, I realized that even such a notion was wrong. A human being can never look away, no matter what, from anything that's essential to his life. For example, it's absolutely impossible to forget, no matter how much you keep deluding yourself, an incident like being abandoned by a parent, or the fact that you're going to die someday. In the end, once a person with my kind of roots gets wrapped up in himself, he begins to get baffled about why he's alive. If I try to attach great importance to myself, the moment I begin to try, I get terrified. And that's why when my younger sister was born, after I entered grade school, I had the idea of taking her away from Momma, and for the next ten years or so, until my sister grew up, I resolved to dedicate my life to her well-being. That way, I'd be able to go on living without being reminded of how worthless I was, right? I told you once, didn't I? That I didn't believe in families? You see, that's because, in my eyes, the so-called ordinary family you see every day isn't a family at all. For a mother to truly be a mother, for a father to truly be a father, for an older brother to truly be an older brother, and for a younger sister to truly be a younger sister, each of them has to make drastic sacrifices for the other. That, I believe, is key. That, I believe, is what makes a family a family.

"Just as Kohei died for Raita, and just as Raita had become convinced that a part of him too, after experiencing Kohei's death, had died, a person should be connected to another in just such a profound way; two people should be swept away into the depths of each other's lives. But in the bonds that form between humans, things like equality, respect, or sacrifice simply can't exist. The same can be said of romantic relationships, right? What's important isn't loving or cherishing someone. Such acts aren't enough for a human being to resolve the heart of the matter of life. While love is about totally ruining yourself so that you could just live for your lover—so that you could just live inside her—nobody's really capable of doing such a thing. Regardless of how passionately two lovers love each other, regardless of how much a husband and wife adore each other, there will inevitably come a time when lovers will lose each other. Now, when that happens, that is, when one lover dies, do you think his sweetheart will be so bereft she'll also die to follow him into the hereafter? Have you ever heard of any such thing actually happening? I, for one, haven't, not even once. But that's how it is for all of us; it's only natural. This is because no person ever has any right to really do something about his life, which is something that's been bestowed on him, you see. If you start thinking that you could really do something about your life by dint of your own will and effort, this fragile and fleeting flower called love, far from blooming into full glory, will immediately wither away and die. In a world where each and every human being believes that his life is his own, there can only prevail violence, discrimination, domination, and subjugation, I believe. Just as you see in this world right now."

We arrived in Suwa sometime past noon and boarded—as per Eriko's plan—the pleasure boat that cruised around Lake

Suwa. Standing on the deck and resting against the rails on the side of the ship, we were gazing at the surprisingly rough, white slipstream trailing in the ship's wake, when Eriko suddenly spoke under her breath. "I've finally done it, haven't I? I've dragged you all the way down to the place I was born."

Although what she said had nothing to do with the story I'd recounted in the train, her words evoked a considerateness that was very characteristic of her. I gazed at Eriko's profile, as she took in the dazzling view of the lakeside.

"But," she went on, "it's been pretty much a one-way street, hasn't it? It's always just been me chasing you. Strange, isn't it? I mean, for all I know you might be really annoyed with me, after all."

Out of habit I felt like telling her, "If you feel like that, even just one tiny bit, why do you continue to chase me?" but I quickly reconsidered, thinking that the unease Eriko was trying to convey wasn't anything so ordinary as that. No, what was making her anxious was probably, in reality, the fact that I was detached; if I was hardly troubled by whatever she did, by the same token, I wasn't happy either.

Without answering her I shifted my gaze toward the faintly misty Yatsugatake Mountains, lying beyond the lake.

"Let's go," Eriko said. "The wind's chilly."

Upon Eriko's further urgings we returned to the spacious cabin with a large panoramic window. Thereafter, my mood sank. It was in such a despondent state that in the evening I was shown to her huge two-story home with a large garden and presented to her parents, who were awaiting my arrival.

21

ERIKO'S FATHER WAS THE proprietor of a company that subcontracted the production of meters for a precision-machine maker based in Suwa. In effect, he was a second-generation president of a subcontracting firm employing around three hundred people, and as such, his company was considered to be a major one in Suwa. The moment I saw him, I thought his face was the kind that anyone would find amiable. At the dinner table, where I sat across from him, the first thing he said was that he'd graduated from the same university as I had, and therefore was my college senior. For a while, he wistfully talked about his memories of the Hongo area in the late 1950s, mentioning the names of several diners, shoe shops, tailors, and bars before asking if I knew any of them.

I didn't. "I haven't heard of or seen any of them."

The father looked glum for a moment; he must have thought that I was a buzzkill.

"Well, I suppose that figures. These days, there must be so many places where you can have fun over there. Back in my day, it was just after the postwar period and there was no money to spend and no places to go, so I really couldn't have fun even if I wanted to. Once in a while these places popped up, where they'd serve cheap booze to students, but they used to get so crowded there was hardly elbow room in them."

"Yukio Mishima, whom Eriko likes," I replied, "also touches on those days in one of his essays. If I'm not mistaken, he was born at the end of the Taisho era, so he belongs to the generation just above yours, Fukasawa-san. Anyway, he said that in his case, the dire circumstances had worked in his favor. They spurred him to devote himself to literature, and so he was happy. But he was angry with the students of later years—meaning, of course, the students of the Showa 40s, or the late sixties and early seventies—complaining that they had no passion. He ended the essay, though, with the utterly dull conclusion that youth, in any age, is bereft of idealism."

The conversation came to a halt and I poured myself some beer and drank two or three glasses in a row, at the same time marveling at the splendid-looking sofa, sideboard, chandelier, and photorealistic paintings hanging on the wall in the spacious living room adjacent to the dining room. The coffee table was lined with plenty of food, which Eriko's mother had apparently spent half a day preparing.

"But it's rather rare," Eriko's father said, "to see someone advancing into journalism from law school."

I repeated what I'd already explained to Eriko. It wasn't particularly because I was interested in joining the mass media, or because I liked books. I didn't mind working anywhere, actually, but I'd heard during a certain lecture, from an assistant professor of literature, who was frequently contributing to a business magazine in those days, a rumor that the company I'm working for now pays the highest salary in Japan. And so I ended up taking the company's employment examination. That's really the only reason.

"Hmm, I see," the father said, sounding impressed, before going on to ask, "I don't mean to pry, but how much are you making?"

"While it's only been eight years since I joined, I make a little north of ten million yen a year."

"That's great!" The father then began to lament that the manufacturing industry was struggling to survive due to the current recession, and that his own company was bearing the brunt of the bad times. We then talked for a while about the economic relationship between Japan and the United States. In the course of this discussion, I elaborated a little on the concept of a key currency; about the fact that Phileas Fogg, the main protagonist of *Around the World in Eighty Days*, had the advantage of being able to shop around anywhere in the world with Bank of England notes; about how in 1931 that became impossible, when the pound abandoned the gold standard; about the emergence of America; about the war; about the story of how Mr. Joseph Dodge talked down GHQ's New Dealers; about the fact that the dollar against the yen was thirty yen weaker when Dodge and Hayato Ikeda fixed the exchange rate in the course of a confidential talk; about the trap of overseas credit obligations a hegemonic nation always falls into; about the contradictions of America's "guns-and-butter policy" during the Vietnam era; about the Nixon Shock in 1971 and the inside story behind the Plaza Accord that transpired when Noboru Takeshita was the Minister of Finance; about the surprisingly tarnished reputation the former vice finance minister for international affairs, who was nicknamed Mr. Yen, suffered within the ministry; about the fact that the financial authorities have absolutely no faith in the role of the Financial Services Agency, with their current plan for administrative reform built on the erroneous assumption that taking away the right to draw up budgets would help reinforce cabinet functions; and about the fact that, at present, it was pointless to believe in the scenario that, with the advancement of interbank trading, the junk loans of Japan could trigger a worldwide recession, because the United States, for these past several years, has been planning the construction of a system that could prevent any financial panic from occurring, even if the Japanese economy were excluded from the global money market; and about the fact that this system was nearing completion already.

The father was listening to me with enthusiasm, and he, in turn, gave a detailed account of the recent achievements of his company and about the price fluctuations of his products. Eriko and her mother, who were on the sidelines, so to speak, looked relieved, seeing that the two of us had finally started to warm up to each other. However, I didn't find Eriko's father's stories all that interesting, so, in fact, I was hardly listening to him at all.

We finished eating and moved to the living room. The father fetched a vintage brandy, saying that it was special liquor, and poured some of it into my glass. As expected, he was seated in front of me, appearing quite relaxed.

"Well, well," he began, "I'm ashamed to tell you this, but last night I wasn't able to sleep that well. When Eriko came home for New Year's and suddenly mentioned you—saying, 'Daddy, there's someone I really want you to meet'—I was dumbfounded, to tell you the truth. If I may say so, that's because I've always thought that this daughter of mine wasn't the type to easily fall for someone."

The father then said, with a tip of his glass, "But I'm absolutely relieved she's fallen for someone like you." He smiled, as if he were slightly embarrassed. Then the mother, who was seated next to him and who hadn't talked that much, added while nodding, "Ordinarily, we'd have invited you here only after our Eriko had first paid a visit to the home of your parents." Just like Eriko, her mother had very pleasing features. "But perhaps because Eriko is our only child, whom we had in our late years, we too, as her parents, may have become rather spoiled, and have therefore ended up reversing the order of the protocol, just for the sake of allaying our curiosity. Please accept my humblest apologies for such an impropriety."

In reaction to this expected development I took a look at Eriko, but she had her face turned toward her parents, with a glass of brandy in her hand. I was silent for a while and waited for the mother to go on, but she was only smiling without appreciating the state of mind I was in; I was at a loss as to how

I should respond to this demure mother. I considered telling her that she was too kind, that she was making much ado about nothing, but such words didn't seem suited for the occasion. It was obvious why Eriko's father and mother were waiting for me to show up today, and I too had half-acknowledged the reason before coming here. So essentially, I had no choice but to meet their expectations. Everything is determined by circumstances. That's life. If they wished it, so be it; I didn't particularly mind settling down with Eriko, and in reality, it was nothing earth-shattering. When I thought of it like that, I felt at ease, at least for the time being. In order to be honest with yourself, you need to just let yourself go, like smooth running water. That's all there is to it.

"Please don't trouble yourself over such a thing," I said. "I don't even have parents, after all."

Eriko's parents looked at me at the same time, surprised.

"How old were you?" the father asked without hesitation.

"I lost my father when I was a year old. Apparently he left the house, abandoning my mother and me. Since then I've never met him. As for my mother, she died just this Monday."

Now it was Eriko who was surprised, growing paler by the moment.

"When you say Monday, do you mean this Monday?" the father asked, after staring at me for a while with a dumbfounded look.

"That's right. She had uterine cancer and was being hospitalized and released repeatedly for nearly three years, but it was no use in the end."

Eriko's father was at a loss for words, wearing a weird expression, and when he turned to his daughter, as if in a panic, he asked, "You didn't know?"

Eriko attempted a nod, but it turned out more like the jerky gesture of a sudden hiccup. The mother, covering her mouth with her hand, raised her refined-sounding voice to say, "Oh my!"

"You were telling me you'd returned home to Kyushu, but that's why you . . ." Eriko's voice was trembling. The disgusted look she had on her face at the time made her look just like her father, I thought.

Without pausing, I began to convey all the interesting details about the funeral, about my funny classmates who rushed over to help, but the three of them weren't even nodding. They had fallen silent, sitting there with their probing eyes transfixed on me.

When I finished talking Eriko's father offered a formal condolence and said, "I see, but you speak of your mother as if she were unrelated to you."

I wondered what to do, but couldn't think of anything other than to laugh out loud and ask for another glass of brandy, if it was all right.

The father poured the liquor, fell silent again, and then let out a moan before asking, "So you didn't like your mother then?" He locked his eyes on mine, looking like a vile drunkard with his cheeks all red. Deep down, I was quite angry about his rude question. You don't often find people who dislike their mother. If you do, you'll most certainly find a legitimate reason behind their animosity.

"Why do you ask such a thing?"

"But I'm right, aren't I? Otherwise, how could you come all the way here to meet us, the parents of your fiancée, just five days after your mother died?"

I immediately tried to tell him, in a loud voice, that he was an ass. But I felt Eriko's piercing gaze on me, and when I turned to her, she was subtly shaking her head to the side, again and again, with a desperate plea in her eyes. I closed my mouth, looked up at the ceiling, fixed my eyes on the light of the chandelier, and thought hard about something else to say.

"I was just feeling lonely," I finally said, without much thought, in a feeble tone, sighing. "Is that wrong? Is it un-reasonable to have such an emotion?"

As expected, something hard inside the father and mother dissolved rapidly, all at once.

"I fear my curiosity got the better of me, and so I ended up rather rudely asking you such a strange thing. Please forgive me," the father continued. "We parents, as human beings, are such inferior creatures, aren't we? We wonder, rather foolishly, whether someone's capable of truly loving our daughter, when he can't even love his own blood relation. It's silly, isn't it?"

"I fully understand your feelings, sir," I responded. "But you know, Fukasawa-san, I've always thought that people with strong, affectionate ties to their blood relations tend to be surprisingly cold to others."

"Come to think of it, you could be right," Eriko's mother chimed in blandly.

We went on to kill time looking at photos of Eriko's childhood days, and when it was past eleven, Eriko and I went upstairs.

22

In the ten-tatami mat room reserved for me on the second floor, the bed had already been made.

I let my body sink into the soft and fluffy futon, set the alarm on my cell phone to go off two hours later, and then fell asleep.

Within those two hours I had a brief dream. I was seated on a sofa, wearing a black, double-breasted suit, in a large room that resembled a school principal's office. For some reason I had a red bow tie on as well.

I heard knocking on the door.

When I said, "Come in," a mother and her child entered, ushered in by a middle-aged woman wearing a uniform-like blue smock. The face of this woman was indistinct, but the mother and child brought in were Tomomi and Takuya.

"Principal," the middle-aged woman called me. At that moment I realized I was the principal of a nursery school. I then wondered—in the dream—whether this woman was one of the childcare specialists working there.

I went on to understand, from the explanation the woman offered, that we were going to have Takuya under our care from tomorrow, and that Tomomi had dropped in to pay a courtesy visit. I urged the three of them to have a seat on the sofa, and then went on to elaborate at length to Tomomi the particular rules of the nursery school, of which I had no recollection after I woke up.

Subsequently, the thread of my talk, which also remains hazy in my mind, led into a discussion about the circumstances of

Tomomi getting separated from her husband and consequently having to work herself. Upon hearing Tomomi say "divorce," the middle-aged childcare specialist interjected by turning to Takuya with a smile and saying, "Oh my, what a bad mother!" I most certainly saw Tomomi change her friendly expression for a moment to scowl at the childcare specialist.

Tomomi then stared at my face, as if to blame me for the remark made by the woman, before saying in a renewed, affable tone, "And so, Principal, I was told by this teacher to be sure to come pick up Takuya by half past four, but is there any way you could somehow extend this to six?"

"Let's see now," I answered, "in your case, your child is under our care from seven in the morning. And taking into account the type of work you do for an insurance company, we've determined that half past four is an appropriate time for you to pick up your child."

"But that gets in the way of my work. There are many customers who visit in the evening, and since I just started this job, I have a hard time creating specs. Couldn't you please somehow allow me to pick up my child at six, just like other parents?"

I was bothered by Tomomi's imposing manner. "Nonetheless, there are rules in place, which we must observe."

"What's the big deal? Are you biased against single moms?"

"No, that's not it, but the size of our staff of childcare specialists who clock in from the morning is modest, and our hands are actually tied; we're only barely managing to run the school right now. But setting aside such reasons, let me point out that this divorce of yours, if I may say so, was entirely up to you and your husband, so you've brought this upon yourself; you're suffering the consequences of your own misdeed. For this reason, you really can't expect everything to go your way, and more importantly, you ought to be thinking a little more about Takuya's welfare."

In reaction to these off-the-cuff remarks, Tomomi blew up and began to rant with a ferocious intensity. "I'm having a tough time making ends meet. Working only until four isn't enough for me to raise my performance grade. And since I don't have any relatives in this town, there's no one around to take care of my boy in the evening. Right now I'm trying to get by with only around 150,000 yen a month—that's 100,000 yen in salary and 50,000 yen in welfare payments. You public servants have no idea how hard it is for someone like me! Just the rent sets me back fifty, sixty thousand yen, and food and clothing expenses are no joke either. You can't lump my household together with households where both parents work."

Tomomi's eyes filled with tears, as she went on to give a breakdown of her monthly expenses and complain about the fact that her ex-husband hadn't been sending her any alimony.

Although I was listening to her story in a daze, I was able to appreciate how difficult it was for a single mother to live on around 150,000 yen a month in this city, so I was seized by pity, and, in the end, simply overcome by the sight of this rather attractive mother, in the bloom of her womanhood, going to pieces in front of me.

Once Tomomi's impassioned speech came to an end, I removed a wallet from the inside pocket of the double-breasted suit, pulled out all the ten-thousand-yen bills inside it, folded them, and then held them out before Tomomi's eyes.

"Well then," I said, "please take this money to support yourself this month. But in exchange, you need to pick up your son at half past four. If you do, you'll see this money again next month."

Even before I was finished, I could see the color draining from her face, as she bit her lip and turned ghastly. Strangely enough, I was thinking, in the dream, that this was the first time I'd seen Tomomi look that way.

Tomomi's enraged face filled my field of vision, as if in a freeze-frame, and in that instant, the folded bills in my hand were knocked out of my grip by her right hand, and my cheek slapped fiercely. Without understanding why I had to meet such a terrible fate, I let out a groan, unable to endure the stinging pain in my cheek.

And then I awoke, crying out loud as I sprang up from my futon bed on the floor.

My cell phone's alarm was going off.

I was sweating bullets and my whole body felt hot as I reflected on how terrible the nightmare was.

Turning the light on, I took out a blue towel from the bag I'd kept by the pillow and stuffed it underneath my pajama top to swab up the sweat.

While catching my breath, I wound the towel around my neck and crossed the edges before tucking the towel under the collar. I sat cross-legged on the futon and surveyed the room, feeling the stillness in the air. Exposed to the coolness of this air, my body temperature gradually lowered. There was a calendar hanging on the wall, featuring a photograph of mountains taken by Yoshikazu Shirakawa. The peaks of a tall mountain range of some distant land, awash in the vermillion glow of the sunset sky, were looking down on me.

I was then struck by the notion that I was experiencing this room I found myself in at the moment, and the current flow of time itself, in the abstract, in much the same way I was experiencing the mountain range of a foreign land in the abstract, never being subject to the terribly cold winds that must have been raging across the summits, where the air must have been incredibly thin. This surreal sense of pristine isolation, which made me believe that everything and anything around me has never really existed from the beginning, was, as always, leading me to a peaceful place.

The bottom of the photograph was lined with the dates of July and August. I looked at July. I wondered what today's date was. Since I believed it was a Friday, my eyes landed on the twelfth. I then wondered when it was that mother died and scanned leftward until I began murmuring in my heart that it was the eighth. Deep inside, I chanted July eighth several times and suddenly realized something. I couldn't believe that I hadn't realized it until this very moment.

An intense wave of emotion surged in my heart.

At that moment, I wanted to cry for my mother. And finding myself with this yearning, finding how instinctual this thing called sorrow was, I wanted also to cry for myself.

When I witnessed my mother's death, no, when I was informed of my mother's cancer, no, ever since I became aware, as a son, of the all-too-animalistic sentient life-form known as the mother, someone has always been attempting to sadden me. Until now, I'd continually withstood, as much as possible, the pressure to bow to this outrageous demand. Oh, what great pains I had to take to protect the childish truth that grieving for somebody is nothing more than grieving for yourself.

Staring at the eight on the calendar, I saw that there's nothing sadder than the death of another person. It's unbearably sad, not just for the deceased, but for anyone else. In the end, however, grieving death can only lead you to sin. Someone who relentlessly grieves the death of another is a person who stands in abject fear of his own death. It's this fear that creates a shameless human being, capable of hurting others without compunction.

I'm sure Mother must have had her own demons. Take that day she abandoned me; Momma must have had her own troubles and worries, while being driven to despair and sorrow. Such things were obvious even in the eyes of the two-year-and-eight-month-old boy that I was at the time. And the more I grew, the clearer these things became inside me. Still, why should I grieve over her predicaments, concerns, despair, and sorrow? The more I grieved over Momma's sorrow, the more I'd then have to grieve over, sympathize with, and feel pity for myself—as if I were a total stranger to myself. In this world, there's no greater sin than whining self-pity, than whining self-commiseration.

My heart was about to explode, and I kept soothing it by clenching my fists and pulling my abs in tight. I gasped to push back the tears brimming in my eyes, ready to gush out at any moment. Chanting like a mantra the date, "July eighth, July eighth," I managed to quell the storm raging in my head, and in a matter of only a few minutes, I regained my composure.

I picked up my cell phone and looked at the time. The display read July 13, 1:25 a.m. I stood up, opened the fusuma sliding door, walked across the corridor, and stood before the door to Eriko's room. I considered knocking, but simply turned the knob instead.

I immediately realized there was no one there in that unlit room which I'd been shown into before going to sleep; it was colorless and lined with large bookshelves, jam-packed with books of paintings and works by Yukio Mishima and Kenzaburo Oe. I'd stood next to Eriko and removed several books from there, and each and every one of them were in such mint condition they gave the impression that they'd never been cracked open and thumbed through. Nonetheless, I imagined Eriko breezily pacing through all these great many words in her school days. After a closer examination, though, I noticed yellow asterisks lightly penciled in here and there. When I asked what these marks were for, she answered that they were for flagging the phrases she used to copy into her diary, which she'd been keeping since her junior high school days. I didn't understand the rationale behind such a habit; was she thinking to use her diary one day as source material she could mine for something she wanted to write? I asked her as much. "I have no such talent," Eriko replied. "I just want to retain them in my memory forever."

I went over to the bed by the window and touched the sheets, but they were cold. I then left the room to search for her.

I checked the Japanese-style room next to Eriko's and then the spacious Western-style room next to mine before deciding to go downstairs.

At the bottom of the stairs was a large vestibule, where a marvelous screen made of Japanese cypress stood.

Right beside this vestibule was a drawing room for visitors, where I saw, when I'd been shown into the room in the evening, an antique white leather sofa, a large glass table, and a genuine Laurencin painting hanging on the wall. Next to the stairs on the other side was an old-fashioned maid's quarters, which had been turned into a storage room. At the front of the drawing room was a tatami-floored room, in which an upright piano and a Victor component stereo of a bygone era were kept. With only the light at the entrance lit now, the large corridors and every room in the house had become lonesome.

I went through a dark corridor leading into the patio and walked toward the living room and the dining room where I'd dined earlier.

Light was leaking through the door of the living room. Somebody was still there. When I stood before the door I heard a voice from inside. It was the father's voice.

"Frankly, you didn't seem to know anything about him."

His voice sounded so stern—so reproachful—he seemed like a totally different person from earlier. In fact, he sounded like an executive scolding his employee. I let go of the doorknob, which I'd been holding, and pricked up my ears.

"I'm afraid you've brought in an awful man. He's not that . . ."

"That person is still a child!" Eriko seemed to be appealing to her father, rather desperately. Her voice was barely audible, but I was able to intermittently hear such words as, "He's not weird!"; "He's always on his toes"; "He's frightened of something"; "He shivered in the nude like a newborn . . ."

"As I've been telling you, you mustn't forget that you're about to make an irrevocable decision. Listening to you talk, it sounds as if you're getting married to the guy out of pity; it's as if you think getting married to him is an act of kindness. Now isn't that abnormal, no matter how you look at it? Now and then, you meet people like him, you know; brainy but apathetic. You're innocent and naive, so you might have this notion that he's unusual, but in reality, there are plenty like him out there. Obviously, he has his own philosophy, or some kind of cosmic rationale. But . . . this father of yours can't help but think that the guy is a bad influence on you."

"No, he's not. That's not the case at all!" Eriko's voice had gotten louder now so I was able to hear more clearly.

"He's not a bad influence. That man has something special in him. It's something you'll never understand unless you try to know him. He has something no one else has. He's extremely free-spirited and has gravitas."

"Since when did you start speaking in such abstract terms? In the old days, you were more clear-cut in your speech. That's the kind of daughter I used to know."

The father suddenly spoke in a soothing tone, as if to pacify her. "Eriko, my dear, if you look hard enough, you'll always find a virtue or two in each and every person, and if you're feeling sorry for him, let me tell you that there are far too many people in this world you could feel sorry for. Look, I'm not really making a fuss about his character in particular. My concern is about the way you think, the way you make choices. That's all. The most important thing for a woman is what could be thought of as the ability to focus on her own happiness, you see. It's an attitude that can help you look reality square in the eyes and secure a modicum of happiness; an honest handful's worth. A woman who forgets this by getting absorbed in fleeting infatuations and thrills regularly fails in marriage. Your father, my dear, has seen many such people in his lifetime. Marriage is like that."

Eriko was no longer saying anything.

"Well, at any rate, the two of you should really have a thorough heart-to-heart discussion on this matter once. There's no use for you to consider marriage at this stage—not with the pathetically miniscule knowledge you have of him. It really is astonishing how little you know!"

The conversation seemed to have broken off, so I turned on my heels in a hurry and quietly shuffled away from the door.

I returned to my room on the second floor, switched the lights off for the time being, and slipped onto the futon. After I heard Eriko passing by the front of my room and entering into her room, I switched on the lights and began to change my clothes, taking off the pajamas that Eriko's mother had provided. After I folded the futon and returned it to the closet and put my towel and my used underwear and socks into my bag, I switched off the lights and stepped out of the room. While I thought about leaving in silence, I decided I should at least say goodbye, so this time I knocked on Eriko's door before pulling it open.

When I went inside, she seemed to be writing something at her desk. Noticing me in my clothes, she looked surprised. I approached where she was seated and looked over her shoulder, when she attempted to hide in a hurry what she was writing.

"Wow! Now, that's something. You're writing about that conversation you had with your father a while ago in your diary, huh?"

The face that had been looking up at me froze for an instant. I, on the other hand, was looking at the small cluster of characters in the diary and realizing the reason why Honoka's handwriting—the handwriting I'd seen on the day of the bonfire—had felt reminiscent: it closely resembled Eriko's handwriting.

"I was going to leave quietly," I said, "but I'm glad I came to say goodbye. Just to be clear, I hate people like your father. Any man who advises his daughter to think only about her own happiness is conceited and an idiot. There's no other way of putting it. But even worse than him is you. In fact, you're the worst. You have the nerve to see me as a child when you're hardly confident about yourself, and to top it all, you're obviously basking in self-pity all the time. Bravo indeed! What a remarkable feat! I'm so impressed I want to keep my head down and never see your face again. Okay then, I have no reason to hang around here anymore, so I'm leaving."

I turned my back on her and ran out. Barreling down the staircase, I heard footsteps behind me so I picked up my shoes at the entryway, hastily unlocked the sliding door, and jumped outside, my shoes still hooked on my fingers.

After that, I just ran, barefooted, toward the left for approximately two hundred meters, and just around the area where a jumble of houses appeared I swerved into a narrow bypath, put on my shoes there, and ran like crazy again. Halfway through, I felt as if I was jogging, so I began to chant.

"Left right, left right, left right . . ."

And before I knew it, I was even crooning the old children's tune, "The Monkey Palanquin Carrier," which put a further spring in my step.

"Essa, Essa, Essa Hoi Sa Sa. There goes the Monkey Palanquin Carrier, going Hoi Sa Sa."

23

I FOUND A TAXICAB parked in front of Kami-Suwa Station; its driver was taking a nap when I asked him for a ride up to Tokyo. It was around eight in the morning when I arrived at the apartment in Morishita.

Although I'd slept in the cab, I still felt groggy.

When I entered the apartment, various things brought in by Eriko stood out, so I decided to send back whatever was valuable. To that end, I first began to rearrange the contents of the refrigerator. But, while steadily gulping down around a half-a-dozen cans of cool beer to cheer myself up, the task turned into a drag, so I stopped tidying up.

Sitting cross-legged on the kitchen floor, I faced the great big refrigerator and emptied the last can of beer.

So essentially she was an academic, I mused. Although I'm no expert, I believe there are far too many women like Eriko in this world; beautiful women who do well in school, and in many cases, go on to become academics. In much the same way they're driven by a brazen curiosity and arrogant confidence to carry out fieldwork, or explore uncharted territories, or toy with dangerous compounds in the laboratory, they pour out their passions on a love interest beyond their control, and invariably flee in the end with their tails between their legs. But even so, they never feel ashamed, nor do they ever reflect on their conduct. When they finish writing a saccharine report in a flowery notebook titled "Experience," they go out to repeat the same mistakes again, or they awaken to—as Eriko's father put it—an honest handful's worth of happiness and go on to work hard at attaining a tranquil marriage or delivering a baby.

Something's terribly wrong.

I mean it!

Wait, no. Something's wrong not with Eriko, but me.

How on earth was Eriko at fault? What wrong did she ever commit?

But the very fact that she didn't commit any wrong is evidence of how truly foul, how truly villainous, she was.

Apparently, I'd somehow become completely drunk.

When I staggered into the bedroom, I collapsed onto the bed. In the dark room there with the curtains drawn, I remembered a time similar to this one. At that time I was still an innocent child. It was a precious time, when I myself was precious. Surely, no matter how harsh the times may be, there must always exist an irreplaceable time like that.

Eriko was telling her father that I was like a frightened baby. But it isn't me who's really frightened; it's Eriko herself. She travels and shed tears, she tries to fall in love and pretends to be hurt. She's completely afraid, having seen the great number of people in this world—several hundred times more than all the strands of her hair. She's groping in the darkness, as it were, for something she can cling to.

I understood all too well, in fact to a sickening degree, what Eriko and her folks wanted to say. As a certain writer of the past wrote with some flair, what they wanted to say was simply one thing: that there isn't a single thing in this world you could ever understand through books and movies alone; that there isn't a single thing in this world you could ever understand without confronting a living, breathing human being.

That's all. And it's such a dreadfully down-market, garden-variety philosophy that continues to incite Eriko and instill a sense of awe in all kinds of people around the world, for all their lives. This philosophy certainly has a point. Surely, even a fifteen-year-old girl can teach me a thing or two. No doubt she could even temporarily shock and bewilder me. I'm well aware of that. And I'm also aware that there are plenty of people who'd be pleased by such an experience—like novelists who never get tired of translating their love affairs into eloquent prose. Simply awestruck, these people never think about bettering themselves, and even though they know full well that, ultimately, it's just their petty curiosity being stimulated, they continue to tell preachy lies and brag about their experiences. I just can't stand the narrow-mindedness of such people, their self-deluding, vapid tricks; you'd think they're being hypocritical, but they're not. Even though nothing changes in a human from the day he's born, he goes on to believe that he has something he could lose, and by the same token, something he could recover. I can't stand such drivel. Eriko's the one who's really frightened. She keeps entering silly thoughts into her diary every day and defends her man against her father's accusations, even though she lacks conviction. If people vary from person to person in the way they wear their shoes, they also vary in the way they sink their teeth into their toast. It's much in the same way that the Inuit and the Cubans and we Japanese differ from each other. But if we try to read into such differences every time, what we'll end up losing is ourselves. Everyone is essentially the same. You really can't find any serious differences anywhere. You exist not for yourself, but purely for others. The self vaguely comes into being for the first time only in the presence of another person. Nonetheless, what binds a person in this world—what restricts and thoroughly dominates him—is fear. It's not love. While love is often compared to light, what gives birth to light is nothing other than the deep darkness of the void. To perceive the world there are two approaches; one approach is to believe in the straight road the light reveals to you, and to live through your brief life by fanatically walking along this road. The other approach is a more elaborate one, requiring you to fixate on the whole world, or in other words, on the deep enclosure of darkness itself, as if to cast yourself out into the void of cosmic space. However, not only is the human being too paltry before the vastness of oblivion, he can never keep his eyes focused on its darkness with just the two eyes he was born with. With hope and love come despair, fear, and death, the three elements that constitute most of life. And as long as death—as an absolute terror—is found at the end of our lives, it's impossible for love to overcome fear. However, the root of this fear is actually not found in death itself. What human beings dread the most is the human condition of being destined to die, of having no other choice but to live in fear of this destiny. Despite having no choice, humans continue to fear death in earnest. The more one fears death, the more death will live in the recesses of the heart, however happy you may be at any given moment, the prospect of it sparking like a sizzling electric current, never letting go of its grip on you—never letting you be released into the sea of happiness. For this reason, what we all must firmly reaffirm is not the meaning of life, but the truth of what it really means to die.

This is what Tolstoy says in his work, *On Life*.

Centuries pass, and the problem of the happiness of human life remains, for the majority of mankind, as inexplicable as ever. And yet the problem was solved long ago. And all who learn the answer to the problem are always astonished that they did not guess it themselves; they seem to have known it for a long time, but to have forgotten it. This enigma, which seemed so hopeless in the midst of the false doctrines of the age, offers of itself its own simple solution.

"Thou wishest that all should live for thee, that all should love thee more than themselves? Thy wish can be fulfilled, but on one condition only: that all beings shall live for the well-being of others

and love others more than themselves. Then only wilt thou and all beings be loved by all, and thou in their number wilt obtain thy desired well-being. If indeed well-being is possible to thee only when all beings love others more than themselves, then thou, a living being, must love others more than thyself."

Only on this condition are life and happiness possible for man; only on this condition can all that poisons the life of man be destroyed: the strife of beings, the torment of sufferings, and the terror of death.

And then he gtes on to say, *"Let man make the happiness of his life consist, not in the well-being of his animal individuality but in the happiness of other beings, and the scarecrow of death will disappear forever from his view."*

I recalled Eriko's face, as my consciousness began to gradually blur.

I'd probably never see her again.

She certainly wouldn't forgive me for being the person I am.

On the evening of President Nakagaki's wake, in bed, hugging me tightly, Eriko said, "For my companion, a plain person would suit me just fine, not a passionate or sentimental person. You find plenty of people like that around. I want to be with someone who's a novelty, someone forever irreplaceable, no matter how hard you try to find a match, because he's peerless. You're that kind of a person. You're a person with a hole in his heart. It's afflicted, and it can never find fulfillment. You may have tenderhearted feelings, but your mind is whimsical and cold, although not so cold as to drive a person into a corner. Still, you throw caution to the wind sometimes, don't you? Behave with wild abandon? But you know what? You live with so much pain. I don't know why I love you, but I certainly can't overlook the fact that there's a hole in your heart.

"When I talk about someone who's peerless, I'm talking about someone who's my one and only soul mate; someone whom I can convince that there's no one else in the world but me who can truly see him, who can truly appreciate him. So if there can only be one man like him, then there can only be one woman like me. I'm sure that's how it goes.

"I can't ever forget you. No matter how old I get, even if I end up with some other person, I think there will be times when I remember you, out of the blue. For instance, when I happen to find myself alone and spot some trees across the street, or when I take a trip to the seashore and get separated from my husband and my children, and find myself floating above the waters of the ocean, alone, thinking to myself, ahh how dazzling the sun is—in that moment, I think I'll suddenly find myself yearning for you. And that person I'll be imagining then will be the same as you are right now: kind and brooding, living with so much angst, so much pain.

"Ha, ha. I'm stuck, you know, like a sweater caught on something. It's no big deal, but I can't even move a muscle anymore."

At that time I just laughed it off, saying, "I guess you're telling me that I'm just a rusty nail on the wall!" But in my heart I was bowing deeply in deference to those words of hers.

It was still dark when I awoke.

I got out of bed and removed the cell phone from the charger I'd kept on the bookshelf. I took a look at the records of incoming calls, but saw that there were none from Eriko. It was 2:00 a.m. exactly. Although I don't recall at what time I'd fallen asleep, I reckon I'd had over twelve hours of sleep. It had been quite a while since I'd slept for so long. The booze was out of my system, but my head felt awfully heavy.

The date had changed to the fourteenth, a Sunday. My precious vacation had turned out to be a disaster. From the next day I'd have to show up in my office again and start handling jobs that aren't fun or interesting.

What the hell am I doing?

It isn't just work that isn't fun or interesting. It's my life itself; I haven't found any joy in it at all, not one bit. So why do I go on living?

One Thursday afternoon, as I recall, I was having a meal in a restaurant at Fukuoka Airport when my younger sister, who had come to see me off, took a dig at me, saying, "Momma often used to cry alone—for three years, that's all she did. And you never came home, no matter how many times she called."

What on earth was making her so sad that she had to cry?

Staring at her baby boy who'd come home after six days, she had a dumbfounded look on her face, as if she were seeing a ghost. And when she turned to face the two social workers standing there together with me, she suddenly bowed her head before murmuring in a small voice—"I'm sorry."

I swallowed the words stuck in my throat, baffled by why Momma had said those words when I believed at the time that it was I who should've been saying them. Suddenly, she crouched down in front of me and took me into her arms, snatching me away from the social worker holding my hand. It was only when she then said, "I'm sorry, I'm sorry" over and over again while crying, that I finally realized that I hadn't done anything wrong. She continued to hug me so tightly that my breath got stifled, and my mind went blank.

At that moment I realized, for the first time, that my mother had abandoned me.

When a human being stumbles upon something truly painful, he reaches his wit's end. He becomes incapable of crying, of even laughing. All he can do is become afraid.

And so, my entire body was shuddering in terror, while I stood there in the embrace of my mother's arms.

24

DURING THE MONTHS OF July and August, I worked tirelessly.

I'd launched a few projects within the past several months to compensate for the loss of the new novel, but a collection of essays by a certain writer, which we'd released at the end of July as a makeshift means to balance the accounts, sold unexpectedly well, so I got extremely busy supporting this book's sales. Accompanying the author on a nationwide book tour, which was arranged on the fly, I was present at every TV station where he made his television appearances, and attended to fine-tuning his ever-growing publicity schedule. When circulation went up, meetings with the advertising department and the business department became frequent, so I began to literally find myself rushing around inside and outside the company; I was that busy.

Amid such a flurry, I moved.

The burden of sending money home was largely reduced due to my mother's death, and my younger sister, who was working in her local area, was going to get married within the year. So since I could expect more financial freedom in the future for myself, I resolved to move to a more spacious apartment. Contacting a few real estate brokers, I had them fax me any information on available properties, after which I found one I liked, so I promptly signed a contract and finished moving sometime around the middle of August. This new apartment was in Kagurazaka, near my office, and overall it was a very convenient place to live alone.

The apartment was brand-new, came with an automatic lock installed, and was sufficiently roomy.

Of course, this time around I got into the habit of properly locking the door.

But every time I locked and unlocked the door, I remembered Eriko.

I didn't contact Raita and Honoka. They'd stopped making their occasional visits anyway, so I don't think they were particularly inconvenienced.

Speaking of Raita, I ran into him at an unexpected place in the beginning of August. At that time, a party was being held in Hotel New Otani to celebrate the seventieth birthday of the former Prime Minister who had released his memoirs during New Year's time, and when I attended this event, I bumped into a well-dressed Raita with a TV camera battery strapped over his shoulder. I was surprised because I never expected to see him in a place like this, but when I asked, he said that after President Nakagaki died, he asked Terauchi for help and ended up working part-time at a TV station. As a member of the shooting crew, he was apparently running around Tokyo every day. He was looking much healthier than I expected, sporting a dark tan. He laughed, telling me that Honoka was still busy as a bee job-hunting. Neither of us touched on the subject of Eriko. After only four or five minutes of talking on our feet, Raita hastily left the hall, saying he had to go to his next assignment.

As for Teruko Onishi, I'd lost touch with her ever since conveying my mother's passing to her. For her too, that must have been the turning point.

As for Tomomi, I broke up with her at the end of July.

A little while after a row over Takuya's hospitalization, Tomomi was in talks with Park for a possible reconciliation. One night during the rainy season, when customer traffic ceased because of the driving rain, Tomomi, in her deserted shop, confided as much to me. It was, if I remember correctly, several days before President Nakagaki committed suicide.

Tomomi was confused, saying, "I'd gone to formally ask him to break up with me, so I really don't know what happened! I don't know how we ended up having a talk like that." According to her, he'd done a complete about-face, resolutely refusing to divorce her, and, in the end, even telling her that he wanted to live together again, as a family, just as they had once been. I was listening to her, thinking that it was typical of Park to behave in such a way, but by the time she'd spoken at some length, I was able to grasp that Tomomi wasn't all that unwilling herself.

I became all the more convinced of this after I was told for the first time the details of the quarrel the two had had in the past.

Although I don't know what Park's side of the story is, according to Tomomi, the reason why she'd originally given up on Park wasn't because of Takuya or the nationality issue, but because a money-related complication involving a woman had come to light. At that time, Tomomi had just had Takuya, had washed her hands of the theater, and was in the middle of preparing to launch New Seoul with the money she'd begged in tears from her parents in Sendai, along with a bunch of other loans she'd obtained from various other places. This was because Park hardly seemed to see himself as a father, even after having had a son, so she thought that it was simply out of the question to leave her future in his hands. Anyhow, just when she'd finally secured all the necessary funds, and the prospect of buying the rights to the shop was in sight, trouble brewed between Park and a woman in his acting troupe, provoking the woman's common-law husband to blackmail Park.

"Suddenly," Tomomi recalled, "he came back out of the blue, looking very pale, and fell on his knees and begged for forgiveness. I pretty much figured out that he was involved in yet another scrape with a woman, but when I asked him anyway about what happened, he said he was being threatened by the husband and had promised to pay him three million yen as compensation. What's more, Park had even promised him in writing; apparently he was confined in a cheap hotel for around two days by the husband's gang of hoodlums, and was apparently grilled, and since he's basically a coward, he ended up giving in to their demand of writing up a signed statement that incriminated him. And there I was, having made an all-out effort to buy the shop, having finally raised all the money. I mean, hell! I'd really had just about enough of him, I tell you! I consulted my acquaintance's lawyer, but he told me that the situation was hopeless since Park had agreed in writing to pay, so the guy was shedding tears like rain and apologizing, but frankly, I was the one who really wanted to cry."

"And so, what did you do about the money?" I asked.

"I paid, but I kicked him out, telling him to never show his face again."

Hearing this story, I felt Tomomi and Park would be able to start over again any number of times, since their falling-out didn't seem that dire. Unlike ages ago, Park's Korean nationality didn't pose an obstacle to marriage or compromise Takuya's future, and in another few years, men and women marrying Koreans and Chinese will certainly cease to be a novelty. Besides, Park, though he was definitely theatrical and pretentious, didn't seem like a bad person at heart.

When I visited Tomomi's shop, after a long absence at the end of July, and told her that I'd be moving, she looked surprised, but took in the news without any difficult.

Of course she asked me for the reason, so I told her it was because my mother had died.

"And so with such a thing happening," I said, "I wanted to change my life a little."

"I see . . ." she said, before surprising me with what she said next. "She was suffering for quite a long time, wasn't she? I mean it was nearly three years ago when I heard from you about your mother's situation. I was always kind of worried myself."

"How did you know?"

I had no recollection whatsoever of speaking to her about my mother's illness. According to Tomomi, however, I'd apparently told her, two or three months after we began seeing each other, that my mother had been admitted into the hospital with cancer, and that there was no hope of saving her.

"But since then," Tomomi said, "you haven't said anything, so I remained silent."

I was genuinely surprised. I must have been very drunk at the time. However, as soon as I supposed so, an eerie doubt flared up in my mind; I wondered whether Tomomi might have heard everything from me about Eriko and about Mrs. Onishi as well. I tried to banish the thought, but the conversation was getting dreary anyway.

Tomomi said, "When a parent dies, you experience all kinds of emotions, especially when your mother dies."

"What are you talking about? Both of your parents are alive and well, aren't they?"

"Oh my, haven't I told you? My father remarried. My real mother died when I was in the eighth grade."

It was the first time I'd heard this story, or perhaps I'd heard it previously, but I just didn't remember.

"Is that so?" I said in a surprised tone.

"Actually," Tomomi said, looking fed up with me, "as I recall, I think I've told you once before."

"Say hello to Takuya for me, won't you?" I said as I was preparing to leave the shop. "And please let him know that I'll always be around for him, to be his mentor, to help him out with anything in his life. But I guess he won't be needing my guidance until he's much, much older."

After I said so, the somber look on Tomomi's face melted slightly for the first time.

"Okay, I'll be sure to tell him. You've taken good care of him until now, haven't you? Thank you."

"Hey, I'm the one who should say thanks. I'm glad I got to know you and Takuya."

When I stepped out of the shop, Tomomi came to the front to see me off. The rainy season was over and it was oppressively hot day after day. Even though it was already past eleven, the town was still enveloped in sweltering heat.

"It's really summer now," I said.

Tomomi nodded slightly, staring down her long skirt at her feet.

"What are you going to do about moving?"

"I've already made all the arrangements with a forwarding agent, so everything's taken care of."

"I see."

I stood in front of her and took her hand. Tomomi looked up and stared at me.

"I've met him only once, so I can't say for sure, but I think he's probably a good person."

Tomomi just smiled without saying anything.

"Well then, goodbye," I said.

"Bye-bye."

I hadn't walked far when I heard a voice behind me. I turned around and saw Tomomi laughing.

"I can say for sure that you're a good person," she said.

I smiled. She gave a big wave. I gave a big wave.

And that's how we parted ways.

I returned to Kokura on August 25, Sunday, to attend my mother's memorial service, which was held, according to custom, on the forty-ninth day after her passing. Since I was able to stay for only one night during the Obon Holidays, this time I took three days off from work.

After the memorial service held at the Koboji temple was over I talked for a while with my sister's fiancé over dinner. We'd exchanged greetings at the time of the funeral, but it was the first time for us to have a leisurely face-to-face conversation. He was working in the same credit loan company my sister was working in, and he was also twenty-six, just like my sister. Wearing glasses and appearing slightly plump, he seemed like a really calm and collected young man. He graduated from Saga University and joined his present company as a local recruit, but since his parents were running a rather large leasing company in Saga city, as the eldest son, he'd eventually be inheriting the company, he explained.

I thanked my sister for picking such an ideal partner. After all, now that she'd be living in neighboring Saga city, the task of carrying out the memorial service for our mother, whose ashes were in Koboji's charnel house, wasn't going to be that much of a challenge.

"The two of us were talking about having the wedding ceremony while Mother-In-Law was well, but I'm truly sorry for how suddenly she left us."

"Please don't be," I said in response to his gracious apology. "I don't know how to thank you for taking such good care of Mother before she passed away. Because of my job, I don't think I'll be returning to Kyushu again, so I believe I'll have to ask you to take care of my younger sister and help manage our affairs with the temple. I'd appreciate your support." I bowed deeply.

There was no friction between him and me. But when he said that he'd like to postpone his wedding from the planned date in October to a date after the first anniversary of my mother's death next year, out of respect, I objected strongly, saying that there was no need to do so.

"There is no better way to pray for the repose of Mother's soul than for the two of you to get married as soon as possible."

"Is that how you feel?" he asked, wearing a thoughtful look. "Actually, Father-In-Law had said the same thing, so she and I were talking about doing so."

"Father-in-law?" I was surprised. "So you've met him as well?"

The father of my younger sister was currently living in Hiroshima with his new family. Although my sister had informed him of my mother's death, I don't believe he'd turned up at the wake or the funeral. My sister, who was seated next to her fiancé, spoke hesitantly. "After the funeral," she said, "Father immediately came to make an incense offering. That's when he kindly met him. Last week, the two of us even went up to Hiroshima, you know. The family warmly welcomed us there. I was so glad." Next to her, her fiancé was nodding. This was news to me.

"I see . . ." I had nothing more to say. The two people in front of me were steadily on their way to building a new family; so be it. Turning a new leaf after her mother's death, my younger sister had gotten back together with her estranged father, and intended to begin a certain level of association with her half-siblings.

"In that case, though, I feel very sorry for Momma," I thought.

If it were me, I wouldn't so easily tolerate the man who abandoned our mother, nor would I so readily accept the children this man fathered with another woman as my own brother and sister.

It was already September, but the sweltering heat lingered in Tokyo. I finally grew accustomed to my new life in Kagurazaka, and work kept me busy as usual. Still, there were a few things that were different. First of all, I rarely went out drinking anymore. I realized—as if taught a lesson—how precious Tomomi's shop was to me, having lost it now. These days, I left the office around nine and returned directly to my apartment. I'd buy food from a late-night supermarket in the vicinity to prepare dinner by myself. But it wasn't anything much; just dishes like stir-fry vegetables, omelet, fried noodles and fried chicken, and I'd eat them as side dishes while watching TV and drinking a can of beer. After getting a bit tipsy, I'd take a bath before getting into bed around one in the morning.

In the brief period before falling asleep, I'd try to think about something but nothing would occur to me.

Whether I thought about Mother or Tomomi and Takuya or Teruko Onishi or Raita or Honoka, or even Eriko, the only things that floated into my mind were past memories, to which I didn't have anything to add. For this reason my thoughts failed to expand, and I couldn't take any pleasure in imagining. Once upon a time, I used to feel that retracing the past was comforting, but I realized that I was only deluding myself. The past is something like a catalyst for enjoying the present, so if you don't have a present, memories become totally worthless.

Right now—in my present—I definitely found myself with a place of my own. But there were no people. And I realized then that without people, time was nothing.

People are time itself, after all. And as such, a space devoid of time may be meaningless to humans. As Machiko-san used to say, everything, including places, people, and time, is merely a different manifestation of a single thing.

What was Eriko doing now?

Were Raita and Honoka getting along well? How did Honoka's job-hunting turn out? Eriko must be mentoring her even now. How did Eriko explain to the two of them about our breakup? I hardly think she's blaming me . . .

September 17, Tuesday.

On that day, when the cool autumn winds began finally to blow through the town, I was at my desk, busy processing the final-proof galley that I had to finish by tomorrow morning. The author was high-strung and he had red-penciled large-scale revisions in what was the final proof, so my work got complicated, and I had to proceed with caution, readjusting the lines and changing the subheadings.

I don't know how much time had passed since I finished lunch, returned to my seat, and began to concentrate on the galley again, but the entire seventh floor, where my publishing division was located, was suddenly abuzz with commotion. This noise was tinged with an indescribably awful and dismal foreboding, so I put down my pen and turned around.

There were a few people at their desks, but they too were standing up and looking in the direction of the noise. We were facing the east window, but the noise was breaking out near the west window, directly across from us. It was where the editorial department of the general monthly magazine, to which I'd once belonged, was situated.

One of us in the division went to see what was happening and returned.

"What's the matter?" someone asked.

While hastily turning on the TV on a worktable, he blurted out, looking pale with shock, "Seems that Udagawa's been stabbed."

All at once, everyone rushed over to the television set, each crying out, "Really?" "You must be joking!" After taking a deep breath, I also walked over to the TV where the anchorman was beginning to convey the news in an anxious voice. As I walked over, though, a vivid image of Raita was projected into my retina. It was a picture of him, just as I'd seen him approximately one and a half months ago at the assembly hall of Hotel New Otani, where I'd run into him; a picture of him dressed in a suit, sporting a tan, and looking elated.

25

On September 17th, at 2:15 in the afternoon, Prime Minister Keiichiro Udagawa (63) was stabbed by Raita Kimura (20), a young, left-wing activist moonlighting on a TV crew in the National Diet building.

The prime minister, who had just returned to Japan after visiting China and Korea over the three-day holiday period that included in the middle the Respect for the Aged Day, was attending a meeting in which intensive deliberations had begun as soon as the holidays ended. The deliberations were being carried out by the Budget Committee of the House of Representatives to discuss the secondary supplementary budget for the economic recovery policy. Emerging from the assembly hall after finishing his energetic address, the prime minister was surrounded by television crews from various stations, who had been waiting for him to appear. It so happened that on that day, the leader of the ruling party had just expressed his intention to resign after being subjected to criticism regarding the matter of the former First Secretary's implication in a massive tax evasion scheme, so the media had flocked into the building to directly elicit Prime Minister Udagawa's comments on the scandal.

According to protocol, Udagawa had stopped in front of the reporter holding the pool microphone, and the moment he was about to make a comment, a thin man suddenly leapt out from the surrounding crowd of camera crews and hurled himself at Udagawa. Of course, there were bodyguards, dispatched from the Metropolitan Police Department, positioned behind the prime minister, but it was totally impossible for them to carry out their duty in this situation; it was all over in the blink of an eye.

After Prime Minister Udagawa wrapped his arms around the young man, who had jumped up to his chest suddenly, he parted his tightly pursed lips, let out a single groan, and collapsed right there and then, together with the young man. Right after that, the bodyguards and the reporters, who were stationed at the front, rushed over to the two and fell all over them.

And that's how the decisive moment of the sudden assault on the incumbent prime minister transpired in front of many cameras.

The wounded prime minister was immediately carried out of the building and transported to the Toranomon Hospital.

The perpetrator, Raita Kimura, was dragged out of the crowd by several bodyguards and was taken, gagged and handcuffed, to the Metropolitan Police Department in Sakuradamon. The TV cameras captured in great detail, and repeatedly televised through news broadcasts, how two police officers amid the turbulent atmosphere were escorting Raita outside, seizing him on either side as they walked down the wide corridor of the building teeming with a crowd of onlookers.

Newspapers released extra editions, while TV stations rescheduled various programs in order to carry out continuous coverage.

Raita's name and age had already been ascertained soon after the incident had occurred, but it was only late at night that day when it was revealed that Raita was the son of an official of the Japanese Communist Party. Although the party promptly held an emergency press conference to disavow any connection to Raita's act of terrorism, Shinichi Kimura, the father of the perpetrator who was also a council member of Inagi City, was conspicuously absent from the conference and refrained from making any statement. So the media's response was terribly cold.

It had been reported that Raita was "cooperating with the

investigation," and it was on the following day, the eighteenth, in the morning editions of newspapers, that the synopsis of Raita's deposition was reported.

While the plan, motive, and background of the crime were apparently going to be disclosed at a press conference to be held by the Metropolitan Police Department on the eighteenth from nine in the morning, the newspapers, thanks to their interviews with various parties connected to the investigation, succeeded in scooping most of the details.

Above all, what shook the world beyond belief was Raita's motive. The morning edition of the Mainichi Shimbun ran his testimony word for word.

"It's not that I wanted to change the world, or that I was thinking that this person (Prime Minister Udagawa) was ruining Japan or anything like that. In the first place, I'm not interested in politics at all, and I hardly ever read the papers or watch the news on television, you see. But it's just that, you know, someone like the prime minister's considered to be great, right? But in reality, he's the same as us, and even if he were to die, the world's, like, not going to change one little bit. Well I guess I wanted everyone to learn this lesson. Ah, heck, I don't know. Basically, all I'm saying is that the death of the prime minister's not going to make any difference in Japan; it's not going to change the nation for the better or worse. Anyway, I'm hoping I get the death penalty or whatever soon. I'm not too confident about committing suicide; I think I'll really suck at it."

Similarly on the eighteenth, the president of the TV station that had hired Raita as a part-timer took responsibility for the incident and resigned. Upon receiving this news, I wondered about the look on Terauchi's face—the look on the face of the man who had been effectively used by Raita.

At that juncture, I hadn't yet been contacted by the police. Obviously, during the investigation, there was no reason for Raita to say anything at all about me or Eriko or Honoka.

However, my friendship with Raita would eventually come to the police's attention from Terauchi's mouth. At that point, though, all I had to do was respond to their questioning in a straightforward fashion.

But what concerned me the most was Honoka. If her relationship with Raita was still intact, it was only natural that the police would end up focusing their attention on her. If she were going in and out of that apartment in Ekoda, her face would be known to the neighbors, and the press was undoubtedly going to sniff out her presence soon. If I didn't do anything, it was inevitable that she'd get mobbed by the reporters and sensationalized, in a news maelstrom, as the lover of the prime minister's would-be assassin.

There was no way Honoka could tolerate such a situation.

On the afternoon of the seventeenth, as soon as I saw the first images of the incident, I called Eriko.

She seemed to have been in a studio for a shooting job, and when I skipped the greetings and told her about Raita's case, she was at a loss for words for a while.

Eriko went on to inform me, though, that Raita and Honoka had broken up in late July. So when Raita laughed and told me in Hotel New Otani that Honoka was very busy job-hunting, he was apparently talking about a time before he split up with her. Eriko also said that Raita had suddenly disappeared from Honoka's sight, vacating the apartment in Ekoda without a warning. This claim was supported the next day, when Raita, in his statement, clarified that he'd been wandering around Tokyo, moving from capsule hotel to capsule hotel, in the months of August and September.

"I'd like you to immediately contact Honoka and tell her to stay overnight at your place tonight," I said.

"Understood. I'll call her now and go pick her up. She's probably heard the news by now. I can't bear to leave her alone."

"Yeah, please. I'm going to wrap up my work and also head over to your place. I should talk to Honoka too."

That evening I rushed over to Eriko's apartment and met, for the first time in a long while, Honoka, who was sobbing, and—snuggled up next to her—Eriko, who was dazed and confused.

The assassination attempt on Prime Minister Udagawa went on to shake the nation for over a month. The Japanese ended up tasting, for the first time in ages, the true meaning of the word turmoil. On the fifth day following the incident, Toshiyuki Onodera, who was the Minister of Finance in the Udagawa Cabinet, was appointed prime minister during a plenary session of the National Diet. While Prime Minister Udagawa had narrowly escaped death, his abdominal region was seriously wounded; the Swiss army knife's fifteen-centimeter-long blade had reached the kidneys and liver. All hopes for a swift return to the post of prime minister were effectively dashed.

In response to the kind of political instability, which hadn't been seen in Japan since the postwar years began, the level of foreign countries' confidence in Japan saw a marked decline. Sparked by a huge sell-off of Japanese stocks, the stock market went into free fall and the yen plummeted repeatedly. Furthermore, Japanese government bonds were downgraded and the money market entered into a state of panic.

The name Raita Kimura came to be etched in the minds of the people with far greater force than the name of the notorious criminal, Otoya Yamaguchi, who had committed suicide in jail after stabbing Inejiro Asanuma. This was because a series of investigations had failed to uncover any mastermind behind Raita's act, confirming, for the most part, that Raita wasn't driven by any ideology. Journalists, politicians, and even legal experts were all at a loss, since, for the life of them, they couldn't figure out what to make of his act of terrorism. This lack of clarity proved to be the source of a malaise that afflicted the whole of Japanese society.

In the end, however, I wasn't called for questioning, and Honoka wasn't summoned by the police either. It was also likely that Terauchi didn't mention my name. Come to think of it, that man was principled enough not to do such a thing. But above all, Raita, apparently, hadn't breathed a word about us. When he moved out of his apartment he'd disposed of all of his personal effects. In addition, he didn't seem to have acquaintances other than us, so unless he himself talked, there was no trail that could ever lead the police to us.

Indeed, you could say that Raita had brilliantly made "this thing that's like a cord that's barely been keeping me tied to this dirty world . . . snap." And to him, his relationships with Honoka, Eriko, and myself may have been nothing more than mere segments of such a cord.

After one and a half months passed, when November came, Honoka gradually started to regain her composure. Ever since the incident occurred, she'd been living together with Eriko. I also made frequent visits to Eriko's apartment and the three of us would cook together, watch TV together, and sometimes even drink alcohol together. The subject of Raita or the incident hardly ever came up.

"I've decided to remain another year in university," Honoka told us at the beginning of November. "I don't think I particularly wish to carry on studying psychology, but then again I really don't want to join the workforce yet, and it's not as if I need to, either. Actually, for a while I don't want to get close to anybody, and I don't want to get absorbed in anything new. I'll pay for my school fees and living expenses by working part-time, so Eriko-san, please continue to keep me here, please?"

Watching Honoka plead in that way and bow, Eriko nodded and said in a carefree tone, "Yeah, I think it'd be a good thing for you to just take it easy for a year and do nothing."

Eriko and I warmed to each other, as if we'd really become friends again, as if nothing had happened between us. And perhaps, in reality, nothing all that significant had transpired. However, I was patiently watching Eriko, and I knew that Eriko herself was also patiently watching me; the two of us were waiting for the opportune moment to arrive to try to settle the matter of our relationship once and for all.

What drives Eriko to be so persistent is perhaps nothing more than mere pride. It may be that she simply can't stand being spurned and ignored by someone like me. But truthfully, I wasn't ignoring Eriko, nor was I thinking lightly of her. Ever since that night I sprang out of the house in Suwa—ever since that juncture in my life—I realized all the more that I'd been yearning for Eriko, from the depths of my heart. However, I understood at the same time that my hope was futile, that it would never bear fruit.

I wasn't qualified to live together with someone else. I lacked that ability.

The showdown for us came on November tenth.

It was a very warm spring-like Sunday, which also happened to fall on my thirtieth birthday.

I visited Eriko's apartment in the evening as usual. Honoka was absent, as she'd left for an overnight trip to Tateshina with her classmates. Apparently, her decision to travel was made just the previous night, but Eriko was nonetheless very pleased that Honoka had recovered enough of her vitality to enjoy a trip together with her friends. Although I hesitated in the doorway for a while before entering an apartment where it'd just be the two of us alone together, she said, rather forcefully, "Well, please come on in," and accepted the wine I'd bought before quickly going back inside.

We cooked dinner together and toasted with wine.

Since Honoka was absent, I talked a little about Raita's current situation. The first public trial had been slated for the end of November, and the full results of a battery of psychiatric tests, which the prosecution and the defense had been requesting the court to disclose ahead of the public trial, had just been released. All results concurred on the diagnosis that he was, of course, "of sound enough mind to assume legal responsibility." However, according to a tip from the defense lawyer, it was believed that Raita was in a terribly deranged state.

Apparently, on top of enduring grueling interrogations over an extended period, he'd been severely shocked by the fact that his father, Shinichi Kimura, the city council official, had hung himself to take responsibility for his son's crime.

"It seems he's gone mostly insane now," I said. "I don't ever want Honoka to know that, but sooner or later, it's going to get covered by the press."

"Yeah, I suppose it's not something we can hide, and besides, she herself has got to get over it. But you know something? In retrospect, I'm grateful that Raita-kun dumped Hono-chan before he committed the crime. Of course, I'm pretty sure that she understands what's going in his heart of hearts—that is, she understands his true feelings for her—but still, the fact remains that he left her without telling her anything, and to Hono-chan, that's reason enough to give up on him."

"Eriko, how serious do you think Raita was about Honoka? Perhaps truly understanding his heart of hearts might, quite to the contrary, end up hurting Honoka even more, you know."

"Hmm. I'm not so sure I agree," Eriko said, tilting her head. "Until recently, Hono-chan was saying that she was going to wait for him to finish his prison term."

"Really?"

"That's right. To her, finding Raita was a miracle. That's what she used to say all the time."

"A miracle?"

"Uh-huh. Apparently it's a miracle to her that the two of

them were able to meet by chance in a world teeming with so many people; the fact that out of all the myriad possibilities, out of all the fish in the sea, the one and only Honoka came across the one and only Raita, that sort of thing. What's important to her isn't the type of person he is or what he's accomplished, but rather the simple fact that the two of them happened to meet. Lately, though, her faith in such starry-eyed notions seems to be finally wearing off."

"That's incredible!" I said, laughing a little. "She might have been thinking about getting married to him behind bars then."

"Maybe," Eriko said, without laughing along with me though. Instead, she went on to say, "It just might be a viable life choice for her, and I don't think she's completely ruled it out yet."

"You're joking, right?"

"Am I? If Hono-chan were to make such a choice, well, in that case I don't think I'd mind. In fact, I think I'd be rooting for her. Now don't get me wrong. I do feel sorry for Prime Minister Udagawa, and I do believe that there's no room for justifying what Raita-kun did. But still, if Raita-kun atones for his sin, then he'll be coming back here someday, right? And when that happens, if there's no one waiting for him, he'll surely die."

Hearing those words, I imagined for the first time how Raita would one day return to this world after completing his sentence. Be it fifteen years later or twenty years later, that day will surely come. And when it does, Raita will still be under forty.

"I'm not too confident about committing suicide; I think I'll really suck at it."

That's what he declared with arrogant indifference during his interrogation, but what he'll find himself really sucking at isn't dying; instead, it's living. The forty-year-old ex-con would surely be struck by this realization, even more than me right now.

"But I wonder why Raita-kun did such a thing?" Eriko suddenly muttered. "After all, it's not as if he could go somewhere, you know."

"What are you talking about? He didn't do it to go somewhere."

"You think? I feel he certainly wanted to go somewhere; somewhere different from here. Just like you want to."

About halfway through our conversation I'd understood that Eriko was using Raita as a pretext to talk about me. And after hearing what she'd just said, I became convinced that she intended to finally have a showdown tonight, to settle the matter of our relationship once and for all.

I asked Eriko, with as much restraint as I could muster, "Where is it that you think that little old me wants to go?"

Locking her eyes on mine, Eriko said, "Wherever you should be."

"And where's that?"

"Who knows? I haven't a clue. But wherever that is, it's a place you'll never find, as long as you stay the way you are today."

"Wow! For you, that's being vague," I said, laughing again.

Eriko remained steely. "I'm not the one being vague at all here. It's you who's being vague, don't you think?"

"Are you talking about our relationship?" I didn't want to say anything else. I didn't want to get entangled in a bitter quarrel like this, not at the end of our time together.

"No, I'm not. I'm talking about you."

But Eriko was cool and composed, like an actress who had thoroughly rehearsed her lines. This detached, lofty attitude got on my nerves.

"Exactly how am I being vague? I think it's you who's being rather vague here, with all your sly innuendos."

At that point Eriko finally showed a smile. It was an edgy smile; edgy enough to slice the human heart.

"Remember what you once said?" she went on. "There's nothing sadder than not having a place to go? That a person exists only when a place exists first? You also said that you didn't believe in families. I thought, what rubbish this man says! And when you fled from my parents' home, I was stunned that you could be so shameless. But actually, haven't you yourself been searching all along for a place where you can belong?"

I let out a sigh. But Eriko was no longer daunted and resolutely went on to add, "Even I don't believe in families."

I stared Eriko in the face with an unrelenting gaze.

It suddenly occurred to me that I shouldn't press her any further.

But there wasn't even a hint of hesitation or vacillation in her expression: it was so resolute it perplexed me a little.

"I've always longed for a place where I can belong," Eriko began. "Everyone longs for such a place. You're not the only one lost, mister. But no matter how much you seek it, how much you search for it, you can never find such a place. You could hang around with all sorts of people, but nobody is ever going to give you a place of your own. I remember you saying that you didn't want to go anywhere because you were tired here. Well, I'd like to ask wherever on earth is this place you call here? What on earth do you mean by here, anyway? I certainly wanted a place where you and I could be together. But by that, I wasn't saying that you and I should join forces to find such a place. Because, if one really wanted a genuine place of one's own, one would stop looking for it; one would stop endlessly wandering about like you and make such a place—all by his or her damn self—in this very place you're so tired of, the one you call here. I never thought about starting a family with you, not even once. It's just that I thought the two of us could build a place where we could be comfortable together. But all you ever did was give up after looking through your self-centered eyes and despairing. You looked so pathetic and pitiful, behaving like that. I got so worried I couldn't stand it anymore. I thought you'd surely end up leading a life of misery, if you didn't change. And not just any kind of misery, mind you, but a misery so epic nobody has ever experienced it yet. And so that's why I couldn't turn a blind eye to you. I'm not the one who's being vague. It's you. Can't you see? There's never been anywhere else but here. Heaven and hell, this world and the next; they're all here. The past and the future all happen here, and will just keep happening again from now on as well. You and I are also here, and were here before we were born, and will continue to be here after we die. I'm sure even God and the Devil are here, without ever having been anywhere else, without ever having a place to return to. There's something I've always wanted to say to you; you're always straining hard to see, looking at things with such intense scrutiny; but just where are you looking anyway? All that you can ever see, all that's ever evident, is the world that's where you find yourself standing, right? So what the hell are you still trying to see? If you take a good look at where you stand, and then if you lift your face and finally open your eyes wide, you'll know that this world stretches out forever, and you'll know that that's all there is to see, that it's this world itself that is the only world you can ever see, and ever should see. But you never even tried to listen to me, did you? You never even tried to imagine my point of view, my feelings! Instead, all you ever did was to try to make yourself disappear, over and over again. I didn't dislike you, I didn't doubt you, and last but not least, I never hated you. I loved you dearly, you know, from deep down inside my heart. I'd have done anything for you; I had my mind set on you. But all you ever did was fear me. You rejected me and fled from me, as if I were attempting to harm you. It then occurred to me that, in my life, I've never even once come across a person as dreadful as you."

Eriko had started to cry midway through her story. In the nearly two years I'd known her, it was the first time she'd shed tears in front of me, for my sake.

As I took in the sight of her on the verge of a breakdown I thought . . . that if I could stay together with her, in the place where she stands, there's no telling how happy I could be.

What peace of mind even I—this worthless thing needlessly born—could attain, if I could only live for a person who weeps for me in this way. Just as I'd once thought about my younger sister, just as I'd once thought about Takuya by that riverbank on that summer day, if I could abandon all of me for this person, Eriko, how wonderful that would be.

But that was impossible, no matter what.

They all universally preach:

The only path to happiness is to love another more than yourself.

But they also preach—at a much deeper level—that when you love another entity more than yourself, you must never love in the way you would a member of the opposite sex.

A man must not love a woman as a woman, nor should a woman love a man as a man; men and women should love one another in the way they'd love themselves.

This is because the love between a man and a woman will inevitably bear the fruits of misery.

And this, in turn, is because each and every one of us living in this world, and not only me, is nothing more than the fruit of this misery.

I was fortunate; I was able to make a firm promise to myself, on July 8th, the day when Mother abandoned me, to never repeat such a mistake. And God too secretly instructed me.

"Love another person," the supreme being said, "at all times, as a parent would love their child."

There wasn't a single thing that was wrong in what Eriko was saying. However, if I may be permitted to say one thing in my defense, the reason I was scared of her wasn't because I thought she was going to harm me in any way. It was just that I was afraid that I myself would surely end up harming her.

And I'd probably hurt her enough already.

The dishes arranged on the dining table, where we were seated across from each other, were mostly cleared away. I had a sip of the remaining wine and stood up, pushing backing my chair. Eriko looked up at me, her wet eyes starting to dry up.

"I have nothing to say to you," she said quietly.

Averting my eyes from her gaze, I regarded for a while, in silence, the huge portrait hanging on the wall.

I sensed that someone was trying to make me sad, yet again.

I left the table, turning my back not on Eriko, but on this image of Eriko.

Then I heard a gentle voice behind me again. "You can't even say goodbye."

With my hand on the doorknob, I stood still at the door, gritted my teeth, and looked back.

Eriko's eyes were wet with fresh tears. When our eyes locked, she slowly stood up and began to approach me.

An intense unease shook my entire body.

The terror of being dragged into a jet-black darkness any moment mushroomed in my mind.

But I couldn't move a muscle anymore. So this is how I was going to meet my downfall, I felt, how I was going to be broken at last. Still, I was helpless, unable to do anything but wait patiently for Eriko to come.

26

On Monday, December 2, at 9:30 a.m., ex-Prime Minister Keiichiro Udagawa left this world, after fighting for his life for two and a half months. Even though Udagawa had released to the media a photograph of him smiling in a hospital ward, in the end, his severe wound never healed, and his last moments saw him deteriorating suddenly overnight due to a liver failure brought on by a massive blood transfusion carried out right after the tragedy, making him meet an end that was all too soon.

It was Honoka who had informed me of Udagawa's death. She'd suddenly reached me at my office by phone, and the first thing she said was, "Sensei! It looks like Raita-san has become a murderer, after all."

She spoke in a monotone that concealed her emotions.

When I asked her "What are you doing now?" she told me that she was on her way to her part-time job. At around ten, it seems she came across the news story in an extra edition of a newspaper that was being distributed in front of Yurakucho Station. Honoka calmly read the article for me.

"Are you still going to your job?" I asked. Because Udagawa's death was so unexpected, even I was greatly upset.

"Yeah, I'm going," Honoka said. "I just can't think about anything else right now anyway. Besides, I don't even want to."

The presence of a bustling crowd crackled through from the other end of the line.

"What time do you get off?"

"I've got a class to attend today, so I'm going to finish working at two."

"After that?"

"I'll just go straight to school from there." After a pause, she added, "But I suppose I've got some free time, since the class starts from the fifth session."

"What time does the fifth session start?"

"4:20."

"In that case I'll drop by the university at about three. Let's have some tea."

"Are you sure that's okay?"

"Yeah, I don't mind."

"All right then. I'll wait for you in front of the main gate."

Honoka hung up. Throughout the entire conversation, there was no indication that she was upset. In fact, she seemed strangely calm. This bugged me.

Last week, Raita's first public trial had just begun.

I moved heaven and earth to secure two passes to the court hearing.

After Raita appeared in court, I believe he clearly recognized Honoka and me seated in the central section of the visitors' gallery, as he made his way across the short distance from the dock to the witness stand. Although there was no change in his facial expression, we sensed that he'd recognized us when our eyes met his for an instant: they appeared to flicker with intent. Contrary to what the news had been broadcasting, Raita didn't appear haggard, nor did he seem mentally unstable. Even though he made his replies in a low voice during the proceedings, he remained composed, clearly denying any intent to kill the ex-prime minister.

After the court adjourned, Honoka and I decided to separate from each other, just to be safe. She left first and slipped away from the crowd of reporters swarming in front of the Tokyo District Court. We met up at a hotel in Akasaka to have lunch together.

At that time, Honoka had said, "I guess if Prime Minister Udagawa recovers now, the sentence probably wouldn't be that severe, especially since Raita-san has denied the intent to kill. Besides, he just turned twenty."

After reiterating such sentiments, she said, "And he wasn't strange or unsound at all."

It had been a while since I'd seen Honoka looking cheerful, and while I gazed on at that radiant look of hers, I reaffirmed the strong bond that existed between Raita and Honoka. This bond was sufficiently evident even from Raita's unflinching, steely expression, though—an expression that didn't allow him to even twitch an eyebrow when he saw her.

Buoyed with such high hopes, Honoka must have been all the more devastated by the news of Udagawa's death.

Eriko simply believed that Honoka would recover with the passage of time, but I didn't see it that way. Regardless of the depth of her connection to Raita, one of her temperament doesn't recover that easily from such a great shock. To put it in Raita's terms, Eriko and Honoka fundamentally differ by the thickness of the cord linking them to this world. And for this reason, it must be difficult for Eriko to understand Honoka.

When I got off from the taxi at exactly three, I saw Honoka standing by Keio's main gate. Before I even began to approach her she came rushing over to me. Although we hadn't talked properly that year, I immediately felt the vibes of the precious intimacy of friendship. It occurred to me then that this person had still been a fifteen-year old girl when I first met her.

"Phew, that's a relief," Honoka said, looking at me with a slight smile.

"What is?"

"Oh, I just thought that Eriko-san might be coming along as well."

"Did you call her?"

Honoka shook her head.

"In that case, she might not have even heard the news yet. Besides, she said she'd be in the studio all day long."

"Shall we?" Honoka said, taking my hand.

After we entered through the gate Honoka took me on a brief guided stroll through the campus. With the end of the year approaching and the classes still in session, the premises were deserted. Giant ginkgo trees were planted here and there, lush with yellow foliage. The paths were filled with vast amounts of fallen leaves, as if a yellow carpet had been unfurled all over the campus.

"Aren't Keio's gingkoes great?" Honoka said. "It seems every year the cleaning people have a hard time, with all the autumn leaves piling up like this. And since ginkgo leaves can't be repurposed as fertilizers, they have no option but to throw them all away, apparently."

Stepping firmly on the ginkgo leaves, I remembered Machiko-san boiling them to prepare a tea substitute, which she used to drink often.

After walking around the small campus for approximately fifteen minutes, we entered a cafeteria called "Fiesta" in the basement of the northern wing of the school building. I bought coffee and Honoka bought a plastic bottle of oolong tea before we settled down at a table in the back. The large cafeteria was quiet, with just a sprinkling of students seated here and there. The window on the left only afforded a view of the protruding section of the concave school building, but the faint rays of the already setting winter sun were reaching all the way up to the timeworn wooden table where we were seated. Behind me, I could hear a male student slurping up soba noodles. In front was a middle-aged woman, wearing an apron and a hood, eagerly wiping up rows of tables. On the white wall at the right was found a poster advertising a co-op's Driver's Ed program and another poster advertising CD and DVD bargain sales.

I took one sip of the lukewarm coffee and asked, "So you always have your meals here?"

Honoka was drinking her tea, which she'd poured from the plastic bottle into a plastic teacup.

"Yes, I usually have my lunches here, since it's cheap."

"Like set meals?"

"Well, set meals are a bit too pricey, and they contain a lot of meats and fish in them, so . . ."

"About how much do they cost?"

"More than four hundred yen. I just make do with small dishes like boiled spinach with dressing or croquette or burdock salad and try to keep my food expenses under four hundred yen as much as possible. Most of us girls around here get by like that."

"Yeah, I guess four hundred yen must be the limit if you're living on part-time wages," I said, laughing.

"Of course it is," Honoka said with a smile. "I'm not as rich as you are, sensei."

"But back in my college days it was even worse, you know."

"Really?"

"Sure it was!"

"Then I'll cut down on my expenses even more!"

"What? You don't have to follow in my footsteps, you know."

At that point Honoka fell silent, and then said, "But even Raita-san isn't eating properly, I think."

"He should still be in detention, so as far as food is concerned, as long as people visit him with gifts, he'll be eating surprisingly well, actually."

"But I don't think there's anyone who'd do such a thing for him, since his father has passed away as well."

"In that case why don't the two of us go pay him a visit, with some presents?"

"How about after a little while longer?" Honoka asked with earnest eyes.

"How much longer?"

"About a year," she said in a clear-cut way.

"A year, huh?" I murmured, looking her straight in the eye. "You knew, didn't you?"

Honoka looked at me in silence.

"You knew what Raita was up to, didn't you? I finally realized that you did when we went to the district court together last week. Until then I didn't understand, although I must say it was rather remiss of me not to."

Honoka lowered her hands from the table to her knees, straightened her posture, and bowed. "I'm sorry, I couldn't stop him. I'm totally ashamed."

"I wish you had at least consulted me."

Honoka apologized again before saying, "I went to your apartment, sensei, on the fifteenth, but you weren't there."

"Is that right?"

"Yes sir."

On that day I was back in Kitakyushu. "It was the first O-Bon since my mother died, so I was in the countryside, in my hometown."

"I see," Honoka said, lifting her teacup and slowly sipping her tea.

"Why the fifteenth?" I said, taking a sip of my coffee.

"I became convinced that Raita would go through with it."

"And what convinced you?"

"Well, on that day, Prime Minister Udagawa paid an official visit to the Yasukuni shrine, right? Raita-san was saying that if the prime minister went to Yasukuni this year also, he'd have no choice but to go through with it."

Indeed, Udagawa had paid a visit to Yasukuni last year on the anniversary commemorating the end of the war, to much harsh protest from Korea, China, and other southeast Asian countries. Nonetheless, he still went ahead with an official visit to the Yasukuni shrine, in brazen defiance.

"Raita-san kept saying that he just couldn't forgive Prime Minister Udagawa after he heard him saying, 'When I think of all those kamikaze pilots I can't sleep at nights, and as an individual citizen I consider it a manifest duty to visit Yasukuni.'

He said that he couldn't accept, in whatever shape or form, any idealization or romanticizing of war, and that even the glorified kamikaze pilots, in the end, were undeniably murderers—they flew out to kill human beings of other nations. It was a mistake to treat them as heroes, he kept saying. He said as long as there's even just one person objecting among the people who were invaded and victimized the prime minister had no right to go to the Yasukuni Shrine in their name. Raita-san believed that it was men like him—men who'd do such a thing so shamelessly— who had driven the youths of that time to commit suicide attacks. And so he said he had to rise up and take action, if the prime minister went ahead and worshipped this year as well."

"So that's what it was all about . . ." I said, sighing. Justifying the stabbing of the Prime Minister on such grounds is a dangerous idea, disproportionate to the political statement made by an official visit. Terrorism is war itself, after all.

"Ever since President Nakagaki passed away, Raita-san began to visit the gym regularly to get himself all pumped up. As for his part-time jobs, he always chose rough stuff like roadwork. I was told of his intention to attack Prime Minister Udagawa at the end of July, when he said that he wouldn't be able to see me again for a long time. But because he said he might not go through with it if the prime minister didn't go to Yasukuni, I prayed desperately every day afterward—I prayed, please don't go to Yasukuni! When I saw the news of his official visit, though, I lost all hope. By then, I could only talk to Raita-san when he'd call me occasionally, and he never told me about his part-time job at the TV station. So on that day I got into a state of panic and went to your apartment, sensei. But you weren't there. I was waiting for you inside until midnight."

"Well, you should've called me, or at least left a note."

"I just couldn't. Raita-san specifically told me to keep my mouth shut. I promised I wouldn't tell a soul. But in return I also made him promise."

"What'd you make him promise?"

Honoka looked down and hesitated for a while. When she finally raised her face her eyes were brimming with tears, ready to spill at any moment.

"Not to die, no matter what. 'If you commit suicide,' I told him, 'I'll certainly follow and die as well.'"

Drinking up my remaining coffee, I averted my eyes from Honoka, who was now crying, and paid attention to the fading light outside the window.

"I'm sorry. That's all I was able to tell him at the time. I really don't know why, now that I think about it; I don't know why I wasn't able to become more assertive and actually stop him. I should've at least told him that I'd die on the spot the moment he committed a crime! I don't know why I couldn't say something like that. I guess I really didn't want to look bad in Raita-san's eyes. I guess I didn't have any self-confidence at all. I guess I was only thinking about myself. And that's why I really couldn't do anything for Raita-san in the end."

For a while Honoka continued to cry quietly.

As I watched her, I thought that both Raita and Honoka, each in their own way, were trying to come to terms with their own death, to make peace with death, and in so doing, find happiness. This was surely the right thing to do. It was far more virtuous and honorable than anyone or anything. In reality, the question of the purpose of life, the question of what becomes of you, is perhaps pointless. After all we humans only live to die, our bodies being reduced to ashes in due time.

The acquisition of material satisfaction, status, fame, victories over your competition, or winning praises from others—such things amount to nothing more than building up a tower, higher and higher. They're only a desperate attempt to escape the collapse of life called death; a bitter struggle to remain far removed from it. As long as you measure your happiness by your distance from death, no matter who you are, you'll have no choice but to keep accruing the fruits of meaningless deeds. But when a person finds happiness only by overcoming material hardships and suffering, in the end—dragged into the dark swamp of death—he'll meet total annihilation.

A happiness that hinges on how far you can remove yourself from a ruinous death, how much you can keep your mind off it, is no happiness at all; it's nothing. The higher such a precarious tower of happiness becomes, the more your inevitable fall—your destiny of falling from a height one day—will end up being rewritten as a tragedy. In our final moment, flung out into the midair of nothingness, during the long, long horror that lasts until we sink into the sea of death, we won't be able to help but resent and curse the day we were born.

Death is something like the surface of the sea.

The moment we pass through the surface we're underwater. What lies there is an utterly new world where the death we fear and the love we yearn for are nonexistent. It's a world that lies past death; one that's difficult to imagine, yet never impossible to imagine.

This is what I believe: that true happiness must be intimate with death, that true happiness is indeed a happiness that is found ever so close to death, ever so close to the surface of its sea.

"You said to Eriko that getting to know him was a miracle, didn't you?" I said.

Honoka had finally stopped crying.

She wore a slightly perplexed look, and murmured, "There are no such things, I think, as miracles in this world." And then she added, "Eriko-san is a very good person, but she's entirely different from you, sensei, and from Raita-san and me."

How right she was, I thought. Compared to us, Eriko was surely a different type of human being.

"What are you going to do from now?" I asked. "Are you working on a seminar paper?"

"Yes. I've got nothing else to do, so I'm putting together a thesis, but I don't know if I'll be submitting it yet. I intend to stay on for another year anyway."

"Oh that's right, so you said."

"What about you, sensei? What are you going to do?"

The question was sudden and I didn't quite understand what she meant.

"About what?"

"About Eriko-san."

"Who knows? I'm not sure really."

"I think Eriko-san's someone who's good at anything, like all sorts of things, you know. There are people like that, aren't there?" Honoka finally had a smile on her face.

"Sure there are," I laughed.

"I'm positive Eriko-san can make the two of you work as a couple, sensei. I think you should just leave the matter in her hands, let her be in charge to work out the kinks, you know."

"What do you mean, let her be in charge?"

"I mean let her do as she likes, and as for you, all you have to do is stay silent and keep still. It'll be good for you. You deserve to take better care of yourself anyway."

She had a condescending look, as if to mock me for not understanding even such a simple thing.

"You think?"

"Yes, I do."

Thereafter Honoka spoke in a pensive tone. "There's something that occurred to me when I started looking for a job. You see, every person in the personnel department of every company inevitably asked, 'Can you continue working even after having a baby?' Although other girls I know seemed to have become fed up, simply replying, 'I'm not going to have a baby,' I plainly told the interviewers, 'I'll have a baby, and when I do I intend to leave the company.' Then the interviewer would say, 'Don't you think that's irresponsible of you and disrespectful to the company? In fact, don't you think such thinking makes you unworthy of being considered as an adult member of society?' There was even one person who said, 'Why did you even think about applying for a job with us in the first place?' My answer to these people was 'I want to join the workforce and learn things that'll help me give birth to a healthy child and raise him or her in a proper fashion, and I also wish to build a solid financial foundation for myself before I give birth to my baby.' Then all of those interviewers would agree, saying something like, 'What you're saying is correct.' And then all the companies ended up keeping me on their shortlist. In the end, though, as expected, none of them accepted me. But then a thought occurred to me: everyone in this world is suffering because, even though they understand the truth, even though they know what's right and what's wrong, they can't do anything about it. I'm really glad I went out searching for a job, you know. Thanks to the experience, I realized that there's nothing for me to do but to find my own way in life. I realized that relying on someone or following the herd wasn't for me. And that's why I decided I want a little more time. When I see Eriko-san I get inspired because I see a person who's living in the way I want to; she has her own approach toward life—she's living life on her own terms. Sure, she's not like us at all, but I can respect her. And that's why I'm also confident that she's quite capable of making her relationship with you work too, sensei."

Without saying anything, I tried to weigh Honoka's words, but it was no use: I just couldn't ponder them too deeply. Lately, I feel as though my interest in other people's expressions, gestures, and words isn't as strong as it used to be. This was particularly true where Eriko was concerned. While I'm not so sure I should let Eriko do as she pleases, as Honoka advises, I no longer find myself taking Eriko too seriously, as I once used to. But that's not to say that my interest in her has waned. Quite to the contrary, since that day of November tenth, we've been in touch with each other, more than ever before, discussing various topics and seeing each other almost every day.

I decided to place the matter of myself on the back burner and, instead, focus on more carefully ascertaining Honoka's state of mind, and to that end I was about to speak, when I heard the brief wail of a siren. I looked around.

"It's the bell signaling the start of fifth-session classes," Honoka said, standing up quickly with her teacup and empty plastic bottle. "Thanks for your time today."

She bobs her head.

I stand up.

Exiting the northern wing of the school building, we followed the path lined with ginkgo trees back to the gateway.

As expected, a cold wind had started to blow. Honoka seemed cold, drawing her coat lapels more tightly around her chest.

"Sensei, are you going back to your office?"

"Yeah, I've got some work to finish up."

"I guess being a salaryman is tough, after all," she said in a relaxed voice, following me up to the main street ahead.

A taxi promptly came to a halt. When the door opened, Honoka said behind me, "Sensei, please don't worry about me anymore."

I turned to face her as I climbed into the car.

"After a year," she went on, "let's all go meet Raita-san, the three of us together. We'll take along plenty of delicious things."

When I said, "Sounds good," her face lit up with a wonderful smile.

The door closed, I mentioned the destination, and the taxi took off.

Honoka was waving with that smile still on her face. I took a deep breath and waved back. After her rapidly receding figure disappeared I leaned back into the seat of the car and felt my energy draining.

One year, huh? . . . I murmured in my mind. At that moment, one year felt like such an unimaginably distant future; lately, at times, the flow of time seemed to slow down suddenly. This sensation, instead of fostering a sense of well-being, was exhausting my mind and body; it was like smelly mud stuck on both my feet, impeding even the tiniest steps forward.

With the passing of each year, even Honoka will find her affection for Raita waning. As long as she goes on living, she herself will keep undergoing drastic changes; there isn't a single thing in this world that can stay fixed and immutable. Whether you die while living, or you live while dying, in the end, there are no serious differences between the lives of people, I suppose. Even if you were to give up on yourself and get drunk on another person, letting him or her take you on a ride, as long as you're in this world, I'm sure, just like me, you'll end up getting bogged down with an apathetic torpor that'll keep weighing down on you with the passage of time, like heavy lead continuing to heap up around your feet until it saps you of all meaning.

So I wonder if Eriko can still keep believing until the very end that everything is to be found in the here and now.

Is she seriously convinced that such a barren world as this one is the one and only world? I, for one, can never believe so.

There must be some other place that's different.

And that's why, no matter how much you devote yourself to something entirely other than yourself, no matter how egoless you become, the true value of such noble aspirations will remain unrecognized and unappreciated. That's because such achievements aren't meant for this world; they only serve their purpose when you take flight for the next, when they transform into luminary wings that light up the future. Neither bliss nor misery can belong to this world alone. They go on in the next world, and the one after that, ad infinitum. We must never allow ourselves to be consumed by self-centered happiness or sorrow or hate. If you're preoccupied with living all the time, like Eriko, you won't be able to find your way into the new world awaiting you. If you're constantly distracted by whatever glitters before you, you'll fail to notice the light of the beacon flaring up in the distance, showing your way.

Whether you love, believe, or long for the good old days, be it for the sake of a person, Mother Nature, or whatever else, all you're doing is fretting about wanting to go on existing in this world.

Honoka said to let Eriko do as she likes. In other words, she was telling me to tolerate precisely that kind of fretting from her, make peace with her sad attachment to the material world.

It had suddenly gotten dark outside. I was reminded that it was winter, since the sunset was happening early.

I suppose whether I stayed together with Eriko until the end, or whether I never met her again, it made little difference to me.

Remembering her gentle face, I vacantly gazed out the car window. The city lights were flickering on one by one in the gloom.

Afterword

Mr. Kazufumi Shiraishi won the Naoki Prize, one of Japan's most prestigious literary awards, for his novel *Hokanaranu hito e* (To an Incomparable Other) in 2009. Yet *Boku no naka no kowareteinai bubun* (The Part of Me That Isn't Broken Inside), which was released back in 2002, remains his perennial favorite even after all these years.

One of the appeals of this title, which has achieved best-seller status in Japan, definitely lies in being an exemplary addition in the stream of "I" novels, a literary genre that first caught fire in Japan during the Meiji Period when Naturalism was introduced to the nation. Compared to the standard first-person narratives found in the West, the "I" novel has a more confessional feel, tending to reveal, as Motoyuki Shibata, the preeminent Japanese translator of American literature, says, "the less savory aspects of a writer's own personal life."[1]

This rings especially true in many of Mr. Shiraishi's works, which offer down-to-earth, even gritty, windows into the lives people lead, often through true-to-life portrayals of the modern Japanese professional. To that end, *The Part of Me That Isn't Broken Inside* is sprinkled with eye-opening scenes that reveal the working milieu of media professionals in Tokyo; a world with which Mr. Shiraishi, who has served for many years as editor and reporter at Bungeishunju, one of Japan's leading literary publishers, is intimately familiar.

But the more significant appeal, as similarly reflected in Mr. Shiraishi's later work, the 2008 *Kono yo no zenbu wo teki ni mawashite* (Me Against the World), where the fruits of his years

---

1   *Ignition*, http://ignition.co/1

of ruminating on life and love culminate and find expression in a powerful philosophy of his own devising (dubbed *Shiraishi Bungaku* [Shiraishi Literature] by Japanese literary critics), is that *The Part of Me That Isn't Broken Inside* is, without a doubt, as John O'Brien has said of the works of Svetlana Alexievich, winner of the 2015 Nobel Prize in Literature, "deeply rooted in a sense of humanity and suffering."

In effect, most of Mr. Shiraishi's novels share with the works of Ms. Alexievich the theme of "the ordinary person at the mercy of the greater evils of our world." Unlike her works, however, where these greater evils visibly manifest as voracious corporate juggernauts depleting the earth's natural resources or, perhaps, as ruthless and reckless tyrants hungry for power and money, in *The Part of Me That Isn't Broken Inside* they make their presences known in trace amounts—in the form of repercussions: as tormented emotions, dazed confusion, and lasting emotional scars, etched deep inside the psyches of lost individuals who endeavor to make sense of their existences—the seemingly random products of some unknown improbability generator at work in the cosmos, as the late Douglas Adams, the doyen of existential science fiction, might say.

The Part of Me That Isn't Broken Inside, as its straightforward, unadorned title suggests, is certainly rooted in existentialism. In fact, Mr. Shiraishi's defining influence is Albert Camus's *The Stranger*; he was so struck by this classic when he first encountered it in his formative years that, for a time, he even made the French existentialist's birth date his credit card's PIN number.[2]

The novel is a portrayal of an unvarnished account of life as it is lived by someone who, without any rhyme or reason, happens to be in Tokyo, making a living as a publishing professional. This sense of abstraction, or this sense of life lived as a "nowhere man," if you will, is heightened even more by the story's occasional, yet remarkable, digressions into explorations

---

2   *Sakka no dokusho michi (An Author's Road to Literature)* April 18, 2012, *http://www.webdoku.jp/rensai/sakka/michi124_ shiraishi/20120418_3.html*

of the meaning of "place"; one that comes to mind is the argument Naoto Matsubara, the "I" narrator of this "I" novel, has with his alluring partner, Eriko, a beautiful career woman three years younger than him who works as a media planner in a fashion-related PR firm. Naoto argues how place—as birthright rather than real estate—relates to identity.

Another excursion into the mystery of place is the scene where Naoto, while staying at Eriko's family home, is lost in thought, pondering the timelessness of a calendar image of a frigid summit in a faraway land, a place to which he feels so paradoxically close.

Complementing such existential flourishes, like resonant undertones ringing throughout the narrative, are notes of Buddhist aesthetics. A case in point—an instance when these aesthetics appear in perhaps their sharpest relief—is when Raita and company are disposing his old household garbage into a bonfire on the occasion of his move to a new residence. Echoing the essayist, novelist, and Buddhism expert Pico Iyer's opening of his book, *Global Soul*, in which Mr. Iyer witnesses his home, and, by extension, his whole world consumed in flames, this scene with Raita and his friends is bursting with the symbolism of renewal, not only in terms of switching vocations—in this case from a yakitori shop attendant to an employee at a construction firm—but also in the spiritual sense of abandoning a worldly existence, a notion that Raita, driven by his passionate disavowal of materialism, seems to embrace more and more toward the climax of the story; this is especially evident when he rejects a talent scout's efforts to lure him into the glitz and glamor of becoming a so-called "idol," or celluloid star, deriding entertainers and politicians as peddlers of the commercialization of self; as people condemned to the psychic strain of managing public personas; as people who sell a brand image of themselves without even giving a thought, to begin with, to the question of the unexamined life—the question of "Who am I?"

This calls to mind, incidentally, a scene in *Me Against the World*, a novel that is decidedly more essayistic, in which its long-suffering narrator remembers how he was amazed, one day

in his childhood, by the funhouse strangeness of so many selves—
so many flickers of consciousness—reflecting on the question of
selves:

> As a child, didn't you incidentally wonder "Why am
> I me?" I did, quite often. Gazing at the large number of
> strangers every day, I would always tilt my head in wonder
> at the inconceivability, the mystery, of the fact that I am I.
> I'd also wonder whether these people were really all that
> different from me, all of them also supposedly thinking the
> thought "I am me."[3]

Another resonant Buddhist chord is struck when Naoto looks
back into his days of youth and remembers his first crush, the
tender and virtuous, Machiko, who instilled in him, among many
other things, a sense of awe and wonder about the mystery of Bon,
the Japanese summertime Buddhist festival honoring the spirits of
ancestors, inside a temple where he met her. He also remembers
how fond she was of an author who explains the purpose of life
from the perspective of a daikon radish, and, just prior to her
passing, how she waxed philosophical about the unbearable light-
ness of being, likening death to a passage through a smooth tunnel. Death, incidentally, figures prominently in the novel. Along
with other episodes revolving around mortality, not the least of
which is about Naoto's mother, Machiko's end underscores the
notion that—as Salman Rushdie's character, Saleem Sinai, says
in *Midnight's Children*—"A death makes the living see themselves
too clearly."

Naoto's relationship with Machiko is one of the several relationships he has that serves as a launching pad for exploring different worldviews, each such worldview colored by the character
of the female other in the relationship. If his platonic love for
the maternal Machiko can be understood as a reminder of the
fleeting nature of life, his avuncular fondness for Honoka (as well

---

3   Excerpted from *Me Against the World*, Kazufumi Shiraishi,
Dalkey Archive Press, 2016.

as Raita), who looks up to him as her mentor, is a recognition, as articulated by the daikon radish parable, of biological life's primary directive: growth. His relationship with Lady Onishi, on the other hand, is clearly demonstrative of a worldview that condones a life of depravity and debauchery, whereas his relationship with Tomomi, the single working mother and owner of a bar, is characterized by an awakening of his paternal instincts and a full embrace of the role of guardian, as he demonstrates with his tender and protective feelings for her son, Takuya.

But the most salient relationship, in his angst-ridden life, is his complicated and thorny, yet true, experience with the love of his life, Eriko. At times sexist in tone, and at times a serene tableau of two peas in a pod, this thread of the narrative is an arresting portrait of how love for another person can become so all-consuming that, more often than not, it ends up becoming a case of flirting with disaster. And perhaps that is why the hero remains reluctant—and too jaded—throughout the story to take the relationship to the next level, even after making up with Eriko after the cringe-inducing fiasco at her family home, where a meeting with her parents ends in a fight-or-flight trainwreck.

In effect, Naoto's relationship with Eriko is an exploration of domestic bliss; a state of existence he never fully warms to, even at the end of the story. After all, what he fears above all is a false sense of security; a state of mind that would lead him astray from his self-avowed mission in life, which is to seek meaning, or to confirm the lack thereof and embrace the absurd. He had learned the painful lesson that domestic bliss is, like the weather, unreliable, when his mother had abandoned him when he was still a child; when the gift of photographic memory, born of the trauma of this abandonment, had fallen into his lap.

In sum, if there is any redeeming quality to Naoto's promiscuity, it is that, for the sake of investigating life's unvarnished truths, he engages each of his lovers with absolute intensity, even with the lady of leisure, Ms. Onishi; what he lacks in emotional connection with her, he more than makes up for by diving deep into carnal depravity; so much so that he attains epiphanies about female sexuality, as evidenced in his experiments inspired by his insider knowledge of a male porn star's techniques.

Undoubtedly, it could be argued that Naoto regards women, in general, through sexist eyes. But whether you relate to his character or not, what softens the blow of this critique, if it doesn't altogether nullify it, is the fact that this narrative—this first-person adventure of being Naoto Matsubara, with the richness of its details and emotional resonances—helps the reader engage in a "deep sense of self," warts and all. In effect, it's a portrayal of an unbounded inner life, which more often than not comes at the expense of likeability. It is, in the end, an exercise in not sympathy, but empathy.

In a morally complex age like ours, perhaps empathy is what we need more than anything else. When so much blood is being shed in the name of one cause or another that promises the individual meaning and purpose—a sense of direction in life— be it a religion, a political ideology, or a lifestyle promoted by an omnipresent, all-encompassing brand touting the promise of instant gratification, perhaps there is no better time than the present for Mr. Shiraishi's stories to remind us that, with the right kind of eyes, we can see that meaning, in a true sense, resides in the absurd, where freedom can take flight on the wings of imagination; where we are free to make whatever we want of our lives; where, as the eminent philosopher of our times, Amartya Sen says, identity can be seen as a choice, and not destiny; where we can experience, even, a brush with eternal recurrence; and where we, in the end, can find, as Mr. Shiraishi says about his feline friend, "an outlet for love and love only."[4]

I owe a deep debt of gratitude to TranNet's senior agent, Mr. Koji Chikatani, my guide and guru for so many memorable years, who so graciously offered me the opportunity to translate not one, but two of Mr. Shiraishi's masterpieces, and whose visionary foresight, encouragement, and patience have been invaluable in bringing the projects to fruition.

---

4   *ilove.cat*, http://ilove.cat/en/11373

My special thanks also goes to Professor Michael Emmerich, the eminent author of *The Tale of Genji: Translation, Canonization, and World Literature,* and the translator of so many exemplary works of modern Japanese literary fiction, including Hiromi Kawakami's *Manazaru* and Gen'ichiro Takahashi's *Sayonara Gangsters,* for helping me better understand where Mr. Shiraishi's oeuvre fits within the larger rubric of Japanese literature.

To Professor Peter MacMillan, award-winning artist, translator, and poet extraordinaire, whose many works, including his highly acclaimed, prize-winning translation, *One Hundred Poets, One Poem Each (Hyakunin Isshu),* and more recently, *Tales of Ise,* are truly doing wonders in bringing Japan to the rest of the world, thank you for being so generous with your time and for pointing me in the right direction for researching Mr. Shiraishi's literature.

A huge thank you also to Mr. Katsunori Hoshi, musician and producer, CEO of Nippop, all around *yushikisha* (man of light and leading) and free-thinker, and my dear friend for allowing me to engage in spirited, eye-opening tête-à-têtes on Mr. Shiraishi's works, often over espressos at a Starbucks in Tokyo.

A huge thank you also to my wonderful, inspiring family for giving me space and strength.

A very special thank you goes to Mr. Nathan Redman, assistant editor at Dalkey Archive Press, for his fine-tuning and constructive comments.

To Sir John O'Brien of the Dalkey Archive Press, no words can do justice to my deep gratitude for taking Mr. Shiraishi and myself under your wing; it is a boundless honor, sir, to be a part of your distinguished and awe-inspiring imprint, home to a truly brilliant and storied constellation of literary luminaries.

And last, but not least, I would like to thank, from the depths of my heart, Mr. Kazufumi Shiraishi himself for his stories, and for letting me help them flow, at long last, beyond Japan.

Yokohama, 2015

Born in 1958, KAZUFUMI SHIRAISHI is a prolific, award-winning novelist who debuted in 2000 to great critical acclaim with *Isshun no hikari* [*A Ray of Light*]. The winner of two major Japanese literary awards (the Yamamoto Shūgorō and Naoki Prize), he currently lives in Tokyo with his wife.

Born in 1965, RAJ MAHTANI is a freelance translator based in Yokohama, Japan. His published translations include *Fujisan* by Randy Taguchi and *I Hear Them Cry* by Shiho Kishimoto, both released by Amazon Crossing.

MICHAL AJVAZ, *The Golden Age.*
The Other City.

PIERRE ALBERT-BIROT, *Grabinoulor.*

YUZ ALESHKOVSKY, *Kangaroo.*

FELIPE ALFAU, *Chromos.*
Locos.

JOE AMATO, *Samuel Taylor's Last Night.*

IVAN ÂNGELO, *The Celebration.*
The Tower of Glass.

ANTÓNIO LOBO ANTUNES, *Knowledge of Hell.*
The Splendor of Portugal.

ALAIN ARIAS-MISSON, *Theatre of Incest.*

JOHN ASHBERY & JAMES SCHUYLER, *A Nest of Ninnies.*

ROBERT ASHLEY, *Perfect Lives.*

GABRIELA AVIGUR-ROTEM, *Heatwave and Crazy Birds.*

DJUNA BARNES, *Ladies Almanack.*
Ryder.

JOHN BARTH, *Letters.*
Sabbatical.

DONALD BARTHELME, *The King.*
Paradise.

SVETISLAV BASARA, *Chinese Letter.*

MIQUEL BAUÇÀ, *The Siege in the Room.*

RENÉ BELLETTO, *Dying.*

MAREK BIEŃCZYK, *Transparency.*

ANDREI BITOV, *Pushkin House.*

ANDREJ BLATNIK, *You Do Understand.*
Law of Desire.

LOUIS PAUL BOON, *Chapel Road.*
My Little War.
Summer in Termuren.

ROGER BOYLAN, *Killoyle.*

IGNÁCIO DE LOYOLA BRANDÃO,
Anonymous Celebrity.
Zero.

BONNIE BREMSER, *Troia: Mexican Memoirs.*

CHRISTINE BROOKE-ROSE,
Amalgamemnon.

BRIGID BROPHY, *In Transit.*
The Prancing Novelist.

GERALD L. BRUNS,
Modern Poetry and the Idea of Language.

GABRIELLE BURTON, *Heartbreak Hotel.*

MICHEL BUTOR, *Degrees.*
Mobile.

G. CABRERA INFANTE, *Infante's Inferno.*
Three Trapped Tigers.

JULIETA CAMPOS, *The Fear of Losing Eurydice.*

ANNE CARSON, *Eros the Bittersweet.*

ORLY CASTEL-BLOOM, *Dolly City.*

LOUIS-FERDINAND CÉLINE, *North.*
Conversations with Professor Y.
London Bridge.

MARIE CHAIX, *The Laurels of Lake Constance.*

HUGO CHARTERIS, *The Tide Is Right.*

ERIC CHEVILLARD, *Demolishing Nisard.*
The Author and Me.

MARC CHOLODENKO, *Mordechai Schamz.*

JOSHUA COHEN, *Witz.*

EMILY HOLMES COLEMAN, *The Shutter of Snow.*

ERIC CHEVILLARD, *The Author and Me.*

ROBERT COOVER, *A Night at the Movies.*

STANLEY CRAWFORD, *Log of the S.S. The Mrs Unguentine.*
Some Instructions to My Wife.

RENÉ CREVEL, *Putting My Foot in It.*

RALPH CUSACK, *Cadenza.*

NICHOLAS DELBANCO, *Sherbrookes.*
The Count of Concord.

NIGEL DENNIS, *Cards of Identity.*

PETER DIMOCK, *A Short Rhetoric for Leaving the Family.*

ARIEL DORFMAN, *Konfidenz.*

COLEMAN DOWELL, *Island People.*
Too Much Flesh and Jabez.

ARKADII DRAGOMOSHCHENKO,
Dust.

RIKKI DUCORNET, *Phosphor in Dreamland.*
The Complete Butcher's Tales.

RIKKI DUCORNET (cont.), *The Jade Cabinet.*
The Fountains of Neptune.

WILLIAM EASTLAKE, *The Bamboo Bed.*
Castle Keep.
Lyric of the Circle Heart.

JEAN ECHENOZ, *Chopin's Move.*

STANLEY ELKIN, *A Bad Man.*
Criers and Kibitzers, Kibitzers and Criers.
The Dick Gibson Show.
The Franchiser.
The Living End.
Mrs. Ted Bliss.

FRANÇOIS EMMANUEL, *Invitation to a Voyage.*

PAUL EMOND, *The Dance of a Sham.*

SALVADOR ESPRIU, *Ariadne in the Grotesque Labyrinth.*

LESLIE A. FIEDLER, *Love and Death in the American Novel.*

JUAN FILLOY, *Op Oloop.*

ANDY FITCH, *Pop Poetics.*

GUSTAVE FLAUBERT, *Bouvard and Pécuchet.*

KASS FLEISHER, *Talking out of School.*

JON FOSSE, *Aliss at the Fire.*
Melancholy.

FORD MADOX FORD, *The March of Literature.*

MAX FRISCH, *I'm Not Stiller.*
Man in the Holocene.

CARLOS FUENTES, *Christopher Unborn.*
Distant Relations.
Terra Nostra.
Where the Air Is Clear.

TAKEHIKO FUKUNAGA, *Flowers of Grass.*

WILLIAM GADDIS, JR., *The Recognitions.*

JANICE GALLOWAY, *Foreign Parts.*
The Trick Is to Keep Breathing.

WILLIAM H. GASS, *Life Sentences.*
The Tunnel.
The World Within the Word.
Willie Masters' Lonesome Wife.

GÉRARD GAVARRY, *Hoppla! 1 2 3.*

ETIENNE GILSON, *The Arts of the Beautiful.*
Forms and Substances in the Arts.

C. S. GISCOMBE, *Giscome Road.*
Here.

DOUGLAS GLOVER, *Bad News of the Heart.*

WITOLD GOMBROWICZ, *A Kind of Testament.*

PAULO EMÍLIO SALES GOMES, *P's Three Women.*

GEORGI GOSPODINOV, *Natural Novel.*

JUAN GOYTISOLO, *Count Julian.*
Juan the Landless.
Makbara.
Marks of Identity.

HENRY GREEN, *Blindness.*
Concluding.
Doting.
Nothing.

JACK GREEN, *Fire the Bastards!*

JIŘÍ GRUŠA, *The Questionnaire.*

MELA HARTWIG, *Am I a Redundant Human Being?*

JOHN HAWKES, *The Passion Artist.*
Whistlejacket.

ELIZABETH HEIGHWAY, ED., *Contemporary Georgian Fiction.*

AIDAN HIGGINS, *Balcony of Europe.*
Blind Man's Bluff.
Bornholm Night-Ferry.
Langrishe, Go Down.
Scenes from a Receding Past.

KEIZO HINO, *Isle of Dreams.*

KAZUSHI HOSAKA, *Plainsong.*

ALDOUS HUXLEY, *Antic Hay.*
Point Counter Point.
Those Barren Leaves.
Time Must Have a Stop.

NAOYUKI II, *The Shadow of a Blue Cat.*

DRAGO JANČAR, *The Tree with No Name.*

MIKHEIL JAVAKHISHVILI, *Kvachi.*

GERT JONKE, *The Distant Sound.*
Homage to Czerny.
The System of Vienna.

JACQUES JOUET, *Mountain R.*
Savage.
Upstaged.
MIEKO KANAI, *The Word Book.*
YORAM KANIUK, *Life on Sandpaper.*
ZURAB KARUMIDZE, *Dagny.*
JOHN KELLY, *From Out of the City.*
HUGH KENNER, *Flaubert, Joyce and Beckett: The Stoic Comedians.*
Joyce's Voices.
DANILO KIŠ, *The Attic.*
The Lute and the Scars.
Psalm 44.
A Tomb for Boris Davidovich.
ANITA KONKKA, *A Fool's Paradise.*
GEORGE KONRÁD, *The City Builder.*
TADEUSZ KONWICKI, *A Minor Apocalypse.*
The Polish Complex.
ANNA KORDZAIA-SAMADASHVILI, *Me, Margarita.*
MENIS KOUMANDAREAS, *Koula.*
ELAINE KRAF, *The Princess of 72nd Street.*
JIM KRUSOE, *Iceland.*
AYSE KULIN, *Farewell: A Mansion in Occupied Istanbul.*
EMILIO LASCANO TEGUI, *On Elegance While Sleeping.*
ERIC LAURRENT, *Do Not Touch.*
VIOLETTE LEDUC, *La Bâtarde.*
EDOUARD LEVÉ, *Autoportrait.*
Newspaper.
Suicide.
Works.
MARIO LEVI, *Istanbul Was a Fairy Tale.*
DEBORAH LEVY, *Billy and Girl.*
JOSÉ LEZAMA LIMA, *Paradiso.*
ROSA LIKSOM, *Dark Paradise.*
OSMAN LINS, *Avalovara.*
The Queen of the Prisons of Greece.
FLORIAN LIPUŠ, *The Errors of Young Tjaž.*
GORDON LISH, *Peru.*
ALF MACLOCHLAINN, *Out of Focus.*
Past Habitual.

The Corpus in the Library.
RON LOEWINSOHN, *Magnetic Field(s).*
YURI LOTMAN, *Non-Memoirs.*
D. KEITH MANO, *Take Five.*
MINA LOY, *Stories and Essays of Mina Loy.*
MICHELINE AHARONIAN MARCOM,
A Brief History of Yes.
The Mirror in the Well.
BEN MARCUS, *The Age of Wire and String.*
WALLACE MARKFIELD, *Teitlebaum's Window.*
DAVID MARKSON, *Reader's Block.*
Wittgenstein's Mistress.
CAROLE MASO, *AVA.*
HISAKI MATSUURA, *Triangle.*
LADISLAV MATEJKA & KRYSTYNA POMORSKA, EDS., *Readings in Russian Poetics: Formalist & Structuralist Views.*
HARRY MATHEWS, *Cigarettes.*
The Conversions.
The Human Country.
The Journalist.
My Life in CIA.
Singular Pleasures.
The Sinking of the Odradek.
Stadium.
Tlooth.
HISAKI MATSUURA, *Triangle.*
DONAL MCLAUGHLIN, *beheading the virgin mary, and other stories.*
JOSEPH MCELROY, *Night Soul and Other Stories.*
ABDELWAHAB MEDDEB, *Talismano.*
GERHARD MEIER, *Isle of the Dead.*
HERMAN MELVILLE, *The Confidence-Man.*
AMANDA MICHALOPOULOU, *I'd Like.*
STEVEN MILLHAUSER, *The Barnum Museum.*
In the Penny Arcade.
RALPH J. MILLS, JR., *Essays on Poetry.*
MOMUS, *The Book of Jokes.*
CHRISTINE MONTALBETTI, *The Origin of Man.*
Western.

NICHOLAS MOSLEY, *Accident.*
Assassins.
Catastrophe Practice.
A Garden of Trees.
Hopeful Monsters.
Imago Bird.
Inventing God.
Look at the Dark.
Metamorphosis.
Natalie Natalia.
Serpent.

WARREN MOTTE, *Fables of the Novel:*
French Fiction since 1990.
Fiction Now: The French Novel in the
21st Century.
Mirror Gazing.
Oulipo: A Primer of Potential Literature.

GERALD MURNANE, *Barley Patch.*
Inland.

YVES NAVARRE, *Our Share of Time.*
Sweet Tooth.

DOROTHY NELSON, *In Night's City.*
Tar and Feathers.

ESHKOL NEVO, *Homesick.*

WILFRIDO D. NOLLEDO, *But for*
the Lovers.

BORIS A. NOVAK, *The Master of*
Insomnia.

FLANN O'BRIEN, *At Swim-Two-Birds.*
The Best of Myles.
The Dalkey Archive.
The Hard Life.
The Poor Mouth.
The Third Policeman.

CLAUDE OLLIER, *The Mise-en-Scène.*
Wert and the Life Without End.

PATRIK OUŘEDNÍK, *Europeana.*
The Opportune Moment, 1855.

BORIS PAHOR, *Necropolis.*

FERNANDO DEL PASO, *News from*
the Empire.
Palinuro of Mexico.

ROBERT PINGET, *The Inquisitory.*
Mahu or The Material.
Trio.

MANUEL PUIG, *Betrayed by Rita*
Hayworth.

The Buenos Aires Affair.
Heartbreak Tango.

RAYMOND QUENEAU, *The Last Days.*
Odile.
Pierrot Mon Ami.
Saint Glinglin.

ANN QUIN, *Berg.*
Passages.
Three.
Tripticks.

ISHMAEL REED, *The Free-Lance*
Pallbearers.
The Last Days of Louisiana Red.
Ishmael Reed: The Plays.
Juice!
The Terrible Threes.
The Terrible Twos.
Yellow Back Radio Broke-Down.

JASIA REICHARDT, *15 Journeys Warsaw*
to London.

JOÃO UBALDO RIBEIRO, *House of the*
Fortunate Buddhas.

JEAN RICARDOU, *Place Names.*

RAINER MARIA RILKE,
The Notebooks of Malte Laurids Brigge.

JULIÁN RÍOS, *The House of Ulysses.*
Larva: A Midsummer Night's Babel.
Poundemonium.

ALAIN ROBBE-GRILLET, *Project for a*
Revolution in New York.
A Sentimental Novel.

AUGUSTO ROA BASTOS, *I the Supreme.*

DANIËL ROBBERECHTS, *Arriving in*
Avignon.

JEAN ROLIN, *The Explosion of the*
Radiator Hose.

OLIVIER ROLIN, *Hotel Crystal.*

ALIX CLEO ROUBAUD, *Alix's Journal.*

JACQUES ROUBAUD, *The Form of*
a City Changes Faster, Alas, Than the
Human Heart.
The Great Fire of London.
Hortense in Exile.
Hortense Is Abducted.
Mathematics: The Plurality of Worlds of
Lewis.
Some Thing Black.

RAYMOND ROUSSEL, *Impressions of Africa.*

VEDRANA RUDAN, *Night.*

PABLO M. RUIZ, *Four Cold Chapters on the Possibility of Literature.*

GERMAN SADULAEV, *The Maya Pill.*

TOMAŽ ŠALAMUN, *Soy Realidad.*

LYDIE SALVAYRE, *The Company of Ghosts.*
The Lecture.
The Power of Flies.

LUIS RAFAEL SÁNCHEZ, *Macho Camacho's Beat.*

SEVERO SARDUY, *Cobra & Maitreya.*

NATHALIE SARRAUTE, *Do You Hear Them?*
Martereau.
The Planetarium.

STIG SÆTERBAKKEN, *Siamese.*
Self-Control.
Through the Night.

ARNO SCHMIDT, *Collected Novellas.*
Collected Stories.
Nobodaddy's Children.
Two Novels.

ASAF SCHURR, *Motti.*

GAIL SCOTT, *My Paris.*

DAMION SEARLS, *What We Were Doing and Where We Were Going.*

JUNE AKERS SEESE,
Is This What Other Women Feel Too?

BERNARD SHARE, *Inish.*
Transit.

VIKTOR SHKLOVSKY, *Bowstring.*
Literature and Cinematography.
Theory of Prose.
Third Factory.
Zoo, or Letters Not about Love.

PIERRE SINIAC, *The Collaborators.*

KJERSTI A. SKOMSVOLD,
The Faster I Walk, the Smaller I Am.

JOSEF ŠKVORECKÝ, *The Engineer of Human Souls.*

GILBERT SORRENTINO, *Aberration of Starlight.*
Blue Pastoral.
Crystal Vision.

Imaginative Qualities of Actual Things.
Mulligan Stew. Red the Fiend.
Steelwork.
Under the Shadow.

MARKO SOSIČ, *Ballerina, Ballerina.*

ANDRZEJ STASIUK, *Dukla.*
Fado.

GERTRUDE STEIN, *The Making of Americans.*
A Novel of Thank You.

LARS SVENDSEN, *A Philosophy of Evil.*

PIOTR SZEWC, *Annihilation.*

GONÇALO M. TAVARES, *A Man: Klaus Klump.*
Jerusalem.
Learning to Pray in the Age of Technique.

LUCIAN DAN TEODOROVICI,
Our Circus Presents . . .

NIKANOR TERATOLOGEN, *Assisted Living.*

STEFAN THEMERSON, *Hobson's Island.*
The Mystery of the Sardine.
Tom Harris.

TAEKO TOMIOKA, *Building Waves.*

JOHN TOOMEY, *Sleepwalker.*

DUMITRU TSEPENEAG, *Hotel Europa.*
The Necessary Marriage.
Pigeon Post.
Vain Art of the Fugue.

ESTHER TUSQUETS, *Stranded.*

DUBRAVKA UGRESIC, *Lend Me Your Character.*
Thank You for Not Reading.

TOR ULVEN, *Replacement.*

MATI UNT, *Brecht at Night.*
Diary of a Blood Donor.
Things in the Night.

ÁLVARO URIBE & OLIVIA SEARS, EDS.,
Best of Contemporary Mexican Fiction.

ELOY URROZ, *Friction.*
The Obstacles.

LUISA VALENZUELA, *Dark Desires and the Others.*
He Who Searches.

PAUL VERHAEGHEN, *Omega Minor.*

BORIS VIAN, *Heartsnatcher.*

LLORENÇ VILLALONGA, *The Dolls' Room.*

TOOMAS VINT, *An Unending Landscape.*

ORNELA VORPSI, *The Country Where No One Ever Dies.*

AUSTRYN WAINHOUSE, *Hedyphagetica.*

CURTIS WHITE, *America's Magic Mountain.*
The Idea of Home.
Memories of My Father Watching TV.
Requiem.

DIANE WILLIAMS,
Excitability: Selected Stories.
Romancer Erector.

DOUGLAS WOOLF, *Wall to Wall.*
Ya! & John-Juan.

JAY WRIGHT, *Polynomials and Pollen.*
The Presentable Art of Reading Absence.

PHILIP WYLIE, *Generation of Vipers.*

MARGUERITE YOUNG, *Angel in the Forest.*
Miss MacIntosh, My Darling.

REYOUNG, *Unbabbling.*

VLADO ŽABOT, *The Succubus.*

ZORAN ŽIVKOVIĆ , *Hidden Camera.*

LOUIS ZUKOFSKY, *Collected Fiction.*

VITOMIL ZUPAN, *Minuet for Guitar.*

SCOTT ZWIREN, *God Head.*

AND MORE . . .